SPROUTING
WINGS

SPROUTING
WINGS

The First Novel in the Alan Ericsson Series

HENRY FAULKNER

TWO HARBORS PRESS, MINNEAPOLIS MN

Two Harbors Press
322 First Avenue N, 5th floor
Minneapolis, MN 55401
612.455.2293
www.TwoHarborsPress.com

ISBN-13: 978-1-935204-60-2
LCCN: 2014913890

Distributed by Itasca Books

Cover Design by Alan Pranke
Typeset by James Arneson

Printed in the United States of America

CONTENTS

AUTHOR'S NOTE

The generally accepted date for the start of the Second World War is September 1, 1939, when Germany invaded Poland. The United States was brought abruptly into the war two and one-quarter years later with the Japanese attack on Pearl Harbor. This novel is set in that intervening period, when the United States continued at peace while most of the other industrialized countries of the world were in a war that was escalating in intensity.

The United States was coming slowly out of the Great Depression, the greatest economic setback the country had ever undergone. Thus, it was a time of rising optimism in the United States, contrasting strongly with the gloom of war in the rest of the world.

This period is also something of a crossroads in the technological history of the country. Mechanical engineering technology had enjoyed seventy years of rapid progress. Most of the machines that are in common use at the start of the twenty-first century, such as the automobile, household appliances, power tools, and construction and farm machinery had been invented and come into common use in the United States during this period. The everyday lives of most people were pervasively affected by this new technology. Development continued in the following decades, but at a slower pace. Electronic technology, on the other hand, was just starting on a period of rapid growth, symbolized by the nascent developments of radar and television in the late 1930s. (This rapid electronic development has continued over the intervening seventy years to give us such devices as computers, the Internet, and smart phones.)

Although they did not affect the everyday lives of most people, the development of aircraft and submarines, and the engines that powered them, embodied the best that mechanical engineering had to offer. The all-metal monoplane, devoid of external bracing and powered by a large piston engine—particularly the light-weight, reliable, air-cooled radial engine—was a remarkable accomplishment. Similarly, the US Navy fleet submarine, powered by compact diesel engines, which would soon achieve reliability, was a significant advance—although it was not able to demonstrate its full potential until the scandalous unreliability of our torpedoes had been remedied. In these military developments, progress was more evenly spread around the world, so our allies and enemies were sometimes ahead of us.

I have deliberately chosen to adhere closely to the rich history of the period in the fact-based aspects of this book. Most of the events involving people beyond Alan's relatives and friends actually happened.

The historical detail is based mainly on the original research and reporting of others, and—to a small extent—on my own experience. In case the reader should like to pursue any topic further, I have compiled a list of the sources of historical information, including a list of references, which is available on the website for the series, **www.alanericsson.com** .

CONVENTIONS

Times and dates listed in the text are local to the action, except as noted. Distances are in nautical miles.

In regard to real and fictional names for historical persons, I have used the real names of persons that are part of the novel's history in two cases:

(1) In the case of prominent persons about whom I have enough biographical information to have some understanding of their character.

(2) In the case of peripheral persons whose part in the story is small enough so that it is not necessary to understand their character.

Otherwise, I have used fictitious names for historical persons, which may have some resemblance to the real names of the persons. In parts of the story, Alan takes on the role of a known historical person. I hope I have not offended anyone by making that substitution.

CHAPTER ONE

Breaks in the Clouds

Wednesday, April 3, 1940

Lieutenant junior grade Alan Ericsson was driving from Newport, Rhode Island, to the submarine base in New London, Connecticut. His duty in Newport was an independent assignment at the US Navy Newport Torpedo Station, and he was required to report to his commanding officer, his "CO," in New London once a month. Although it was only about forty miles as the crow flies, he had to take two ferries to get to the west side of Narragansett Bay, so the trip took about two hours. In spite of the gray, cool weather, he enjoyed the trip. It was a respite from his work at the Torpedo Station, and he could let his mind wander. It gave him time to think about the events of the past year, which had brought about an abrupt change in his navy career.

Although it had been more than ten months since the submarine *Squalus* had sunk, he remembered the event as if it had happened yesterday. The normal test program for a newly built submarine had been going well. It was mid morning, Alan was in the conning tower, and *Squalus* was starting her nineteenth test dive. The bow of the submarine tilted down and entered the water. He watched as the sea covered the eye ports in the conning tower. He could hear orders being given calmly in the control room below. The boat began to level off as it approached periscope-depth.

The voices of both the captain and the civilian superintendent from the Portsmouth Navy Yard simultaneously announced, "Mark!"

Alan could hear them discussing the diving time, which had been just over sixty seconds, and they seemed pleased. The submarine leveled off completely, just as he felt an odd, small fluctuation in the air pressure inside the submarine.

Suddenly the control-room talker, the man assigned to relay telephone messages to and from the other compartments, shattered the calm. He shouted, "The engine rooms are flooding, sir!"

A cold wave of fear washed over Alan. This was the submariner's worst nightmare—water coming in fast when they were fully submerged. *How could this be happening? Everything had been going so smoothly!* He glanced at the quartermaster, the only other man in the conning tower, and saw that the man's face was frozen with fear.

There was complete silence from the control room for about a second, and then the voices of the captain and the executive officer erupted, issuing a rapid series of shouted orders to blow all the ballast tanks. Alan could hear the roar and whoosh of the compressed air going into the tanks, pushing the water out and making the submarine more buoyant. He felt the bow of the submarine tilt upward. Alan stared at the depth gauge and saw it move upward. He eagerly grasped at this positive sign. *Maybe we'll get out of this.*

The bow continued to tilt up, but the depth gauge started down again. Alan realized that the weight of the water coming in aft was overcoming the buoyancy of the air in the ballast tanks. The boat was starting to slide backward, out of control. He and the quartermaster struggled to hold on as the bow continued to tilt up. The deck steadied, bow up, at what Alan guessed was around forty-five degrees—far steeper than would happen in any normal operation. As fear gripped him more strongly, Alan heard hissing and splattering sounds from the control room below. There were curses and grunts as the men there struggled to close valves that were letting in water. Alan guessed that water was getting into the ventilation system, so he clung to a periscope shaft, reached up, and closed the valve on the ventilation pipe which came into the conning tower before water got to it.

Alan knew that the flooding in the after part of the submarine had to be bad. The watertight doors probably had not been closed in time to prevent the flooding from spreading from the engine rooms into the after torpedo room and the after battery. Men were getting hurt or killed back there.

The lights flickered, flared briefly, and went out. The emergency lights came on as they should have, but they also flickered. Alan could hear new voices from the control room. He recognized the voices of men who were stationed further aft. If they were coming into the control room, the after battery compartment must be flooding, and the watertight door to the control room had not been closed. He remembered that it opened by swinging aft, so it would be hard to pull the heavy steel door closed against the steep angle. He hoped that the men there would be able to do it. If not, the control room would flood. He heard more grunts, then the door closed with a clunk, and the captain said, "Well done." He wondered if anyone was still alive aft of that door.

Alan watched as the depth gauge moved steadily downward—100, 150, 200 feet. At around 220 feet, the bow started to tilt back down. He braced himself. Luckily, the deck angle stopped at around ten degrees bow up with no list. He looked at the depth gauge, which had stopped at 243. Alan realized that the *Squalus* had come to rest on the bottom; first the stern, then the bow. The emergency lights went out.

It had only been five minutes since they had been on the surface.

At that moment, he was preoccupied with his and the crew's predicament. It was only later that he realized that the event had triggered big changes in his life.

From what he could hear, thirty-three of the fifty-nine men aboard were uninjured and in the forward half of the submarine. (He later learned that no one had survived in the after half.) No one in any navy had ever escaped from a sunken submarine, except at shallow depths. Nevertheless, Alan knew of two slim rays of hope penetrating the terror. Everyone in the US Navy Submarine Service knew that there were two recent inventions, developed by Charles "Swede" Momsen, to help submariners escape from sunken submarines. Neither, however, had ever been used in a real emergency.

The captain wanted to refloat the submarine with compressed air from the surface. He felt that it was too risky to use the first device, the Momsen Lung, to swim up to the surface because the water was too cold. Once the rescue operation got underway, however, the Navy Yard decided to send for the second device, the McCann Rescue Chamber. The chamber was designed to be brought to the scene on a rescue ship, lowered down onto the submarine, and sealed over a hatch. Up to nine men could fit into it at a time, riding it back up to the surface, and getting out onto the rescue ship. The nearest rescue chamber was on an old minesweeper based in New London, Connecticut, so it would be hours before it arrived.

The inside of the submarine was dark, damp, and—above all—cold. As the hours went by, the cold penetrated everything. The crew, many of whom were also wet from the earlier leaks, was huddled together under blankets. The oxygen in the air was being gradually depleted, and Alan felt his breathing becoming labored. He was determined to take all of this stoically, though, and so were all of the other crewmen. Alan had always been proud to serve with submariners, but this crew rose above the rest.

About eight hours after the sinking, the crew's morale began to inch upward. New, positive signs that they were going to be rescued became apparent every few hours. In the middle of the night, Alan was greatly encouraged to hear that Swede Momsen himself was on the scene and in charge. About twenty-four hours after the sinking, everyone aboard was overjoyed to hear the sound of a diver walking on the deck of the submarine.

During the next fifteen hours, the rescue chamber took them to the surface in four groups. Alan was in the third group. His enormous relief on reaching the surface was tempered by a fervent desire to see that the last group, which included the captain and the executive officer, was safe on the rescue ship. He watched in horror as the steel cable that had been raising the chamber, which was holding the last group, was stopped and lowered all the way back down because the cable had frayed to a single strand. He stood in awe as Momsen calmly directed one attempt after another to remedy the situation. Finally, there was no choice but to try a risky procedure, which worked only because Momsen directed every detail.

Alan remembered hearing, later, about all the other obstacles the rescue operation had overcome that were unknown to those aboard the submarine. Momsen had pulled off a miracle.

He was glad to have been appointed to serve under Momsen in the salvage operation after the rescue, which brought the *Squalus* back to a pier in the Navy Yard. Like the rescue operation, the salvage operation overcame one setback after another, although it was not under the same kind of time pressure. It was hard work and took almost four months, but working under Momsen had been inspiring.

✈

The long reminiscence came to an end as Alan recognized that he was approaching Groton.

It was pouring rain as he crossed the bridge from Groton to New London at dusk. He had arranged to have dinner with an old friend, Lieutenant j.g. Mark Gallagher, and was due to report to his commanding officer early the following morning. This was the first chance that Alan and Mark had had to get together in almost two years. They had picked one of their favorite restaurants from their sub school days.

Mark had been one of Alan's classmates at the Naval Academy and at submarine school, which all submariners attended before serving on submarines. Mark was staying with his in-laws on his way to join the new submarine *Sailfish*—the refurbished *Squalus*—at Portsmouth, New Hampshire, as gunnery and torpedo officer. Mark's assignment was a reward for his long service in the old S-boats.

Alan walked into the restaurant just before 1900—seven o'clock to the civilians who greeted him. He hung up his dripping raincoat amid the usual odor of wet wool. The restaurant was cozy and dark, with lots of wood paneling. Alan saw that Mark had already arrived and gotten a table. Alan relaxed immediately as he saw Mark wave to him.

After they had exchanged greetings and ordered drinks, a friendly grin appeared on Mark's face as he asked, "Have you found the love of your life, yet?"

Alan grimaced. At almost twenty-eight and unmarried, he was becoming tired of the question. "No. I've dated three gals long enough to get to know them pretty well. You remember Maureen from sub school days. Then I got to know another nice gal in Portsmouth while working on the *Squalus*. When I went to Newport, I ran into a girl from my high school, who had had a crush on me then. We had a good time but I broke up with her about two weeks ago. None of them quite filled the bill, and it didn't help that they all decided that they wanted a man who was not going to be moving around a lot." Alan knew that Mark could understand. He was happily married, and his wife, Mary, was pregnant with their first child, but she was still in Norfolk, where Mark had previously been assigned, supervising the packing of their belongings for the move to Portsmouth.

"I guess those women don't realize that if we get into the war, they won't have much choice about that. Hmm . . . So, you're on the prowl again," Mark announced.

"Yeah." There was a pause and Alan changed the subject. "How do you feel about joining the former *Squalus*?"

"It's a remarkable coincidence, isn't it? I've been assigned to your former ship. I'm happy about it. They're incorporating all they've learned from the design of the other boats in the class in the refit."

"You're lucky. I'd like to be aboard her, myself."

"From what I hear, the new captain wants to have a clean slate. He's taken no officers and only a few enlisted men from the *Squalus* crew. But you should've gotten assigned to another sub. Instead you got put ashore in a desk job? What happened?"

"After the *Squalus* sank, each of the crew members had to write a report on it," explained Alan as Mark nodded. "As engineering officer, I knew I should come up with an explanation for the flooding. Shortly after the *Squalus* sank, I heard about what had happened on the *Skipjack*. You probably heard that they also had trouble with the main induction valve, but they managed to surface with only a little flooding. After that, the *Skipjack* crew was wary of the main induction valve; the engine-room personnel always kept the manual inboard induction valves well oiled and they were closed quickly for each dive to prevent flooding. Those valves are not easy to operate, so they had been more or less neglected on the *Squalus* and most of the *Salmons*."

"Yeah, I heard about it. Too bad the word didn't get out until after the *Squalus* sank."

"That's just it. Not long after I heard about the *Skipjack*, I heard that the *Snapper* had also almost sunk, and their main induction valve stayed open longer than during the *Skipjack* incident. For some reason, they had adopted a routine of closing the inboard valves before diving, which saved the ship. Knowing this history, I was pretty angry about the loss of my shipmates. That information should have been shared throughout the fleet boats. My report was much too frank about how the disaster could've been avoided; it made some of the top brass look bad, and—from a career standpoint—it was probably a huge mistake. The desk job is my punishment. I was assigned to New London, and sent to the Torpedo Station. My luck in the navy seems to have sunk with the *Squalus*."

"Wow. At least you survived. I'm sorry that your career sustained damage, though."

Their drinks arrived, and Alan went on. "At least my job hasn't been as boring as I thought it would be. Before, I had always taken torpedoes for granted. I figured that the torpedo just had to be launched at the right place and the right time with the correct settings. After that, if the torpedo had received reasonable maintenance, it should just do its job as advertised. Because of this assignment, I understand what a delicate piece of machinery a torpedo is, and how many things can go wrong. I'm beginning to doubt that our torpedoes are adequately reliable, actually. Because we're not allowed to use live torpedoes for practice, the only chance to find out how well a real, live torpedo works is the testing at Newport. That testing is much less extensive than what is needed to establish reliability."

"That sounds bad. I gather your commanding officer is here in New London? Where do you fit in?"

"Officially, my CO is the base exec, but he has me report to none other than Butch Ludlow."

Ludlow had been two classes ahead of Alan and Mark at the Academy, and had harassed both of them unmercifully when they were starting out as plebes. Ludlow thrived on spit and polish, while although Alan took pride in achieving a smart appearance occasionally, he thought that one's appearance should never be allowed to interfere with more important activities. Ludlow was also a bully, and Alan had hated him for that. Just before Ludlow's attendance at the Ring Dance at the Academy, Alan, Mark, and two other classmates had conspired to have Ludlow's uniform liberally sprayed with cheap perfume. Ludlow had had no recourse but to wear it. He could not take revenge before he graduated, because there were too many suspects. Alan knew that Ludlow would always regard him as an enemy because of that incident, though.

"I see what you mean about your luck sinking with the *Squalus*. He probably treats you like dirt."

"You said it."

There was a pause, and Alan suspected that Mark was searching for a more cheerful topic. Mark brightened as he glanced toward the door. "Oh my, here comes a sweet patootie!"

Alan turned around to look toward the door. A shapely woman had come in, dressed to kill, and had just taken off her coat. "You called that one right. Wow, is she all dressed up," Alan proclaimed. "Oh-oh, look who she's with: Bob Harris."

Bob was another classmate from the Academy and sub school. He had recently been made the engineering and navigation officer on the *Tambor*, which was based at the New London sub base. The *Tambor* was the first of a new and improved class of submarine—about a year newer than the *Squalus*.

Bob and his date were shown to a booth on the other side of the restaurant. They were still visible to Alan and Mark, but far enough away that Bob was unlikely to notice them. The waiter brought Alan and Mark's food, and they began their meal.

Mark glanced over at the couple between bites and said, "Bob still loves to play the field. He'd make a terrible husband, unless he changed a lot and settled down." It was no secret that Bob had gotten engaged not long after their sub school class had started, but had broken off the engagement about nine months later.

"You're right," Alan agreed. "In the long run, Bob probably did Jennifer a favor by breaking off the engagement, although I heard it made her miserable."

Jennifer Warren. Her name brought memories flooding back to Alan. He'd met her for the first time at a cookout for his sub school class, in July 1936. She was tall and graceful, beautiful in an understated way, and she had a sturdy and resolute air about her that only added to her beauty, in Alan's eyes. Her thick hair that was so dark it was nearly black. She parted it in the middle, and it came down almost to her shoulders. Her blue eyes were darker than most; they were not as dark as sapphires, but equally fascinating.

Not only was she good looking, but she was also intelligent, in an unobtrusive way. She was a Radcliffe graduate and had majored in Asian history and minored in math. She had been going into her senior year at Radcliffe when Alan had met her at that cookout. Her father was a scientist of some sort, working at the Massachusetts Institute of Technology.

Alan remembered fondly that she often expressed her sense of humor in a good-natured, bantering, jostling way, which he particularly liked. In fact, he was not aware of anything about her that he had *not* liked.

Mark spoke again, bringing Alan back to the present. "Sad, but true. It was partly that it was so sudden, I suspect. Jennifer had no warning. He dropped her right after he ran across someone new and intriguing." Mark brightened and continued. "As you may know, Mary and Jennifer keep in touch. Did you know Jennifer got her Master's degree? She was hired by ONI before she'd even finished it."

"So she finished her studies at Harvard and got hired by ONI? Good for her." Alan had no problem believing that the Office of Naval Intelligence would have hired her.

Mark said, "You had a crush on Jennifer in sub school, didn't you? Have you seen her since then?"

"Only once. It was during that huge hurricane in September of '38. Where were you at that time?"

"I was on *S-26* down in the Caribbean, but I heard all about it later."

"Did you hear about the train that was nearly wrecked? It was over in Stonington, near the Rhode Island line."

"Yeah, that was quite a story. It came close to being washed away. But what has that got to do with Jennifer?"

"She and I were both on that train, although I didn't know she was there at first. They wanted the passengers to move to the front of the train so they could leave most of the cars behind. It was very slow going through the cars so many of us got out to wade up to the front of the train. I saw her helping other people—strong and brave. It really rekindled my admiration for her." Alan felt a surge of nostalgia. "I asked if I could see her again. Even though it had been a year since Bob had broken the engagement, she said she still wasn't ready to start dating again."

"Yeah, I heard she waited a while. She apparently buried herself in her studies and helped to take care of her grandmother, withdrawing from the social scene. Her grandmother died last October, and Jennifer got her degree in February. Last we heard, she was headed for Washington. Mary was hoping to catch a glimpse of Jennifer on her way up here. I'll ask her to send you Jennifer's address in Washington."

"That would be good," said Alan, hiding his disappointment at hearing that Jennifer had moved out of reach.

"You're still fond of her, aren't you?"

"Yeah, I guess."

They finished their dinner and left the restaurant. The rain had lightened as Alan drove to the Bachelor Officers' Quarters on the submarine base.

Thursday, April 4, 1940

The night's rain had tapered off to a drizzle as Alan left the BOQ. He walked into the headquarters building of the submarine base around 0750. It was a typical navy office building, austere and lacking in style. He walked down the corridor to Ludlow's office. As he removed his raincoat, he noted proudly that his uniform had remained unwrinkled. Before leaving the BOQ, he had groomed himself and dressed carefully to minimize the chance of Ludlow finding fault with his appearance.

"Lieutenant j.g. Ericsson to see Lieutenant Ludlow," he told the yeoman.

There was a long pause before the yeoman looked up languidly. "Yes, sir. I'll tell him you're here." The young man finished something on his desk and then rose slowly and sauntered into Ludlow's office and closed the door. He reappeared a few minutes later. "Lieutenant Ludlow is busy. He'll see you when he is free." Alan was fairly certain that Ludlow had carefully chosen this particular yeoman for his ability to be rude with selected people.

The routine was the same every month when Alan reported to Ludlow's office. Ludlow made the appointment at his convenience, but still he always kept Alan waiting for some time.

Forty minutes later, Ludlow appeared in his doorway, pointed at Alan, and crooked his finger for Alan to enter his office. Alan went in, handed his latest report to Ludlow, and stood at attention. Ludlow put the report on his desk without looking at it and began to inspect Alan closely. He walked around Alan twice. "Your hair is a mess, your uniform's wrinkled, and there's mud on your shoes. You're still a discredit to the US Navy, just like you were at the Academy. You never learn, do you, Ericsson?"

Alan had become used to this during his previous meetings, and he remained silent. He wondered if the effort he put into his appearance when reporting to Ludlow did any good. Ludlow went behind his desk, sat down, and wrote comments on Alan's appearance in his file. When he was done with this, Ludlow sighed and picked up Alan's report. He leaned back in his chair with his feet on the desk. Alan wanted to watch him, to see if he was actually reading, but he knew he had to keep his eyes straight ahead. Ludlow seemed to turn the pages pretty quickly. After about twenty minutes, Ludlow tossed the report on his desk.

With a sneer, he barked, "You will report again May 14 at 0800. Now get out!" Alan was happy to oblige. It was still drizzling as he walked to his car.

As Alan started the return trip to Newport, his mind drifted to the war in Europe and what he knew of the deteriorating relations between the United States and Japan. After the German invasion of Poland the previous September, some people in the country seemed to have forgotten about the war. To Alan, it seemed likely that the United States would be pulled into the war one way or another, eventually. Would Hitler be satisfied with half of Poland? His recent history and large army said he wouldn't. Why would he wait for Britain and France to get better prepared, now that spring was reaching Europe? It was more likely that Hitler would end the quiet of this "Phony War" soon. The Japanese might not take no for an answer to their expansion plans, either. Alan knew that war would mean a huge military expansion, possible promotion for him, and excitement, but also much suffering, hard work, and danger. War was what Alan was trained for, but he was not sure that he was truly ready. *Am I a coward?* he couldn't help but wonder.

He was particularly worried about how unprepared the United States was for war. Roosevelt was anxious to accelerate rearmament, but he was frequently stymied by the powerful isolationist block in Congress, and Alan thought that the United States would not be ready for war for at least two years. He knew that the Germans, with the help of the Russians, had easily rolled up the Polish army, even though the Polish army was larger than the US Army at the time. Also, much of the US Army was stationed in garrisons outside the United States, and those troops would be difficult to call back. Fortunately, important steps toward rearmament had been taken during the last several years, but so far, there had been little increase in the men and equipment ready for combat. He was not confident that the military brass were telling the civilian leaders how bad it was, or that the civilian leaders were taking what they were hearing to heart. He shuddered when he thought about what could happen if events moved too quickly.

CHAPTER TWO

A Very Pleasant Surprise

Sunday, April 14, 1940

Alan was taking a drive around Newport on a beautiful, clear spring morning. He had not been able to resist the temptation to put the top down on his convertible for the first time that spring. Even though it was still a bit too chilly for comfort, he enjoyed being able to hear and see things in all directions and to smell the pleasant scents from the many gardens around town.

Alan had been invited to Sunday dinner at the Peckhams' house in Newport that afternoon. The Peckhams were old friends of Alan's parents. Dr. Peckham had served with Alan's father in the Naval Reserve at the Newport Naval Hospital during World War I. In 1938, he had been looking for a change and volunteered for active duty again, and was assigned, again, to Newport. The Peckhams rented a spacious house in town and rented out their own house in Brookline, Massachusetts. Alan had stayed with them when he first came to Newport, while he was looking for an apartment. They liked to host Sunday dinners, and they invited Alan occasionally.

The Peckhams had a daughter, Victoria, who was five years older than Alan. When Alan was growing up, she had babysat him from time to time. She had taken full advantage of the situation and bossed Alan around, and he had hated her. She had grown up to be quite a lady, though, graduating with high honors from Vassar. She had gone to work for the Naval War College, located on Coasters Harbor Island in Newport Harbor—about a mile north of the Torpedo Station on Goat Island—and had worked her way up to the position of head librarian. She had her own apartment, but she visited her parents frequently. When Alan first stayed with the Peckhams, he had wondered whether Victoria and he would get along. She was cordial from the start; their mutual respect grew as they came to appreciate each other's accomplishments. They became friends and played tennis once a week.

Alan could not quite figure out why Victoria was still unmarried. She was attractive and intelligent, though Alan thought of her more as an older sister than girlfriend material, because of his childhood memories.

Victoria had called him two days earlier to tell him that the Peckhams were particularly glad that he had accepted their invitation for Sunday dinner. Among the invited guests was an Army Air Corps pilot that the Peckhams did not know—friends had asked that they invite him. They were aware that Alan was interested in aviation, so they thought he would be good company. Alan had a high respect for all military pilots, and he looked forward to the occasion to speak with one.

At Victoria's request, that afternoon the Peckhams were also welcoming three young people who had recently started work at the Naval War College: one man and two women, all in their twenties or early thirties, and all unmarried.

Victoria had also informed him earlier that her father thought their guests would like to hear the story of the sinking and rescue of the *Squalus*. The previous Tuesday, however, Germany had invaded Denmark and Norway, ending the "Phony War" abruptly, and Britain was moving to try to defend Norway. This topic might eclipse everything else.

Alan had timed his arrival at the Peckhams' for noon. As he entered their affluent neighborhood on the southeast side of Newport, he couldn't help but marvel at the truly enormous mansions that served as summer houses for extremely wealthy

New Yorkers. These "summer homes" dwarfed the Peckhams' gray Victorian, even though it was both large and formal, as well. As he approached the house, he slowed down and enjoyed the sweet scent of the daffodils and forsythia as they mixed with that of the neatly manicured lawn. Their colors stood out in contrast to the gray house with its white trimmings, making Alan pause to smile for just a moment.

In the driveway by the front door was the Peckhams' stately Packard. He watched as Victoria and several other people climbed out of it; apparently, the others getting out of the car were the guests from the War College. One of the women looked familiar. It took him a moment to place her, but then he realized that it was Jennifer Warren. He quickly pulled over to the curb and stopped, getting a better look.

Sure enough, there she was. Waves of emotion washed over him in rapid succession: complete surprise, amazement at the coincidence, pleasure that he would be in her company again, and a feeling that he was totally unprepared. He was suddenly keyed up and nervous. *Calm down, this could be a nice opportunity*, he told himself. It dawned on him that her presence meant that she was working at the War College, which meant that she was living in Newport, and there might be other opportunities to see her in the future.

He pulled into the driveway. While he had been collecting himself, Victoria and her guests had gone inside. He parked his car, got out, and rang the doorbell.

Victoria opened the door. "Welcome, Alan! Come in and meet our guests."

As he entered the house, he noticed that Victoria had been talking to Jennifer, who was standing nearby, but the other guests had started moving down the hallway. Alan had never mentioned Jennifer to Victoria, so she had no way of knowing that they were acquainted. Alan and Victoria embraced, and Alan found himself looking over Victoria's shoulder into Jennifer's deep blue eyes. Alan was gratified that she, too, seemed taken aback by his presence at first. She smiled warmly back at him.

After greeting Victoria, Alan turned to Jennifer . "Jennifer, what a pleasant surprise! It's been a while," he said, offering his hand.

"It's very nice to see you again, Alan," she replied, grasping his hand with some pressure. She looked apprehensive, almost embarrassed.

"You two know each other, I take it," Victoria chimed in, casting a reproving look at Alan. Victoria was a busybody, never content unless she knew everything about her friends' social lives.

"Yes, Jennifer dated one of my classmates when I was in sub school a few years ago."

Jennifer smiled and seemed relieved at Alan's response. Alan had a feeling that Victoria was watching him closely. *Does she see right through me?* he wondered, slightly embarrassed.

"Well, let's join the rest of our guests," Victoria suggested, taking Jennifer's hand and leading her down the hallway while Alan followed.

Jennifer had not changed. Now that he was looking at her, she was much more than the sum of his slightly hazy memories. Her erect, graceful, posture and her lively, penetrating eyes added to her attraction. He found it hard not to gape at her.

He followed them into the living room where Dr. and Mrs. Peckham were greeting the guests, a large formal room furnished with antiques. Alan always felt out of place in the sumptuous setting of the Peckhams' dinners, but he enjoyed them anyway. He was introduced to the other guests from the War College.

After the introductions, Dr. Peckham asked, "What do you think, Alan? Are the Germans going to take Norway?"

"I'm afraid they will," Alan replied. "The British don't seem to be able to get ahead of the Germans and take the initiative. What do you think, sir?"

"Maybe the British will be able to come up with a surprise and stop the Germans. If they don't, I think Norway may be doomed."

"If they take Norway, do you think they will move on and attack somewhere else, Alan?" asked Mrs. Peckham.

"I hate to think about it, but I think they might."

"It could be the World War all over again," interjected Mrs. Peckham.

"Armies are more mechanized and air forces are much more effective now," Dr. Peckham replied. "I don't think the front will bog down like it did then."

"It sounds pretty grim anyway," said Mrs. Peckham.

"Yes," Dr. Peckham agreed, "but in some ways, it's better to have the uncertainty over with. Maybe now we'll take rearmament more seriously."

Just then the doorbell rang and Mrs. Peckham went to answer it. She returned and introduced First Lieutenant Delbert "Deke" Harrelson of the Army Air Corps, the pilot that the Peckhams thought Alan would enjoy talking to. Alan noticed Deke's West Point ring, mentally noting that he was regular army.

Deke started the conversation with, "So, you're a submariner? I guess that's about as far *below* my job as you can get in the military. I'm a fighter pilot." He laughed at his little joke.

Alan was not amused, and he winced at Deke's joke. For the Peckhams' sake, though, he would try to take it in stride. "What airplane do you fly?" asked Alan.

"The P-36," replied Deke, smiling. "I'll be moving up to the P-40 in a few months."

Since Alan followed aviation, he knew that the P-40 was really just a new version of the P-36. It was faster, because the Pratt & Whitney radial engine had been replaced with a newer, more powerful, sleeker, liquid-cooled Allison V-12. Alan had always been amused that the "P" stood for "pursuit," which was the term the army used to designate fighters, because it suggested following, rather than leading, and possibly culminating in failure. It also suggested that the only way to attack another airplane was from the rear, which he found to be symbolic of the army's narrow view of fighter tactics. "That should be fun," Alan answered. "I've heard the P-36 handles like a sweetheart."

Deke's eyebrows went up and his eyes narrowed. "It is definitely hard to beat the P-36 for handling. The P-40 doesn't handle quite as well, but it's much faster. Where does a submariner hear about army airplanes?"

"Well, I've always been interested in aviation as well as submarines. I still sometimes wonder whether I picked the right specialty."

Deke relaxed and smiled. "I've never had any doubts. Of course, if you went into aviation and got into fighters in the navy, you'd be stuck with the F4F at best. The P-40 will leave the F4F in the dust."

He sure is pushy, Alan realized. He'd heard that was a desirable characteristic in fighter pilots, though. He countered, "It's true that the P-40 is faster below 15,000 feet, but going above that, the P-40 slows down fast. The F4F just keeps getting faster because of its two-stage supercharger, so above 18,000, the F4F will leave the P-40 in the dust. In fact, above 25,000, I doubt the P-40 could even keep up with a B-17."

Deke ignored this last comment and rebutted, "But the army has the turbo-supercharged P-38 coming along. The navy doesn't have anything close to the P-38."

"Maybe." Alan knew he sounded cryptic and skeptical. He had heard a little via the grapevine about the new XF4U-1 fighter that Vought was developing for the navy. "I mean, I know some things about new navy developments that I'm probably not supposed to know. But I imagine that the army may have a few new things up its sleeve, as well."

"You bet! The P-38 is so clean, though, and following versions will have more power, so it'll be the fastest for a long time."

Alan knew that the P-38's speed was largely due to its two engines, but the extra weight on the wings made it a lot slower in rolling maneuvers. "It should do a fine job intercepting bombers," Alan informed him, "but it might have trouble against single-engine fighters with its slow roll response." *That ought to take some of the wind out of his sails.*

Deke's eyes narrowed again. For a fleeting moment, his smile changed to a frown, but he quickly forced a smile again. "We have ways of dealing with that," Deke replied.

A pretty lame reply, Alan thought.

Just then, Mrs. Peckham rang a small bell and asked the guests to take their seats at the table in the dining room, which was almost as large as the living room and lit by large windows. Alan found that Victoria's hand-written place cards indicated that Victoria was on his left and Jennifer was opposite her, across the table from them. The other woman from the War College, Louise Funkhouser, was on his right.

Louise seemed to be in her early twenties and just out of college, too young for Alan to look at as a serious dating prospect. She was attractive, but had a serious, studious manner.

Dr. Peckham offered a brief prayer before standing and carving the ham. The plates were passed around to the other end of the table, where Mrs. Peckham served the vegetables and potatoes. Bottles of Chateau Latour 1936 circulated among the guests.

When Dr. Peckham had finished carving, he tapped the side of his glass with his fork before addressing the company. "All of us here work for the navy or the army, except for my good wife, so we're keenly aware that we seem headed toward war. The events in Europe this week are probably going to push us faster in that direction.

"Some of you may not be aware that one of our company has already had an experience that was as terrifying as combat, in my opinion. Our friend Alan Ericsson, here," he said, gesturing toward Alan, "whom we have known since he was a small child, is a submariner. He was the engineering officer on the submarine *Squalus*. The *Squalus,* as you may remember, sank to the ocean floor, out of control, last May. Our navy succeeded in rescuing the surviving crew members, which brought international prestige to our navy. Until then, no navy had been able to rescue men in sunken submarines unless they had sunk in very shallow water. Many navies sent congratulations, including the German Navy. I thought you might be interested to hear the story, so I've asked Alan to tell us about it."

There was a murmur of assent.

Alan cleared his throat and got started. He had told the story enough times that he could do it now with little effort. He kept his eyes moving around the table as he talked. He had decided that he would not look at Jennifer, because he might become distracted, but after a while he unintentionally glanced at her. He found that she was staring at him with rapt attention; he could not help staring back. Her deep blue eyes seemed to be searching into his soul. He suddenly realized that he had paused in his story, and everyone had noticed that he and Jennifer were staring at each other. He blushed, averted his eyes, cleared his throat, and continued with the story. He was aware that Victoria continued to stare at him for some time after the pause. She would be sure to question him about it later, in private. He wrapped up the story with a summary of the salvage process.

"Well, that's a most amazing story, Alan," Mrs. Peckham announced. There was a murmur of agreement around the table.

By the end of the story, most of the others had finished their main course, but Alan had hardly started. Talk turned back to the war in Europe, and Alan did not mind that he had to forgo conversation to catch up on the rest of his meal. He noticed that Jennifer did not contribute to that conversation, either. When the meal was finished and chairs were pushed back, Mrs. Peckham announced that coffee would be served outside on the terrace. The guests slowly made their way out into a beautiful, sunny afternoon. Alan took a cup of coffee and turned around to find Jennifer standing next to him. He was unable to suppress another blush.

"Do you remember the last time we saw each other?" she asked, smiling warmly.

"Like it was yesterday. You were helping a perfect stranger; you were so brave. About ten days ago, I had dinner with Mark Gallagher, and I mentioned it to him. He was down in the Caribbean on *S-26* at the time and missed the hurricane."

"You were the one who was brave." She looked him in the eyes. "I felt much braver knowing you were there." There was a pause, and Alan didn't know what to say. She continued, "The Gallaghers seem to be doing well; he is looking forward to *Sailfish*, and Mary's pregnancy has gone well so far."

"Yes, they seem to be in great shape. Mark told me you'd gotten your Master's degree and that you had been hired by ONI in Washington. Congratulations!" He beamed at her.

"Thank you," she said, smiling warmly again.

"Mark thought you were in Washington, but now you're at the War College? Can you tell me anything about what you're doing?"

"I'm working in the library. In fact, Victoria is my boss. Recently, I've been studying the Fleet Problems. My boss at ONI is Commander McCollum, the head of the Far East desk, and he wanted me to learn more about the navy before getting into intelligence work. He thought I might learn faster at the War

College than at ONI, where everyone is too busy to spend time helping a neophyte, so ONI is loaning me to the War College for the time being."

"What a coincidence that you're working for Victoria, whom I've known since I was a little kid! Studying the Fleet Problems is a great way to learn about the navy. They're far from perfect, but they're the best chance we have in peacetime to find out how well things really work."

"How about you? I had no idea you were in Newport. I've been wondering where you ended up after the *Squalus* sank. The last time I'd heard from them, the Gallaghers didn't know you were here."

Wow, he realized, *she was thinking about me!* He explained how he had gotten assigned to the Torpedo Station. When the Peckhams, Victoria, and the other guests moved off as a group to walk around the grounds, discussing the flowers and shrubs, Jennifer did not seem anxious to join them. Alan saw that this was his chance to have a moment alone with her.

Alan gathered his courage and asked, "Jennifer, could I take you out to dinner next weekend? Maybe Saturday or Sunday? I'd like to take you to one of the old restaurants here in the city."

She turned, smiled, and looked directly into his eyes. "That would be very nice. I think Saturday would be best for me." Her smile grew as she said, "It has taken almost four years for you to get a date with me, hasn't it? I'm glad you don't give up easily."

He grinned. "I'll pick you up at 1800." Alan was aglow inside at the prospect of their date. They exchanged addresses and telephone numbers. He realized that her apartment was on the mainland near the War College, which was only about a mile away from his apartment and the ferry to the Torpedo Station.

By then, the other guests had returned to the terrace and were starting to thank their hosts and prepare to leave. Jennifer turned to him and winked, saying, "Very nice to see you again, Alan."

Alan got the message and said, "It was a pleasure, Jennifer. I hope to see you again soon." Deke and Alan thanked the Peckhams and said good-bye at the same time, exiting the front door together, as the War College guests followed them.

Alan noticed that behind his car was a bright yellow 1933 Ford coupe that looked brand new. Alan had always loved cars. He had always loved anything mechanical, really, but cars were something he had learned about on his own from a young age. He fondly remembered his days of working as a mechanic at a car dealership in the summers between school years.

"Is that your car?" Alan asked, pointing to the Ford.

"Yep," Deke replied shortly.

"Very nice. It looks like new."

Deke smiled and looked at Alan's car. "Is that your car in front of mine? I noticed it when I arrived. What is it?"

"It's a Tatra, from Czechoslovakia," Alan replied as they walked down the driveway toward Alan's car.

"It looks awful low. What kind of an engine does it have?"

"It's air-cooled, like a Franklin, but the four cylinders are opposed, like the engine in a Piper Cub. This one has fifty horsepower, instead of the stock thirty, because our gas is so much better that their racing engine works fine."

"Won't keep up with my Ford, even though it's seven years old, now," Deke bragged. "A car that low couldn't ride as well as my Ford, either."

Victoria and the other guests stopped to listen to their conversation.

"My Tatra is seven years old, too," Alan replied, "and it won't keep up with your Ford in a straight line, but on a curvy road, especially if the road is bumpy, it'll leave your Ford behind. It rides better than your Ford because it has independent suspension on all four wheels. Your Ford has solid axles at both ends and a much higher center of gravity."

Deke smiled and said, "You gotta be kidding. I could leave that little foreign contraption in the dust on *any* road. You wanna race?"

Alan almost took him up on it. He glanced up and saw Victoria behind Deke, shaking her head. She drew her finger across her throat in the "kill it" signal. *Ever the babysitter*, thought Alan. "Your car stock?" Alan asked, continuing the conversation as he saw Victoria beginning to fume.

"Pretty close."

"Let's see." Alan walked back to Deke's car, and Deke followed him. Deke opened the hood, and Alan gaped. Everything was spotless. Many of the parts were polished and gleaming. On top of the V-8, there were three big carburetors instead of the little one that Ford provided.

"That's one of the prettiest engine compartments I've ever seen," Alan said, defusing the situation, "but it's not anything close to stock. I bet you have a hot cam, too."

"Well, shucks," said Deke. His face turned red and a big grin appeared.

"Beautiful car," said Alan, as he turned and walked toward his car. Victoria smiled and gave Alan a thumbs-up signal.

"Yours is kinda pretty, too," called Deke.

Dr. Peckham appeared in the doorway and beckoned to Alan to come back in. When Alan went back in, Dr. Peckham said, "I just wanted to thank you for entertaining everyone today with your story. You told it well." Alan glanced at Mrs. Peckham, who was smiling and nodding.

"Thank you, sir," he politely replied. "It was the least I could do in return for all your hospitality."

Dr. Peckham continued the conversation about the prospects of war and US rearmament for a bit. Alan had nothing planned for the afternoon, so he stayed and talked. The prospect of having a date with Jennifer had put him in a genial mood.

Soon Victoria returned. She quickly took him by the hand and led him onto the grounds for a stroll before turning to him and saying, "Really, Alan, I thought I knew you. Now it seems that you've concealed a long history with one of my employees. I was glad to let you two reminisce, but I sensed it went way beyond that. Are you in love with her?"

It's confirmed, Alan realized, *to Victoria, I'm transparent.* "I had no idea that she was one of your employees, or that she was even in Newport, until today," he said. "Maybe I *am* in love with her. I'll admit that I've admired her since we first met, but she was engaged. Now she has resurfaced, and I'm hoping to get to know her better. If that's being in love, then the answer is yes."

"Sounds more like a crush, I guess. Wow, I had no inkling. *You're* a sly one. When are you going to see her again?" she asked, her smile friendly.

"Next Saturday."

"Well done. Good luck."

"Aye, aye, madam," he said, smiling back.

As he drove back to his apartment, Alan turned the day's events over in his mind several times, savoring several moments. Jennifer was in town, and she was willing to see him! It seemed like his good luck was starting to come back, just like the *Squalus*.

Saturday, April 20, 1940

It had been another beautiful, sunny spring day, but still cool. Now it was evening, with a cloudless sky and the temperature in the fifties. Even after having relationships with three women, Alan felt like a kid on his first date. He was scrubbed clean and dressed in a jacket and tie, and his blue eyes looked out under black hair that was carefully combed. If ever there was an occasion for a smart appearance, this was it. It was hard for him to accomplish this with ready-made civilian clothes, though. He was 6'1" and 155 pounds, which was why he had acquired the nickname Stringy at the Naval Academy. Luckily, tailored uniforms could accommodate his shape, unlike ready-made clothes.

He felt a tingle of nervousness as he turned onto the street where Jennifer's apartment was. He found her apartment building, parked, and pressed the doorbell. He heard a door close upstairs, and Jennifer appeared a moment later. She was as beautiful as ever, wearing a tailored light-blue dress. They started out the door.

She pointed to a royal blue Chevrolet coupe by the door. "My parents gave me a car when I finished my Master's, and here it is," she told him.

"'37 Chevy Master De Luxe Business Coupe. Very nice. I like the features Chevy offers. Your father made a good choice . . . Or did you pick it out?"

"We worked on it together."

"I like the color, too; it reminds me of your eyes." Alan walked around her car.

She smiled and blushed slightly. As they walked back to Alan's car, she said, "I saw your car in the Peckhams' driveway. I like the look of it. It's very low and sporty. Too bad it's still too cool to put the top down. And it has right-hand drive?"

"Yes, so you'll be sitting on the left. I hope you don't mind." He took her hand to guide her around the front of the car.

"Not at all," she said. "I've ridden in a couple of other cars with right-hand drive. What a beautiful paint scheme." The paint was original—sky blue for the body and wheels, with black fenders.

"Thank you. I like it a lot, too." Alan opened the door for her and she settled herself into the seat. He went back around the front of the car and climbed in on the right side.

He was about to put the key in the switch when she smiled and said, "Okay, Alan, out with it: What *is* this crazy car? It has right hand-drive, but nothing is written in English. The speedometer even says 'kilometers'."

Alan felt a wave of affection for her. He turned and beamed at her. "That joshing manner of yours—I just love it! It's so nice to hear it again." She reddened as he answered her question. "It's a Tatra, made in Czechoslovakia. They drove on the left like they do in Britain until Hitler took over."

"I know the Czechs are quite industrialized, but I haven't heard much about their cars. Why do you like it?"

"Tatra is located in Moravia, away from Prague and at the eastern edge of the central European-industrialized region, which I think might have something to do with the independence of their thinking. Their vehicles are quite innovative and advanced, really. In this car, the engine has horizontally opposed cylinders, which gives the car a low center of gravity, and the engine is air-cooled, so it cannot boil, freeze up, or leak away its coolant. The car has fully independent suspension; when any wheel hits a bump, it doesn't cause the other wheels to tip or bounce. The Tatra is the only make that has these features, except for the new German Volkswagen, which I suspect stole some of its ideas from Tatra . . . Am I talking Greek to you?"

"Not at all. It makes me wonder why more car companies aren't following their lead. What year is this car?"

"1933."

"Seven years old, and still ahead of its time. I like that you know where Tatra is located. I suspected your interests went well beyond just machinery. Where did you get this car?"

"My uncle left it to me in his will three years ago. He had no children, and I guess I was the only one he knew who shared his enthusiasm for it."

"Well, I think we should find out how well the car drives by actually using it," she joked, smiling at him.

It was Alan's turn to redden. He grinned and said, "You're right," turning the key on and pulling the starter lever. They headed for the restaurant.

"It doesn't have synchromesh, I see," she added, watching him pump the clutch twice at each shift.

He was delighted to find that she knew so much about cars. "Yeah, you're right, but it does have overdrive, so in effect, it has eight speeds forward and two in reverse."

"That might be too many," she said, laughing. "It does have a comfortable ride. The engine sounds different, though—a little more clickety-clack. Is that because it's air cooled?"

"Yes. The internal sounds don't have a water jacket to muffle them."

They found a parking spot near the restaurant and were shown to a dimly lit booth near the back.

Jennifer liked his suggestion of a bottle of red wine. After he ordered it, she said, "Now tell me more about what you've been doing since the hurricane, other than escaping from a sunken submarine."

"Well, let's see . . . The reason I was on the train during the hurricane was that I'd completed my duty on *S-24*. I had orders to report to the *Squalus*, which was under construction at Portsmouth, with two weeks' leave before I had to be there. I went home to my parents' house in Brookline and helped them and some neighbors with the hurricane damage. When my leave was up, I drove up to Portsmouth. The hurricane didn't hit Portsmouth as hard as the Boston area, so the mess was mostly cleared up by the time I got there. For the next six months, we worked on getting the *Squalus* fitted out and learning her systems, since none of us had served in a fleet boat before. Then we began her sea trials."

"During which disaster struck," Jennifer supplied. "That was a chilling story you told. It must have been a terrifying experience.

You said you worked on the salvage until the middle of September. What happened then?"

"The navy decided they were going to refurbish the *Squalus*, so the survivors of the submarine worked with the Yard to get that effort underway. The Court of Inquiry that had started in June was reconvened to consider all new evidence that could be found on board the *Squalus*, and then it drew its conclusions. All the survivors were exonerated, but the Secretary of the Navy barred the captain and XO from further submarine duty, which was a major setback in their careers. It was his prerogative, but it doesn't seem right to me for a civilian to meddle in the careers of mid-level officers. They renamed the submarine the *Sailfish*, and, as you know, Mark Gallagher got assigned to her as gunnery and torpedo officer."

"Yes, Mark seems quite pleased with the assignment. On the other hand, I also know that you were exonerated, but you were sent to a desk job because of your embarrassing report." She paused, and then continued. "You've probably had more time for your social life, though. Have you met anyone interesting?"

"There was one girl, but we broke up about a month ago." Alan paused. "How about you? The Gallaghers said that you hadn't dated for a long time."

"It took me a long time to get over Bob breaking the engagement." She paused and swallowed hard. Alan reached out and put his hand on hers, and she smiled back at him. "I plunged into my studies; a few months later, my grandmother had a stroke that left her partially paralyzed. I moved in with her, in Lexington near my parents, and shared her care with my mother. She was a wonderful woman to get to know. Last October, she suddenly died. Under the circumstances, it was probably a blessing, but it came as a shock to me. I woke up to the fact that I'd been hiding from the world, and it was time to face it. I made some forays into the social scene in Cambridge last winter—I met a few guys who *seemed* nice, but as soon as they found out that I was a graduate student, they backed away. It seems that most men are disconcerted by the idea of a well-educated woman." Her expression had turned to a frown.

"I'm afraid that's true, and it's shameful. Your accomplishments make me admire you more," Alan said, looking into her eyes.

She looked back into his eyes. "Thank you, Alan."

The waiter served the wine and took their orders for dinner.

"Your degree is in Asian History, right?" Alan pursued.

"Yes. Well . . . That's sort of a catchall. Individual students usually have a much narrower focus within that subject. I studied Japanese history and culture. When I was applying for graduate school, one of the professors thought the navy might be interested in me. I had an interview, and the officer said that the navy would pay my tuition plus a small stipend if I agreed to two commitments: that I would learn the Japanese language, and that I would work for the navy after getting my degree, sticking with it for five years even if I got married. That didn't seem unreasonable, because I knew they'd be making a big investment in my education.

"The three professors at Harvard who knew Japanese had studied the language in Japan, although none of them were fluent. I knew I couldn't go to Japan, so I began to push for instruction from someone who *was* fluent. They knew a Japanese gentleman who agreed to do it. In the end, I think I became closer to fluency than any of those three—both in speech and writing. It's a tough language for Westerners, but I found I enjoyed the challenge. At first, it was sort of like code breaking." She blushed and added, "I have an interest in code breaking that I got from one of my undergraduate math professors, but that's a separate matter . . . . Anyway, learning Japanese added quite a bit of extra time to my degree program."

"Wow, I can see why the navy was interested in you. I suspect they made a smart investment. Tell me a little more about what you've been up to since the hurricane. Or is it all secret?" She smiled and seemed to relax, relieved that he genuinely appreciated her unusual career.

"Some of it is. The reason *I* was on the train during the hurricane is that I was going home to start the fall term after visiting the Gallaghers in New London. They had told me you were headed for duty on the *Squalus*, but they didn't say when, so I was surprised to see you on the train.

"Last fall, I knew I would finish up in February so I started looking into what part of the navy I would work for. One of the professors told me that the head of the Far East desk at ONI would be interested in me. In December, I went to Washington and had an interview with that gentleman, Commander McCollum. I also had an interview with a woman who works in the Office of Naval Communications—the only woman working as a professional in the Navy Department. She has been working there since the First World War, and she has some exceptional skills that I am *not* allowed to discuss. She described what it was like to work in an all-male office, and she wanted to know if I was really ready for that. Apparently, I convinced her that I was, and I was hired. After I graduated, I went to Washington. They told me right away that they wanted to send me to work at the War College, so I didn't get an apartment there. I started working here about three weeks ago, and I've been busy setting up an apartment."

"How long will you be at the War College?"

"I expect to be here between six months and a year, and then I'll go to work at ONI in Washington. How about you? How long will you be at the Torpedo Station?"

Alan was thrilled to hear that she would probably be around for another six months. He savored the thought for a moment before replying, "Another five or six months, I think. I've been advised, by an officer I have a lot of respect for, to stick it out for nine months or so at this assignment. After that, I am considering transferring to aviation."

Her response was tinged with anxiety. "That sounds like good advice, but aviation, Alan? After submarines, isn't that like jumping from the frying pan into the fire?" She had a point, but he tried to reassure her.

"All the fighting parts of the navy have quite a bit of risk. During my two-year surface tour after graduating from the Naval Academy, I served on the battleship *Pennsylvania*, which was the flagship of the Pacific Fleet. I thought a lot about what it would be like to serve on her in combat, and I didn't feel very safe. In submarines, you're part of a much smaller unit, so you feel that you have more influence over the outcome. This is even truer in aviation, where the fate of one airplane is largely determined by its small crew."

"Hmm. I need to think about that." After a pause, Jennifer asked, "Tell me a little about your family. Do you have brothers and sisters? What does your father do?" *It's a good sign that she's interested in my family*, Alan thought happily.

"My dad is a doctor—a urologist. My mother is a nurse, and she went back to work after I and my siblings were out of the house. I have an older brother who is also a doctor, but he's a cardiologist. He's married and has a two-year-old daughter. I have a younger sister who is about your age. She is a nurse. She married a mechanical engineer last June, and he works for General Electric in Lynn. My brother-in-law and I are the black sheep of the family, since we aren't in the medical profession. How about your family?"

"My dad is a physicist; he works at MIT. He's been working on some hush-hush project having to do with high frequency radio waves. My mother is a schoolteacher who went back to work recently, like your mother. I have an older sister who is also a schoolteacher. She's about your age and not married. My younger brother is a senior at MIT, studying electrical engineering."

Their food arrived, and they ate in silence for a few minutes.

Jennifer leaned back and took a sip of wine. She turned to a new subject. "It's hard for me not to think about world events these days. Naturally, I've been thinking mostly about Japan. Most people are so worried about what's going on in Europe that they aren't paying much attention to the Pacific. It seems to me that things are headed toward war there, too."

Alan smiled and said, "It's nice to talk to someone who really knows about Japan. Like most people in this country, I don't know much about their culture, but it seems like their government feels it's their right to expand and take over other countries and ter- ritories, just like Germany. As they keep expanding their territory, we keep putting more pressure on them, but it doesn't seem to be having any effect. If we cut off their oil, they'll be forced to give in or fight. I know that most people assume they'll give in, but it seems like a big risk, especially when we don't have the forces to back up our threat."

"Exactly. Most Americans don't understand the Japanese idea of honor. If their honor is threatened, they will fight—even if they have no chance of success. The idea of backing down is foreign to them. Perhaps that is because their country is small enough that there is not much room to retreat. Also, the Japanese have been intent for a long time on joining the club of colonial powers. They're extremely sensitive to the colonial powers looking down on them, and are aware that most of those powers consider them racially inferior. Now their army is working on taking over their government, which would get rid of any chance for negotiation."

"Very interesting. It sounds even worse than I thought."

Jennifer continued, "Of course, the people at the War College are thinking about both potential theaters. If we get into a war with both Japan and Germany, we won't have enough navy to charge across the Pacific for a quick showdown with Japan, the way some strategists advocate."

"The people advocating that fast-charge strategy have had to ignore logistics, as well. I think it was a mistake when they eliminated the Logistics Department at the War College in 1928."

"I didn't know they used to have a logistics department. It does seem like logistics are often neglected." She looked thoughtful for a moment, and then continued. "Naturally, the navy would play a bigger role in a war in the Pacific than in the Atlantic."

"Unless Britain falls," said Alan.

"Very true. In that case, it could get pretty grim." She smiled and said, "You know, you'd fit right in at the War College, but they don't take anyone below full lieutenant, and not many of those. They're starting to worry about keeping enough students and faculty, though, as the expansion of the navy pulls people away."

"So, now might be a good time to apply," said Alan, chuckling. "It seems to me that many of the top brass in both the army and the navy don't take the Japanese threat very seriously. They seem to think that the Japanese victories in China don't mean much because China is weak. And the Russians did defeat the Japanese at Nomonhan last summer. They seem to think that the Japanese aren't good fighters and that their technology is third-rate, but the aviation magazines have some ominous reports about their new airplanes. What do people at the War College think about Japanese capability?"

"I really don't know yet, but if I did, I couldn't tell you. You know we should be careful not to tempt each other to be too revealing," she said with a smile, shaking a finger at him.

"But it would be okay to tempt each other in other ways," he said with a big grin.

She blushed and smiled again, saying, "Watch it."

He reached out and squeezed her hand, saying, "Okay."

They ate in silence for a few moments, finishing their main course before Alan resumed his line of questioning. "Here's another big question: If we went to war with Japan, do you think we would use unrestricted submarine warfare like the Germans do? It would negate all our past denouncements of the German policy, but it could be very effective. Do you hear anything at the War College about that?"

Jennifer paused and replied. "Again, if I knew I couldn't say. But I haven't heard any discussion of that, and I agree that it's a big question. It would be a lot easier to do that if the Japanese did it first."

"That's true. I'm inclined to think that this type of warfare would be considered tolerable if the sailors in the merchant marine who are threatened by submarine attacks were treated as part of the military. It's a new type of warfare, so a new military organization could be created; the merchant sailors could be brought into it in wartime. Their pay and benefits could be made more comparable to that of navy sailors."

"That *seems* logical, but it would be a huge change."

"Very true."

Jennifer changed the subject. "It's so nice that the weather is getting warmer. I'm looking forward to getting to know the beaches here."

"There are four nice ones close by: First, Second, Third, and Bailey's Beach. When we leave here, we could take a drive down to First Beach, if you'd like. It would be nice to take a stroll on the beach tonight . . . but neither of us wore the right shoes for it, did we?"

"You're right about that."

The waiter appeared with the check and Alan paid.

"Thank you for a delightful dinner, Alan."

"You're very welcome. It was my pleasure."

It was still warm, and it was not completely dark when they walked out. After the short drive down the hill on Bath Road, they came to First Beach on their right. Alan parked at the sea wall and switched off the engine. The side windows were open, letting in the gentle northwest breeze. Alan put his arm around Jennifer's shoulders, and she leaned over and put her head on his shoulder. He smelled her perfume and listened to the gentle sound of the surf.

They remained there, quietly enjoying each other's company, for some time. Finally, Jennifer broke the silence. "You know, we really don't know each other very well, but sometimes I feel like you are very familiar, like I've known you for a long time."

"It's the same with me. In a way, it's true; we've known a little bit about each other for four years."

"True."

He leaned over and gave her a quick kiss on the cheek.

She turned her head, smiled, and returned the quick kiss, then put her head back down on his shoulder for a while until it started to get cooler. "I think I'm starting to get cold. Let's go back," she suggested.

"Sure."

They drove back to her apartment, and Alan helped her out of the car and walked her to the door. She turned and looked into his eyes.

"Alan?" She paused, then smiled and said, "It's been a wonderful evening. I . . . I hope I'll see you again soon."

"How about tomorrow afternoon?" he asked her. "We could do some beach exploring in more appropriate clothes." He grinned.

"I think that might be just barely soon enough, you rascal." She laughed. "I could make us a picnic lunch."

"That sounds very nice. Can I pick you up at noon, you scalawag?"

"No. *I'll* pick *you* up at noon," she replied, grinning.

They came together and embraced, noses almost touching. She cocked her head and unexpectedly kissed him on the mouth. He felt his body responding as she squeezed him and he squeezed back. Their tongues touched and began to explore each other before she drew back and looked him in the eyes, smiling. He could see that there were tears in her eyes.

"Let's leave it at that for tonight," she suggested huskily. "Good night, Alan. See you tomorrow."

"Good night, Jennifer. I'll be waiting at noon."

She turned and disappeared into her building. He returned to his car filled with so much joy that he could barely drive. He knew he was falling head over heels for her, but why shouldn't he? He had admired her for a long time, and it seemed like she might be falling for him, too.

CHAPTER THREE

More Good News

Friday, May 17, 1940

Alan had gotten notice that the base exec had been relieved by Commander John Ellsworth. He was ordered to report to Ellsworth at 0800 instead of reporting to Lieutenant Ludlow. Alan had heard through the grapevine that Ellsworth, known as "Cracker Jack," was tough and demanding, but also fair and inspiring. He sounded to Alan like just the kind of person that was needed as the base exec, because he could rein Ludlow in. Maybe a little more of Alan's lost luck was about to resurface.

It was damp and cloudy, the result of the onshore wind that was common that time of year. Alan walked into the office of the Base Executive Officer at 0754. "Lieutenant j.g. Alan Ericsson to see Commander Ellsworth," he told the yeoman, ready to be kept waiting.

"He's expecting you, sir. Go right in."

Alan walked into the Commander's office. Ellsworth had a crew cut of salt and pepper hair, dark eyes, and a firm set to his jaw. Alan thought he projected a no-nonsense air, perhaps more so than any other officer he had met. Everything in the office was neat and austere, echoing that no-nonsense attitude.

"Lieutenant j.g. Alan Ericsson reporting as ordered, sir."

Ellsworth came around his desk, and his forbidding face suddenly broke into a welcoming smile. He extended his hand and gripped Alan's hand almost painfully firmly, saying, "Very good, Ericsson. Have a seat." They both sat down, and Ellsworth started filling his pipe. Alan was among the minority in the navy who did not smoke, but he did enjoy the occasional whiff of aromatic pipe smoke.

Ellsworth explained, "I always try to get to know my officers as soon as possible when I get reassigned. In your case, I couldn't do it informally, since you aren't stationed here, which is why I called for this interview. Let's start at the beginning. Where did you grow up, and where did you go to school?" Ellsworth opened a file, which he added to from time to time. He started to light his pipe.

"In Brookline, right next to Boston, sir. I went to public and private schools, graduating from Milton Academy."

"That's a top-notch school. You probably had no difficulty getting into the Academy, unlike many bright boys from other schools. What did you do in the summers?"

"After seventh, eighth, and ninth grades I worked at a local car dealer, working my way up to mechanic. My parents did not like my becoming a grease monkey, so they made me an offer. I could keep my earnings, instead of putting them towards Milton tuition, but they would get to choose what kind of job I took. They had me work on a farm in West Virginia after tenth grade, and I was a cowboy in Wyoming after eleventh grade. I'm grateful to them for pushing me to get away. It was a great experience, once I got used to being away from home."

"Interesting variety. What's your father's occupation?"

"He's a doctor, sir."

"I see. And what made you want to go into the navy?"

"Well, I've always been interested in machinery and travel to faraway places, and the chance for adventure was a plus. I knew I didn't want to go into medicine or law. Engineering was a possibility, but I was afraid that I didn't have the patience for it. I was leaning toward applying to the Naval Academy when the '29 stock market crash hit. My father told me about what happened to a few people he knew who were hit hard by the crash, and I was worried about getting caught in a financial failure if I worked in civilian business. That settled it for me."

Ellsworth had gotten his pipe going, and he said in between puffs, "The economy has influenced quite a few applicants. How did your parents feel about you applying to the Naval Academy?"

"They were against it at first, sir. They felt I was too smart and well-educated for the navy, I'm sorry to say. I kept arguing with them, though, and they gradually came around. My older brother was already headed to medical school, so I think they felt they could take a chance with me."

"And you graduated in '34, a little below the midpoint in class ranking. You did very well academically, but you were hurt by your disciplinary record," Ellsworth said, glancing over several sheets in a folder that was open on his desk.

"Yes, sir." Alan smiled to himself as he remembered the worst offense: He was caught climbing over a wall to get back on campus in the middle of the night. After that, he learned to be more careful.

"You were lucky you weren't in the class of '33," Ellsworth reminded him.

Alan remembered well that the bottom half of the class that year had not gotten their commissions when they graduated. They had been discharged from the navy, although they had all been given a chance to come back and get their commissions the following spring. That debacle was the unintended result of a congressional limit on the number of navy officers.

"Yes, sir. Luckily, Congress rectified their mistake before we graduated."

"Did you have a car at the Academy, Ericsson?" Midshipmen were forbidden to have cars, but everyone knew that some did, anyway.

"Yes, sir."

"I thought you might have," Ellsworth said, grinning. "After the Academy, your mandatory two-year surface tour was on the *Pennsylvania*. You did well in gunnery. Did you ask for a battleship?"

"No, sir. By the time I graduated, I was pretty sure I wanted to go into submarines or aviation—the three-dimensional navy, as I call it. I felt that battleship duty might not help my career, and that it would be less rewarding."

"The three-dimensional navy? I haven't heard that one before. There are a lot of parallels between submarines and aviation, but they don't seem to get along well with each other. You chose duty in the submarine service."

"Yes, sir. It wasn't easy for me, choosing between submarines and aviation. It was partly the stealthy nature of the submarine that tipped me in that direction. I didn't like the biplanes the navy was using on carriers at that time, either, because they seemed old-fashioned. I knew that biplanes saved space on the carriers, so I thought that the navy would stick with them for a long time. It seemed like carrier airplanes would always be inferior to army planes, and submarines were already making a big step forward with the arrival of the fleet boat."

"Hmm, that sounds logical. You did exceedingly well in the submarine school here, and then served eighteen months on *S-24*. You qualified in submarines in the minimum time. You progressed well, and your fitness reports look good. You earned a place on a fleet boat. What do you see the role of the fleet boat in future conflicts being, Ericsson?"

"The S-boats aren't fast enough to operate with the fleet, and they don't have enough range to do effective long-range independent patrols. The fleet boats can do both, in theory. They can operate well with a fleet from the last war at twenty knots, but not with the fleet of the next war, which will operate at around thirty knots in combat. Long-range independent patrol has to be the role of the fleet boat."

Ellsworth sat back suddenly, pointed at Alan with his pipe stem, and said, "Jesus, Ericsson, are you bucking for admiral or professor at the War College? How do you know that I'm not one of those officers who thinks the fleet will continue to be built on the twenty-knot battleships for a long time to come? It happens that I believe you're right on the money, but that's not the point. Your views are heresy to some high-ranking submariners. Not only would they disagree vehemently, they would think you were a smartass for making the argument sound so simple. I can see that tact and discretion aren't your strong suit, and I suggest you work on that when you talk about these things with officers you are unfamiliar with. You need to trim your sails. That way, you might get promoted far enough that you could put some of that thinking to use." He puffed on his pipe. "Let's get back to nuts and bolts, here. How were the early days on the *Squalus*?"

Alan was a little stung by the rebuke, but he knew that Ellsworth was right: he did lack tact and discretion. He was beginning to warm to Ellsworth, because the man seemed to genuinely have Alan's best interests at heart. "She came along very well. Lieutenant Naquin and the other officers were very good, and so were the crew. We got to know the *Sculpin* crew pretty well, also. The two boats were in constant competition, and compared closely."

"I know about the sinking and the rescue, and I've read your report. I thought it was an excellent report, although a little blunt in its conclusions. Did you know someone on the *Skipjack*?"

Alan was shocked and pleased that Ellsworth had read his report on the *Squalus* sinking. "Yes, sir. The navigation and engineering officer on the *Skipjack* at the time was a good friend, an Academy and sub school classmate. When he heard about the *Squalus* sinking, he called me long distance from San Diego and described what had happened on the *Skipjack*. I also heard later about what happened on the *Snapper*."

Ellsworth remarked, "A good friend, indeed. Instead of being appreciated, your report got you a big black mark and assignment to a desk job. What happened?"

"At the time, I was furious about the loss of my shipmates. I felt that my duty to them was to pull no punches in laying out what the problem was, what the fix was, and how the sinking could've been prevented. I thought the rest would take care of itself." Alan paused and continued. "Later, I realized that my report would embarrass the brass. I should have known that. They were angry, and that damaged my career. It also slowed getting the fix on the submarines, though, fortunately, not by too much. It was a lesson I should've learned earlier, but I hadn't."

"Tact and discretion again, Lieutenant. At least you figured it out afterward. You participated in the salvage of the *Squalus*. It took almost four months; so it didn't go smoothly?"

"It was pretty bad, sir. Just about everything that could go wrong did. The good part was that I had the privilege of getting to know Commander Momsen."

"Swede's a very fine officer. We could use a few more like him. But he also took a while to learn tact and discretion. I'm sure you learned a lot. With the salvage completed and the *Squalus* decommissioned, you were assigned in November to the submarine base, with independent duty at the Newport Torpedo Station. How did that work?"

"I was ordered to report to Lieutenant Ludlow, sir. He requires me to present written reports to him in person once a month here at the base."

Ellsworth was writing more, and his pipe was going out. "What happens during your monthly visits? What kind of comments and evaluations have you received on your reports?"

"Lieutenant Ludlow has me stand at attention. He inspects me, finds something unsatisfactory, and makes a note of it. He then sits down, reads my report, and sets the date for the next report. After that, I'm dismissed."

Ellsworth was writing faster. He put his pipe aside, and his frown was becoming steadily more intense. "He inspects you every time?"

"Yes, sir."

"While he's reading the report, what are you doing?"

"I'm standing at attention, sir."

"What? For how long?"

"Usually about twenty minutes, sir."

"And what does Lieutenant Ludlow say to you about your reports?"

"Nothing, sir."

"Are you telling me that you've *never* received any evaluation of your work from Lieutenant Ludlow, or, for that matter, anyone else?"

"Yes, sir. That's correct."

"Thank you, Lieutenant. From now on, you will report directly to me and not to Lieutenant Ludlow. Officially, your assignment at Newport was to become thoroughly versed in torpedo development and improve communication between the submarine base and the Torpedo Station. Obviously, this assignment was cobbled up as a punishment, and I know it wasn't very clear what your duties actually were. From what you've told me, no one, including Lieutenant Ludlow, has given you any guidance. Now I'd like you to summarize in five or ten minutes what you've done with this vague assignment, and what you've learned at Newport." Ellsworth began to relight his pipe.

While this was not an easy request to fulfill, it was one that Alan had anticipated and prepared for. He realized that he *could* offend an officer he did not know if he was too frank about the seamy side of the station, so he had to be careful as he told his new CO about what he'd been researching. He had *some* tact and discretion, contrary to what Ellsworth might think. "I assume you're familiar with the general history of the Torpedo Station, sir?"

"Yes, I am."

"The buildup of the navy under Roosevelt has created a need for a lot more torpedoes. The number of employees at Newport has tripled, and they work in three shifts, but they have still not reached their goal of 600 torpedoes a year. With the Bliss Company out of the torpedo business and the Torpedo Station at Alexandria, Virginia, closed, there is no competition or standard for comparison. The Rhode Island congressional delegation is aware that the station is the mainstay of the Newport economy, so they tend to protect the station's interests against its detractors."

"Speaking of the congressional delegation, I've heard that if an employee of the station is fired, he can often get reinstated by appealing to one of the delegation, even if he was fired for good reason. Is that true?"

"I've heard the same thing, sir."

"Why didn't you say so when you mentioned the station personnel?"

"I thought you might not be that skeptical about the station's operations, sir."

"Good, Ericsson. You're learning. Go on."

Alan was relieved that he had found the channel through the shoals this time. He continued. "When the war started in Europe last September, the Rhode Island delegation finally gave in to pressure to reopen the Alexandria station and to build a new station in the northwest, which should add capacity and an element of competition, but they only agreed on the condition that the Newport station would be expanded further."

"I heard about that. Go on."

"Naturally, the Torpedo Station people were suspicious of me at first. I tried hard to win over a few of them, and think I've had some success. I tried to be helpful and to use my repertoire of submarine stories to bring a little more interest and purpose to their work. I even get together socially with a few of the younger engineers about once a week.

"Overall, I wasn't surprised to find that the place isn't very efficient. I was more disturbed, to find that, in my opinion, they also tend to not do thorough testing of their torpedoes. It affects most of their work. As far as I know, torpedoes are one of the few weapons that are never exercised in peacetime, so the testing done by the station is all there is."

"That's right."

"Apparently the Bureau of Ordnance does not insist on thorough testing. Obviously, testing torpedoes is very expensive, and the expense occurs right away. Having unreliable torpedoes could be much more expensive, but that expense only comes later, when the torpedoes have to be used."

"You're right. I think BuOrd understands that the torpedoes should be tested thoroughly, but the cost of torpedoes is too high. Until recently, budgets have been very tight, and big guns are their top priority."

"There's one more thing, sir. I've noticed that there's some kind of secret activity going on at the station, and only certain personnel have access to it. I sense that many people at the station know enough about the project to value it highly. From what I can gather, they think that some kind of breakthrough has been made. Since I'm learning everything I can about the station, I think it would make my work more complete if I were let in on the secret. Obviously, that means that someone here, such as you, would also have to be cleared so I could pass the information along. I made this request to Lieutenant Ludlow in January, and he rejected it. I know it may be difficult, perhaps impossible, and could involve some delicate negotiation with BuOrd, but I'm making the same request to you."

"Do you have any idea what this activity is?"

"I've got a rough idea of how many people are involved and how much floor space the project occupies. It seems to me that it isn't a big enough activity to build a complete torpedo, which means that it's probably a new torpedo part that could be substituted into existing torpedoes. I think it could be a new type of propulsion, or guidance system, or a new type of firing mechanism."

Ellsworth had been making only an occasional note during Alan's summary, but now he was writing a longer one. "It's a reasonable request, Ericsson. I've no idea whether it's possible, but I'll make some inquiries and let you know." Ellsworth paused before continuing. "That was a good summary. I know, because I've read your reports. I think that you've done well to try to accomplish something in a strange situation. I think your time could have been better spent doing something else, but I know that wasn't your decision."

"Thank you, sir." Ellsworth had not only read his reports, he'd liked them. Alan was both amazed and gratified. Suddenly, the last five months did not seem like such a waste.

"By the end of September, you'll have been at the station about ten months, so I think that you should apply for a new assignment to begin around that time. If I recommended you for another billet on a sub, would you want it?"

Even though Alan had anticipated this question, he was not sure how to frame his reply. He decided on the simple truth. "I'd be very pleased to be on a sub again, sir, if I stay in the submarine service, but I wonder if my career in submarines can ever recover from that report on the *Squalus*. I've been considering requesting a transfer to aviation."

Ellsworth paused and stared out the window for a moment before replying. "Well, the question of whether your career in submarines can ever recover is a good one. I think it can, but it isn't certain. There's always a risk. You had a very good record prior to the *Squalus* report, and I think you could do very well in submarines. For the good of the submarine service, I hope you'll stick with it, but under the circumstances, I don't blame you for considering a transfer to something else. I think you should make up your mind within the next couple of months."

"Thank you very much, sir. I'll do as you recommend and decide within two months. If I may say so, sir, your arrival here has brought a tremendous breath of fresh air."

"Thank you, Ericsson. I'm aware that my style of command is quite different from my predecessor's. As I said earlier, from now on, you'll report directly to me. Unless you think something different would work better, I would like for you to continue to come back to the base once a month with your reports. Let's make it a little earlier next month, though, say, June eleventh."

"Yes, sir."

Ellsworth paused, looking thoughtful. "I wonder what will have happened in Europe by then. Things are really happening fast there now. The Germans seem poised to invade France, and the British have put Churchill in charge. I think the Germans were hoping, with some justification I'd say, that the British would decide that fighting wasn't worth it. Churchill sure put a stop to that idea, though. That was quite an acceptance speech he gave Tuesday."

"Yes, sir, I heard it too. It was very inspiring. The president has asked for 50,000 planes per year; maybe, now, Congress will be willing to speed up our rearmament."

Ellsworth remained pensive. "Let's hope so. Events in Europe are weakening the appeal of the isolationist ideas, it's true, but will they really let us get moving? I don't know." Ellsworth looked down at his papers and then stood up. Alan quickly followed suit. "That will be all, Lieutenant," Ellsworth dismissed him. They shook hands before Alan left the office.

As Alan walked back to his car, he noticed that the clouds were beginning to break up and there were small patches of blue sky. During the drive back to Newport, Alan reviewed both his interview with Ellsworth and its implications. Suddenly, things were looking up in a big way. Ellsworth appeared to be the kind of officer who could really inspire his men. It was too bad that he would not be Alan's commanding officer much longer. It also sounded like Ellsworth was not impressed with Ludlow, but the six months of negative comments from Ludlow would still be in Alan's permanent record.

Saturday, June 15, 1940

It was late afternoon on a beautiful early-summer day. Jennifer had invited Alan for supper at her apartment, and he had walked over from his place. He was already starting to feel at home where she lived. They were working together on dinner preparations while a radio provided background music.

At 1700, the music was interrupted for the hourly news broadcast. "Today, the Germans completed the occupation of Paris; it seems unlikely that France will be able to hold out much longer. The fall of France would leave Britain alone among the major powers to face the Axis. The United States is remaining neutral, but Congress has been considering many bills to accelerate the pace of our rearmament in light of the bad news from Europe. Today, a bill was passed that increases the navy by eleven percent. It was sponsored by Congressman Vinson of Georgia. This bill contained an increase in the authorized strength of naval aviation to 10,000 airplanes. Only yesterday, the strength of naval aviation was increased from 3,000 to 4,500 planes. Similar expansion—"

Alan interrupted, speaking over the news broadcast. "Holy smoke! Did you hear that? Authorization from 3,000 to 10,000 planes in two days! It's enough to make your head spin. The navy is being rapidly expanded, and naval aviation is being expanded even faster, which means more opportunity for me if I make the transfer to aviation."

"That's true."

He paused and grinned. "Have you ever thought of taking up flying?"

Jennifer suddenly stopped tossing the salad, and blushed as she said, "What? Me? Take up flying an airplane? No, Alan, I haven't given much thought to that. I've already done enough things that girls aren't supposed to do."

"You'd be good at it, you know," he said earnestly.

She smiled. "Do you really think so? It *does* sound like fun."

"You have a feel for machinery, which many people do not. Last weekend, I found out that you know how to sail, so you have a feel for the wind. You're smart and you're good at math. You'd be as good as Amelia Earhart or Beryl Markham."

"Thank you, Alan, but that's enough flattery. I imagine you got an introduction to flying at the Naval Academy, like Bob did?"

"Yes, I did some flying at the Academy, but no solo time. Right after I graduated, I had some leave, and my uncle—the same one that owned the Tatra—got me to take flying lessons. I got a few solo hours that way. It was a lot of fun. It was a cute little airplane that I took up. Two people could just fit in it side by side, but you were really squeezed together. It would be fun to go up in it with you."

"That sounds exciting in more ways than one, you rascal," she said, sliding up against his side and giving a quick kiss on the cheek. Then she went back to tossing the salad.

"Speaking of aviation, when I met with Commander Ellsworth last week, he reminded me that I should decide whether I want to stay in submarines or transfer to aviation—and to let him know my decision when we meet again in July. I think I'm going to go for aviation. It'll be hard to leave submarines, though, since my career was going well until last spring."

Alan had been interested in military aviation since he was a little boy, and he had followed the evolution of carrier aviation as he grew up. The idea of flying from an airport that could move all over the world had fascinated him for a long time. Flying from a carrier was challenging and dangerous, and as a result, the carrier pilots were an elite group within military aviation. He hoped to qualify for membership in that group.

"I think I understand why you're struggling with the decision to leave submarines. It isn't easy to leave something that you know, that you are used to, and then embark on something new and unknown. But wouldn't it look good on your record later on if you become proficient in both submarines and aircraft?"

"I think that's true, but I have to balance that against the possible appearance of having left in disgrace from the submarine service."

"Well, your record here in Newport should look good, now that Ellsworth has replaced all of Ludlow's negative entries with his own positive comments. That should help to erase the effect of your report."

"Good thought, thank you," Alan said, leaning over and kissing her on the cheek.

She smiled, paused and said, "Ludlow must be a colossal nitwit to leave himself open to getting demoted and sent to the Aleutians."

"That's right. He reaped what he had sowed." Alan went back to making gravy. Then he stopped and looked at Jennifer, saying, "It sounds like you aren't as afraid as you were of having a boyfriend who's a pilot."

She stopped, looked into his eyes, and said, "I've thought about it, and I think you're right that none of the fighting parts of the navy are very safe, but please be very careful. I once heard someone say there are old pilots and there are bold pilots, but there are no old, bold pilots."

She faced him with a pleading look that he hadn't seen before. He went to her and they embraced and kissed.

"I've heard that saying, too. I promise not to be too bold."

CHAPTER FOUR

Meeting the Family

Friday, June 28, 1940

It was early evening on a sultry day, and Jennifer and Alan were driving up from Newport to Boston in the Tatra. Three weeks earlier, Jennifer had gone to her parents' home in Lexington, a suburb northwest of Boston, for the weekend. Her brother had graduated from MIT, and she attended his graduation. Her parents, sister, and brother had all seemed intensely interested in her new boyfriend. Under pressure, she had agreed to bring him home for a family review, soon. Alan's family had also become anxious to meet his new girlfriend, as they had detected a higher level of attraction and commitment than he'd had for any girl in the past. Jennifer and Alan settled on a plan to visit both families on the last weekend in June, which had arrived quickly.

As they drove along, Alan realized that he had been dating Jennifer for two and a half months. Not only had she lived up to his expectations from the start, but he had also found more things to admire about her as time went on. He hoped that visiting her family would not cast a shadow on anything for either of them.

Jennifer explained that her parents had moved to a smaller house when she had gone to Washington in February, and were starting to feel settled there. The house was nicely situated on a hill south of Lexington Center, within walking distance of the train, which stopped near MIT on its way to North Station in Boston. Alan's feeling of anxiety increased as they entered Lexington. He felt like he was about to present himself for an oral exam.

Due at 1900, they pulled into the Warrens' driveway about ten minutes early. "That's David's cute little car." Jennifer pointed to a '38 Willys coupe in the driveway. She took Alan by the hand and led him to a side door between the garage and the house. It opened directly into the kitchen, where Jennifer's mother and sister were busy with dinner preparations. Jennifer's mother looked up, smiled, and rushed forward to embrace her daughter as the couple came in.

Jennifer's mother turned to Alan and grasped his hand in both of hers, smiling warmly. "Hello, Alan. I'm Marjorie, Jennifer's mother. We're very glad you could come for a visit. We've been looking forward to a chance to get to know you a little bit. Jennifer says very nice things about you."

She looked somewhat like Jennifer—not quite as tall, but just as trim. She had a rounder face, light blue eyes, and dark hair, which was showing some gray; there was something innately graceful about her. She made him feel welcome, and Alan liked her at once.

Meanwhile, Jennifer had greeted her older sister Gertrude, whom she introduced to Alan. She was even taller than Jennifer, who was about five foot ten, and seemed slightly hunched forward, as if she were very self-conscious about her height. She was a brunette with a round face and hazel eyes. Alan immediately noticed that she was very shy, although she did manage a smile when greeting him.

Jennifer took Alan by the hand again and led him along a short hallway into the living room to meet her father and brother. The two men rose from their chairs. Jennifer's father, Roger, stepped forward and embraced his daughter. He was an inch shorter than Alan, and not as thin and wiry. He had crew-cut gray hair and glasses, and his narrow face held hazel eyes. Though he said nothing, Alan felt intimidated by his intense, serious air, as if he was meeting a captain or an admiral.

After they exchanged greetings, Jennifer introduced Alan to her brother David. He was handsome, with a brown crew cut and blue eyes, and seemed like a pleasant young man.

Roger offered Alan a drink, and he asked for Scotch and water. Jennifer excused herself and returned to the kitchen.

As Roger made Alan's drink, he said, "Jennifer tells us that you're a submariner, but you're thinking about getting into naval aviation?"

"Yes, I think I *will* ask for the transfer to aviation. I have to tell my commanding officer in about ten days."

"Good for you. If you're accepted, what happens?" Roger handed the drink to Alan.

"Thank you," Alan responded, taking a sip to calm himself under Roger's questioning. "I'll be ordered to report for flight training in Pensacola, Florida, for six or seven months at that point. Can you tell me anything about your work, or is it all secret? Jennifer said it has something to do with high frequency radio waves."

"Well, I can't give you any details, but I've been working on RADAR."

"RADAR," repeated Alan. The acronym was a new term recently invented by the US Navy, and Alan had only heard it used a few times. He did know that it stood for radio direction and range finding. "That's very important to the navy. Probably every navy combat ship needs it, but I'm betting it'll be years before they all get it. It should revolutionize tactics, though, once our officers have time to learn how to take full advantage of it."

"Well, we just try to make it better. You know, more range, better resolution, easier to use and understand, more reliable, smaller, and lighter. We leave it up to you guys to decide how to use it."

"I'm sure every improvement will pay dividends," Alan replied. Turning to David, he changed the subject. "Jennifer said that you're working at MIT on some kind of giant computing machine?"

"Yeah, that's right. I'm working on automatic computing machines, which are part of an activity started by Vannevar Bush when he was at MIT. It's a lot of fun. We don't need to keep it secret, though, because nobody understands what we're doing, anyway," David joked, grinning.

Roger gazed proudly at his son. "When David talks to his colleagues, I am quickly lost. I think he's headed to graduate school, but he's so busy now that he may have to put if off for a while."

"I have read about Dr. Bush. He seems like a very versatile scientist, as well as brilliant," said Alan.

"You're right. He's an amazing guy," Roger affirmed.

"Dinner is served!" Marjorie's voice came from the dining room.

The men joined the ladies in the dining room, and Alan's mouth watered as a dinner of lamb chops, potatoes, and fresh peas was served.

Turning to Gertrude, Alan said, "Jennifer told me you teach at the Park School. I went there through sixth grade. I left in 1924. I wonder if any of my teachers are still there."

Gertrude brightened and said, "I think Bill Thayer might have started by then, and perhaps Sandra Wilder."

"Yes. They were both there, but I didn't have Miss Wilder. I remember Mister Thayer well. He was demanding, but fair, and hard on troublemakers like me."

Gertrude broke into a big smile. "He's still like that. He's now the assistant to the headmistress."

Marjorie interjected, "Jennifer told us you went to Milton, which is a very good school. We would've seriously considered sending our children there, but it was too far, and we didn't want them to board. Where did your parents grow up?"

"My father grew up in Needham, then moved to Roxbury and went to Boston Latin, Harvard, and Harvard Medical School. My mother grew up in the North End and went to English High

School, and then to nursing school at Mass General. Shortly after she started work as a nurse, she met my father. They got married and she stopped working when she became pregnant with my older brother, Alfredo, who goes by Fred. Fred followed my father's footsteps to Boston Latin and Harvard. Like you, my mother went back to work when my younger sister, Megan, graduated from Milton and started college at Jackson."

Marjorie asked, "Your mother grew up in the North End. Is she Italian?"

"Italian and Portuguese."

"So she was brought up in the Catholic church?"

"Yes."

Jennifer had warned Alan that her parents would question him about his religion. They were devout Episcopalians, and that was their expectation for their children. Jennifer thought they would be upset if they knew that her boyfriend had been brought up without a religious tradition. Alan would have preferred to be frank and open about his views on religion, but they decided that revealing them now would probably create strife, and nothing good was likely to come of it.

"And your father, is he Catholic?"

"No, although his mother was. She and my mother's parents never left the church, but they were far from devout. My grandmother Alvares once told me, 'The Church is old and venerable, and has done many wonderful things for people; don't ever forget it. The Church is old and stuck in its ways, though, and has also done many terrible things. Don't ever forget that, either.'"

"Far from devout is an understatement," Marjorie agreed. "So what religion does your father belong to?"

"He's a Unitarian."

"And you?"

"Unitarian, also."

"How often do you go to church?" asked Roger.

"Several times a year." Alan hardly ever went to church and he didn't like lying about it.

"You don't sound very religious," Roger remarked pointedly.

"It's true that I don't put a lot of time into it."

"And I haven't, either, since high school," Jennifer reminded her father.

"I know that," said Roger, with a disappointed frown.

Marjorie deliberately changed the subject. "Tell us a little more about your brother and sister, Alan."

"Fred is three years older than me. As I said, he followed my father's footsteps. He graduated from medical school in 1935 and got married in 1937, and he has a two-year-old daughter. Fred and I don't have a lot in common, but I respect what he has accomplished."

Marjorie smiled and replied, "So you steered an entirely different course. And your sister?"

"Megan is three years younger than me, the same age as Jennifer." He glanced at Jennifer and she smiled back at him. "She got married last year to a mechanical engineer. He has a job with General Electric in Lynn, and they moved to Swampscott. She's a nurse, and she found a good position in Salem. Megan and I have been good friends since in our teenage years. I also have a lot of interests in common with her husband."

Marjorie reached out and put her hand on Alan's. "You can relax now. The interrogation is over." They all smiled, except Roger, and Alan did relax some.

Gertrude and Jennifer got up and cleared the table while Marjorie got dessert ready. Soon, Alan was savoring the aroma of a fresh-baked blueberry pie and coffee.

"I had to make room in the deep freeze for this year's blueberries, which should be ready for picking in a month," Marjorie explained as she sat down to serve the pie.

"It's one of my favorite desserts," said Alan, "and this one smells particularly delicious."

"Thank you, Alan," said Marjorie.

Jennifer said, "What about you, David? Are you still dating Carol?"

David's smile faded and he said, "No. She and I haven't been getting along. We broke up a couple of weeks ago. I just joined a square dance club in Concord, and there seem to be some nice girls there."

"I'm sorry to hear that. Just don't get sucked into spending all your time on your work," said Jennifer.

"That's the pot calling the kettle black." David smiled.

"True. I speak from experience."

Marjorie turned to Alan and said, "Jennifer did bury herself in her graduate studies for quite a while, you know. I think she said something about running into you on a train a year or two ago, while she was in the middle of all that?"

"That's right. Your daughter was a true heroine that day, but I'm sure she told you all about it."

"No, she didn't say much about it at all."

Alan looked at Jennifer, who shrugged her shoulders.

"Well, I think you ought to know about it," he replied.

"Tell us about it." Roger smiled, sounding friendlier.

"It was in the middle of that big hurricane in September of '38. Do you remember the train that was nearly washed away near Stonington, Connecticut?"

Roger replied, "Let's see . . . That does ring a bell, but I've forgotten the details. There were so many amazing stories from the hurricane."

"The train was the Bostonian—the 1100 Shore Line Limited from New York to Boston. I had boarded the train in New London to go home to Boston on leave. The train was late, and it crept out around 1600, excuse me, four o'clock, way behind schedule. By then, the wind was really blowing. There were a lot of leaves, twigs, shingles, and things like that in the air."

"So you and Jennifer were actually on this train?" Gertrude interjected.

"That's right, although at first I had no idea that she was on it. The eye of the hurricane moved north along the Connecticut River, so east of the river, the wind and tidal surge were stronger. Sections of the railroad to the east of New London are very close to the ocean. The train was going slowly, because the engineer was worried about the roadbed. We had reached a point just short of Stonington when the train stopped. The train was sitting on an exposed section of raised roadbed and trestle, right next to the ocean, and the water was already right up to the rails.

"The last car was the luxury parlor car. Shortly after the train stopped, that car began to tip toward the ocean because the roadbed was being undermined. The people from that car came forward to the next car, where I was. People started to panic and push and shove to go forward to the next cars. The conductor opened the door on the left side so some of us could move forward by walking beside the train. The water was up over my knees.

"When I got about halfway up to the locomotive, there were quite a few people wading forward by then. I could see that the train had stopped for a red light on a signal tower a little farther down the track. All of a sudden, I realized that the person in front of me was Jennifer. She was helping a woman with three children. They were each carrying one child, and they were pulling a bigger boy along. I shouted to Jennifer that I could take the bigger boy. Jennifer turned and recognized me, and she shouted to the woman to let me take the boy. The woman nodded, I put the boy on my shoulders, and we started forward again."

Marjorie interjected, "So, you and Jennifer were helping this woman? Did you know her, Jennifer? How old were the children?"

Jennifer replied, "No, I didn't know her, but I could see that she needed help. I'd guess the children were maybe three, five, and seven years old. Of course, we were all scared, the children most of all, but I felt much better when Alan miraculously appeared."

Alan continued, "We reached the passenger car behind the tender, which had become very crowded. I saw one of the train crew deliberately submerge himself in the water next to the coupling at the back end of that car. By then, the current coming between the cars from seaward was really strong and full of debris, so going underwater took a lot of courage. It looked like he was trying to uncouple the rest of the train so that it could be left behind. We found out later that was exactly what he was doing. It was a hell of a job, but he did it and survived.

"We hoped the engineer would decide to ignore the red signal and move the train forward to higher ground, which we could see was only a few hundred yards ahead. It was clear that the best chance to survive was to stick with the train if it could be moved ahead, because the depth of water, strong current and debris made drowning likely if anyone left the train.

We kept on to the front of that car and saw that there were already a lot of people on the tender. This was a very strange sight, but every square foot was needed to carry all the passengers. We kept going to the cab of the locomotive. There were already a couple of passengers in the cab, but the engineer motioned us to come up. Jennifer climbed up and sat on the floor of the cab, and I lifted the children up to her one by one. She passed them up into the cab, then jumped off and helped me lift the woman up to the cab. We helped some other mothers and children up, as well. By then, the engineer was blowing the whistle and shouting to everyone that he was getting ready to move the train. The cab was full of people and there was no room for Jennifer or me."

"What happened? Did you and Jennifer get left behind?" asked Marjorie.

"Almost. I shouted to her that we should try for the front of the locomotive, and we waded to the front end of the locomotive as fast as we could. The whistle blew again, and I was pretty sure that meant the train was about to start. I shouted to Jennifer that the silver-painted part at the front of the locomotive might be hot, so she should get on the gangway that ran along the side of the boiler, above the driving wheels, and go further back. Then I boosted her up on the cow catcher. The wind coming around the front of the locomotive caught her and nearly blew her off, but she held on to the railing and pulled herself to the right, behind the front end and out of the wind. Then she went up the steps and back along the gangway. I was right behind her, and I nearly got blown off the cow catcher, myself. On the gangway, we got down out of the wind and flying debris."

Alan recalled the scene like it had just happened. Jennifer had lain down flat on the gangway, both to get out of the wind and because she was exhausted. He lay down on top of her to protect both her and himself. He still remembered the feel of her body and her hair in his face. Jennifer had thanked him afterward. He left this part out of the story; the Warrens did not need to know all the details.

Jennifer supplied the details. "I was exhausted, so I lay down on the gangway. Alan lay down on top of me—for a second, I thought he was taking great liberties, but then I realized that he was shielding me from all the debris that was flying around. I was very glad he was there."

Alan glanced at Marjorie and Roger, and saw that their eyebrows were coming back down from the heights they had reached. He continued. "As the train started to move, the steam shot up through the stack with the usual roar, and it was a very welcome sound, I can tell you. We heard later that everyone on the train cheered at the sound, but we couldn't hear it over the wind.

"The front of the locomotive snagged some low-hanging wires. As it moved forward, the wires became taut and began to pull over the poles. Luckily, we were far enough back along the locomotive that the wires didn't touch us. We did feel several thumps resonate through the locomotive as large boats bounced off the other side. The locomotive slowed, and I turned to look forward. I watched as the locomotive began nudging aside a house that had come to rest partly across the tracks."

David exclaimed, "Horse feathers! There was a house on the tracks?"

"Just about everything was drifting in the water and crossing the tracks, but the locomotive pushed the house aside like it was nothing. A little farther, there was a large sailboat on its side across the tracks, and the locomotive came to a stop against the sailboat. It was jammed in the tracks somehow and wouldn't move. I could feel the driving wheels slipping against the rails, and I got really worried that we were stuck. We were still exposed to wind and water. I heard a loud crack, and the sailboat swung around and went off to leeward. The locomotive surged forward until we were completely onto the high ground, not far from the middle of Stonington."

"Phew. You made it," Marjorie exclaimed.

"The town put us up in the Town Hall and the Catholic Church, and the townspeople gave us food and dry clothing. The next day, the railroad got us buses to Providence and Boston. Jennifer got on the first bus and went on her way. I didn't see her again until this spring."

"Well, that is quite a story, Alan, thank you for telling us," Roger said, smiling again. Alan thought that Roger might be feeling more welcoming toward him after that story, in spite of their religious differences. He fervently hoped so.

After dinner, the group sat down on the small back porch and enjoyed the summer evening. The conversation revolved around the fall of France and the war in Europe. Alan noticed that Jennifer was ready to say something several times, but caught herself and remained silent. After an hour, Roger drove Gertrude back to her apartment in Brookline. David left to spend the night with a friend. Alan and Jennifer helped Marjorie clean up the kitchen. When Roger returned, they all went upstairs to bed. Alan got to use David's room, while Jennifer had the guest room. After making sure they were comfortable, Marjorie and Roger said good night and retired. Alan and Jennifer kissed and said good night, then fell into their beds and a sound sleep.

Saturday, June 29, 1940

After a full and delicious breakfast, Roger wanted to take a close look at the Tatra, and Alan was glad to oblige. Roger asked questions until he understood all the unusual features of the car. He instantly accepted Alan's offer to let him drive it. Alan was not surprised to find that Jennifer's driving instructor was also an expert driver.

In the afternoon, Alan and Jennifer went to Alan's parents' house in Brookline. Jennifer had long since demonstrated her competence driving the Tatra, so she drove, so that along the way she could show Alan the house in Arlington in which she'd grown up. A cold front had gone through, followed by the usual brisk northwest wind, but it was still warm enough to put the top down on the Tatra.

As they started out, Jennifer said, "Well, Alan, you made a very good impression. My father didn't like the fact that you are not very religious, but I think he likes you in other ways. They haven't criticized me too much about not going to church, so I thought they might have mellowed and become more tolerant. I'm sorry that wasn't true."

"I'm sorry, too. I guess it's something we'll just have to live with. My family should be more tolerant. Fred became a Catholic when he got married, and my parents accepted it, although I think they were secretly quite disappointed."

"It's interesting that it's my father who is troubled by your lack of religion, but it was my mother who had the most trouble with Bob. She sensed his lack of commitment right from the start; of course, I wasn't ready to accept anything like that. I was going to prove her wrong where Bob was concerned."

"You're the first girl I have brought home to meet my family, so I can't make any comparisons. My family seems much more anxious to meet you than any of my previous girlfriends, though."

The car swerved to the left, and Jennifer quickly brought it back. "You didn't tell me that before," she said, blushing and glancing quickly at him.

Jennifer pulled up in front of a wooden Victorian and shut off the engine. "Well, this is it. It is so familiar; it's still hard to accept that it doesn't belong to our family anymore."

"I like the rambling style, and it seems plenty large enough. You each had your own room, did you?"

"Yes. Mine was on the second floor, in the front, on the right."

"Very nice! Thank you for showing it to me. I should tell you that my parents' house is even larger, though. It's kind of formal and formidable-looking inside and out, but it's old and has never been renovated. It has electric lights, but it still has gas lights, as well, and there's only one electrical outlet in the whole house. When Megan moved out last year, my parents should have moved to a smaller, more modern house, like your parents did, but they're very attached to their big, funny old house."

"Sounds intriguing." Jennifer started the car and they continued on their way to the Pill Hill neighborhood in Brookline, named for the concentration of doctors that lived there, convenient to several large hospitals in Boston. They pulled into the horseshoe driveway in front of Alan's parents' house at about 1545. Jennifer looked at the house and gasped. "Oh my, it's definitely more formidable than funny."

"Give it a chance to show its quaint side."

Alan noticed that Jennifer remained apprehensive as they approached the front door. Alan's father, Larry, a blond, blue-eyed man who was a little shorter than Alan, answered the doorbell. Alan was surprised that Larry had dressed for the occasion in a coat and tie. There was a cry from the kitchen, in the rear of the house, and Alan's mother Joanna came running into the front hall. She was covered in white from her neck to her knees, which contrasted sharply with the natural, swarthy complexion of her face. The others went in to meet her in the front hall, and the familiar scents of the house welcomed Alan home. Joanna saw that they were all staring at her in amazement.

"I must be a sight," she said, starting to chuckle as she looked down at herself, "but I'm not going to let a little accident keep me from welcoming our special guest." Soon, the whole group was laughing.

"What happened?" asked Alan.

"I had a big pile of sifted flour in front of me, next to the open window. When Larry opened the front door, the wind blew in through the window, and a lot of the flour landed on me." She laughed again. Alan made the introductions. Joanna was thin; she was inches shorter than Jennifer, but still tall for a woman of Mediterranean descent. Her piercing black eyes were kind as her face assumed her usual friendly expression. She stepped forward and clasped Jennifer's hand in both of hers. "We're so happy you're here. Relax and enjoy yourself." Jennifer was smiling. Her eyes twinkled in cheerful anticipation, her apprehension gone.

In spite of her clownish appearance, Joanna took charge. She sent Alan and Larry to bring the luggage in from the car and showed Jennifer upstairs to Megan's old bedroom.

By 1800, Joanna had cleaned up and made dinner and Alan had given Jennifer a tour of the house. He'd started with the third floor, which was mostly the unused servant's quarters—small, dusty rooms with peeling wallpaper.

When they were alone, Jennifer smiled and said, "Your blue eyes and dark complexion are an unusual and extremely handsome combination. Now I know where they come from."

Alan blushed and said, "Thank you. Your dark hair and blue eyes are unusual, too, and so beautiful."

She blushed and they kissed.

As they started back down, Jennifer said, "I see what you mean now about the house being old-fashioned. I don't think I've ever been in a house quite like this. Our house in Arlington is older, but it had been renovated."

They came to Alan's old bedroom last in their tour. Alan was pleased to see that Jennifer was interested in the mementos of his boyhood. She looked closely at each of the old photographs.

"You must have been a handful when you were younger, you rascal," she joked, turning toward him with a big grin.

"I suppose I was, you scalawag."

She stood in the center of the room and looked around, smiling. "I guess it's not so different from David's old room."

When Alan's brother Fred and his wife Michelle arrived for dinner, Alan could tell that his mother was disappointed that they had not brought their daughter. They'd left her with a babysitter, instead. Perhaps it meant that they did not want any distractions, which could be taken as a vague compliment to Jennifer. Fred was shorter than Alan and a little overweight. He had an unctuous manner that had always come across as insincere to Alan. As Jennifer was introduced to him, Alan could see that she was stiff, and her smile seemed forced; it appeared that Fred's manner had the same effect on her.

A short time later, Alan's sister Megan came bouncing in, followed by her husband, Nat Steele. With blonde hair, blue eyes, and freckles, Megan did not look at all like her mother. She had inherited Joanna's liveliness and charm, however. Jennifer looked relaxed again after meeting them.

The pattern of the dinner conversation was similar to that at the Warrens'. This time, Jennifer was quizzed about her background. Alan saw eyebrows go up as Jennifer described her graduate school program, getting hired by ONI, and being sent to the War College.

Joanna joked, "Well, Alan, you and I are the only lackluster characters around here without graduate degrees." They all laughed, dissolving the gravity that had crept into the conversation.

Jennifer picked up the mood. "So, now I am working under Victoria Peckham, whom I gather you all know?" There were nods around the table, and Jennifer continued, with a big smile, "She has told me all about how incorrigible Alan was as a child." Everyone grinned.

"Did she tell you why Alan left the Park School?" asked Fred. The grave expressions returned.

There are good reasons for not liking Fred, Alan thought. Alan had been dismissed from Park after his practical jokes had become increasingly impractical. They had culminated in his secretly driving a hated teacher's car to a spot some distance from the school.

Jennifer quickly replied, "I heard all about that from Alan. Victoria never mentioned it."

After dinner they all gathered in the large living room. The conversation was again mostly about the fall of France and its implications. Among people she had just met, Jennifer had no trouble refraining from participating, and she politely declined to answer questions. Around 2030, Megan and Nat started on their drive back to Swampscott. A little later, Fred and Michelle left for their home nearby on Pill Hill, while Alan and Jennifer helped Joanna clean up the kitchen.

Sunday, June 30, 1940

When he was dressed and ready for breakfast, Alan could hear that Jennifer was awake and getting ready. He waited a few minutes and welcomed her with a kiss as she came out of her bedroom. They went downstairs to find Joanna ready with a sumptuous breakfast of bacon, eggs and English muffins.

After breakfast, Joanna invited Jennifer to help her with cooking something for lunch. Larry asked Alan for some help with the rewiring project he had started in the basement. He said that he had put off rewiring the house for as long as possible, and now he was anxious to get on with it, because he had found some places where the old wiring was in danger of catching on fire.

Joanna and Jennifer had produced a tasty lasagna for lunch, with homemade pasta that Joanna showed Jennifer how to make. After lunch, Jennifer and Alan were ready to start back to Newport. Alan was pleased when Joanna gave Jennifer a hug before they left and said, "Please come back soon."

Alan drove. It was drizzling, so they kept the top up. "Well, you made a marvelous impression. If we ever part, I think I'll be put in the dog house."

Jennifer grinned and turned toward him. "Oh, Alan, I'm so glad, but I think you're exaggerating."

"I'm not. My parents think you're wonderful, but I had also hoped that Megan would like you. She said—and these are her words: 'You've hit the jackpot, Alan. She's a gem. I hope you two stick together.'"

Jennifer's voice trembled as she said, "Oh, Alan, that means so much to me."

Alan glanced at her and saw that there were tears in her eyes. She was reaching for a handkerchief. His heart went out to her. "I love you, Jennifer," he said, reaching out and squeezing her hand.

CHAPTER FIVE

Long-Term Commitments

Thursday, July 11, 1940

It was about fifteen minutes before noon when Alan arrived at Commander Ellsworth's office for his regular monthly meeting. He carried his report in a briefcase.

"Lieutenant j.g. Ericsson to see Commander Ellsworth," he told the yeoman.

"Please have a seat, sir, and I'll tell him you're here," said the yeoman. He got up and went into Ellsworth's office.

A minute later, the yeoman emerged and said, "It'll be a few minutes, sir."

Alan's mind wandered to the recent news from Europe. The Germans had started an air offensive against Britain. Goering had announced that, within a month, the Royal Air Force would be destroyed and England invaded. However, it sounded like the British fighter planes were having some success shooting down the bombers. This tended to confirm the views of outspoken US Army Captain Claire Chennault, who contended that unescorted bombers could not stand up to fighters. Chennault's recent experience in China tended to bear this out. Alan suspected that RADAR, which the British had put into service a little faster than the US, was also giving warning of impending attacks and helping the Royal Air Force to direct their fighters efficiently.

Ellsworth's office door opened and he appeared. "Come in, Ericsson," he said as they shook hands.

Alan followed him into the office. Ellsworth closed the door, and they both sat down. Alan opened his briefcase and put his report on Ellsworth's desk.

"How about if you try to summarize what's in your report?" Ellsworth suggested, loading his pipe. "I'll read it carefully later."

"Yes, sir. I've found out that the secret activity that we've been talking about is a new exploder, the Mark VI. It's designed to be used on all the current torpedoes—the Mark XIII for aircraft, the Mark XIV for submarines, and the Mark XV for surface ships. This exploder has a magnetic detonator as well as the normal contact detonator. The magnetic detonator is designed to go off in response to a ship's magnetic field. The idea is that if the torpedo goes under a ship instead of impacting it, the torpedo will explode under the ship. It's expected to do at least as much damage as it would if it exploded by contact with the side of the ship. Of course, this could happen if the running depth of the torpedo was set low deliberately, or if there was an error in estimating the draft of the ship."

"Hmm, I never thought about damage coming from an explosion underneath a ship. It just *might* do more damage, especially if the ship is armored," said Ellsworth.

"Yes, sir. Development of the Mark VI started in the 1920s. It was redesigned a few times, and then they had a big test in 1934 in which over a hundred test shots were fired underneath the *Indianapolis*. In theory, the magnetic exploder works better at high latitudes because of the shape of the earth's magnetic field. The tests were done in the least favorable latitude—near the equator, off the west coast of South America—to show that it would work well in unfavorable circumstances. The position of the torpedo relative to the hull of the cruiser was measured when the magnetic exploder was tripped, and it seemed to work well. Neither live warheads nor contact detonators were tested, however.

"While this was going on, the Torpedo Station commander put in a request to the navy for a hulk for live tests. After a lot of correspondence, the CNO agreed to provide a decommissioned destroyer, but he put in a condition that any damage to the destroyer must be repaired at the Torpedo Station's expense. Obviously, that made it, in effect, a refusal."

"Seems like a bad decision. Go on."

"After the tests with the *Indianapolis*, they decided the Mark VI was ready for production, and no other tests have been done. Production has all been done at Newport; the units are locked away, along with the maintenance manuals, to maintain secrecy. If we go to war, the Mark VI can be substituted in the field for the Mark V contact exploder, which is currently on the torpedoes in the fleet.

"Based on my research, it appears to me that the testing hasn't been adequate to ensure reliability. There still seems to be some doubt about whether the magnetic exploder will perform in the same way in different parts of the world, where the earth's magnetic field isn't the same. It isn't just that the torpedo could fail to explode—it might explode prematurely. At the same time, the contact detonator is not the same as in the Mark V, and has never been tested. Frankly, it gives me the willies, sir."

"I have to agree with you, based on what you've told me. Go on."

"The Torpedo Station people seem to think that we're the only navy that has tried to develop a magnetic exploder." *This could sound harsh and tactless, so I need to phrase it right,* Alan realized. "Our magnetic exploder evolved from magnetic mines, so it seems a bit rash to me to assume that no other navy has thought of it. It would be useful to know if our intelligence has caught a whiff of anything." Alan paused to take a breath and let it all sink in. "That's the gist of what I've found out."

"Well, that's an earful, Ericsson. Your evaluation seems sound to me, though, and I look forward to reading the whole story in your report. I'll see what I can find out about other countries developing something similar, and after that, I'll see what action the base commander recommends." Ellsworth paused and looked out the window for a moment, and then turned back to Alan and asked, "Now, in regard to your next assignment, what have you decided?"

Alan looked him in the eye. "I have reluctantly decided to transfer to Naval Aviation and apply for pilot training." *Well, now I've done it*, he thought. He felt relieved that he'd taken the plunge, though.

"I'm sorry to hear it, but I understand your reasoning. My recommendation will be favorable."

"I appreciate that very much, sir."

"Did your evaluation of the Mark VI exploder have any bearing on your decision?"

"Yes, sir. I was leaning toward aviation, anyway, but this exploder business gave me a definite push."

"It seems that your punishment for being too frank was to be assigned to dig into what turned out to be a lot of dirty laundry, which has discouraged you further from the submarine service—too bad." He paused. "I had the yeoman start the paperwork for your transfer so that you wouldn't have to come back if you decided on the transfer. See him your way out and sign the request for transfer. We'll get the paperwork completed and submitted right away." He grinned. "You'll be spending the winter in Pensacola, you lucky dog."

"Yes, sir."

Ellsworth paused, becoming serious again. "What happens if you get assigned to a torpedo squadron? You could, you know."

"I'll try to avoid it if at all possible, sir. If it happens, I think I'd owe it to the squadron skipper to tell him that I have a morale problem with torpedo bombing, and why. I would not mention the exploders, of course. As far as I know, the aircraft torpedoes have all the problems of the submarine torpedoes and some more of their own. I *do* think that torpedo bombing could be very effective, however, if the torpedoes work properly."

"Well, let's hope you don't get assigned to a torpedo squadron. As you finish out your present assignment, keep digging and see if you can find out any more about the reliability of the complete Mark XIV torpedo, including the Mark VI exploder. A list of all the tests conducted to date would be helpful. Obviously, it's a crucial weapon for the submarine service. Let's set Tuesday, August thirteenth, as the date for your next visit."

"Yes, sir. Thank you again, sir."

"That will be all, Ericsson. Good luck and good digging."

Alan stood and shook Ellsworth's hand and then left the office, reflecting on how lucky he was to have a CO who was interested in helping his officers with their careers.

Alan had made arrangements to have a cup of coffee at 1430 with Mark Gallagher in New London. He went south from the submarine base into Groton and took the bridge across the Thames River to New London.

After a pleasant visit with Mark, Alan started driving back to Newport. He was on the west side of the Thames this time, so he decided to take a different route back. He usually followed the Thames south to Groton and then went east to Narragansett Bay. This time, he decided to go north on the west side of the Thames, cross the river in Norwich, and then go east from there. It was a warm day, but there were low clouds. Rain threatened, so he kept the Tatra's top up.

It was late afternoon when Alan approached Thamesville, just south of Norwich. It was raining off and on. Suddenly, he glimpsed an airplane flying very low and heading north on his right. He might not have seen it if he had not been sitting on the right side of the car. The plane was a big single-engine monoplane with a small canopy over the cockpit. It looked like a single-seater—a fighter. As it continued ahead, he recognized the unique inverted gull wing he had seen in a picture and realized it must be the XF4U-1, nicknamed the "Corsair"—the hot new navy fighter from Vought.

Thoughts raced through his mind. *What is it doing here? Why is it so low? You never want to fly a brand-new experimental airplane solely on instruments in the clouds. With all the pressure to test a major new weapon, they must have sent out a test flight on a marginal day.* He saw the landing gear come down. The pilot had to be getting ready to land somewhere, but Alan couldn't remember an airport around Norwich. It looked like the pilot was making a forced landing. Alan wondered if there were any big open fields around Norwich. He remembered that he had seen a sign for the Norwich golf course ahead, where the fairways might provide a chance for a forced landing with minimum damage.

Alan continued north, following the plane, and came to the entrance of the golf course on his left. Instinctively, he turned in. He saw a dirt maintenance road leading west out of the parking lot, and he took it. The road wound through bands of trees and opened into a clearing. He saw the Corsair heading south, beyond the far side of the golf course. *Maybe he's circling to land to the east or north*, he thought. There was hardly any wind to favor a particular direction for landing. The road ended at a fairway running to the west, so Alan stopped the car, switched off the engine, and lowered the window to listen. He heard the rumble of a big radial engine, and then it faded. In the quiet he could hear the moisture dripping from the trees. Suddenly, he saw the Corsair on the ground, rolling north across the far end of the fairway. It was apparently undamaged. He gasped as he realized that it was going much too fast to stop before hitting the trees on the north side of the fairway. The trees moved violently as the Corsair disappeared into the woods.

Alan's adrenaline spiked. He threw caution to the wind and sped down the edge of the fairway in his car. He saw the tracks of the Corsair and turned to follow, heading toward the tree line. He stopped his car at the point where the tracks entered the trees, jumped out, and ran after the plane. Just beyond the tree line, the ground dropped off steeply. He started down and saw the Corsair. Somehow, it had flipped upside down, its nose pointed back up the slope. It was resting mainly on its tail, which was wrecked. One wing had been torn off. Alan ran down to the cockpit. The canopy was slid back, but it was resting, inverted, on the ground. The side rails of the canopy were not too far above the ground, leaving an opening about a foot and a half high.

"Hello? Are you okay?" he shouted.

"Not sure." A voice came from the cockpit.

Alan pulled some tree branches away, and he could see the pilot wriggling inside. He broke off a tree branch and began using it to dig the earth away, enlarging the opening. The pilot's head emerged through the opening. The pilot kept inching his way out, grunting and cursing. Alan dug away more earth to make it a little easier. When the pilot had made it out, Alan saw that he was a big guy, well over six feet.

"Are you hurt?" Alan asked.

"Not much, I guess. We better get away; there could be a fire," the pilot responded.

Alan helped him up, and they started up the slope. Alan looked the pilot over and saw that he was bleeding from some cuts on his face, though they seemed minor. He'd probably gotten some hard knocks and would have some sore spots, at least, Alan thought. When they got to the top of the slope, they turned and looked back at the Corsair. Even in its wrecked condition, the airplane inspired Alan. It had clean lines; its engine and propeller were enormous. It evoked the idea of speed and power more than anything he had ever seen before.

"This is the worst day of my life," the pilot said, breaking into Alan's euphoria, his expression grim.

Alan realized that the pilot might want to be alone, and he edged away, toward his car.

The pilot sat down and put his head in his hands. Alan thought he might be quietly crying, which was understandable. After about fifteen minutes, the pilot got up and came over to Alan.

He extended his hand to Alan and said, "Booth Gurdon, test pilot for Vought-Sikorsky."

"Lieutenant. j.g. Alan Ericsson, submarine service. I just put in my application today for a transfer to aviation."

"Maybe you'll change your mind after seeing this." Gurdon gave a hint of a grin. "Thanks for your help. How did you happen to get here so fast?"

"I was driving north and happened to see you flying by. I recognized the Corsair from a picture, and, naturally, I was fascinated. I saw your landing gear go down, and I knew there was no airport around here, so I figured that you had to be making a forced landing. I'd seen a sign for the golf course and guessed that was a possibility. When I got to it, I drove in and saw you go into the woods. I bet this grass is slick after it rains—no wonder you couldn't stop." He paused. "Even though it's upside-down in the woods, I think I'm falling in love with your airplane."

"You figured it all out mighty fast. I guess I'm pretty lucky that you were going by . . . You seem to know a lot about aviation for a submariner. Have you done some flying?"

"A little. I've soloed in an Aeronca C3, which is about as far from the Corsair as you can get and still be a single-engine monoplane, I guess."

"There's something lovable about the C3. I wanted to fly one, but I'm too tall. I've heard that some pilots are able to get their foot over the cockpit edge to step on the left main tire for braking on the ground, but you'd have to be both small and agile," he said, grinning at the memory.

"Yeah, I couldn't do it either, but I agree that there's something lovable about an airplane so basic and humble."

Just then, a small, motorized cart with fat tires appeared. A man hopped off and strode across the grass, visibly irate. "What the hell do you think you're doing, driving on the course?" he yelled.

Alan was going to start explaining when Gurdon spoke, authority in his voice.

"My name is Booth Gurdon. I'm a test pilot for Vought-Sikorsky Aircraft, and I just made an emergency landing on your golf course. I couldn't brake on the wet grass, and the airplane went into the woods—you can see the tracks of the wheels right here. You'll be compensated for the damage to the golf course. I'm going to give you a telephone number at Vought-Sikorsky, and I want you to go back to your office and call the number, give them my name, and tell them what happened. I also want you to call the police. I want this area sealed off from the public."

"Who's this, your copilot?" the man asked, pointing to Alan.

"No, this is Lieutenant Ericsson from the navy. He's monitoring our flight tests," replied Gurdon.

Gurdon was dressed as a pilot, and Alan was in uniform, so the story seemed plausible. Alan felt strangely honored, even though Gurdon was just making it up. Gurdon had a quick mind, which is what you'd expect in a test pilot. He waited patiently as Gurdon wrote a phone number and his name on the page of a notebook he had pulled out of his flight suit.

The man eyed the Tatra with suspicion, but then seemed to decide to play along. He took the page from Gurdon, hopped onto the cart, and disappeared.

"Thanks for the promotion. Let's get in my car and out of the rain," suggested Alan.

"Good idea. Oh, it has right-hand drive!" Gurdon went around to the left side and got in. When they were settled and out of the rain, Gurdon sighed and said, "It's going to be hard to even show my face at the plant again."

Alan decided to go out on a limb a little to try and cheer up Gurdon. "Well, let me guess a little here. I suspect that you were under a lot of pressure to squeeze in as many flight tests as possible. In a plane that is that fast, I imagine that it's probably hard to stay near the plant. Either something went wrong with the airplane, or you got low on fuel. You couldn't make it back due to the weather. It's not really your fault."

"Thanks for the kind thoughts. You might be right, but I'm not that optimistic. I nearly ran out of fuel. A problem with the airplane would make a better excuse, though."

"The Corsair has an R-2800 with a two-stage supercharger?" Alan asked.

"Yes."

"It's very clean. It should be fast."

"Very."

"More range than an F4F?"

"Much more."

"I just hope I get to fly one someday. I hope they keep you on flight test, too, so the job gets done more quickly."

"Hell, they may cancel the program," said Gurdon.

"With France gone and the British demonstrating the value of top-notch fighters every day, I would think the Corsair has got to have top priority . . . Unless it has some crippling problem."

"It's a fine airplane. It has a few rough edges, but nothing major. You're probably right."

Two police cars appeared, with their blue lights flashing.

"Well, I guess the authorities have been informed, so you should be free to go. The police will want your name and address, but I better take it, too," said Gurdon. He took down Alan's information before they both got out of the car.

Alan said, "Good luck. After the police get what they want, perhaps I'll go. Is there anything else I can do for you?"

"I don't think you'll be able to do much for me now, but thanks for your help and good thoughts."

They shook hands and parted.

Saturday, August 10, 1940

It was going to be a hot, sultry, hazy day. Alan and Jennifer had decided to meet and walk on First Beach at 0700, while it was still cool. The southwest breeze off the water made it quite pleasant.

As they started walking, Alan said, "Well, I have big news. I got my acceptance for transfer to aviation and flight training yesterday. I was given leave starting September 7. I'm ordered to report in at Pensacola on September 30. With Naval Aviation expanding so fast, I'm glad to be accepted, but I hate the prospect of leaving you."

She turned to him, a wistful expression on her face. "Well, I've been assuming that you'd probably be leaving Newport during September, one way or another. Now it's definite. After that, we may not see each other for quite a while."

He searched for something cheerful to say, but couldn't find anything. "That's right, I'm afraid. Even if I stayed, you probably wouldn't be here a lot longer, either."

"True. You'll be in Pensacola for the winter, you rascal. I imagine they'll keep you quite busy, though, since they recently condensed the curriculum from a year to seven months." She stopped, faced him and held him with her hands on his upper arms. "Please be extremely careful, Alan. Aviation is a dangerous business, like submarines."

"I promise."

"We've been having a great summer together, and we should be grateful for that, I suppose."

"Yeah, let's try to make the best of what's left of it."

"Will you have leave to come home for Christmas?"

"I hope so."

"Of course, I'm not sure where I'll be by then—probably here or Washington, so I don't know if *I'll* be home for Christmas. It's going to be a little hard to leave the War College, while I'm still enjoying my work here so much. I'm a little surprised that it seems to suit me so well."

"You and the navy are a good fit for each other."

As the sun rose higher, it began to get hot. They decided to separate for the rest of the morning to get their Saturday chores done and then meet in the afternoon to go for a sail.

As Alan drove back to his apartment, he thought about Jennifer. His affection for her had grown even stronger over the summer. The nervousness that he felt on their first few dates had gradually faded away. He was relaxed and comfortable with her, and she seemed to feel the same way. He had been thinking about asking her to marry him. With the news of his transfer, there didn't seem to be much point in waiting longer. He was pretty sure she would say yes, but the only way to be sure was to ask.

Alan had rented a graceful Herreshoff sailboat for the afternoon, which had plenty of room for the two of them, some extra clothes, and the picnic supper that Jennifer had said she would pack. Alan picked her up a little after 1500, and they drove to the harbor, as they had done several times during the summer. They had gotten rained on once and becalmed once, but each sail had been fun anyway.

A thunderstorm came in from the west as they arrived at the harbor, causing them to wait in the Tatra until it cleared out. They chatted in the car as it went over, clearing out the sultry air and lowering the August humidity. As they carried their things down to the wharf, the breeze steadied and the sun came out, leaving the sky crystal clear and littered with puffy cumulus clouds. Alan thought that it was perfect weather for a sail.

They got everything stowed and sailed over to Bonnet Shores, on the west side of Narragansett Bay, dropping anchor a little before 1800.

After enjoying their supper, they started back. They were running before the northwest wind. The sun was sinking low and the wind was dying as they rounded Beavertail Point. Alan was propped up at the aft end of the cockpit, his left arm on the tiller and his right arm around Jennifer. She was lying against him with her head on his chest. The wind dropped to nothing, and the boat slowed, then gradually turned toward the north, bobbing on the gentle swell. Off to the west, a magnificent sunset was unfolding. Tall cumulus clouds seemed to be on fire. Alan had been looking for a particularly pleasant moment, and this seemed to be it.

"Jennifer, are you awake?"

"Oh, yes. I'm watching the beautiful sunset and listening to your heart."

"What's it saying?"

"Now it's beating faster. Is everything okay?"

"Yes. Does it say it wants to ask a question?"

"A question?"

"Yes—a very important question."

She pushed herself up and looked into his eyes. "What, Alan?"

"Jennifer, will you marry me?"

Her eyes widened, her jaw dropped, and she stared into his eyes for what seemed like an eternity to Alan, but was probably only a second.

She put her hands on his shoulders. "Yes, Alan, I will." She broke into a huge grin, shook his shoulders, and said louder and louder, "Yes, yes, YES!" She drew him to her, kissing him long and hard.

They both sat back and held hands. She said, "I have been hoping that you would ask that question soon. I think my heart has known the answer since that day back in April, when you looked over Victoria's shoulder and directly into my eyes for the first time in a long time."

Alan was jubilant—and relieved.

The sun sank and a zephyr came again from the northwest. It felt chilly, so they pulled out sweaters and put them on.

He looked at her and said, "You're so foxy." He paused and smiled widely. "I love the way you look, but that's just the tip of the iceberg."

She reddened and said, "Thank you, Alan. I know you like the way I look. I can tell because of the way you stare at me. I don't think I'll ever tire of you staring at me."

"Good."

"When we first met four years ago, I was struck by how handsome you were. I just wasn't able to admit it to myself until I saw you again last April."

They embraced and kissed again.

The zephyr turned into a breeze, still coming from the northwest, and the mainsail announced its impatience by flapping. Alan sheeted in and steered in reverse until the sails filled on the port tack, and then he bore off and started on the reach northeast back to Newport. It was still faintly light when they eased into the wharf. Alan paid for the rental, and they put their things back in the car.

"How about a little libation to celebrate the occasion?" he asked.

"Great idea."

They walked to a waterfront bar and went in, sitting down and ordering a bottle of champagne.

"Here's to you, Jennifer, love of my life."

"Here's to you, Alan, my true love."

They touched glasses and drank.

"I think my family will be very pleased," said Alan.

"I think my family will, too. I think Dad really likes you. In regard to religion, I think he came to realize that it wasn't quite right to expect more of you than he does of me." She paused and gazed into his eyes before suddenly saying, "You know this will start a whole train of events, though. We'll need to make a lot of decisions, and pretty darn quick."

"None tonight, though. Let's walk on Bailey's Beach tomorrow morning, before it gets hot. We'll talk and start figuring it all out."

"Why do you always know just what to do?"

"I don't."

"We're having our first argument, you rascal," she said, grinning widely.

"You're right, you scalawag."

They kissed and took another drink.

They left, taking most of the champagne with them. Alan was so euphoric that he crunched the gears twice on the way to Jennifer's apartment. They said good night tenderly, and he forced himself to drive slowly and carefully back to his apartment.

CHAPTER SIX

Carriers vs. Battleships

Sunday, September 8, 1940

Alan picked up Jennifer to drive to the Peckhams' for dinner. She was wearing a bottle-green skirt and a white blouse with a silver necklace and bracelet. *Sunday dinner at the Peckhams' is reason to dress up a little more than usual,* Alan thought. She looked wonderful, as always. He knew that not every man would consider her especially beautiful, but to him, her beauty was magical.

Jennifer had told Alan earlier that Victoria had found a new boyfriend, who was a student entering the War College. Alan knew that Victoria had cultivated friends in the housing office, and she looked over each list of new students before they arrived. She had always paid close attention to each of the few students who were unmarried and arranged to show them around the college when they arrived. Alan remembered that this had resulted in a few dates, but no really appealing candidates. Now, at last, she had found one, Lieutenant Seth Stephenson, Academy class of '28, that she considered promising. They had been dating, and he had already met her parents. In fact, she was bringing him to join them for Sunday dinner. Also invited were two professors from the War College, who were friends of Victoria, and their wives. Alan eagerly looked forward to hearing what they had to say about the war in Europe, and to meeting Seth.

Jennifer had also told Alan that, because she was actually employed by ONI, she would listen eagerly to discussions of naval matters, but could not offer opinions. Alan was not about to take on any War College professors in a debate, either—even if he disagreed strongly. The need for tact and discretion was obvious.

It was a beautiful, bright, clear day. The northwest wind was cool and temperatures were in the seventies, marking the winding down of summer, which is also why the Peckhams were back from their annual vacation in Maine. Mrs. Peckham greeted Alan and Jennifer at the front door and escorted them into the living room to greet Dr. Peckham. Victoria, Seth, and the other guests had not yet arrived.

Mrs. Peckham exclaimed, "We were thrilled to hear that you two are engaged! How exciting! Congratulations! We're very much looking forward to the party in two weeks."

Alan thought it was wonderful that his parents had offered to host the engagement party since the Warrens would be putting on the wedding. The Warrens had gratefully accepted the offer.

"I know, it's coming up fast," Jennifer agreed.

"And you, Alan, are off to Pensacola at the end of the month! That's very exciting, too," said Mrs. Peckham, "but we're very sorry to see you leave Newport."

"Thank you. I'm pleased and looking forward to it," said Alan, "but I'll miss your hospitality very much."

Victoria, Seth, and the other guests arrived, and introductions were made. Jennifer had told Alan before they'd arrived that Seth's nickname was Spuz, the slang word for dressing up, because he seemed to thrive on formal dress and affairs. He was a cruiser man, and he had spent some time in the Office of War Plans at US Navy headquarters. Alan thought he looked the part. Alan was introduced to Dick Burgess and Walter Hyde, the two War College professors, and their wives, as well.

Turning to Alan, Dr. Peckham said, "Now is an excellent time to get into aviation. They've increased the authorized strength of naval aviation all the way up to 15,000 planes since we saw you last."

Burgess joined in. "Our rearmament is finally picking up speed. It's way overdue, but better late than never. Right now, we couldn't help the British much if we wanted to, but that trade of old destroyers for leases on bases announced last week seems very good for both the British and us. I'm sure the isolationists are upset again, but the crucial thing right now is the war in the air over England. Did you hear the news from England yesterday? The Germans attacked London at night instead of the RAF fighter bases during the day. Civilians in London and other English cities may have a very bad time now. It seems to me, however, that the switch in targets is a sign that the Germans have been unable to gain air superiority. That means they cannot sustain precision targeted bombing in daylight, which is the only way they can attack the RAF bases. As long as Britain can prevent Germany from getting control of the air, I don't think the Germans can invade. It could be a major turning point." Alan had heard about the Germans changing of targets, but had not recognized the significance it. Burgess had made a crucial point.

Hyde said, "Maybe, but another thing holding up the Germans is that they lost several of their important combat ships during the invasion of Norway."

"True, but without control of the air, their fleet would be vulnerable," said Burgess.

"Dick and I differ on that point," Hyde said, looking at the others. "It's one thing to hit stationary buildings and troop concentrations with bombs, but is quite another to damage a maneuvering armored naval vessel that is armed with anti-aircraft weapons."

"Dinner is served," interrupted Mrs. Peckham firmly, and she herded the group into the dining room. Alan thought her interruption must have been deliberate, and it left him a little disappointed that the discussion was interrupted just as it was coming to a head.

The table was beautifully set, as always. Alan found that he was seated between Jennifer on his right and Mrs. Burgess on his left. They sat down and Dr. Peckham said a brief prayer, then stood and began carving the salmon. Bottles of Pouilly-Fume went around.

Burgess addressed Alan, "Which branch of naval aviation do you want to get into?"

"My preference would be for carrier aviation," answered Alan.

"Good for you. I think that will be a very rewarding place to serve," said Burgess.

Dr. Peckham finished the carving and sat down. The last few plates were passed to the other end of the table, where Mrs. Peckham added vegetables and potatoes until everyone was served. There was a pause in the conversation as everyone began the meal.

Hyde looked at Alan and said, "You have been in submarines, and now you want to go into aviation. What's wrong with the good-old surface navy?"

"Well, since my days at the Naval Academy, I've been interested in the two parts of the navy that have a vertical component to their operations—operate in three dimensions, in effect—which are submarines and aviation," answered Alan. "When my surface tour was over, I considered both and chose submarines."

"What ship did you serve on for your surface tour?" asked Seth.

"The *Pennsylvania*."

"Flagship of the fleet," said Hyde. "You can't do much better than that. Unlike Dick, I think that battleships still rule the waves, and the people that run the navy come out of them. What department were you in at the end of the tour?"

"Gunnery. I was in number-four turret."

"Very good. I bet that was rewarding," Seth commented.

It seemed to Alan that Seth and Hyde were members of the "Gun Club," the informal name for the men who were devoted to traditional surface ships with heavy guns. Alan remembered that the Gun Club had been the impetus behind the original development of the aircraft carrier. Tests done shortly after the World War had showed that the accuracy of naval gunfire could be greatly improved by having aircraft report where the shots were falling, so the Gun Club pushed the development of the carrier. As aircraft improved, the possibility emerged that the aircraft themselves could deliver projectiles more accurately and much farther than the battleships. Thus the aircraft carrier had gradually turned into a rival of the battleship. This had resulted in a long-running controversy, which had divided the navy into two camps: the Gun Club supporting battleships, and the aviators and their friends supporting aircraft carriers. Obviously, Alan was in the latter camp, as apparently Burgess was also. He was pleased, however, at the prospect of hearing both sides of the argument put forth by War College professors.

Burgess said, "Well, Walter, as you say, you and I differ on some topics. I think that Alan may be headed for what has become the new capital ship, the aircraft carrier."

Hyde replied, "The aircraft carrier can be a huge help in scouting for the fleet; that's why control of the air is important. Aircraft can also be helpful in harassing the enemy fleet during the approach to battle. In the end, though, it takes the heavy guns of another battleship to sink a battleship."

Burgess countered, "As I see it, there's been no battle experience to tell us for sure whether or not a battleship could survive an attack by an aircraft carrier. The best test we have is the Fleet Problems. Looking at the results of those, I think that our aircraft have improved to the point that a determined squadron of either dive-bombers or torpedo bombers could sink a battleship, even when it's surrounded by other surface ships that lend supporting anti-aircraft fire. For that to happen, it has to be daylight and reasonably good weather. If there's enemy fighter opposition, the attack must be escorted by our fighters. It might take more than one attack wave to get the job done, but the damage from the first wave will make the job of the second wave a lot easier."

Alan was surprised to find that this sounded very much like the gospel according to Ericsson.

Dr. Peckham smiled and asked, "What is your opinion, Seth?"

"I am inclined to agree with Professor Hyde," Seth replied, smiling and glancing at both professors. "I would extend what Professor Hyde said to include heavy cruisers, because I think their higher speed and maneuverability would offset their thinner armor during an air attack."

Spoken like a cruiser man, thought Alan.

Dr. Peckham said, "What do you think, Alan?"

As the most junior officer present, Alan was certainly not going to preach the gospel according to Ericsson. "As a prospective carrier pilot, I am biased in favor of carriers, so I would have to agree with Professor Burgess."

Seth glanced at the others and said, "Well, let us assume for the moment that Professor Burgess and Alan are right. What's to prevent battleships or heavy cruisers from sinking enemy carriers at night?"

Burgess replied, "If a battleship can get within range of a carrier without its main battery being seriously damaged, it could probably sink the carrier faster than the carrier aircraft could disable the battleship—unless the carrier's aircraft were already in the air and there was enough light for them to attack—but it's hard for a battleship to get within range without being attacked first. Say we have a small fleet with battleships and no carriers going against a small fleet with carriers and no battleships. At dusk, the battleship fleet is just out of scouting range of the carrier fleet, say 300 miles. Night falls with the battleship fleet as close as it can get without being detected and attacked, but to get within firing range of the carriers—say twenty-five miles—even the new thirty-knot battleships or heavy cruisers will have to steam most of the night in exactly the right direction to reach the carriers before dawn. For this to happen, the battleship fleet has to know precisely where the carriers will be when the battleships arrive, without the carrier fleet having detected them. That seems like a very unlikely situation, since the air reconnaissance of the carrier fleet is likely to be much better than that of the battleship fleet."

Alan was surprised again to hear the same argument he had used in discussions with his peers.

"I hadn't thought of it that way, but that makes a lot of sense," Dr. Peckham chimed in.

Hyde countered, "In reality, both fleets will have both battleships *and* carriers. The friendly carriers will keep control of the air over their friendly battleships until the battleships of both fleets come within firing range of each other."

Burgess replied, "If one fleet can disable the other's carriers, however, they'll have a huge advantage. They'll be able to severely damage, if not destroy, the other's battleships before the battleships get within range of each other to attack. In that case, when the carriers get within range of each other, which will be long before the battleships are in range of each other, the opposing carriers will seek each other out and attack. Thus, the battle becomes carriers versus carriers, and the role of the battleships is to provide supporting anti-aircraft fire. The only way the battleships can fight each other is if there are no operational carriers left."

"I doubt it," said Hyde.

Burgess continued. "There is one situation where the battleship could still be crucial, and that is when one side has an air base within gun range of the sea. The air base is, in effect, an unsinkable, but immobile, aircraft carrier. Knowing the location of the air base, fast battleships could attack the air base at midnight, but be nearly out of range of air attack the afternoon before and the morning after. The battleships couldn't destroy the air base completely, but they could put it out of action for days. The only defense against this type of attack would be heavy coast-defense guns, which take a long time to install, or countering the attacking battleships with friendly battleships in a night battle."

Alan had not considered this point, and he was intrigued. Burgess's argument sounded very logical.

Hyde said, "Well, it's nice to know that you think that battleships can still play a role beyond anti-aircraft support. *I* still think that aircraft cannot be relied upon to mount an effective attack on maneuvering, armored, surface ships."

"Well, it seems that the experts from the War College disagree, and the rest of us are hardly in a position to argue with them," said Dr. Peckham with a smile. "I guess we'll have to leave it at that."

After dessert, the gathering moved out to the patio for coffee. Alan felt a wave of nostalgia as he remembered talking with Jennifer in the same spot on a beautiful spring day five months earlier.

"Are the British going to hold out, do you think?" Mrs. Peckham asked the group.

Hyde replied, "Things are definitely looking up, so I would say yes, although it isn't over. It looks like it's too late in the season to mount an invasion for this year, which will let the British catch their breath to some extent during the winter, although the air attacks on the cities may continue. Also, the Germans might decide to try something else next spring, instead of just going back to the attack on Britain. The submarine battle in the Atlantic could get worse, though."

Burgess was nodding.

"After going through hell with the German submarines in the last war, why weren't the British better prepared?" asked Dr. Peckham.

Burgess replied, "It's the same in their navy as it is in ours. In a democracy in peacetime, it's easiest to get money for things that sound important and take a long time to build, like battleships, cruisers, and carriers. Escorts, tenders, and oilers tend to get left out. Because of this, we're very short of all of those, and the British are very short of escorts. Also, right now, the British are holding many of their destroyers in home waters in case of an invasion."

Hyde nodded. Burgess and Hyde seemed to be in agreement about Britain's prospects, Alan realized.

The guests finished their coffee, thanked the Peckhams, and got ready to leave. Alan and Jennifer stayed to say good-bye to the Peckhams after the other guests had left.

"What a nice time of year to be in Florida," Mrs. Peckham said to Alan. "Will you live on the base? Will you take your car?"

"Yes, there's a BOQ on the base where I'll live. I plan to take the train down there and leave my car behind. After I get there, if I find that I could use a car, I might pick up a local rattletrap to use, and sell it when I leave."

"I guess there's some value to being a certified grease monkey," agreed Mrs. Peckham, smiling. They all laughed.

"You'll arrive right in the middle of hurricane season," Dr. Peckham said.

"That's right, but I'm sure they're prepared for it," said Alan.

"We'll see you briefly again in two weeks, but we *will* miss you," Mrs. Peckham commented.

"No more than I'll miss you and Victoria," Alan assured her. "You've been my second family, and I'm deeply grateful to you."

"Jennifer, we hope you'll visit us after Alan has gone," said Mrs. Peckham.

"That would be very nice, thank you. I will look forward to it," Jennifer promised, after a departing hug.

CHAPTER SEVEN

The War Comes Home

Tuesday, September 10, 1940

Alan was having a quiet supper with his parents at their house. The day before, he had moved out of his furnished apartment in Newport. He had just barely been able to stuff all of his belongings into the Tatra to bring them home.

The doorbell rang. "Who's at the door at this hour?" Larry wondered aloud as he went to the door, returning a minute later, carrying an envelope.

"It's a telegram," he said, opening the familiar yellow envelope. He groaned as he scanned the message. His face became stern and resolute as he cleared his throat and read it aloud.

```
MARGUERITE KILLED AIR RAID LONDON 9 SEPT
STOP COULD WINNIE AND JENNY COME FOR LONG
VISIT STOP LETTER FOLLOWS STOP

COLIN ERICSSON
```

Joanna put her hands to her face as her eyes quickly filled with tears. "Oh, how horrible! She was such a good woman and a wonderful mother," she said, dabbing her eyes with her napkin.

Larry's eyes reddened as he spoke. "She was a marvelous person. It's terribly sad. This really brings the war home, doesn't it?"

Alan felt a wave of sadness as he was struck by the truth of his father's remark. He winced as he remembered hearing at the Peckhams' that the German switch to civilian targets could be good news. It was true in the strategic sense, but civilians were being hurt and killed. Colin was Larry's first cousin, the son of Larry's father's younger brother. He was an officer on a Royal Navy destroyer, so he would probably not be allowed much leave at this critical time, even in a family emergency. Alan had met Colin once when he'd visited Boston, and had been very impressed. He had only seen pictures of Marguerite, his wife of ten years, and their two young daughters Winifred and Genevieve, who were Alan's second cousins. He felt a kinship for them, anyway.

After a few minutes, Larry and Joanna had outwardly recovered from the shock and composed themselves.

"I wonder what he means by 'a long visit,'" Joanna queried.

"I suspect it's an English understatement. It could be for the duration of the war," Larry speculated.

"Oh, my. Let's see, we last saw Winnie and Jenny in '36, I think—sweet girls. Winnie was five and Jenny was three, so they'd be nine and seven now. I think it would be fun to have them here. That's all settled, then," Joanna proclaimed, smiling at Larry.

"Well, I can't think of any reason why we couldn't do it. I'm sure they'd want do the same for us if the situation was reversed, but we could probably find other places for them. It's really up to you, because you'll effectively be their mother," said Larry.

It was clear to Alan that his mother was becoming more delighted with the idea by the minute. As his initial surprise faded rapidly, he came to understand that his mother was eager to take on a second set of children. After all, he knew that she would love to spend more time with her granddaughter, but Michelle would only share her daughter so much.

Joanna's thoughts began to tumble out rapidly. "Let's see, I'll have to cut back my hours at the hospital, but I think I can do that. They can even have their choice of bedrooms. We'll need to find places for them in school."

Larry said, "Well, if it's all settled, I think we shouldn't waste any time. School will start in a week or two. I think we should try tomorrow to get an appointment with Miss Cole."

Joanna nodded her agreement. An appointment with Miss Cole, the head mistress of the Park School, would have to be a priority.

"Remember that Jennifer's sister Gertrude is a teacher there," said Alan.

Joanna replied, "That's right. She could be very helpful. Alan, call Jennifer and tell her what's going on. She's coming up next weekend, right? Let's invite her and Gertrude for dinner on Saturday."

"Good idea," agreed Larry.

"Aye Aye," said Alan.

Larry declared, "If it's really settled, we should not keep Colin in suspense."

"It is settled," said Joanna firmly.

Larry said, "I think Marguerite would be pleased. We should wire Colin back right away, saying something like this: 'Deepest sympathy for your loss. Glad to have children for as long as you want. Joanna waits eagerly.' What do you think?" He was writing the message out on a piece of paper.

Joanna smiled warmly. "You have no trouble reading me, do you? Add 'Letter follows', and I'll write it."

Larry smiled and added the two words. He glanced at Joanna and Alan for any more thoughts and then rose to go to the telephone and send the telegram. Alan could only admire his parents' quickness to rise to the occasion.

Tuesday, September 24, 1940

The engagement party for Jennifer and Alan had taken place the previous Saturday. They had truly enjoyed the party, although neither was used to being the center of attention at parties. Alan was glad to see old family friends again, and he was able to meet much more of Jennifer's family. The party had been catered, so the cleanup afterward was fairly simple. Jennifer had been able to take the week off, and was staying with her parents to spend as much time with Alan as possible before he went off to Florida.

After the party, the imminent arrival of the English children had very quickly become the center of attention in the Ericsson household. Winifred and Genevieve Ericsson were scheduled to arrive in New York from England by ship that morning. Joanna had left the previous day for New York in order to be on the wharf to meet the children and return with them by train to the Back Bay Station at 1650.

Jennifer arrived just after 1600 at Alan's parents' house, having offered to make supper for everyone in Joanna's absence. Shortly after she arrived, Larry left to pick up Joanna and the children at the station. Alan helped Jennifer find everything in the kitchen, even though he found he was a bit rusty.

Shortly before 1730, there was a *beep-beep* in the driveway to announce Larry's return with his passengers. Jennifer and Alan went to the front hall to meet them. The door opened and in walked the two children, closely followed by Joanna and Larry. Joanna made the introductions, and the children responded formally and properly.

"Now, we have two hungry and very tired guests, so let's have supper soon," suggested Joanna.

"Would 1800—excuse me, six o'clock, be soon enough?" asked Jennifer.

"That would be just right. I'm going to take Winnie and Jenny up to their room, and they can have a chance to wash up. You gentlemen bring up the luggage, please."

Although it was a momentous occasion for both the English girls and their adopted family, Joanna let everyone know that it was to be a quiet dinner. The girls answered a few questions about their voyage across the Atlantic over dinner. They said the woman who had been their guardian for the trip was very kind, and they enjoyed the trip. It seemed clear, however, that the sudden loss of their mother and their move to a new world, away from everything familiar, had left them very bewildered and subdued. After a dessert of ice cream, they both found it difficult to suppress yawns.

Joanna whisked them upstairs right after dinner. She could be heard reading a bedtime story for a while, and then she reappeared downstairs.

"The poor darlings," she told everyone. "It may take them awhile to come out of their shells, but I'm sure they will. They seem like nice kids—intelligent, too."

Those girls are in good hands, Alan reflected.

CHAPTER EIGHT

Off to Flight Training

Friday, September 27, 1940

Alan was ready to start on his train trip to Pensacola. Just for the fun of it, he had found out what the cost and travel time would be to go to Pensacola by the airlines. He would have had to fly to New York, change planes for Atlanta, change planes again for Mobile, Alabama, and then take a bus back to Pensacola. It would cost almost as much as a new car, and it would take about twelve hours. The train would cost about one tenth as much, and take about forty hours. Of course, the navy was willing to pay for his train fare, but not for the airline trip.

Joanna had announced the previous evening that breakfast would be at 0600. Alan got up at 0515 and came down to his favorite breakfast of fried eggs, bacon, sausage, English muffins, grapefruit, orange juice, and coffee. A little before 0700, Jennifer arrived in her car to take Alan to the train station. He had shipped most of his belongings, but he still had two large suitcases. Alan loaded his luggage into the Chevy before they went back into the house. He knew that Larry and Joanna would have preferred to see him off at the train station, but they realized that Jennifer would like to have that moment to herself. There were long hugs and stifled tears as Alan bid farewell to his parents.

Joanna glanced up the stairs and saw two small faces staring down. "Oh, Winnie and Jenny, I told you yesterday that Alan was leaving for Florida very early this morning, but I didn't want to wake you up. Since you're awake, come down and say good-bye."

The two girls came running down the stairs. "How long will you be gone?" asked Winnie.

"Until next May. I'll possibly be able to come home for a little while at Christmas, though," said Alan.

"That's a very long time," Winnie responded.

"Are you really going to learn to fly?" asked Jenny.

"Yes, I hope so."

"Are pilots all heroes?" asked Jenny.

"No, they're just like everybody else. A few are heroes, most are fairly good, and a few are no good."

"Alan will miss his train if he doesn't leave now," said Joanna firmly. Alan knelt and the two girls came forward. Each gave him a hug.

"Be good, have fun, and listen to your Aunt Joanna. She's very wise," Alan instructed them.

"Whew, I hope that was for the record," muttered Joanna.

They all said good-bye, and Alan and Jennifer went out and got into her car for the ride to Back Bay Station. She found a parking space and they were inside the station by about 0745. Alan found the listing and track number for the Murray Hill for New York, which was scheduled to depart at 0805. With his suitcases, Alan decided to take the elevator down to the platform below the main concourse.

Alan felt torn between opposing emotions. He knew that going off to Pensacola for flight training was one of the best things that had ever happened to him, but leaving Jennifer was one of the most difficult things he had ever done. What made it worse was that he could see that it was hard for her, too. He had never seen her dejected before, and his heart went out to her.

"Remember to write," Jennifer instructed.

"Don't worry, I will—and keep me posted on your life. Take good care of yourself, and don't get carried away with your work. I love you, Jennifer."

"I love you, Alan, so be very careful and come back in one piece," she said, smiling and trying to cover up the tears forming in her eyes.

Alan's eyes suddenly became very damp. They embraced and kissed as long as possible, and then he slowly picked up his bag and boarded the train. He found a window seat and waved to Jennifer on the platform. She waved back and then abruptly turned and walked to the stairs. As he watched her, he was overwhelmed by how much he was going to miss her.

CHAPTER NINE

Settling in at Pensacola

Monday, September 30, 1940

Alan was woken up at 0615 by the roar of an airplane taking off nearby. He had slept deeply, and it took him a moment to remember where he was—in the Bachelor Officers' Quarters at the Pensacola Naval Air Station. The BOQ was housed in several buildings that were on a small rise overlooking Chevalier Field from the west. The buildings were adapted to the climate, with two-story screened porches on all sides. To his delight, Alan had been assigned a room on the east side of the second floor with a view of the field. That side was considered the least desirable because of the noise from the field, but for the time being, the sound of aircraft engines was music to Alan's ears.

He had arrived in Pensacola late Saturday afternoon after spending a day and a half on a series of trains. He'd had to change trains in Washington, Atlanta, Montgomery, and the nearby little town of Flomaton, Alabama, where he got the dedicated shuttle train to Pensacola. It all went smoothly, but all the switching was tiring.

The weather on Sunday had been showery. He had spent most of the day getting his permanent room assignment, collecting his shipped luggage, and getting moved in. He met some of his neighbors, who informed him that the first six weeks of the course would be spent entirely on ground school, with no flying—a big letdown since he had been looking forward to flying soon.

Monday dawned bright and sunny. Alan reported to head-quarters as ordered at 0800 and learned that ground school would start the following day, so he had the rest of the day to look around. He began by walking around the base. The naval air station was on a peninsula, with Pensacola Bay on the south and east sides and a bayou to the north.

Chevalier Field was a beehive of flying activity on weekdays. The field had many runways in all directions that were generously long for smaller airplanes, but too short for large, modern ones. The larger ones had to use Corry Field, which was close by, but across the bayou. The main facilities of the base, including the hangars, were on the south side of the base, between Chevalier Field and the bay. The seaplane operations were located on the bay. Alan saw many different types of navy airplanes on the ground and in the air as he walked. He found himself caught up in the excitement of the place. On weekends, there was little activity, although some aircraft maintenance activities took place then, so it had been fairly quiet when he arrived. With war looming, he wondered how much longer the navy shore installations would remain mostly shut down on weekends.

The base was extensive, and it had more of an air of permanence than his image of a typical air base. He saw large buildings and hangars, many of them brick. There were big trees with Spanish moss between the buildings. It felt good to stretch his legs as he wandered around, although it was hot. The Officers' Club was in a prime location on the beach. Alan began to learn about the history of the base from signs and displays in some of the buildings. It had begun operations early in 1914; until the 1930s, it was the only naval air station in the world.

He had already found out from his neighbors in the BOQ that many pilots enjoyed visiting off-base watering holes across the bayou or in the city, beyond walking distance. He noticed that most of the students seemed to have cars or motorcycles, so he decided that he would look for a cheap car among the things that were advertised on a bulletin board in his building. He looked over the ads, and one for a 1924 Buick caught his eye. It was the same make and year as his first car, so it would be familiar, which was a big advantage. A car that old shouldn't be expensive, either.

Alan had fond memories of his first car. It had been a dark green six-cylinder roadster, which an old lady in the neighborhood had put up for sale. In addition to being a nice car, it was one of the very few cars available that had an advanced feature that he particularly admired: an overhead valve engine. It had been only four years old at the time, but he could afford it because it needed a lot of work—it had been in an accident and left to sit for three years. Although he was not old enough to have a driver's license, he recognized the rare opportunity and persuaded his parents to let him buy it. He'd put his mechanic's skills to work after school and had it in operating condition shortly after he got his driver's license. He had reluctantly sold the Buick ten years later when he had inherited the Tatra.

Alan found the student who had placed the ad in another building of the BOQ, and they went out to the parking lot to view the Buick. Alan did not expect it to be in great shape, but he was a little surprised at what he saw. It was a dark blue six-cylinder touring car that had been modified by cutting out the back of the body and getting rid of the rear seat. It had a roadster convertible top covering just the front seat, which made it sort of a makeshift pickup truck. Overcoming his doubts, they took it for a spin around the base. It was fairly rusty, but everything seemed to work and it ran well. Alan decided that it was a good fit for his modest needs and negotiated a price of fifty dollars.

Saturday, October 5, 1940

After breakfast, Alan was thinking of Jennifer, and he decided to write his first letter to her.

Pensacola Naval Air Station
October 5, 1940

Dear Jennifer,

How are you? I am fine. Except for missing you extremely, I am enjoying being here in the aviation world. I'm glad you're still enjoying being at the War College. Please keep me posted about your plans.

I got settled in the BOQ pretty fast. My alarm clock here on weekdays is the roar of airplanes taking off. So far, that has not bothered me at all, since I like the sound of airplane engines so much.

Most of the students here have cars or motorcycles, so I picked up an old car. It is a 1924 Buick, like my first car, so it is familiar. It is sort of a jalopy, so you might not like it, but I think it will fill my needs here. I have enjoyed the sensation of driving an old open car like that again, especially with the warm weather here. I sit up high in the breeze and I can see all around me with the top down. It might not be so much fun to take a real trip in it, though, because it's drafty and the old-fashioned suspension gives a bouncy ride.

Although the weather is hot, there's often a good breeze. I like the fact that it is seldom cloudy all day. Fairly often, there are beautiful tropical sunsets, with cumulus clouds glowing orange and red.

I quickly found out that the curriculum is all ground school for the first six weeks—no flying. That was quite a disappointment, but perhaps it is best to get the bulk of the ground school out of the way at the beginning. So far, some of it, like navigation and weather, is pretty old hat for me, and my attention wanders. I hope that we soon move on to less familiar stuff.

Naturally, the curriculum was changed drastically when the whole course was shortened from a year to six or seven months. Before that, all the students followed the same course, with training in land planes and seaplanes. Now, after about six weeks of flight training, each student is assigned to one of the three categories of navy airplanes: carrier planes, observation floatplanes on battleships and cruisers, or multi-engine flying boats for long-range reconnaissance. After that, the students get specialized training in that category for the rest of the course. We get to put in our preference before the selection, but they don't always follow it. You know I want to get into carrier planes.

Before I got here, I wasn't completely sure that I had what it takes to be a navy pilot. I've gotten to know some of the other students well enough to feel now that I am reasonably well qualified.

Yesterday, I joined a bunch of guys from my class on a bar-hopping trip. As you'd expect, jazz is the most common type of music down here. I was pleasantly surprised that some of the bars also included occasional forays into hillbilly music, which you know I love. We're a long way from any hills here, but I guess that music has appeal throughout the South.

I think that's all my news. My greetings to the Gallaghers. Mary should be having her baby soon. Please also give my greetings to Victoria and the Peckhams. Most of all, please write very soon.

All my love,

Alan

Friday, October 11, 1940

When Alan returned to the BOQ in the late afternoon, he was glad to find a letter from Jennifer. As he opened it, he smelled her perfume and it felt almost like she was standing there, watching him open her letter.

Newport, R. I.
October 4, 1940

Dear Alan,

It has been only a week since you left, and already I miss you badly, you rascal. I sure hope you can come home for Christmas.

I am fine, and my work here continues to be fascinating. Now I know enough about the navy to feel much more like I am part of it.

It looks like I will be at the War College a few more months, and then I will be moving to Washington and starting work for ONI.

Last Friday, after I dropped you off at the train, I came back down here to Newport. On Sunday the Peckhams had Victoria, Seth, and me over to dinner. Victoria and Seth are still going strong. They and the Peckhams send their greetings. It felt like I had hardly been away when I started back to work at the War College on Monday.

That day I ran into an old friend, Albert Hindmarsh. He had arrived at the War College as a lecturer while I was away in Boston. He was a professor of government at Harvard, and one of the Japan experts there. He encouraged me to consider working for ONI. Then last summer he volunteered himself for active duty at ONI and Commander McCollum took him on. It was good to see him again and catch up with him.

Yesterday evening I got a call from Mark Gallagher, saying that Mary had her baby—a girl—yesterday morning. Mother and daughter are doing fine, and I'm so glad everything is ok. Her name is Elizabeth Rose Gallagher. Mark is as proud as a peacock.

That's about all the news here. By the time you get this, you will have probably been flying several times. PLEASE be VERY careful, and tell me all about it. Please write soon. I want to hear all about Pensacola is like.

Much love,

Jennifer

It was a short letter, but it made Alan feel much more in touch with the world he had left. He was glad that he had written her a week earlier, and that it was time to write her again.

CHAPTER TEN

Getting Off the Ground

Thursday, November 14, 1940

The day that Alan was to begin flight training dawned clear and cool, as forecast. He had gone to bed early the night before. He was excited and had woken up earlier than usual. He liked to have breakfast, and he had had time to have a quick one in the cafeteria near the BOQ. He was wearing his newly issued flight suit and carrying his leather flying helmet as he headed to his first flight training session.

For Alan's class, primary flight training—known as Squadron One—would be held at Saufley Field, about eight miles north of Chevalier Field. They had just moved part of Squadron One there, so Alan's class was among the first primary students to be based there. There had been a briefing on it in ground school, and they were told that a shuttle bus would take the students out there in the morning. Saufley Field was a big field with lots of runways, concrete aprons, and hangars—and plenty of room—all of which had been built on land that the navy had acquired only the previous February. It was hard to imagine getting all that built in such a short time. *At least some rearmament activities are moving fast*, Alan observed.

In his excitement, Alan found himself squirming like a little kid on the shuttle bus. They arrived at Saufley Field about 0600, a little before dawn. He got off the shuttle bus with his classmates and immediately heard the growl of airplane engines warming up. He looked around and saw that Saufley had a very different atmosphere from Chevalier Field. The buildings were new and modern, but strictly functional. He noticed that some trees had been planted, but they were tiny.

He went into a large hangar and found other members of his group milling around a large blackboard. Airplanes were listed by number down the left side, with columns for the student and instructor for each of the first two periods. The first period was at 0700 and the second period was at 0900. Alan found his last name listed in the first period, along with his instructor's last name, Allard. There was also a diagram showing where the airplanes were parked on the apron.

The chief instructor for Squadron One climbed onto a table and gave a short speech to welcome the new class and issue some instructions. He told them where things were in the hangar and where to collect their parachutes and said that they should meet their instructors at their airplanes before the start of each flying period. After that, he wished them good luck. Coffee was set out on a table nearby, and Alan had a cup before gathering his parachute and walking out along the flight line. There was a vague odor of hydrocarbons wafting around, which was probably from aviation gasoline. He could see mechanics warming up engines. The last time he felt this excited was the first time he'd headed to sea in a submarine. *This is it*, he thought, *I am really going to get to fly*.

Students normally started off in the N3N, which was made by the government's Naval Aircraft Factory in Philadelphia. It was a big, rugged biplane that was reputed to be forgiving. After a few weeks, students moved on to the N2S, which was similar, but a little more responsive and less forgiving. The N2S was made by the Stearman Company in Wichita, Kansas. These primary trainers were all painted a bright shade of yellow and known as Yellow Perils because of their inexperienced pilots.

Alan knew that a fair number of students failed to learn fast enough, or got scared, and they were eliminated from flight training—"washed out." Alan realized that from the navy's point of view, if a student was going to wash out, it was better to have it happen early, before the navy had invested a lot of time and expense in training him. Alan's group was told that they would start out in the Stearman as an experiment, and he guessed that this change was made to try to get the wash-outs to happen even earlier in the training. Alan could see, however, that some students might be overwhelmed by the more difficult airplane and appear to be poor pilots, even though they were good prospects.

He found his airplane, but it was only 0630 and his instructor was not there, yet. The aircraft type was painted on the tail: N2S-3. Like all primary trainers, it had two separate, open cockpits, one behind the other. Alan began looking the airplane over, standing behind the lower wing on the left side. His first impression was that it was big, tall, and old-fashioned. It reminded him of the seaplanes that he had flown seven years earlier at the Academy. The typical biplane structure, with the two wings connected with struts and wires, was strong and light, but each little piece had wind resistance, which added up to a lot of drag. The covering over the wings, fuselage, and tail was cloth fabric, which always seemed more fragile to Alan than even the thinnest metal. The seven-cylinder Continental radial engine was mounted on the nose with no cowling, exposing the cylinders, while the simple fixed-pitch propeller was made of wood.

Alan understood that the Stearman was a good primary trainer for the military, but he found it hard to admire. He had been looking forward intensely to flying, however, so he was going to be anything but fussy about what aircraft type he would fly.

"Lieutenant Ericsson?" A voice called from behind him.

Alan turned around to find a lanky young man in a flight suit. He had a welcoming smile and his hand was extended. Alan had been told that rank did not count for much in flight training, where the student might outrank the instructor, and that there was no saluting. "That's me," said Alan, shaking his instructor's hand. *No Academy ring, so he must have been an AvCad,* thought Alan. The Aviation Cadet program took in college graduates and gave them military training to become officers while they were getting their flight training. The combination was quite rigorous. When they finished flight school, AvCads were commissioned as ensigns in the reserve. Alan thought this fellow was probably a "plowback," assigned as an instructor right after finishing flight school.

"Ensign James Allard."

Being instructed by an officer junior to me will be a new experience, Alan thought.

"We're supposed to be formal with our students, but if you don't mind, I prefer first names. I go by Jim."

"Fine with me, Jim. I go by Alan."

Jim looked a bit surprised and said, "Okay, Alan. Your information sheet says you've soloed in a light aircraft in addition to instruction in seaplanes at the Academy."

"That's right. I got a few solo hours in an Aeronca C3 about six years ago," Alan informed him. "It's about as different from the Stearman as a trainer can get, I suspect. Certainly it's much smaller."

"Razorback or Master?"

"Razorback," answered Alan. *Flying must be more than just a job to him if he's familiar with the early Aeroncas.*

"There's something lovable about the C3 Airknocker," Jim said with a smile.

Alan knew that the nickname Airknocker came at least partly from the staccato bark of the little two-cylinder engine that powered the C3. Alan broke into a grin. "You know, a test pilot from Vought said the same thing to me a few months ago, and I agree."

Jim's smile disappeared. "You were talking to a test pilot? This sheet says you were a submariner."

I blundered into that one, Alan noted, chagrined. "My conversation with the test pilot had nothing to do with the navy." He stretched the truth slightly.

"As for submarines, I don't want to get anywhere near them, because my father was killed in one. I do have to admit that the German submarines have been very effective," said Jim. He turned toward the airplane and said, "Well, let's get started. Climb up and put your parachute in, and then we'll start with the preflight inspection." Jim put his own parachute in the front cockpit.

The instructor flew in the front cockpit because it was nearer the center of gravity of the airplane. When it was time for a solo flight, therefore, his absence would not affect the balance of the airplane very much. They walked around the airplane clockwise, stopping while Jim described the things to check and watched Alan check each item. To Alan, he seemed to be careful and conscientious, not flaunting his teacher status. Alan was starting to like him.

Jim said, "Okay, get strapped in."

Alan climbed in. He fastened his parachute harness and his seat belt, and then plugged the rubber Gosport tube on his helmet into the socket, so that Jim could to talk to him, like a voice tube in ship, but he could not talk back. Alan had become familiar with a typical military cockpit in the seaplanes at the Academy. The cockpit resembled that of a racing car more than one in a normal automobile: there was no upholstery, and nothing was concealed. There was a multiplicity of dials in the panel, and control knobs and levers were scattered around. The big control stick stuck up between his legs as he sat down. Behind the controls and instruments, there was a framework of steel tubing, as well as electrical wires and control rods. As in the Academy seaplanes, there were aluminum strips for his feet to rest on. Otherwise, there was no floor in the cockpit, and he could see the bottom of the fuselage. The usual faint odor of gasoline was mixed with the smell of sunbaked paint and fabric and something unpleasant—probably vomit. He grasped the throttle with his left hand, the control stick with his right, and put his feet on the rudder pedals.

Jim stood on the lower wing and leaned over the rear cockpit. He went over the controls and indicators. "Okay, we're ready to go," he said with a smile. Jim stood up and waved his hand to signal that he was ready for a starter crew, and then climbed into the front cockpit.

Two ground crewmen appeared. One ground crewman stood by the left landing gear and pushed the starting crank into the cowling. The other ground crewman stood about ten feet in front of the left wing with a big fire extinguisher on wheels, watching for fuel spillage or a fire. From the Academy, Alan was familiar with the procedure of starting the engine with a flywheel inertia starter, which was being cranked up by the ground crewman. Like most radials, the engine started unevenly, with coughs and puffs of smoke from the exhaust before it settled into a steady idle. Alan enjoyed hearing the rumble of the radial engine a few feet away. He also felt the vibration coming through the fuselage and smelled the exhaust blowing by.

Jim coached Alan through the taxi out to the runway. "In most military land planes, you can't see straight ahead when the tail wheel is on the ground, so we always use S-turns while taxiing to be able to look ahead."

Alan began to make shallow S-turns along the taxiway, which did allow him to get a glimpse down the taxiway along either side of the fuselage at the end of each swing.

"We've got a northwest wind today, so we'll be using runway three two."

Alan could see the approach end of the runway ahead to the left. An airplane was turning onto it to take off. A number of airplanes were lined up ahead, waiting to take off, and Alan stopped at the end of the line. While waiting, Jim showed Alan how to do the run-up to check out the engine before taking off. They ran through the takeoff checklist and were ready to go.

"I'll do this takeoff," Jim told him, "but I want you to follow me through on the controls."

Alan knew that meant to touch the controls lightly to feel their movement, but not interfere with what Jim was doing.

Soon, it was their turn. Jim taxied onto the runway. As they lined up straight with the runway, Jim instructed, "Wait for the green light from the tower. There it is."

Alan gently held the throttle and stick, and placed his feet on the rudder pedals. As Jim slowly pushed the throttle all the way forward, a loud roar came from the engine and the wind from the propeller increased dramatically.

"Oil pressure, okay," Jim said.

Alan was too busy taking in what was happening to look at the oil pressure gauge.

"Let the stick come forward, and when there's enough speed, lift the tail a little, but keep the tail low and let the airplane fly off," Jim instructed.

As they gathered speed, the tail lifted off the runway a little. Alan glanced at the airspeed indicator, which was showing about fifty-five knots and climbing fast. Suddenly, the runway started dropping away. *Airborne!* Alan felt the same thrill he had felt in the C3 and in the Academy seaplanes. He loved seeing the ground drop away, feeling the rush of the wind past the cockpit, and hearing the roar of the engine.

"We'll climb at sixty-five knots. Trim as needed," Jim continued.

Alan glanced quickly at the instruments, but he could not help taking in the view. It was a beautiful day, with good visibility, and he could see all around Pensacola. He had known flying would be fun, and it was.

"We're going to head north to one of our practice areas and climb to 3,000 feet."

Alan felt the stick and rudder pedals move as Jim made a shallow right turn. Alan glanced at the altimeter; they were passing through 1,500 feet.

"Okay, you got it," Jim informed him. Alan quickly gripped the stick and felt Jim let go. He began by practicing turns as they climbed, and then he leveled off at 3,000 feet. He pulled the throttle back until the engine was turning at 1,850 rpm for cruising, and the sound of the engine dropped an octave. Alan used the trim lever to relieve the steady force on the stick as the airplane gradually accelerated to cruise speed in level flight.

Jim asked Alan to lean the gasoline and air mixture going into the engine for minimum fuel consumption in cruising flight, using a procedure taught in ground school. When he finished that, Alan glanced around at the scenery. He felt like he had the ability to go anywhere in three dimensions, which gave him an enormous sense of freedom and mobility. The fields and forest below were still mostly green. He looked back and could still see the Gulf, but they were about thirty miles inland.

When they got to the practice area, Jim had Alan do 360-degree turns to the right and left. After each maneuver, Jim would critique it and offer suggestions. On the second 360-degree turn, Alan had the satisfaction of feeling the small bump that meant he had flown through his own wake, indicating a precision turn.

Next, Jim demonstrated stalls, in which the airplane was pulled up into a steep climb until the air flowing over the wings was so slow that the wings suddenly stopped lifting and the nose plunged down sharply. The pilot was expected to let the stick move forward and let the airspeed build back up to recover, while losing no more altitude than necessary.

Finally, Jim announced over the Gosport, "Okay, that was very good. Nice job. I think we should head back to Saufley now. You take me there."

Alan looked at his watch. It was already 0810. Alan was aware that they had been flying alternate north and west legs, so they should have traveled more or less northwest. They were currently headed north, so he started a right turn toward the southeast. As they turned, he scanned the shore in the distance to the southeast and thought he recognized Pensacola Bay. He rolled the airplane level and headed toward it. As they got closer, he recognized the north end of Perdido Bay. He remembered that Saufley Field was just northeast of that.

"Descend to 1,000 feet," Jim ordered him.

Alan pulled the throttle back to 1,000 rpm, and the engine was almost quiet by comparison. The Stearman began a steady descent. Some minutes later, Alan brought the rpm back up to 1,850 and pulled the nose up, leveling off at 1,000 feet.

"Very good, nicely done," Jim encouraged him. "We're about five miles from the field and headed for it, so I guess you know where you're going. This time I'll coach you down until we're on final, and then I'll take it from there. We can see from traffic that runway three two is still the active runway. We know that runway has a left-hand traffic pattern. Keep a lookout for other airplanes, and approach the field from the west to enter the downwind leg at roughly a forty-five-degree angle."

Alan did so. He remembered airport traffic patterns from his own flying, so he had a picture of what their path to the runway should be.

"When we're about a mile from the center of the field, turn right and fly your downwind leg, parallel to runway three two on the southwest side. Throttle back to 1,400 to slow down, but don't lose altitude."

Alan throttled back and re-trimmed. He was about to turn onto the downwind leg when another airplane suddenly came up from the southwest and cut in front of them, quite close. Alan hesitated.

"It's okay," Jim assured him. "We can work around him. Turn to fly your downwind outside of him, further from the runway. He may not have seen us, but he should have."

The other airplane was turning downwind, and Alan deliberately carried his right turn further to pass behind. He turned left briefly to place their plane on a parallel path. Jim coached Alan through the landing checklist.

"Good. Keep an eye on Hot Pants over on our left. We'll need to extend our downwind leg to get enough spacing behind him."

Alan glanced at the airplane to the left and slightly ahead. They were passing the threshold of runway three two off their left wing. In a few moments, the other airplane turned left ninety degrees onto the base leg.

"Keep going downwind. I'll tell you when to turn base." After twenty seconds, Jim said, "Now turn your base."

Alan made a ninety-degree left turn onto the base leg, well outside of the other airplane.

"We'll have a long final, so we won't close the throttle yet. Remember to lead your turn onto final, or you'll overshoot."

Alan watched the runway and judged when to turn. He led the turn, but not enough, so he overshot a little.

"Not bad at all. I got it."

Alan felt the stick move as Jim took over.

"We should get a light from the tower. There it is—green, so we're cleared to land. I'm pulling the power back to idle. Now we establish a steady descent at sixty knots. Remember to watch both sides using your peripheral vision; don't look at one side or the other. Watch the end of the runway and see whether it's moving up or down. If it's moving up, we'll be short and we add power. If it's moving down, we'll be long and we reduce power. If we're already at idle, we slip to steepen our descent."

Alan knew that in a slip, the rudder and ailerons were moved in opposing directions, causing the airplane to go slightly sideways. The extra drag caused the airplane to drop more rapidly. Their glide path looked good to Alan as it was, and soon they were over the end of the runway.

"About twenty feet above the runway, I start the flare," Jim informed him.

Alan saw the nose come up as they flared out to end their descent. The wind noise tailed off as they lost speed rapidly. The nose continued coming up until it was well above level. Alan thought that the wheels were still about five feet above the runway and that Jim was going to drop it in, landing hard, but just then, to Alan's amazement, they touched down on all three wheels—a perfect three-point landing. As they rolled out along the runway, Alan felt the rudder pedals twitch occasionally as Jim kept it straight with the rudder at first, then by using the toe brakes at the top of the rudder pedals to apply braking to one main wheel or the other. The airplane continued to slow down rapidly. When they reached the large paved rectangle that surrounded the runway intersection in the center of the field, they were at taxiing speed.

"Okay, you got it. Unlock the tail wheel," Jim commanded. Alan pulled the stick fully back and unlocked the tail wheel, and then he taxied back to their parking spot. He pulled into their spot and set the parking brake and then Jim led him through the engine shutdown procedure.

"Okay, let's climb out and have coffee while we talk about how this lesson went," Jim suggested. By the time Alan had unplugged his helmet, and unfastened his seat belt and his parachute, Jim was already jumping off the wing. Alan climbed out, hoisted his parachute out, and jumped down. He realized that he had been so busy flying that he'd hardly had time to think about how he liked it. He loved it! Again, he felt reassured that he had what it would take to be a pilot. He knew there was a long road ahead before he became a real pilot, but he relished the prospect.

He followed Jim back to the hangar, where they each got a cup of coffee. There were folding chairs scattered around, and other instructors were talking to their students. They found two chairs and sat down.

Jim started the discussion. "Okay, I think things went very well for the first lesson. Obviously, your flying experience has put you way ahead of those who came here with no experience. We get a variety here: The AvCads usually come from an E-base, where they have done at least ten hours of flying to get past elimination. A few students have a lot of civilian experience, and some have no experience. We've found, though, that in the long run, flying ability depends on innate skills and a willingness to practice—neither of these is related to experience. We try to adjust for each person and pick up at the right level. I think I'm more or less tuned in to your level. What do you think?"

Alan replied, "I really enjoyed it, although at times I was struggling a bit. The fact that the Stearman is so big hardly makes any difference in the air. The controls seem responsive, but it will take a while to get used to being so high off the ground. It feels sort of like the floatplanes at the Academy. Just before we touched down, I thought our wheels were still five feet up, and I thought you were going to really drop it in, but you got it just right."

"Yeah, the Stearman is high compared to many small civilian airplanes, and your C3 is one of the lowest there is, but most of the planes you'll be flying from now on will put you up pretty high. The carrier planes may be a little closer to the ground, but they have a bigger fuselage and you're sitting at the top of it. If you fly floatplanes, you'll be even higher." Jim pulled some papers out of his flight suit and continued. "We're required to write comments after each flight. I'm writing, 'First flight. Student has some previous solo flying and is able to control the airplane when airborne.' Do you have any questions about the flight?"

"Not that I can think of. I'm a little worried about how high the center of gravity is, though. If it starts turning on the runway, it must be difficult to keep it from tipping and rubbing a wing tip."

"It isn't all that difficult to keep it straight, but if you get a little careless and don't keep it straight, it will rub a wing tip in the blink of an eye. You're right about that."

"Okay."

"We fly again at 1100. See you then," said Jim, smiling as he got up.

"Okay, see you at 1100, and thanks," replied Alan, also getting up.

Their second flight also went well, and Alan decided that Jim was indeed a good instructor.

During ground school in the afternoon, a rumor spread rapidly that a few nights earlier the British had conducted a daring and successful night attack on the Italian fleet anchored at Taranto by using torpedo bombers from an aircraft carrier. The details provided by the scuttlebutt were sketchy and inconsistent. This exciting news made it difficult for Alan to pay attention to the ground school session. If it were true, this would be the first time that he knew of that aircraft had successfully attacked battleships, and the first time that aircraft had attacked a fleet in harbor. It was widely believed that fleets were safe in harbor, even from an attack by aircraft, because they could be defended by strong shore-based anti-aircraft defenses. It was also believed that most harbors were too shallow and too confined for successful torpedo-bomber attack. He resolved to try to pick up anything he could from the newspapers in the Officers' Club at suppertime.

Before supper, Alan scanned the newspapers and found an article on the front page of the *New York Times*. He was glad to see that the paper also thought this was big news, putting the article under a six-column headline. The attack had occurred three nights earlier, but the news hadn't broken until the carrier reached port. The Italians had the advantage in that there weren't many attacking aircraft, and those that were attacking were obsolete biplanes. The Italians also had torpedo nets, barrage balloons, plenty of searchlights, and anti-aircraft guns. At the same time, the British had the advantage of surprise, and the Italian fleet was at anchor. The attack was conducted at night, which showed that the British had undertaken more than token training at night, unlike the US Navy. However, Alan suspected that once the attack got underway, flares and fires had provided some light. The report of the attack indicated that the British had reliable aerial torpedoes, as well. The audacity of the British was inspiring, and it was a great antidote to the notion that the Axis always had the initiative. The bravery of the pilots was also inspiring. *Bravo!* Alan silently cheered. He guessed that, back in Newport, the War College would be buzzing. He hoped Jennifer could tell him something about how the news was received there.

Jennifer and Alan had been writing to each other about once a week, and he had last written her the previous Sunday. Now with his first flight and the Taranto raid on his mind, he couldn't wait any longer.

Pensacola Naval Air Station
November 14, 1940

Dear Jennifer,

How are you? I am fine and happy because I had my first flight today. It went well, no serious mistakes, and I loved it! What a feeling to zoom around the sky! The weather was quite nice, still warm in the middle of the day. The plane was a Stearman N2S, a big rugged biplane, something like the planes I flew at the Academy. Even though we stuck to simple maneuvers, there were a few times when I struggled a bit, so I have a lot to learn. Things are still green here and there was such a beautiful view that it was hard sometimes to focus on the flying. My instructor made the landing, but it won't be long before he lets me try it. It helps that I have a little experience. I think I have a good instructor. I like him already, although it feels odd that he is an ensign and younger than me.

We flew from one of the auxiliary airports here. It's a nice big airport with long concrete runways and many big hangars, all built on land the navy did not even own until last February. That shows that at least some rearmament activities are moving fairly fast.

I think I mentioned to you last summer that I have some Academy classmate friends in aviation, but I've lost track of them. Well, last week I was very glad to run into Harry Tolman. It turns out that he is an instructor in the next phase of training, called Squadron Two. Naturally most of the pilots would like to be in an active combat squadron, so they don't like being instructors here, even though I suspect it looks good on their records. Having a friend among the instructors will help me to get the inside story. He confirmed that they started us off in the Stearman to try to get the washouts to happen earlier.

Tomorrow night a bunch of us student pilots are going to unwind at Al's Castle Bar, a very informal place across the bayou from the base. It's too far to walk, so I usually drive my jalopy. There are six of us that have become friends and go there on Friday or Saturday night. It's a geographically diverse group here: none of the other five are from the northeast, and they come from states all over the country.

The other big news is the Taranto raid. You probably know more about it than I do, you scalawag. It's exciting to hear about the British taking the initiative with an audacious raid. It seems that any fleet in harbor is very vulnerable unless they have good long-range reconnaissance to detect a carrier sneaking up before it gets within striking distance. I think this is a fairly radical notion, and one that some of our top brass might be inclined to dismiss, but ignoring it could mean taking a big risk. The raid also showed the British have decent aerial torpedoes.

Now I am very sorry to tell you that they have cancelled leave at Christmas and New Year's. We get one extra day off each at Christmas and New Year's, so I will not be able to come home. I wish you could come down for a visit and see everything here. I miss you so much! As a substitute, I think we should at least have a long phone call together sometime near Christmas. How about the Winter Solstice, Saturday December 21st? That is probably when Christmas was intended to be anyway, but I could do it any day in the evening.

On a happier note, I have found out that I should finish the course here on the weekend of May 17, so our wedding could be May 24. Let me know if there is any problem with that date. I think I will have leave for at least the week after that, so we could have that week for the honeymoon.

I hope you are still enjoying the War College. I imagine news of the Taranto raid stirred things up there. Please tell me what you can about it.

Write soon and let me know what your plans are.

Tons of love,

Alan

Wednesday, November 20, 1940

Inevitably the schedule in Squadron One had slipped some, and to keep from falling behind, the pace picked up to about three flying hours per day, in spite of the shorter days. Alan returned to the BOQ in the late afternoon quite tired. Jim had put him through a lot of maneuvers making sure he was ready for the twenty-hour check flight. In Squadron One, there were two check flights: one after twenty hours of flight and another near the end, after about sixty-five hours of flight. A check flight was like an exam. The student flew with a check pilot, who was a god-like person with whom the student had not flown before. The student was required to demonstrate the various things he was supposed to have mastered, and the check pilot gave him an "up" or a "down," which was equivalent to a pass or a fail.

Tired or not, he perked up as always when he found he had a letter from Jennifer.

Newport, R. I.
November 14, 1940

Dear Alan,

How are you? I am fine, but I miss you as much as ever. Please let me know whether you can come home for Christmas. I think I will be able to work around your dates so we can spend as much time together as possible. For a Christmas present, I would like a good picture of you in a nice frame that I could put on my desk, maybe even in color?

The War College continues to be fulfilling, but now I know I will be here only one more month. My last day will be December 13, and I am required to report to work at ONI in Washington on January 6, so I will have three weeks for vacation and moving. I'm not really looking forward to the move itself, because it means having to get everything packed and unpacked. I am looking forward to being settled in Washington, however. I am also looking forward to working at ONI and not being a perpetual student for a change.

I'm also starting to get excited about our wedding. My parents are about ready to send out the invitations, so please let me know as soon as you can when you think you will finish at Pensacola.

By now you have heard about the British raid on the Italian Fleet at Taranto. As you know, the War College is usually a staid and dignified place. Not this week! Closer to a disturbed ant hill, I would say. It was exciting to be there. The usual quietly simmering controversy over the battleship vs. the aircraft carrier erupted in full force. I actually heard professors shouting at each other behind closed doors. Victoria was horrified, but I think the place benefitted by being stirred up. I hope the obvious lesson is not soon forgotten.

It has been six weeks since you started, so by now you are probably about to start your flying instruction. How exciting! In fact by the time you get this, you will probably have flown a number of times. Please be VERY careful. Write soon, and tell me all about it.

Oodles of love,

Jennifer

Alan reread the letter. He had noticed how many serious accidents there were around Pensacola, and he had no trouble taking to heart her advice to be careful. It was reassuring to Alan to hear that at least some of the War College faculty seemed to be taking the news of the Taranto raid seriously. She sounded a bit daunted by the prospect of finding an apartment in Washington and moving there. Alan was sympathetic. She could not travel light and live in a BOQ like he could. Alan thought ONI would be a very interesting place to work; he hoped that she would be able to give him some idea of what it was like at ONI without compromising secrecy. Her mention of the wedding started Alan dreaming about their honeymoon. *Tomorrow is Thanksgiving*, he thought, *there will be lots of time to enjoy writing a reply.*

Friday, November 22, 1940

A few of the check pilots were not able to live up to their roles as "gods." There were some that gave almost every student an "up," and they were called Santa Clauses. There were also some that were the opposite, and they were called Down Checkers. Neither of these types of check pilot was doing his job.

On the day of Alan's twenty-hour check, he was well rested from having the previous day off for Thanksgiving. That was a good thing because his check pilot was Lieutenant Sykes, a notorious Down Checker. Alan's friends had come to him with long faces and said he was a "dead gosling," suggesting he call in sick. Alan tried to mentally prepare himself. He had been warned that the worst thing you could do with a Down Checker was to indicate any anger or resentment.

Sykes was rude even before they got into the airplane. Nothing Alan did was correct or good, and Sykes harangued him during the whole flight. Alan thought that he was not an outstanding student pilot, but Sykes's remarks were so uniformly negative that they soon began to lose their intimidating aspect. Instead, Alan felt his anger building. During the flight, he was able to conceal his anger because he could not talk back. They flew for an hour, and then Sykes abruptly grabbed the controls and took them back to base without further comment. As they parked the airplane, Alan was surprised to see a lot of students and a few instructors gathered around the area. *Are they gloating over my bad luck?* he wondered angrily. Alan climbed out, tired and soaked with sweat. Sykes announced in a booming voice that Alan had flown one of the worst check rides that Sykes had ever experienced, and that he hoped Alan could explain why he was so bad to the Hearing Board. Alan found it more difficult to contain his anger, but he managed. He knew that he would never be washed out for one down check, but it was a chilling experience, nevertheless.

Sykes then turned around and walked away. He hadn't gotten far when he came face to face with the skipper of Squadron One, an experienced officer who commanded everyone's respect.

The skipper had a very forbidding expression on his face. He asked, "Lieutenant Sykes, has this student flown a down check for you?"

Sykes was taken completely by surprise. He replied, "Yes, sir, he flew a down. He did very poorly."

The skipper replied very coldly, "I thought so. I'll check the abilities of this student myself, and then we'll discuss this matter in my office. Until then, make no entries in this student's flight record. Is that clear?"

By this time, Sykes's face was beet red. Sykes said, "Yes, sir," saluted, and walked away.

Alan found out later that the scuttlebutt had circulated that there was going to be a showdown between the skipper and Sykes, and that was why a crowd had gathered when Sykes and Alan came back in. The rumor was that Sykes's wife had left him, and that after that happened he was so angry that he rarely gave any student an up. Apparently, the skipper had grown tired of it.

The skipper approached Alan. "Lieutenant Ericsson, I know you have had a grueling flight, but do you think you would be able to handle a second check ride with me?"

"Yes, sir, I would appreciate a second chance."

"Okay, while the plane is being refueled, take a short break. Come back in twenty minutes."

Alan had a great flight with the skipper. He was an inspiring instructor—he knew how to minimize Alan's anxiety and get him to do his best. At Bell's Farm, which was one of the auxiliary training fields, he got out and watched Alan shoot five spot landings, in which Alan was required to land as close as possible to a particular place on the runway. Alan thought that the landings were pretty good. When Alan came back in to pick the skipper up, the skipper told him to get into the front cockpit for the flight back to Saufley—the traditional way of indicating that the student had just earned an up. When they taxied back in at Saufley, the skipper held his hand up with the thumb up, confirming the result to everyone present. Alan saw that Jim Allard was beaming. He had signed off that Alan was ready for the check ride, so Jim had to be pleased that Alan had done well with the skipper.

Relieved, Alan was looking forward to unwinding at Al's Castle Bar that evening, as he and five of his friends had become accustomed to doing. After supper, Alan left the BOQ and went to his car. He liked to drive his own car to the bar so he could choose his time to come back to the base. He swung by the AvCad quarters to see if Frank Evans needed a ride.

Frank had become one of Alan's best friends among the students. He was a classic good-looking Westerner—tall, dark and handsome. He was the son of the owner of a general store in Cody, Wyoming, it turned out. Frank had gone to Stanford and majored in ancient history, and Alan had soon realized that Frank was very bright. Alan had spent the summer after eleventh grade working at a ranch near Dubois, Wyoming, only about seventy miles south of Cody, but it was on the other side of a rugged wilderness, so he was not familiar with Cody. Nevertheless, Frank was surprised that anyone not from Wyoming knew where Cody was, and it gave them something in common.

Frank was happy to have a ride, so he and Alan headed north off the base and across the bayou, turning left onto Winthrop Avenue in Warrington. A few more blocks, and he turned into the parking lot next to Al's Castle Bar. As he and Frank started walking toward the bar, a big four-cylinder Indian motorcycle rumbled up. A big guy was riding it, whom Alan recognized their friend Rudi "Tank" Fischer.

"Fancy meeting you here," Alan said to Rudi as Rudi parked the Indian next to Alan's car.

"Well, if it ain't Stringy and the Cowboy! Stringy, you look like you've been keel-hauled, and the evening's just beginning," Rudi said with a grin. Rudi had played varsity tackle at the Academy, where he acquired the nickname "Tank." He never seemed to run out of enthusiasm. He had been in the class of 1938, and he had gone into aviation right after his surface tour—the same age as Jim Allard.

"Well, Rudi, I had a busy afternoon, but I think I'll be able to keep my chin above the table," replied Alan, grinning as the three of them went into the bar.

The background odor of beer was alleviated somewhat by the scent of flowering tropical plants. The décor was sort of marine rustic, with lots of weathered wood and a few aviation items thrown in. There was a large two-bladed wooden propeller hanging over the bar and a fabric-covered vertical stabilizer on the opposite wall. A local jazz band was playing Glenn Miller.

They saw that three of their friends had already gotten a table, and joined the group.

"Good evening, gentlemen," said Ed Miller. Ed was built like a fire hydrant and very outgoing. Also at the table were Les "Craggy" Travis and Wade "Judge" Buckner.

"Whad'ya think, Judge, can we handle all these Yankees?" said Les in his western North Carolina drawl. Les and Wade were classmates of Rudi at the Naval Academy. Les was tall and thin like Alan. He hadn't really warmed up to Alan until he found out they had a shared interest in mountain music.

"They look like half-pints to me, Les," replied Wade with his smooth Mississippi accent. He had put on a poker face, but a slight twitch of his mouth gave away his good humor. Wade had a placid manner that gave him his judicial nickname, but his cherubic face hid a fiercely competitive spirit.

Rudi, Frank, and Alan sat down. Their usual waitress, June Burch, approached. June was attractive, although a bit rustic, in Alan's eyes. She stood behind Frank, and put her hands on his shoulders, leaning over him. Everyone at the table knew that June and Frank were fond of each other.

"What's it gonna be, Frankie?" she asked.

Frank tilted his head back and looked up at her face, grinning. "A pint of Ace High, June, my belle," he said.

Most of the beer in Pensacola came from a local brewery named Spearman. Fortunately, they offered about eight different beers and ales. June glanced at Alan.

"I'd like an Ace High, also." Alan usually preferred this smooth ale.

Rudi ordered a Straight Eight beer, and June headed for the rear of the bar.

"Les was telling us about how he got into an inverted spin yesterday," Ed explained.

Les described, using the hand movements that all pilots used to help illustrate, how he had gotten into an inverted stall at the top of a loop. Somehow, he had inadvertently put in the rudder so the airplane started to spin. Luckily, he realized what was happening and was able to recover.

"That sounds like fun! I might try that," said Rudi with a big grin. "But maybe not as much fun as a tail slide. My instructor showed it to me Wednesday, and I can't wait to try it solo." Like Les, he was demonstrating with his flat hand as the airplane, how he had pulled straight up until the airplane started falling backward. He smiled as he said, "You know, you don't get too many chances to go backward in an airplane. It's quite a feeling, sliding backward before the plane flips over to nose down."

June reappeared with the three pints. She served Rudi and Alan first, and then she went over to Frank and deliberately spilled a little on his head before setting the beer in front of him.

Frank reached around and grabbed her, pulling her next to him. "I'm not that hot yet; I need you to warm me up," he said.

She smiled at him and said, "Not now, I got customers waiting." She pulled away and disappeared.

Turning to Alan, Rudi said, "I'm guessing they put you through the ringer for your twenty-hour check. What happened?"

Alan proceeded to tell the story, to everyone's amusement. None of the others had encountered a Down Checker yet, but they were glad to hear that the Down Checkers did not always get away with it.

The jazz band gave way to the Shirttails, a local hillbilly group that aspired to revive the music of The Skillet Lickers. Alan was very fond of the original band and thought that this group was not bad. This type of music was unknown in the northeast, where Alan grew up. His acquaintance with it started when his relatives from West Virginia brought it to his parents' house when he was growing up. He really came to enjoy it during the summer that he spent on their farm.

After they all had taken a good swill from their beers, Ed said, "Another six weeks, and we'll move on to Squadron Two and the SBU. What do you guys think of it?"

"The SBU is huge: it's like flying a barn," said Wade.

"I like 'em big," said Rudi. "At least it's a real carrier plane."

"That's true, but the landing gear is even narrower than the Stearman," Les reminded him.

"I like the smoothness of that fourteen-cylinder engine," said Frank.

"It should be different to have a controllable pitch propeller," Ed chimed in.

"It's more modern than the British Stringbag, roughly two dozen of which put a big dent in the Italian fleet about ten days ago," Alan reminded them. "Stringbag" was the popular nickname for the plane that the British navy called the Swordfish.

"But the Stringbag is a torpedo bomber," said Rudi. "Torpedoes sink ships."

"And thousand-pound bombs don't?" asked Les.

"Not like torpedoes, because torpedoes make big holes below the water line," said Rudi.

"Very true," admitted Alan. "But bombs can be armor piercing. They can penetrate inside the ship before detonating, which could cripple the ship."

"That will cause a lot of damage, but not likely make a hole in the side of the ship, which would cause it to sink," countered Rudi.

Alan said, "True, although a completely disabled ship is not much better than a sunken one. You may have heard about the Record Gunnery Exercises scored by Bombing Six in October and Torpedo Six in November. Bombing Six did pretty well—twenty-five to thirty-one percent hits on a maneuvering target with fighter opposition on one exercise. Torpedo Six did their best, but only one out of the ten torpedoes dropped ran hot, straight, and true. Four sank and five ran erratically." *And that was without the questionable Mark VI exploder*, Alan said to himself.

Rudi replied, "That was the first RGE with the Mark XIII torpedo, though. You have to expect problems with a new weapon."

Alan was thinking of arguing further with Rudi, but it did not feel right to push his doubts on others, however well founded they seemed to him.

Nearby, there was a table with a group of instructors clustered around it. Alan had noticed that Harry Tolman was among them. As the instructors were standing up to leave, Harry glanced over at Alan and Alan motioned him to join their group. He smiled and came over. Alan introduced Harry, mentioning that they had been classmates at the Academy and that Harry was an instructor in Squadron Two. Harry sat down, and June appeared and took an order for another round of beers.

Harry said, "I like to ask students at the start of Squadron Two which type of airplane they'd like to fly when they graduate. Do any of you want to fly observation or long-range patrol?"

They all looked at each other. "No one in this bunch," answered Ed.

Harry smiled and said, "I thought you guys would all prefer carrier planes."

The beer was served and there was a pause in the conversation as they each took a drink or two and listened to the music. During a pause in the music, Harry asked, "Can I ask each of you which type of carrier plane you'd prefer to fly?"

Alan thought he should reply first, in case there was some hesitation from the others to directly answer this question from someone they didn't know. "I'd like to fly either fighters or dive-bombers, but I haven't decided which yet."

Rudi immediately said, "Torpedo bombers for me. I want to sink ships."

Les replied, "No tor*peckers* if I can help it. I think I'm leaning toward dive-bombers." Frank agreed with Les.

Ed said, "I want to fly fighters," and Wade agreed with him.

"Well, that's a nice distribution. Usually about half our students choose fighters. Not many choose torpedo bombers," said Harry.

Looking at Harry, Frank asked, "How did starting the students off in the Stearman work out?"

"Mixed results, I'd say," Harry answered. "It was a little hard for some of the guys who didn't have much experience—mostly the Academy men. Stringy here was the exception, probably because he had some civilian experience. The AvCads did better because they had more recent experience. I think they're going to go back to starting students in the N3N."

When the band stopped for another break, Ed spoke up. "Squadron Two is supposed to be nearly all formation flying. Seems like a lot of time to spend on it."

"Formation flying is harder than it looks, and it takes a while to get the hang of it," Harry replied.

"Pretty easy to collide while you're practicing, too," said Frank.

Harry replied, "It sure is. That's why it takes a while. We start with plenty of separation. We only begin to tighten it up when the students are getting consistent. The hard part is holding back the hot shots who want to plunge ahead with tight formation work." He paused to emphasize his point, and then went on. "Well, gentlemen, it was nice to visit with you, but it's been a long day and I'm ready for the sack." He glanced around the group, said goodnight, and left.

"Goes for me, too," said Alan, standing up. "Frank, you got a ride back?"

"We got Frank covered," said Ed. Frank gave him a thumbs-up.

"Good night, gentlemen," said Alan, as he headed for the door.

Saturday, December 21, 1940

At 0845, Alan was sitting in the lobby of his BOQ building, near the two telephone booths. He wanted to make sure one of them was available at 0900, the time he had arranged with Jennifer for their call. The previous evening he had arranged the call with an operator, which she was able to do because the circuits were not so busy on Saturday.

Marjorie answered the phone, "Hello?"

"Hello, Marjorie. This is Alan Ericsson. May I speak to Jennifer?"

"Oh, Alan, what a nice idea to have a phone call. Jennifer is right here."

Jennifer came on, "Hello, Alan, How are you?"

The sound of her voice made him so happy that it almost brought tears to his eyes. "I'm fine, Jennifer, except that you're not here. I miss you so much. He made a loud kissing sound. How are you?" Alan remembered that the Warrens' telephone was on the kitchen counter, and he visualized Jennifer sitting next to it.

"Oh, Alan, you rascal! I am fine, except that I miss you terribly. I couldn't wait for the phone to ring. It's wonderful just to hear your voice. At least you're almost half way through your time in Pensacola."

"That's right. I think I can be in Washington the evening of May 19, you scalawag."

"Oh, Alan, you've got it all figured out. That doesn't sound so far away now, does it?"

"No, it doesn't."

"Speaking of Washington, guess what! I found an apartment, and it's within walking distance of ONI, about ten blocks."

"Wow, that's wonderful. How did you find one so fast?"

"Well, I got the movers to pick up my things in Newport on the fourteenth, and then I drove home to Lexington. I took a train to Washington on the fifteenth, and started looking early on Monday the sixteenth. I rented the apartment on the eighteenth and then headed back to Newport. I just got home yesterday. I'm a little tired, but I'm so glad I got it done."

"Is it big enough for two?

"You bet, you rascal," she chuckled. "There is a bedroom, living room, small kitchen, and even a small study and balcony"

"When do you move in?"

"I think I will spend New Year's Eve with the Gallaghers in New London, and hope to make it all the way to Washington on the first. They won't be sleeping in with a new baby, so I can get an early start. The movers will come on the second to move me in, unless I let them know to hold off. That gives me three days to get halfway settled before starting work on the sixth."

"Wow. That's a long drive." Alan admired her spunk, among her other virtues. Most young women would not attempt that, especially in winter.

"Yes, it is. If I hit bad weather, I'll have to take another day. But my trusty Chevy is ready for it, I think."

"ONI should be a very interesting place to work. I think I'm a little bit jealous."

"You'd give up warm sunshine and lots of flying? I think I'm the one who should be jealous," she chuckled again. "Your mother said to tell you that Winnie and Jenny have made friends and are doing very well. They're losing their accents, which she thinks shows they're feeling at home."

"That's great to hear. They deserve to settle down and be at home."

"I agree. Now what's your news?"

"Well, I'm close to being done with Primary Training, Squadron One. The final check ride will be before New Year's. Then we have some night flying before Squadron Two.

"You're making progress. What kind of flying are you doing right now?"

"We're doing acrobatics, which is a lot of fun. Loops, rolls, flying upside down, that sort of thing."

"It sounds like you might be having too much fun, you rascal."

"You know there's no such thing as too much fun, you scalawag."

"What comes next?"

"Basic Training. The first part is Squadron Two, which is formation flying in the SBU. It's an obsolete scout-bomber, a biplane like the Stearman, but quite a lot bigger. It has a greenhouse canopy over the cockpit, which will be welcome because now the weather is turning chilly. After that we move on to instrument training in Squadron Three."

"What is instrument training?"

"You learn to fly the plane by watching only the instruments, without being able to see outside. So you can't see the horizon, to tell if you're flying level, or how close you are to the ground. You actually sit in the rear cockpit with a cloth hood over you, so you can't see anything outside the cockpit."

"That sounds awful. What if you run into something?"

"There is an instructor in front all the time watching out. He makes all the takeoffs and landings."

"Well, that sounds better. It still sounds pretty bad, being cooped up in the rear cockpit all the time."

"I don't expect it to be fun. But it is necessary, because you have to be able to fly in the clouds or at night in places where there are no lights."

Their conversation turned to the plan for the wedding and settling some remaining details. Then Jennifer gave Alan her new Washington address. Finally, after they had talked for half an hour, it was time to say goodbye.

"I love you very much, Jennifer. Write soon and tell me as much as you can about ONI."

"I will, and Alan, please write and tell me all about your flying. I love you very dearly, so be careful. Goodbye."

"I will. Goodbye."

Sunday, January 5, 1941

Alan was relaxing in his room and reviewing the pilot's operating manual for the Vought SBU. He was pretty familiar with it at this point. He was finished with Primary Training and would be starting Basic Training in Squadron Two the next day.

Basic training would consist of three weeks of formation practice in Squadron Two, followed by three weeks of instrument flying in Squadron Three. After that, they would have ten weeks of advanced training, consisting of training in gunnery, dive-bombing, and fighter tactics. The training would be getting more exciting with each phase.

Training was going reasonably well, and Alan was enjoying the friends he had made, but he was not really happy, because of how much he missed Jennifer. The telephone conversation they had arranged for the winter solstice had helped a lot, but it had a huge void to fill.

A few days after Christmas, Alan had received Jennifer's Christmas present to him. It was a beautiful photo of her taken on a sunny day in front of the Naval War College.

CHAPTER ELEVEN

Squadron Two

Monday, January 6, 1941

It was a bright and clear, but cold, day. The temperature at dawn was in the high 30s. The start of the training day had been moved to 0630 because the sun did not rise until 0640 in January. It was a pleasant twenty-minute walk from the BOQ, which was on the west side of Chevalier Field, down to the Squadron Two hangar on the south side, so Alan had decided that would be his routine.

As he approached the field, a lone SNJ was rolling down the runway, taking off with the usual roar, probably doing a maintenance check flight. A few seconds after it lifted off, the main landing gear retracted, a little unevenly, as usual, but neatly tucked away in the end. Alan felt inspired, and then wondered why that was. Was it the idea that the airplane was getting cleaned up and squared away for its intended purpose of flying? Or was it that the airplane was resolutely starting out, no matter what it might meet up with? He wasn't sure—probably both. For some reason, it reminded him of a sailing vessel leaving harbor and starting to catch the wind, although there was no physical resemblance.

He entered the hangar at 0625, and the scene was much the same as at the start of Squadron One. He said hello to Ed Miller and Les Travis, but did not see his other friends. On the blackboard, he found his name, his aircraft number, his instructor's name (Crawford), and his flight time of 0730.

At 0645, the chief instructor addressed the class and welcomed them to Squadron Two. He said that, in formation flying, there was a high potential for collisions, which were likely to be fatal to both parties, whether they had parachutes or not. This fact and the more complex aircraft they would be flying required a dedication to perfection, he told them. As he finished, he wished them good luck.

Alan had a cup of coffee and then collected his parachute. He had been issued a new leather helmet that was different from the one used in the Stearman; it had real earphones and a wire with a plug to connect it to an intercom between the cockpits. He had been warned that it would be cold in the cockpit at this time of year, even though it was enclosed by a greenhouse canopy, so he had put his flight suit on over the warmest clothes he had brought to Pensacola. He was also wearing the fleece-lined leather flying jacket he had been issued as he walked out along the flight line.

He found his airplane and began looking it over while awaiting his instructor. The SBU was made by the company which had been known as Chance Vought, though it later merged with Sikorsky to make Vought-Sikorsky, a division of United Aircraft in East Hartford, Connecticut. Rather than the all-yellow scheme of the primary trainers, the SBUs had the traditional navy carrier plane paint scheme. Its wings were yellow on top and silver underneath; the fuselage was silver with "US NAVY" painted in big letters on the fuselage near the tail.

The SBU was much like the Stearman, but bigger. The engine was the Pratt & Whitney Twin Wasp Junior, which had a second radial array of seven cylinders behind the first. That and larger cylinders gave it three times the power of the Stearman engine. He was glad to see that the propeller had modern aluminum blades.

Alan became aware that an odor of stale cigar had suddenly replaced the usual background gasoline smell. He looked around and saw a man in a flight suit and battered leather jacket approaching him. His dark hair had streaks of gray, and he had a weather-beaten face with brown eyes. The stub of an unlit cigar was clamped in his teeth.

"Ericsson?" he asked.

"That's me," said Alan. He had long since learned that rank was secondary on the flight line, but this fellow had no indication of rank showing at all. He did have an Academy ring, however.

"Lieutenant Clyde Crawford." There was the hint of a smile as they shook hands.

Alan realized that this lieutenant was probably in his late forties and he must have had a very disappointing career.

"Preflight," said Crawford, motioning for Alan to begin.

Crawford coached him through the preflight inspection with nods, grunts, and the occasional single word or two. "Climb in," said Crawford before he walked away.

Alan climbed onto the left lower wing, slid back the front canopy section, heaved his parachute into the seat, and climbed into the front cockpit. As he sat down, he almost bumped his head on the big telescopic gun sight that was used for both bombing and gunnery. It was a tube about two inches in diameter and two feet long, mounted in the center of the windshield, above the glare shield that was over the instrument panel. The rear of the gun sight extended behind the glare shield, allowing the pilot to bring his eye to it by simply leaning forward. Alan was disconcerted that it could be difficult to keep his face from hitting it hard in a crash landing.

He adjusted his seat and the rudder pedals and strapped in. Crawford appeared outside the front cockpit and went over the controls, using one or two words to describe each. The dead cigar was about a foot from Alan's nose, and the odor was nearly overwhelming.

The starting procedure was similar to that of the Stearman—a ground crewman cranked up the inertia starter, and soon the engine was idling contentedly. Alan noticed that the now-familiar vibration of the radial engine was smoothed out considerably by having twice as many cylinders. By this time, about a dozen SBUs had started up, and ground crewmen were directing them onto the taxiway. Alan heard crackling in his earphones. After a while, he could hear the control tower giving instructions to airplanes over the two-way radio. Alan began gently taxiing toward the runway.

After the run-up, Crawford said over the intercom, "You need to understand the throttle response of big radials. Open the throttle halfway as fast as you can right now."

Alan jabbed the throttle lever forward abruptly to halfway without really thinking about it. There was a startling silence for several seconds because the engine had quit. Instead of rapidly speeding up, as he'd expected, it was coasting down! The engine caught again, and sped up rapidly. Crawford pulled the throttle back. Alan was aghast.

"Remember that if you need power in a hurry, like on a go-around. Always open the throttle gently." The need to go around— to climb away at the last minute instead of landing—would only happen due to something going suddenly wrong. Alan would have to remember to be gentle with the throttle.

Crawford handled the radio communications with the control tower, and Alan made the takeoff. The big engine accelerated the airplane rapidly, and soon they were climbing away.

"Climb power, airspeed 100, climb to 4,000," Crawford ordered. Alan throttled back to climb power.

Crawford slid the rear canopy back and Alan slid the front canopy forward to close it. The wind in the front cockpit dropped to a zephyr, but Alan was glad that he was dressed warmly. He noticed that they were climbing at about 1,000 feet per minute, which was a lot faster than in the Stearman.

When they reached 4,000 feet, Crawford had Alan practice the typical maneuvers for getting familiar with a new airplane. He started by having Alan do 360-degree turns both ways and then went on to climbs and descents. After these, they did a series of stalls with the power on and off.

After about an hour, Crawford told Alan to go to Corry Field to practice takeoffs and landings, and again Crawford handled the radio communications with the tower. As Alan turned downwind, he went through the landing checklist. He left the microphone in his lap so he could grab it quickly to announce each step. By now, they were abeam the runway. He decided to keep his base leg close in, as he had been taught to do if spacing was adequate. He pulled the throttle back to idle and turned onto the base leg. He had not lost much altitude when he turned his final, leading the turn nicely.

"Flaps down," Crawford reminded him.

Alan held the stick with his left hand while he cranked the flaps down quickly with his right. They were headed for a position just beyond the runway numbers. The flaps steepened their glide, so they were at the right height to start their flare just before the numbers.

Alan flared out the same way he had in the Stearman. With less wing for its weight and having wing flaps, the SBU lost speed more rapidly. Alan lowered the nose briefly to make sure that he was close to the ground when the stall came and saw that they were over the threshold. When the stall came, the main wheels touched right away, but the tail was a little high. The mains bounced once before rolling on all three. The SBU was not slowing as fast as the N2S on the ground, and Alan braked gently, carefully keeping it straight with first the rudder, then differential braking.

"Flaps up, cowl flaps open, and go right into takeoff," Crawford instructed him. They continued with two more full stall landings and two wheel landings, in which the airplane was landed in a level attitude on the main wheels only, without a stall, and then slowed down until the tail could no longer be held up by the elevators. Then Crawford told Alan to return to Chevalier Field, where he returned to the same parking spot. Alan went through the shutdown procedure and climbed out to find Crawford waiting.

Crawford said, "Nice job. First formation practice tomorrow."

He was relieved that at least the transition from the N2S to the SBU had gone smoothly. "Thanks. See you tomorrow."

Tuesday, January 7, 1941

In the morning, Alan and Crawford met for his first practice formation flight. They climbed in, and Alan got the engine started.

"We're going to practice formation with the airplane on our right, Number Nine. Follow him; keep him in sight. Let's go." Crawford's gruff voice came through the earphones.

They taxied out, took off, and headed west, following Number Nine to 5,000 feet. Alan saw that they were approaching Mobile Bay.

"Level off. We'll fly wing on their right, stepped down. Keep this power on to catch up."

Ground school had covered the purpose of formation flying, and the basic concepts. Formation flying was the technique of flying close to another airplane on a parallel path. This could be extended to groups of more than two planes, and served several purposes. First, visual signals could be used to communicate between planes to maintain radio silence and avoid detection. Second, planes were better able to see each other in poor visibility, and thus stay together, even when flying through clouds. Third, it was easier to defend a dense concentration of airplanes against fighter attack. As a part of formation practice, the students would learn to use visual signals, such as rocking the wings or giving various hand signals, to communicate with other airplanes.

A pair of airplanes consisted of a leader and his wingman. The leader's duty was never to worry about the wingman's position; that was the wingman's problem. The leader had to make all his maneuvers gently so the wingman could follow and be sure to fly precisely on course and altitude. It was the leader's duty to watch out for other airplanes and ground obstacles. At the same time, the wingman's sole duty was to keep his position on the leader. He did not need to pay any attention to where they were going or to what they might run into, as that was the leader's responsibility.

Alan leveled off, and the airspeed built up to 120. They began to catch up with Number Nine. They were about 100 feet away, slightly behind and below the leader. "Pull it back to around twenty-two inches, shift to high pitch, lean it, and then vary the throttle to stay in position," Crawford reminded him. "Stay about two wingspans away to start with."

Alan continued to correct, but he passed quickly through the correct position over and over. He would swing too high and too low, too far out and too close in, too far ahead and too far behind. After about fifteen minutes of correcting and never staying in the correct position, he was frustrated and sweating.

The two planes separated briefly and Alan became leader, Number Nine flying wing on him. Number Nine's pilot seemed to have about the same amount of trouble staying in position as Alan had. They switched roles several times, with only a slight improvement by the end of practice.

Crawford suddenly said, "Formation practice over. Hold your course and they will break formation. Back to base."

Number Nine turned away abruptly and Alan flew back to Chevalier Field. He felt tired and dissatisfied with his performance, even though he had heard that formation flying would be difficult at first. Crawford again handled the radio with the tower, while Alan landed, taxied in, and climbed out. Crawford was waiting for him.

"Didn't have to save it, even once. Unusual. Nice landing. See you at 1130." Crawford turned and walked away.

Alan thought, *Well, I guess that is as close to a "well done" as I will ever get from this character. Maybe I didn't do as poorly as I thought.*

Sunday, January 12, 1941

The previous day he had gotten a letter from Jennifer, telling him about her holiday activities and her move to Washington. She had followed her plan and spent New Year's Eve with the Gallaghers in New London. Their big news was that the *Sailfish* would be departing for Pearl Harbor on January 20. She said that Mary was prepared for Mark to leave, but subdued. Jennifer had driven by herself all the way to Washington on New Year's Day. By the time Alan got her letter, she had already worked for a week at ONI. He was sure that office would be humming. He had just heard that graduation for the Naval Academy class of 1941 had been advanced to February 7, four months early. It seemed that the sense of urgency was starting to be felt in many parts of the navy.

Thursday, January 16, 1941

At the end of Squadron One, Alan and his classmates had put in their preferences on which type of airplanes they would like to fly. Assignments had just been announced, and Alan and his friends had all gotten their preference: carrier planes. The students speculated that their records in Squadron One had something to do with which type of plane they were assigned, but nobody, not even the instructors, seemed to know how the selection was actually made.

By now, Alan's class had become fairly proficient in formation flying. He found that it was a bit like learning to play tennis or ski. It was awful at first, but as he persisted, he eventually got good enough to do it reliably and even enjoy it. Flying close to another airplane and trying to maintain his position relative to it required patience, vigilance, and a firm, but gentle, hand on the controls. The rest was drill and remembering how to reshuffle the formation safely.

He was glad that he had gotten his feet wet in Squadron One with a good instructor and not many bumps in the road outside of that twenty-hour check. Squadron Two had been different. He had to quickly adapt to Crawford's minimum usage of words. Harry Tolman had told Alan that Crawford had always been like that. Alan felt like he had learned mostly on his own, although he knew that Crawford would probably have said something if Alan had done something really dangerous. *Perhaps that was good experience*, he thought.

He only had two more formation practice flights with Crawford before solo practice began. Alan went to the airplane a little ahead of time and started the preflight inspection. Suddenly he smelled something unusual—a whiff of strong whiskey, he thought. He turned around and saw Crawford right behind him. His eyes were bloodshot, and he seemed a little unsteady on his feet. Alan realized that he was drunk.

Alan continued with the preflight inspection as he quickly tried to decide how to handle this surprise. On one hand, Crawford had no business going up in an airplane in his condition, and he should have known better. On the other hand, Alan liked him, in a way, and was sympathetic to his overall situation. He decided he was going to handle it as quietly as possible, hopefully without involving anyone else. He finished the preflight inspection and then approached Crawford.

"The airplane is ready to go, but you are not, sir. I recommend that you call in sick." Alan had never addressed him as "sir" before, although Crawford did outrank him, because nobody was supposed to pull rank on the flight line unless it was absolutely necessary. Alan felt that such an address in this situation might soften the blow. Crawford jerked upright and glared at Alan, and it seemed for a moment that Crawford was going to start a fight, but then he turned and walked away without a word.

Alan hoped he had handled the situation right. He occupied the time by sitting in on an extra ground school. He was apprehensive all day about what kind of mood Crawford would be in for their final flight the following day.

Friday, January 17, 1941

Crawford showed up for his last session with Alan quite sober and more cheerful than usual. *Phew!* Alan was pleased that he had gotten through another shoal unscathed.

Wednesday, January 22, 1941

The morning had been taken up with ground school. They had started practice formation flying without their instructors two days before, flying with one other airplane in a pair. This afternoon they would start flying with four airplanes in a group.

Alan saw that he was grouped with Frank Evans and Ensigns Haggler and Runkle. Alan thought about what rotten luck it was that he and Frank were paired with them. Formation flying meant that Alan had to trust the pilots who would be flying close to him. He had plenty of confidence in Frank, and he felt okay about the majority of his classmates, but he did not trust these two. Like Frank, they were big, handsome Westerners. That was where the resemblance ended, though. They seemed to be fairly skillful pilots, but they were always eager to show off and take risks. Alan thought that their loud and brassy style was probably covering up some kind of insecurity.

The group started off with Frank and Alan flying lead and wing alternately on each other. Haggler and Runkle did the same. Frank and Alan were the lead pair, and Haggler and Runkle were the wing pair, which flew to the right and stepped down and back relative to the lead pair. Alan glanced at the other pair a few times and noticed that they were flying closer to each other than he had ever seen in practice.

When it came time to mix it up, Haggler flew wing on Alan as the lead pair, while Runkle flew wing on Frank as the wing pair. Within the lead pair, Haggler was stepped down and back to Alan's right. As the leader of the wing pair, Frank was farther to the right and stepped down and behind Haggler, with Runkle farthest to the right. Thus when Alan glanced to his right, he could see the other three airplanes roughly in a line stretching away from him, sloping down and to the rear.

Haggler started off at a normal distance from Alan and then steadily moved in. Alan felt more fear gripping him than he'd felt since the *Squalus* sank. He found it difficult to focus on being lead man as Haggler's wing began to overlap his.

Alan suddenly realized that flying this close was folly, not practice. He decided to break away from Haggler, but he had to decide quickly which way to do it. Haggler was stepped down on his right, so up and to the left looked best to him. He moved the stick violently to the left and back, and opened the throttle. As the g-force of the turn caught up with him, he sank into his seat and his vision narrowed to almost nothing. His airspeed dropped. He eased the stick forward. His vision returned and the airspeed started back up. He glanced quickly to the right to see that Haggler was not there, and he felt relieved. He rolled right and kicked the rudder to throw the airplane into a hard right turn, then leveled off and looked around. Haggler was well away, left behind by his evasive maneuvers. Alan felt his tension easing rapidly.

When he looked around for Frank and Runkle, they seemed to have disappeared. He put the airplane in a left turn to get a different view, keeping an eye on Haggler the whole time. He looked down, and his heart sank. He saw two airplanes spiraling down below him, apparently out of control and trailed by fluttering pieces that had broken off of them. He watched, hoping with all his might to see parachutes. None came. Shortly after, there were two splashes. Both airplanes hit the sea, disappearing without a trace. Alan swallowed hard and felt a lump in his gut. His adrenaline high had subsided, leaving him exhausted, but calm.

He called Chevalier Tower on the radio and reported the accident, giving cross bearings off some prominent landmarks. He decided he had to do a search because there was a tiny possibility that Frank or Runkle had survived. He used the same landmarks and bearings to stay in the right area. Then he closed the throttle and put his airplane into a slip to lose altitude quickly. He leveled off at 100 feet above the sea and flew back and forth, both east and west and north and south for about half an hour. He was surprised that Haggler did not join him, but it was just as well not to have another airplane to worry about as he searched. He saw nothing on the surface, so he gave up and flew gingerly back to Chevalier Field and landed.

Alan knew that he had to report the accident immediately to the skipper of Squadron Two, Lieutenant Commander Scott, even though he had probably already heard from Haggler. As Alan approached the skipper's office, Haggler came out and glared at Alan. "Shit," he exclaimed as Alan passed. Alan tightened his jaw and clenched his teeth. *Easy*, he told himself. He walked into the skipper's office, shut the door, and stood in front of the desk.

Scott informed Alan of the situation. "As I told Haggler, you are both grounded until we can have a formal inquiry. We will need all four instructors present, so it may take a while to get it scheduled. At that time we will hear testimony about why the collision happened. Now I would like to get your description of what happened after the collision."

Alan described what he had seen, reporting the accident, and his search, as Scott made notes.

"Did Haggler come on the radio or join you in the search?"

"No sir."

"Hmm. It seems like he may have panicked." The phone rang and Scott answered it. He listened and said with a sigh, "Ok. Thanks for passing the word." He turned to Alan. "That was Search and Rescue. The search boat already reported in. They found an aileron, so they were in the right place. Nothing else. That will be all for now, Ericsson."

Alan left the squadron office and started walking back to the BOQ. He could no longer suppress his grief and anger. Frank was a great guy, and he deserved to come through training. He hated Haggler and Runkle and the system that allowed them to endanger others. He began to wonder if he wanted to continue his training anymore. The more he thought about it, the more he realized that what was really bothering him was the loss of his good friend, though. He had not felt quite as close to the friends he'd lost on the *Squalus*. He was in the navy, and if war came, he could easily lose other friends. He got to his room, sat down, and gradually unwound. After a while, he pulled himself together, got cleaned up, and changed his clothes.

He suddenly realized that, as Frank's best friend, he should write a letter to Frank's parents. He sat down and wrote it, saying little about the accident itself. After this, he felt a little better. It was 1730, and he was trying to decide if he wanted any supper when another thought struck him: June Burch. He would have to tell her in person.

He drove to Al's Castle Bar. The bar was empty and June was sitting at a table as he walked in. She looked up and smiled, and then her face fell as she read his expression. He told her what had happened, and by the end of his story, she was crying. He put his arm around her and tried to comfort her, and she put her arm around him and hugged him. She was the only person around who might miss Frank more than he would, and his heart went out to her.

June gently rose, went behind the bar, and returned with two glasses and a fifth of bourbon. As they drank, they celebrated what they had learned about Frank in the short time they had known him. Alan told her about the part of Wyoming in which Frank had grown up and what it meant to go from that region to a prestigious college like Stanford. She told him how kind and gentle Frank was with her, and how he liked hillbilly music. As she spoke of his love of the genre, Alan was surprised to find that she had a fund of knowledge about hillbilly music, including how it related to English folk music. He recognized that she was more than smart enough to have gone to college if she had gotten a better start. *Frank found a diamond in the rough*, he realized. The bartender took care of the few customers that came in, and they talked for quite a while.

Eventually, the bartender left, leaving June to close up. Alan was exhausted, and he was too drunk to drive, so June showed him to a little bunk in the back room, said good night, and walked unsteadily out.

Thursday, January 23, 1941

Alan awoke around 0410 and drove back to the base. He handed a five-dollar bill to the sentry at the gate and hoped that would secure the man's silence. He slipped into the BOQ a little after 0430 without attracting attention. As long as no one knew for sure that he had spent the night off base, he would probably get away with it. He took a shower, shaved, and felt fairly presentable at breakfast. His appetite had returned, and he felt better after breakfast. He was glad that he would not be flying, however.

Ground school in the morning kept Alan occupied. During a break, an orderly told him that the accident inquiry would be held at 1630 that afternoon. In the afternoon, while his friends were flying, he took a slow walk past the hangars where much of the maintenance was done, which he had gotten into the habit of visiting on nights and weekends. There was much less activity during weekdays because most of the airplanes were needed on the flight line. Most of the activity that was occurring was routine maintenance, and did not involve major disassembly, which is what Alan found particularly interesting. Disappointed, he was about to head back toward the BOQ when he spotted an engine suspended from a crane in the back of one of the hangars, and the crane was moving. He started walking in that direction and saw that an overhauled engine was being installed on an SBU. Only two men were in the hangar, and they were moving the crane up to the nose of the airplane. As he walked up, he recognized Clay Hodge and Glen Goff, mechanics he had gotten to know during his previous visits.

"Howdy, Clay, Glen. How's it going?" Alan greeted them. Using their first names was the signal that navy formality could be dropped.

"Okay, Alan. You playing hooky today? Since the two SBUs went in the bay yesterday, they want this one on the line, but they only sent two of us," said Clay.

Alan's face fell and he said, "Yeah, I saw those two SBUs hit the water. The pilot of one of them was a buddy of mine. There were four of us practicing formation. The other pilot and I are grounded. The inquiry is at 1630."

"Oh shit. I'm sorry," said Clay, looking embarrassed.

"Me, too," said Glen.

"Thanks. There's no way you could have known." He changed the subject, "Two does seem like a small crew to install a Twin Wasp Junior."

"Yeah. Could you ease the crane up and down real slow while Glen and I get the mounting holes aligned?"

"Sure." He glanced around and saw a pair of welding gloves on a nearby table. He donned those to protect his clean uniform as he watched the two mechanics expertly maneuver the engine up to a position close to where the mounting holes would line up and the bolts could be inserted. They picked up some mounting bolts and went back to the rear of the engine. In response to their coaching, Alan eased the engine up and down very slightly with the crane until all the mounting.bolts were in.

"Thanks, Alan. Wait 'til I tell the chief a Ringknocker filled out the installation crew," Clay said with a mischievous grin.

"You better get your story straight. I don't see a Ringknocker anywhere in the building," Alan said, shading his eyes and peering around.

Clay and Glen chuckled. "Your story is safe with us," Glen said.

"Okay, see you guys later. I better start heading for the inquiry."

Lieutenant Commander Scott presided at the inquiry, and he would make any decisions regarding disciplinary actions. Haggler walked in and glared at Alan as he sat down. Crawford was there, looking rumpled as usual, but minus his unlit cigar. Alan nodded to Harry Tolman, who happened to be Frank's instructor. He did not know the other two instructors. There was also a yeoman present to act as stenographer during the inquiry. Alan did not know what to expect, and he feared the worst.

The inquiry started off with statements from Alan and Haggler, who each described the accident. Alan was called on first, and he tried to describe what happened both carefully and thoroughly. When he described both how close Haggler's formation flying was, and the evasive maneuver he had used to break away, Haggler became visibly angry. Alan wondered if Haggler had expected him to cover up what had really happened.

Haggler's story confirmed Alan's in some respects, but he stated firmly that neither he nor Runkle had at any time flown in formation closer than normal, which was with a wingspan between the closest wing tips. He said that he had seen Frank starting to fly erratically, making it very difficult for Runkle to stay in position. He claimed that Frank had abruptly turned into Runkle, causing the collision. Scott asked him repeated questions about the details of the collision, and Haggler answered in detail. Alan sensed that Scott was setting a trap, and he felt some hope that the truth would prevail.

Scott queried, "You were flying wing on Ericsson, stepped down and to the right and back. Is that correct?"

"Yes, sir."

"Evans and Runkle were the second section, stepped down and farther to the right and back. Is that correct?"

"Yes, sir." Alan thought he saw Haggler starting to get nervous.

"How could you see what was happening to Evans and Runkle in detail if this was the case? You would have had to turn away from watching Ericsson, your leader, and look in the opposite direction." *Haggler fell right into the trap.*

"Well, I . . . I looked back and forth."

"In fact, you could not have watched Evans and Runkle closely, and you probably do not know how the collision occurred. You *could* have noticed how close Runkle was flying to Evans, though."

"Runkle was at the normal close-formation distance," Haggler repeated stubbornly.

"Okay, Ensign Haggler, that will be all for now." Turning to the four instructors, Scott asked them to give a brief summary of their students' abilities and attitudes. He called on Runkle's instructor first.

"Runkle had good innate ability and was a skillful pilot. He was also very competitive—to the point of being impetuous and rash. In formation flying, he frequently wanted to fly closer than his ability would allow." The description of Haggler's flying and attitude by his instructor sounded similar. Harry Tolman said that Frank was very thorough and steady, always glad to practice until he had more than mastered each skill. Finally, Scott called on Crawford.

"Good student, steady and careful," was all Crawford said.

Alan thought that Scott already knew it would be hard to get more out of Crawford.

Scott thanked the instructors and then asked Haggler and Alan to leave while he conferred with the instructors before reaching a judgment. As they sat outside, Haggler glared at Alan fiercely. Alan glared back at him defiantly at first, but then turned his attention to the voices inside the room, even though he was unable make out what they said. He thought he heard Crawford put in something once or twice, and he tried in vain to detect which way they were leaning. Although he was fairly certain that Scott did not believe Haggler, he knew that justice did not always prevail in situations in which there was a conflict of testimony. *If they believe Haggler, they would have to conclude that I am a liar.* Alan's mind plunged into gloom. He began to envision being disciplined, perhaps even washed out. *With two black marks on my record, I would never get very far in the navy. I could resign, but then I would be in the Reserve, and I would just be called back when the war started. Either way, I would end up in some dead-end position. How could I have avoided all this?*

After about a half hour, they were called back in to hear Scott's judgment. Alan rose and went back in, dreading what could happen.

Scott announced his judgment. "By far, the most likely cause of this collision was that Ensign Runkle was flying too close to Ensign Evans in formation." He paused, shuffled his papers, and continued. "Ensign Haggler, I could recommend a court-martial for you for lying to this board, but I have decided to give you another chance. In my judgment, however, you are unsuited for carrier aviation. Since the navy has already invested a lot in teaching you to fly, I am transferring you to scout-observation. If you don't learn some caution, however, I assure you that the navy has plenty of shore jobs in which you will be less likely to get into trouble. Lieutenant j.g. Ericsson, carry on." Scott stood up and everyone followed. The inquiry was over.

Whew! Justice was done after all. Alan couldn't help feeling elated for a moment, but then he remembered Frank. As he started to walk away, Scott called Alan back into his office.

"Have a seat and relax, Ericsson," Scott said as he closed the door. "I gather that you were a good friend of Ensign Evans?"

"That's right, sir."

"I share your grief. This is the second time that one of my students has not come back, and it doesn't seem to get any easier. Have you thought about writing something to his parents?"

"Yes, sir. I did that yesterday. He had a steady girlfriend in Warrington, and I told her about what happened, as well."

"Good work. I'm not looking forward to writing his parents. Do you know anything about his background?"

Alan described what he knew about Frank's parents and where Frank grew up, and Scott thanked him sincerely. Alan began to warm to Scott, who had seemed stiff and aloof prior to this point. Then he realized that until the accident inquiry was concluded Scott had to keep the participants at arms length.

Alan said, "I keep asking myself what I could have done to prevent this, but I haven't come up with a good answer."

Scott looked thoughtfully at Alan. "Nothing, I'm afraid. In theory, the instructors should notice the students who lack judgment and hold them back, but it is a very difficult call to make."

"Yes, sir."

"Now, Ericsson, I would like to give you a word of caution, out of friendly concern for your career. I have heard that you have been spending time in the maintenance shops on nights and weekends. As an Academy man, you should know that fraternizing with enlisted men is considered unbecoming in an officer."

Alan knew that Scott meant well. Maintaining distance between officers and enlisted men was a part of the navy that Alan had been taught at the Academy. He usually conformed to this, but never really accepted it.

"Yes, sir, I am aware of that. However, I would like to point out that I understand the insides of our airplanes a lot better as a result of my time in the maintenance shops."

"Really? I thought that was covered in ground school."

Alan decided that he would stay away from the shops until he had finished Squadron Two the following week. At that point, he would no longer be under Scott's command.

Saturday, January 25, 1941

Alan found the expected letter from Jennifer in Saturday's mail. They had fallen into a routine of writing each other on weekends. Washington being a little closer to Pensacola than Newport was enough to allow the mail to get through reliably in five days.

Washington, D. C.
January 19, 1941

Dear Alan,

I got your letter of the twelfth. That was wonderful that you did well on your final check ride in Squadron One. Now you can tell me all about Squadron Two and formation flying. I am a LITTLE jealous.

I am enjoying my work at the Far East desk, under Captain McCollum. (He got his promotion recently.) ONI is extremely busy, as you might expect, with war looming in both the Atlantic and the Pacific. It is an exciting place to work, and I do have access to a lot of interesting stuff. The other professional woman, Mrs. Driscoll, who interviewed me when I first got hired over a year ago, has been very helpful. She and I have gone to lunch together a couple of times. She is very nice to me and has helped me understand some of the undercurrents. I want to tell you all I can, but in return I must ask you from now on to treat my letters as "for your eyes only," and destroy them or keep them well hidden.

Historically, the gathering of one type of intelligence, communications intelligence, has been under the Office of Naval Communications, where Mrs. Driscoll works, not under ONI. This has led to a long feud between the two offices, which was finally settled last fall by an edict from the CNO, Admiral Stark. Now, however, there is a new conflict brewing, which I do not yet understand.

On a lighter note, I really like my apartment, now that I am getting pretty well settled in. I have been adding little items, and that will probably continue for quite a while. I am looking forward to using the balcony when it warms up in the spring. I've been pretty busy with my apartment on the weekends. Now I need to get out and meet more people and get more exercise.

Be careful with your formation flying, and write soon.

Oodles of Love,

Jennifer

Alan was very glad she had told him something about the workings of ONI. He was intensely curious, but he respected her for not going any further. He decided to write her back right away. He dreaded telling her about Frank's death, but there was no choice.

Pensacola Naval Air Station
January 25, 1941

Dear Jennifer,

I just got your letter of the nineteenth. I am not too surprised at the bureaucratic infighting in Main Navy. Please continue to tell me all you can. Your letters will be kept well hidden. I am very glad you like your apartment. You have worked hard to get where you are, and you deserve to enjoy your home.

I am already most of the way through Squadron Two. My training has been going well with one major exception. I am suddenly facing the horrible side of flying.

My best friend here, Frank Evans, was killed in an accident. I was there and saw the whole thing. After you get enough formation training with an instructor, it is time to start practicing it on your own. Frank and I were assigned to practice formation flying with two other students. They were hot shots that liked to fly a lot closer than we are supposed to. Frank and the hot shot that was flying as his wingman collided and their planes went spinning straight down into the ocean, shedding pieces as they fell. They were unable to parachute and both were killed by the impact. This is the usual result after an aerial collision. At first I was very angry, then very sad. Frank was the guy from Wyoming that I wrote you about, that went to Stanford, a very nice and very bright fellow. I will never forget him.

Of course there was an official inquiry. I was afraid they might believe the surviving hotshot, who told a complete lie to protect his friend, the hotshot who was killed. But they saw the inconsistencies in his story, believed me, and reassigned him from carrier aviation to scout-observation planes, which do little formation work.

I am not giving up on flying, but you will never have to tell me to be careful again, because I will never be light-hearted about it again. We start Squadron Three, instrument training, in a few days, and I hope that will help me to stop thinking about the accident all the time.

In Squadron Three we will be flying the SNJ. It will be the first truly modern airplane that I have flown. It is a low wing monoplane with no struts or wires, and it has retractable main landing gear. It also has a reputation of being fun to fly, so it is a shame we have to spend all the time under the hood in the rear cockpit.

I love you very much. Write soon.

Tons of love,

Alan

CHAPTER TWELVE

Squadron Three and the God of Naval Aviation

Tuesday, February 4, 1941

Alan had completed his first week of Squadron Three. This part was all taught on the ground, using a simulator device called a Link Trainer, instead of an actual airplane. The student sat inside a closed wooden box that vaguely resembled a very small airplane fuselage, which was mounted on a swivel, with bellows that rotated and tilted the box in all directions to simulate the motion of a real airplane. The inside of the box looked like an airplane cockpit and had real instruments and controls, but no windows. As a student moved the controls, the apparatus figured out what a real airplane would do and displayed the appropriate readings on the instruments, while an instructor sat at a table outside that had a duplicate set of flight instruments and could talk to the student over a two-way intercom that simulated the airplane radio. The apparatus even had a mechanical arm that drew the student's flight path on a map on the table for examination after the simulation.

Alan's instructor for both the Link Trainer portion and the flight portion of instrument training was Lieutenant j.g. Dave Peters. Dave was an AvCad from Los Angeles who was a year younger than Alan. He took naturally to gadgets, including the Link Trainer. It was clear that he loved instrument flying, and he was probably good at it.

Alan had heard going into Squadron Three that many students found the Link Trainer to be quite difficult, and he soon found that he was one of those. It was a new sensation to be shut up in a black box. All he could see was the instruments. It felt eerie when the box moved and the instrument readings changed—what he felt and what the instruments showed seemed at times to be completely unrelated. While he was struggling, Dave's breezy, cheerful manner had been irritating, but he eventually passed.

Wednesday, February 5, 1941

By now, Alan knew where most everything was located on Chevalier Field. It was a bright, clear day. Spring was in the air, and the temperature at dawn was in the mid-forties. He walked down from the BOQ and entered the Squadron Three hangar at 0620, to be greeted by the usual scene: his class gathering around a large blackboard with a flight schedule. He waved to Rudi Fischer and Les Travis, and thought of Frank Evans. He found his last name, aircraft number, instructor's name, and flight time of 0730, and then studied the aircraft parking diagram.

Alan was glad to be done with Link Trainer, and he was ready to start the flying part of instrument training. The view from the rear cockpit was restricted, so the students were not allowed to takeoff or land. In the air, the view outside would be cut off completely by a cloth hood, which extended from behind the seat up to the glare shield—sort of like the top on a baby carriage—so he could practice instrument flying. The instructor in the front cockpit would be the one to watch for other airplanes and correct any mistakes.

At 0640, the chief instructor welcomed them to the flying part of Squadron Three and told them where to find everything before imparting these words: "You may think that because the SNJ is smaller, lighter, and less powerful than the SBU, it will be a cinch. Not so. The SNJ has less wing area for its weight, so you'll need to treat it with respect. You won't be able to horse around in it safely until you get to know it well. The SNJ will also provide you with the opportunity to land with the main landing gear retracted. You might think that's the instructor's responsibility, but you would be wrong. Students have been making too many gear-up landings here, and we're determined to put a stop to it. We've decided that in Squadron Three, even though the instructor will always land the plane, the responsibility for seeing that the landing gear is lowered before landing will belong to the student, not the instructor. If the landing gear is not lowered before the landing, it's your fault. And, believe me, everyone will know about it. On turning final, you're to call out the gear position. If it's up, you'll need to lower it yourself. If you forget, your name will be mud. Keep sharp, and good luck."

Alan had a cup of coffee, collected his parachute, and walked out along the flight line before his flight time. He found his airplane and began looking it over. It was an SNJ-2, made by North American Aviation in Inglewood, California. Alan already liked the appearance and reputation of the SNJ.

The SNJ was quite modern looking, and Alan thought it had a striking resemblance to the navy's new dive-bomber, the SBD, even though the SNJ was about ten percent smaller and the empty weight was about thirty percent less. Since both were designed in the Los Angeles area, Alan thought that it was possible that the lineage of both designs could be traced back to the same designers, most likely including Jack Northrop. Northrop was a pioneer in the use of the aluminum semi-monocoque structure, in which the aluminum skin was reinforced so that it could act as a framework instead of just acting as a cover. Alan could see that the SNJ used this type of structure for the wings and tail.

The main landing gear swung inward when it retracted. When lowered, the main wheels were much further apart than those of the Stearman or the SBU. The low wing also lowered the center of gravity, so Alan suspected that the ground handling of this airplane would be much better than that of the other two. With retractable gear and no struts or wires, it was aerodynamically much cleaner than the N2S or SBU.

The engine was the nine-cylinder Pratt & Whitney Wasp air-cooled radial. Alan remembered reading about the original Wasp, Pratt & Whitney's first engine, when it had come out in 1926. He had been entering high school then. The first version had 425 horsepower, which seemed like a lot at the time. He thought it was amazing that continuous refinement over the past fifteen years had made it possible to reach 600 horsepower while making the engine more reliable and durable at the same time.

He had learned, however, that this was not unusual for an aircraft engine—at least for the air-cooled radials. The forces on the many parts of the engine were so complex that they could only be roughly estimated by the design engineers. For this reason, the initial version of the engine had to be restricted to a conservative power rating to achieve acceptable reliability. As experience with the engine accumulated over the years, the parts that failed or wore out could be replaced by stronger ones, and the power rating increased.

Alan climbed up on the left wing, put his right foot on the small step protruding from the fuselage below the rear cockpit, and swung himself and his parachute into the rear seat. As in most trainers, there was a pretty complete set of controls and instruments in the rear cockpit. Between the cockpits there was a rollover structure, consisting of a framework of steel tubes that would hold the airplane up if the plane flipped over on the ground, so the crew could crawl out—a function performed by the upper wing in a biplane. Alan looked up and saw Dave Peters approaching.

"Hello, Alan. Ready to fly?" he asked, smiling.

Alan smiled back. "Yup. How about you?"

"I got the eagers. Let's start with the preflight."

Alan climbed out and Dave coached him through the routine, which was similar to the SBU's preflight. There were a few new items to check off on the landing gear, but there were no wires or struts to check. Alan climbed back into the rear cockpit, and Dave jumped on the left wing. With his right foot on the step, he leaned into the rear cockpit and went over all the controls and instruments with Alan. When that was done, Dave climbed into the front cockpit and got the engine started. The inertia starter was cranked up by the airplane's electrical system, so no cranking by a ground crewman was needed.

Dave told Alan that the radio was Alan's responsibility. It felt strange to Alan to have nothing else to do as Dave began taxiing for takeoff. Alan looked out and noticed just how restricted the view really was from the rear cockpit. The forward fuselage blocked the view forward, and the wings blocked the close-up view out the sides of the plane because they were only a little below his eyes when the tail wheel was on the ground. *This view might be worse than what Lindbergh had in the Spirit of St. Louis*, Alan realized. He remembered reading about that plane having had a fuel tank blocking the forward view.

As they were taxiing out around the southeast corner of the field to runway two seven left, Dave explained the lesson plan, which consisted of basic air work for the day. It sounded roughly like a repeat of the first lesson in the Link Trainer.

After the tower cleared them for takeoff, Dave opened the throttle and they were on their way. The SNJ accelerated rapidly, like the SBU. When the tail wheel came off the runway, and the fuselage was nearly level—a situation called a "level attitude"—the rear cockpit was well above the wings, making the view out the sides a lot better. The front cockpit and rollover structure still blocked the view directly forward, though. The airplane made something of an S turn on the runway before the main wheels left the runway and they were airborne. Even with wide landing gear and a low center of gravity, Dave seemed to have trouble keeping the airplane straight on the runway. Dave raised the landing gear and brought the engine back to climb power.

"Close the canopy and put up the instrument hood," Dave instructed Alan over the intercom.

Alan complied. His eyes adjusted rapidly to the dim light in the cockpit. But, without the wind through the cockpit, the usual trainer odors became fairly strong.

They followed the lesson plan that Dave had given. Alan flew straight and level at cruise and approach airspeeds and then performed standard rate turns at cruise and approach airspeeds, both with and without climbs and descents. He had been taught to continually scan the airspeed indicator, artificial horizon, altimeter, turn and bank indicator, directional gyro, and rate-of-climb indicator. When he did this, Alan found that he could manage simple maneuvers fairly well on instruments alone. When a turn was combined with a climb or descent, though, his performance was more ragged. He realized that it would be even more difficult if he had to do something else in addition to flying, such as talk on the radio or review a chart. It did, however, seem a little easier than his first lesson in the Link Trainer.

He also noticed that he was not including the artificial horizon instrument often enough in his scan of the important instruments. The artificial horizon instrument provided the nearest thing to the cues that the pilot got from seeing the actual horizon outside the airplane. Alan gradually realized that when he kept the pitch and bank angles close to where he wanted them by checking the artificial horizon often, the airplane did not wander and everything else was much easier.

Alan could tell that the controls in the SNJ were lighter and more responsive than those of the N2S or the SBU, which made the airplane more fun to fly visually, but a little harder to fly on instruments. *This is one sweet bird*, Alan couldn't help but think. *I'd really like to do some solo visual flying in this airplane. I wonder if there's a way to wangle a checkout.* He'd have to look into that.

At the end of the lesson, Dave gave Alan headings, altitudes, and speeds until they were back in the pattern at Chevalier Field. Alan lowered the landing gear on the downwind leg so he could call it out before landing. Dave told Alan when to turn onto the base leg, and then when to turn onto the final leg. Dave took the controls and told Alan to stow the hood and take a look at their position. Sure enough, Alan saw right away that they were on the short final for runway two seven left. He called out that the landing gear was down.

Dave's landing was wobbly, like his takeoff. *Dave does not seem to be a great stick-and-rudder pilot*, Alan observed, *but he must have done better than this to get through his own training.*

Saturday, February 22, 1941

Alan was happy to find he got another Saturday letter from Jennifer.

Washington, D. C.

February 16, 1941

Dear Alan,

While instrument training may be difficult and tedious, you are obviously enjoying the SNJ. I am glad you were able to find an airplane and an instructor so you could get checked out for solo in the front cockpit. I can see how that might give you some relief from hours cooped up in the rear cockpit.

At my work, the continued fighting between ONI and other offices is hard to ignore. I now have some understanding of what is going on. The Director of War Plans, Admiral Turner, is attempting to take over the evaluation of the strategic situation and prediction of enemy intentions from ONI. He insists that ONI supply him with all intelligence, and he will make any evaluations. This is clearly contrary to what the policy manuals say, and to Stark's edict of last fall. So now it is a battle between ONI and War Plans. The current director of ONI is only in charge temporarily, until a new director arrives in April. Turner is taking full advantage of the situation to encroach on ONI in the meantime.

In spite of this, I continue to enjoy my work at the Far East Desk. I seem to get along well with Captain McCollum. It is a fascinating place to work, even better than the War College. Here I'm not an onlooker; I'm one of the players.

Guess what! Victoria and Seth just announced their engagement. It seems like a good match to me. They are planning to get married on September 6 in Newport. I can probably get to the wedding from Washington, but who knows where you will be in September.

Speaking of weddings, we should start thinking about where we want go on our honeymoon. North? South? West?

I have gotten to know the wives of some of my colleagues, and through them met other women who I am looking forward to getting to know. One of the wives was looking for a partner for doubles tennis, so I am enjoying getting some exercise once a week.

Don't get carried away with the SNJ, you rascal. I would love to have a ride in it. Maybe someday you will be able to give me a ride in some airplane. I miss you so much.

Oodles of love,

Jennifer

Sunday, February 23, 1941

Alan wrote his reply on Sunday.

Pensacola Naval Air Station
February 23, 1941

Dear Jennifer,

That was quite an earful you wrote about Admiral Turner. It certainly goes along with his reputation. What I hear is that he was so upset at being only fifth, and not first, in the class of '08 that he needs to constantly dominate those around him to prove his superiority. I hope he is only a minor distraction and not having an adverse impact on the output of ONI. I am glad to hear you are enjoying your work in spite of the fighting.

That is great news about Victoria and Seth. I agree they do appear to be a good match.

For our honeymoon, how about going south? The third week in May is still a little cool north and west, and we would be heading in the general direction of Washington, which might turn out to save time. But I am open to anything. We don't get our orders for where we will be going from here until the day of graduation, so I won't know where I'm going until a week before the wedding.

I have continued to have a good time with the SNJ on weekends. I had twenty hours in the front cockpit by the end of last weekend. This weekend my instructor suggested I could get checked out in the rear cockpit if I wanted. I did it and it was extra satisfying to master the difficulty of the poor view. After it was over I realized I might have made a mistake. Checking out in the rear cockpit shows you have one of the qualifications to be an instructor. Like all the other pilots graduating, I would rather not become an instructor.

I would LOVE to give you a ride in the SNJ, you scalawag. But even better would be some airplane where we sit side by side, squeezed close together, don't you think? I miss you every day.

Tons of Love,

Alan

Monday, February 24, 1941

It was late afternoon. Alan had completed his last training flight with Dave Peters, who had declared Alan ready for his instrument check ride. Alan was relaxing while Dave talked to squadron operations to see when and with whom the check ride would be. Suddenly, an orderly came up to Alan and told him to report to the squadron skipper's office right away. *Now what?* Alan asked himself, worried. He told Dave that he was wanted in the skipper's office and then he climbed the stairs and went into the waiting area in front of the squadron offices. He knew the yeoman; he had dealt with him before.

"There you are, sir. Admiral Powers is with Commander Ewing in his office. Commander Ewing just asked for your folder, so I took it upon myself to send for you. Chances are that they have something in mind for you."

Holy smoke! Admiral John Powers, the top-ranking and highly-respected naval aviator? Naval Aviator Number 3, if I remember correctly. He is currently the chief of the Bureau of Aeronautics. What could he want with me? Alan was aware from official notices that Powers was visiting the base from BuAer, but he had not heard anything about his coming to Squadron Three.

"Good thinking, and thanks for the heads up. Do I look ship shape?"

"Yes, sir."

Alan sat down in the waiting area. A few minutes later, Ewing's door opened and Ewing spoke through the opening. "See if you can get Lieutenant j.g. Ericsson up here right away."

"He's here now, sir," the yeoman informed him.

"Dammit, one of these days you're going to get so far ahead of me that I'm going to get vertigo," Ewing said, grinning at the yeoman as he came out of his office.

Alan stood and they shook hands.

"Come into my office, Lieutenant. Admiral Powers would like to meet you."

"Yes, sir," Alan replied as he followed Ewing into the office where Admiral Powers was standing.

"Admiral, this is Lieutenant j.g. Alan Ericsson," Ewing said by way of introduction as the two men shook hands.

He looks a little older than I remember, but not too much, thought Alan. He remembered Powers from a lecture at the Naval Academy. He was three inches shorter than Alan, and heavier than Alan remembered, but he had an erect posture that seemed to add to his stature.

"Sit down, Lieutenant, and I'll tell you why we've called you in," said Powers. "I grew up in Rome, Georgia, and my best friend from those days is still living there. He's very sick, and he will probably die before too long. I'd like to make a brief visit there, leaving tomorrow morning and coming back on Wednesday. The weather people are expecting good weather on that route over the next two days. I could go in my plane, but it seems to be a good opportunity for me to get some time in a trainer. I've only gotten one brief hop in the SNJ in the past, so that was my first choice. Commander Ewing says he can supply an airplane, and he offered to have an instructor go with me, but I told him that I'd prefer to go with a student to give me more insight into how the training program is going. He told me that none of the students are checked out in the airplane anymore, because it's all under the hood, except for you. For that reason, he suggested that you accompany me."

"I see, sir."

"Commander Ewing tells me that you got checked out in the front cockpit on your own time on weekends, and then you flew an additional ten hours and got checked out in the rear cockpit, again on your own time. I understand that flying in the back seat of the SNJ is not easy because the view outside is not very good. Don't you get enough flying during the week?"

"Well, sir, the truth is that the instrument work was very intense for me. The stick-and-rudder flying on the weekends provided a nice break from the instrument flying and helped me to relax. I think it would have been harder without that break."

Powers paused and looked thoughtful. "That makes a lot of sense, Lieutenant." Turning to Ewing, he said, "Something to keep in the back of your mind, Commander, for the next time the curriculum comes under review. Even airline pilots don't fly solely on instruments, day after day."

"Yes, sir, I'll keep that in mind," Ewing replied, writing a note.

"Well, Lieutenant, are you ready to take a hop up to Rome?" asked Powers.

"It would be a great honor, sir, to serve you in any way that I can."

"Good. Now let's get down to some details. Rome has a little airport that I know well, but they don't have gas there. It might be a stretch for the SNJ to make the round trip without gassing up once. We could fly into Chattanooga for gas on our initial flight and then fly back to Rome."

Ewing said, "Okay, sir, let's see how far it is up to Rome."

They rose and walked over to a large aeronautical chart on the wall that was equipped with a string attached to a pin at Pensacola and a scale to measure distances. Ewing said, "260 nautical miles to Rome, 520 nautical miles round trip. About three and one-half hours round trip, if there's no wind. The SNJ-2 carries a lot of fuel, over six hours at normal cruise, so you should have plenty of reserve."

Powers said, "Okay, we'll plan to go directly to the airport at Rome. I'll call a friend and check on the field conditions, and I'll arrange ground transportation with friends."

Powers and Ewing discussed the necessary arrangements, and then Powers was given a pilot's manual for the SNJ-2 before he thanked Ewing and left. Ewing had the yeoman send for his executive and operations officers.

Alan wondered if he was having a bad dream. *A three and one-half hour check ride with the God of Naval Aviation? This is what I get for having too much fun in the SNJ.* He said, "Sir, this seems like a two-edged sword if ever there was one. Any suggestions or hints you could offer would be welcome."

Ewing smiled and replied, "Remember that the admiral is the pilot-in-command unless he turns it over to you. The admiral will know that you'll be nervous, so just try to remain calm and do the best you can, which is very good, according to your record. Study the chart and the weather briefing this evening, get a good night's rest, and be back here by 0800 with a small overnight bag. We will go over the latest weather and anything else you need with you then."

"Yes, sir. Thank you, sir."

Tuesday, February 25, 1941

Alan arrived at Ewing's office at 0745. He had not slept very well, but he felt fit. The scuttlebutt had gotten around, and some of the other students thought that he had sucked up to the skipper and gotten a plum. Others thought that he had gotten what he deserved for showing off in the SNJ. His friends were more sympathetic, but not jealous.

It was a clear day. The temperature at dawn was in the low fifties, like late April in New England. Shortly after 0800, Alan met the squadron exec and went over the route. The direct route would take them close to Montgomery, Alabama, which was a little less than half way. That would provide an easy place to stop if there were any problems. Birmingham was also available, although it was a little farther on and a little farther off their direct route. Chattanooga was a third alternative, though it was a little beyond Rome. He also went over the latest weather forecast, which remained excellent.

The exec paused and told Alan, "You know, the admiral might want to make a practice instrument approach somewhere along the way, or he might ask you to make one. Montgomery would be the logical place. I'll get you instrument approach plates for both the military and civilian fields, and I'll throw in Birmingham and Chattanooga, too."

"Thank you, sir," Alan responded, thinking again of the check ride aspect of the flight with foreboding.

Powers arrived promptly a little before 0900, and the exec held a similar, but more condensed, briefing for Powers and Ewing. The exec gave Powers copies of the same set of instrument approach plates he had given Alan, and Powers was given a parachute and helmet. Then Ewing, the exec, Powers, and Alan went out to the airplane. Alan could see that it had been washed down and was noticeably cleaner than the others on the flight line. Two ground crewmen, who had been wiping off smears from minor oil leaks, quickly disappeared. A small crowd of students and a few instructors had gathered.

The squadron operations officer was there, and he said to Powers, "Sir, we've given your plane a thorough preflight inspection, and she's topped up with gas and ready to go. I also put a few tools and spares and some engine oil in the baggage compartment, along with chocks and the canopy cover."

Alan squeezed his and Powers's overnight bags into the remaining space in the small baggage compartment behind the rear cockpit as Powers said good-bye to Ewing and climbed on the left wing. Alan followed.

"I'll take the front cockpit going up to Rome. I'd like you to make a practice approach to Maxwell Field at Montgomery along the way."

"Yes, sir."

"Okay, let's get started," said Powers. Powers climbed into the front cockpit and Alan climbed into the rear. The operations officer went over the controls and switches with Powers while Alan strapped in, arranged his charts, and waited. He felt self-conscious in front of the crowd of onlookers; they reminded him of the time he returned from his Squadron One down-check flight.

Powers got the engine started. While it was warming up, Alan heard a crackling in his earphones, and Powers came on the intercom.

"Here's what I want to do on this flight: You do the first takeoff, but we'll stay in the pattern for two touch-and-go landings. You do the first landing, and then I'll take over as we roll out and make the takeoff. I'll make a landing and another takeoff, and then we'll depart. I'd like you to take us to Montgomery under the hood and shoot a practice approach to Maxwell Field. We'll go at 7,000 feet to be above most of the training activity. I'll navigate to Rome after that and make the landing at Rome. Okay?"

This sounds like a check ride and then some, thought Alan. "Yes, sir. There are certain things I cannot do from the rear cockpit, though. I can lower the gear, but not raise it, so I'll have to ask you to do that."

"No problem. Just say, 'Raise the gear,' and I'll do it. While we're flying, I'd prefer to drop the naval formality, if you don't mind. Please call me Jack."

"I'll try to remember, sir . . . I mean, Jack. Please call me Alan. Would you like the first landing to be a wheel landing or a full stall?" Alan prayed that he'd ask for a wheel landing only. In a wheel landing, the airplane was landed in a level attitude on the main wheels only, and then slowed down until the tail could no longer be held up by the elevators. There was no stalling, and it made for a lot easier landing when flying the SNJ from the rear seat because the view was much less restricted when the tail was up.

"I'd prefer a full-stall landing, Alan. I think we're ready to taxi. You handle the radio with the tower."

So, I'll be lucky not to screw up right away. Flying from the rear cockpit with an admiral in front is not my idea of fun—more like a nightmare. If I don't screw up, however, it should earn me a few points. Alan called the tower and got clearance to taxi to the runway.

Powers eased the SNJ onto the outer taxiway in front of the flight line and turned right. The outer taxiway circled around the entire perimeter of the field, and they were alone when they got to the threshold of two seven left on the east side of the field. Powers stopped and did the run-up and the pre-takeoff checklist while Alan quietly double-checked everything.

After getting clearance from the tower to take off, Alan made one more S-turn as he taxied onto the runway to make sure he would not hit anything. He lined up with the runway and locked the tail wheel. His adrenaline was pumping and he was sweating already. He opened the throttle and the airplane accelerated rapidly. He eased the stick forward to pick up the tail while looking out both sides of the cockpit—his feet poised on the rudder pedals, making small corrections to keep the airplane straight on the runway.

As the tail came up, he had a better view. He kept the tail a little low, and soon they were airborne. Alan could see the runway at the departure end approaching. He asked Powers to raise the landing gear, and then reduced power to the climb setting. After he had gained enough altitude, he turned left into the landing pattern.

Alan quickly went through the landing checklist, announcing each item for Powers's benefit as he did so. Opposite the middle of the runway, he got clearance from the tower to land. Abeam the threshold of the runway, Alan lowered the landing gear and pulled the throttle back to maintain eighty knots in a gentle glide. He checked the landing gear indicators to see that the wheels had come down. Soon he turned ninety degrees left onto the base leg. Knowing that he would not be able to see the runway from the rear seat after turning onto the final leg, he looked at the runway now and noted what he would be able to see on both sides to mark the threshold as he was coming in. The outer edge of the outer taxiway provided a good marker for the threshold.

Alan turned ninety degrees left onto the final leg and lowered the flaps. He could not see the runway, but he could see the outer taxiway clearly on both sides, just as he'd planned. He aimed to start the flare a little short of the threshold, adjusting the throttle for the correct glide angle at eighty knots. Glancing out both sides, he judged when to start the flare. He started the flare and closed the throttle, and the runway became visible, close by, on both sides. The nose came up slowly to the attitude for a three-point touchdown. The airplane hung there for a second, stalled, and dropped about two inches onto all three wheels simultaneously in what Alan considered a very good landing.

Whew! Relief flooded over him. *Not too bad.* He felt the sweat dripping down inside his flight suit now that the tension had eased slightly. Immediately, he began small movements of the rudder to keep the airplane straight, continuing to watch both sides. He braked gently, and the airplane slowed to taxi speed.

Powers came on the intercom, "Very nice landing. That's going to be a hard act to follow, Alan."

Well, he sure knows how to make me feel good. Alan beamed to himself.

Powers proceeded to take the airplane around the pattern again, following the same procedure. He had the huge advantage, however, of a much better forward view. Powers's landing was also nice, but he stalled a little farther off the runway and came down a little harder.

Powers took off again, climbing out straight ahead and turning right to head north. Alan reported to the tower that they were departing to the north.

Powers came on the intercom, "I like the way this airplane handles—quick and responsive. I can see why you like it, Alan. Okay, put up the hood and take us to Montgomery at 7,000 feet."

The God of Naval Aviation agrees with me about the SNJ. Maybe I really do know *something about airplanes.*

Alan quickly put his mind back to flying as he closed the rear canopy and put up the hood. He began to scan the instruments, making sure he glanced frequently at the artificial horizon. They were climbing at 100 knots. Powers closed the front canopy.

Alan had already tuned in the Pensacola Range, one of a network of air-navigation radio stations. Each station put out four directional radio beams that linked with beams from other stations to form radio airways between cities. Using these radio beams, a pilot could navigate between cities without needing to see the ground. Each directional radio beam consisted of the Morse A signal on one side and the Morse N signal on the other. If the plane was centered on the beam, the pilot heard both signals in his headphones. Because they were opposite signals, they made up a continuous tone when blended together. Alan had his chart unfolded on his left thigh to reference when he needed it, as well. Listening to the A and N Morse signals, he tracked the beam inbound to the Pensacola Range and then picked up another beam that headed outbound toward Montgomery.

He continued climbing until they reached 7,000 feet, at which point he leveled off, noting the time, pulling the power back to cruise, and leaning the fuel/air mixture. He knew he was expected to estimate their time of arrival at the Montgomery Range, so he estimated where they were and how far it was to Montgomery. He corrected the airspeed for altitude, temperature, and wind to estimate ground speed. He used his E6B computer, a specialized circular slide rule that the pilots called a "whiz wheel," to get the time en route to Montgomery. He made sure to switch back and forth every few seconds between these calculations and flying by instruments, but the airplane still wandered a couple of times. He brought it back on course and altitude each time, but he knew that Powers must have noticed. He announced his estimate to Powers when he was finished with his calculations.

As they flew on, Alan began to feel isolated in his cocoon. When the signal from the Pensacola Range faded, Alan switched to the Montgomery Range. Alan got out the instrument approach plate for Maxwell Field at Montgomery and reviewed it in snatches between scans of the flight instruments.

They crossed the Montgomery range two minutes ahead of his estimate. Alan called the Maxwell control tower on the radio and got permission to make a practice instrument approach and then he followed the instrument approach procedure to the airport. The purpose of the procedure was to get the airplane safely down fairly low, usually under 1,000 feet above the runway, and in a position to land straight ahead on the runway without it being necessary for the pilot to see anything on the ground until that point. At that point, if the ceiling and visibility were above the minimums specified on the approach plate, the airplane should have descended below the clouds and the pilot should be able to see the runway and land.

Alan started the procedure by flying directly away from the airport on one of the range beams; then he reversed course while descending, intercepting the same beam again, inbound this time, back to the range. During this time, he completed the landing checklist. He felt trickles of sweat running down his face and flight suit as he concentrated on keeping track of everything. After crossing the range a second time, now headed along the beam for the airport, he began the final descent. This was the part of the procedure where getting off-course more than a small amount could result in hitting something. He leveled off at 800 feet above sea level, according to the altimeter—about 400 feet above the runway. He timed their approach from the range to estimate when they were close to the runway.

"We should be there," he said.

"Stow the hood and take a look, Alan. I have the controls. Very nice approach."

After Alan felt Powers take the controls, he opened the hood and looked around. They were just passing over Maxwell Field at 400 feet above the ground, exactly where they should have been. For the second time that day, Alan felt an enormous sense of relief. Powers set climb power, raised the landing gear, and turned right, toward Rome.

As they continued on, Alan noticed that Powers held the heading closely, telling himself, *This is the man who commanded the flight that crossed the Atlantic from Newfoundland to the Azores in the open-cockpit NC-4 flying boat in 1919, when I was seven years old. There were no autopilots then. No wonder he can hold a heading!* Soon, Powers leveled off at 7,000 feet, pulled the power back to cruise, and leaned the mixture.

They continued on for a while, and then Alan noticed a ridge off to the left. *The southern tail of the Appalachian Mountains*, he thought. The ridge gradually got taller and closer as they went on. Alan could see another ridge beyond it. The deciduous trees had not leafed out in the mountains, so they were not as green. It was nice to see some mountains again. He was starting to enjoy the trip.

About twenty miles south of Rome, Powers started their descent. After a few minutes, Alan could see Rome ahead. Powers found the little airport on the northwest side of the city, which was basically two runways cleared out of the forest in the shape of a large X. Powers made a near-perfect three-point landing, and the airplane rolled out smoothly on the brown, oiled dirt surface. He turned left off the strip in the middle of the field, heading toward a small hangar with an office. He taxied up to the office as two men appeared and waved to him. The shorter man directed Powers toward a parking spot for the plane, where he shut the engine down, and he and Alan climbed out.

The man showing Powers where to park was the airport manager, and the other was another of Powers' friends, Tad Hemphill, who made the introductions. Hemphill was there to pick them up in his car. After calling in to Squadron Three on the phone in the office to report their arrival, Alan made sure that the airplane was tied down and the control locks and canopy cover were in place. They climbed into Hemphill's airy Pierce-Arrow touring car and Alan was dropped off at his hotel. Powers told Alan to meet him at the hotel lobby at 1300 the next day. As Powers disappeared, Alan let out a long sigh of relief at not being in the company of an admiral. *On the other hand, he seems to be a pleasant gentleman*, he thought.

Alan enjoyed his brief stay in Rome. He spent the afternoon walking around the town and visiting some of the historic sites.

In the evening, he found a small watering hole that had hillbilly music playing, and he stayed for quite a while. The band was from Charlottesville, Virginia, where the University of Virginia was located. To Alan's surprise, they also played some English, Scottish, and Irish folk music. He was again struck by the similarities running through all these genres.

Wednesday, February 26, 1941

It was another beautiful day, with temperature in the upper thirties at dawn. It was probably warmer back at Pensacola. Shortly after noon, after a little more wandering around in town, Alan called Squadron Three collect from the hotel to check in and get a weather briefing. The forecast remained excellent. He checked out of his room, had a light lunch in the hotel restaurant, and waited for Powers in the lobby, as instructed.

Powers appeared shortly after 1300. He greeted Alan and asked, "Have you checked on the weather, Lieutenant?"

"Yes, sir. Clear and light winds."

"Glad to hear it. We should have a nice flight back, then."

"How about your friend, sir? How is he doing?" asked Alan.

"He was in bed and obviously very ill. The cancer had spread all over his body. We had a pleasant chat yesterday afternoon, and I had dinner with his family. I was glad to see that they seemed to have gotten used to the idea that he might die soon. After dinner, when I said good-bye, he still seemed to be in a good mood from our chat." The admiral paused before continuing on. "This morning I telephoned and found out that he'd died peacefully during the night. It's a shock, but, in hindsight, I think it's a blessing. He'd suffered long enough. I paid my respects to the family, and they understand why I can't stay for the funeral. I'm glad that I came, though; I don't think I could have come at a better time."

"Well, I'm sorry to hear of your friend's passing, but I'm glad to hear that your visit worked out well, sir."

"Thank you. Now, Tad Hemphill should be here shortly to take us back to the airport."

Alan hoped that he would not screw up on the flight back and undo the good impression he seemed to have made with the admiral. When they got back to the field, Alan went right to the airplane, taking off the canopy cover, unlocking the controls, and beginning the preflight inspection. He expected the engine oil to be down about a gallon, and it was, so he topped it off with a gallon from the baggage compartment. Powers stowed their bags and chatted with Hemphill while Alan called in to Squadron Three on the office telephone to say they were ready to take off.

When Alan returned, Powers said, "Let's have you take the front seat on the way back, Lieutenant."

That's a relief.

They climbed in and fastened their seat belts. Alan started the engine and went through the pre-taxi checklist.

Powers came on the intercom, "Okay, Alan, I'd like the flight back to be more or less the reverse of the flight out. You take off from here and navigate back visually to the Montgomery range at 6,000 feet. From there, I'll put up the hood and take us back to the Pensacola Range on instruments."

"Okay, Jack."

The flight back to Pensacola was uneventful. Being unfamiliar with the landmarks, Alan used mostly dead reckoning to get close to Montgomery, and then he picked up one of the beams to go directly over the range. Powers put up the hood and took over from there. Again, Alan enjoyed the beauty of the scenery along the way as Powers flew the radio airway to Pensacola.

After they passed over the Pensacola Range, Powers stowed the hood and said that he would like to practice some maneuvers from the rear seat. Alan called the Chevalier tower, reported their position, and got permission to head out over the Gulf south of the field to practice some maneuvers. Powers practiced steep turns, stalls, and slow flight.

Powers said that he would like to try a landing from the rear seat, so Alan managed the radio with the tower and Powers brought the SNJ in for landing. The plane bounced slightly on the main gear before the tail wheel touched, then settled down and decelerated gently to taxi speed. A landing that good on the first try from the rear seat convinced Alan that Powers was still an expert pilot. Alan was amazed at this, because he thought Powers's duties would not leave him much time to keep up his flying skills. Powers turned it over to Alan for the taxi into the hangar.

Apparently Squadron Three had anticipated their arrival, because a small crowd had gathered. A ground crewman was waiting for them, and he directed them to a parking space. Ewing and the squadron officers were also there, along with Powers's flag lieutenant. Alan noticed that behind them were Dave Peters and the instructor who had checked him out in the SNJ.

Alan knew he was in the spotlight, and he resolved to be careful for the last few steps. He shut down the engine and turned off all the electrical switches, then unstrapped and stepped out onto the wing. Powers had already stepped off the wing with his parachute, and Alan followed. Ewing came forward and shook Powers's hand.

"Welcome back, Admiral. How did the trip go?"

"It was a pleasant and informative trip, and I got to see my old friend just before he died. It really couldn't have worked out better, for which I thank you, Commander."

"I'm sorry to hear about your friend, sir."

"Thank you, Commander, but it was really a blessing. He'd suffered long enough."

"I see, sir." Ewing paused and then smiled. "Those were some beautiful landings you made yesterday, sir. Ericsson's today was very good, but not as pretty."

Alan thought he noticed a twinkle in Powers's eye and a subtle twitch of his mouth.

"Today's landing wasn't as pretty, I have to agree. Which landing yesterday did you think was the best?"

"Well, they were both very nice, sir, but the first one was damn-near perfect."

"I thought so, too. Now I'd like to tell you who was actually flying. The first landing yesterday was made from the rear seat by Lieutenant Ericsson."

He turned and smiled at Alan, who flushed bright red. Alan saw Ewing's eyebrows shoot up as he glanced at Alan. Dave Peters looked baffled, and his checkout instructor beamed, giving a thumbs-up sign.

Powers continued. "I made the second landing yesterday." There were nods and smiles. "I also made the landing today, but from the rear seat."

Immediately there were big smiles and words of approval all around. Ewing reached out and grasped Powers's hand again, saying, "Congratulations, sir. You can add the SNJ to the many airplanes you have mastered."

"Thank you, Commander. I should add that Lieutenant Ericsson also took us from here to Montgomery and shot an excellent approach under the hood. He seems well qualified for instrument flight," said Powers, turning again toward Alan and smiling. Alan smiled back.

"I'm very glad everything went so well," said Ewing.

Powers replied, "Well, the fun's over and I better get back to work. Thank you again, Commander, for arranging everything, and thank you, Lieutenant. It was a pleasure flying with you."

Ewing and Alan shook hands with Powers before he was herded away by his flag lieutenant.

Ewing turned to Alan with a grin. "Well, Ericsson, we aren't going to have a check ride that might contradict the judgment of the admiral. Congratulations, you have completed Squadron Three." He shook Alan's hand.

"Thank you very much, sir." Alan basked in the moment. He realized that he owed this very satisfactory outcome largely to his checkout instructor, so Alan found him in the onlookers and thanked him again before he headed for the BOQ.

CHAPTER THIRTEEN

Gunnery and Dive-Bombing

Thursday, February 27, 1941

Alan's first day in Advanced Training arrived only three weeks after he had started Squadron Three, but it seemed like it had been a much longer time. He felt that he had passed a milestone by making it to this stage. Harry Tolman had told him that Advanced Training was a little different from the earlier training phases because the instructors began to see the trainees as colleagues rather than beginners. He was eager to get started.

It was a clear day, though the morning was a little hazy, and the temperature at dawn was in the mid-fifties. Alan arrived at the Advanced Training hangar on Chevalier Field at 0605. Once again, he found many of his classmates milling around the flight schedule on a large blackboard. He said hello to Ed Miller and Wade Buckner, and found his name with his aircraft number, instructor's name—Lieutenant Earl Walker—and flight time of 0700.

At 0620, the chief instructor climbed onto the wing of a TBD torpedo bomber in the hangar and addressed the class. "Welcome to Advanced Training, in which we really find out if you have the right skills and temperament to be a navy carrier pilot. For most of the training in this phase, you'll either be flying the F2F-1 or the F3F-1. The F3F-1 is very similar to the F2F-1, but it's a little less compact and a little more forgiving. Don't confuse these airplanes with the later F3F-2 and F3F-3 airplanes, which have the larger Wright Cyclone engine. The F2F-1 and F3F-1 have the same engine and the same wing loading as the SBU you've flown, but both of these fighters are much lighter and more compact than the SBU, so things happen faster. From now on, precision and perfection will be required to keep out of trouble. For these initial flights, your instructor will follow you in another airplane of the same type, which you'll find parked next to your airplane. Keep sharp, and good luck."

Alan had time before his flight, so he sat down and had a cup of coffee. He was joined by Ed and Wade.

"Fighters at last! I can't wait," said Wade.

"Yeah, this should be a lot more fun, especially after riding around in the back seat of the SNJ," Ed agreed.

"At least flying a barrel should be better than flying a barn," said Alan with a grin, remembering Wade's description of the SBU, and the fact that the F2F and F3F were known as Flying Barrels because of the chunky shape of their fuselage.

"Damn right," Wade agreed with a twinkle in his eye.

Alan knew that both Ed and Wade continued to be focused on fighters. They had both been reprimanded for dogfighting in the SBUs, and they had missed being able to continue that in Squadron Three. Alan had also done a little dogfighting in the SBU, but he was more discrete about where and when he did it.

Ed and Wade were soon having an animated discussion about the finer points of dogfighting, particularly about how to break up a Lufberry circle, which was a defensive maneuver in which several airplanes flew in a circle, nose-to-tail. Alan thought that he would be likely to learn much faster from an experienced instructor than from two pilots who had no training in dogfighting, so after awhile he decided to go out to the flight line.

He found his airplane and began looking it over. Alan had followed the evolution of the Grumman fighters, starting with the two-seated FF-1. His airplane was an F2F-1, as he had hoped. He was not sure where his preference came from, but maybe it was simply that the F3F was a refinement of the F2F and hence not the pure original. Although both the wings and the fuselage of the F3F-1 were slightly longer, providing additional stability, careful attention to aerodynamic detail had enabled the F3F to reach the same maximum speed with the same engine. The F2F-1 was a lot smaller than the SBU—six feet shorter and having a wingspan five feet less. It was also about thirty percent lighter. With the same engine as the SBU, he figured it should be nimble.

Alan could see that the fuselage was certainly short and squat like a barrel, but it was actually tapered a little at the front and a lot at the rear, making it shaped more like a teardrop, except for the blunt nose—a good shape for maintaining low drag. A sliding canopy enclosed the cockpit, and the tail wheel retracted with the main wheels. Grumman had obviously put a lot of effort into making the fuselage clean, but it was still a biplane with the usual dirty arrangement of struts and wires between the wings, like the Stearman and the SBU. That was the price of keeping the compactness of the biplane arrangement to save space on aircraft carriers. The main wheels retracted into wells in the fuselage, leaving only the outer side of the tire and wheel exposed. Alan realized that the biplane wings were too thin to house the retracted main landing gear, so the fuselage was the only logical place for it. With the gear down, the main wheels were close together, as they were in the Stearman and the SBU. He hoped he hadn't been spoiled by the much-easier ground handling of the SNJ.

After he looked the airplane over, he stepped onto the left lower wing and slid back the small canopy, heaving his parachute in and climbing into the cockpit. He avoided the big, tubular gun sight, which was just like the one the SBU had. That reminded Alan of the navy's reluctance to install shoulder harnesses, in combat airplanes at a minimum. A shoulder harness would keep the pilot's face from hitting the gun sight in a crash landing.

The cockpit had a different feel from those of the previous air-planes he had flown. The fuselage of the Grumman fighters used aluminum semi-monocoque construction, unlike the Stearman, SBU, and SNJ. As a result, all the structure that was visible in the cockpit was made up of sheet aluminum pieces that had been riveted together, instead of steel tubes welded together with a fabric or aluminum cover placed over everything.

The upper wing on the F2F was lower and farther forward than on the SBU, so it obstructed the view forward and upward much less. The two fixed .30-caliber machine guns were enclosed in the top of the nose and fired over the engine and through the propeller. The synchronizing gear, which made sure the bullets passed between the propeller blades, limited the rate of fire to less than that of guns that did not fire through the propeller. Alan knew that this was the typical armament of US fighters in the mid- to late-1930s. It was also the armament on the first Corsair, the XF4U-1. It was now obsolete, however. By 1940, the use of much heavier fighter armament in Europe had forced American aircraft designers to follow suit.

A movement outside the plane on the left caught his eye, and he saw a man in a flight suit approaching. "Not wasting any time getting familiar, I see," the man commented. "Keep at it while I preflight my airplane." Alan continued looking around the cockpit. A few minutes later, the man came back and Alan scrambled out of the cockpit.

"You must be Alan Ericsson. My name is Earl Walker. Please call me Earl."

"Pleased to meet you, Earl. Please call me Alan," he said, shaking hands.

"It's got a lot more horsepower and a lot less inertia than the SNJ. Any questions or concerns so far, Alan?"

Alan replied, "It looks small and powerful, all right, and I see that it's back to narrow main gear."

"A friend of mine once said that it's like going down your driveway in a barrel on top of a single roller skate." Walker laughed. "Actually, it's no worse than the SBU. It's just that things happen a little faster."

"What's it like cranking the gear up and down?" asked Alan. Ground school had described the unusual Grumman retraction mechanism, which consisted of a big crank in the cockpit that was connected by shafts, gears, and chains to the landing gear. The crank was used for raising and lowering the gear. It was a reliable and robust system and not subject to leaks like hydraulically actuated mechanisms were.

"Not much to it—more of a nuisance, I think. Raising the gear takes a fair amount of force on the crank, but there's a ratchet to prevent the gear from going back down again. On the other hand, lowering the gear is easy; it wants to go down by itself due to gravity. The tricky part is that the friction brake must be adjusted so that the gear goes down fairly easily, but not so easily that the crank pulls itself out of your hand. If the friction is light and the crank comes out of your hand, the crank will come around so fast that it could break your arm."

"Wow, I'll remember that. I hear the airplane spins very easily, as well—maybe too easily?"

"Yes, it spins easily, but it comes out again reliably when you get the nose down and reverse the rudder. We'll try to avoid spins at first. For that reason, I want you to refrain from any acrobatic maneuvers until I tell you otherwise. Trust me—the great maneuverability of the airplane will tempt you to do acrobatics, but hold off for now." Walker paused. "Well, Alan, I think we ought to see if this old girl has any obvious flaws," he said with a smile.

So far, Alan liked Walker's genial, relaxed manner. Walker stood back and watched and commented while Alan did the preflight inspection, and then Alan climbed back into the cockpit and Walker went over the controls and instruments with him.

Finally, Walker said, "Okay, let's go flying. I'll take off behind you. We'll go west and practice over Mobile Bay at around 5,000 feet. Just come back here if we get separated and lose radio contact." Walker got down off the wing and walked over to his airplane.

Soloing in an unfamiliar airplane right off the bat could not be avoided with single-seater plane types. Alan thought it was an additional challenge, but nearly all the students seemed to be able to handle it.

The starting procedure was similar to the SBU, and the two ground crewmen were waiting to begin. When the engine was idling contentedly, Alan looked over at Walker's airplane, and saw him make the hand signals to go ahead and taxi out. Alan started taxiing toward the active runway, two three left, and Walker followed. S-turns were required, as usual. There was a small queue at the end of the runway, and they both did their run-ups. When they got to the head of the queue, Alan contacted the tower, which cleared him and Walker for a formation takeoff.

Alan taxied out onto the runway, with Walker closely following. He locked the tail wheel, and opened the throttle. The acceleration was exhilarating; it was quite a lot faster than either the SNJ or SBU. He lifted off and, at 800 feet, he pulled the power back to climb, switched the control stick to his left hand, and then began cranking up the gear with his right. As he threw his whole upper body into turning the crank, he could not help moving the stick back and forth slightly with his left, so the airplane bobbed up and down as it climbed. This characteristic movement told everybody watching that the airplane was a Grumman. The crank took almost thirty turns. When he finished, his right arm was tired and the airplane was already at 2,000 feet. With the gear stowed away, the little fighter shot up into the sky. Alan found himself smiling.

He turned right and headed due west. Before long, Walker was close by on his right. They were five miles out, and Alan switched frequencies and contacted Walker. He continued climbing to 5,000 feet and leveled off. It was springtime in western Florida, and everything was lush and green.

When they were over Mobile Bay, Walker had Alan do the usual maneuvers to get familiar with a new airplane. Walker skillfully stayed in loose formation with Alan. He started with 360-degree turns both ways, and then he had Alan do a series of stalls with the power on and off and the gear up and down. Alan sweated as he worked the big landing-gear crank for the first few times, but then he opened the canopy and soon began to feel more comfortable with it. Following this, Walker had Alan do short climbs and descents, some with turns.

When they were through with the air work, they headed for the Clay Pits, which was another of the outlying practice fields, for some landings and takeoffs. Landings were a lot like those in the SBU, except that everything happened faster in the F2F. The F2F tended to wander more quickly on the runway, but it also came back more quickly when corrected. After five takeoffs and landings, Alan was starting to feel somewhat familiar with the airplane. It was quick in every way, and he found that he was starting to like it.

Once those were done, Walker had Alan return to Chevalier Field, where they taxied back to their parking spaces in front of the Advanced Training hangar. They shut down and climbed out, and went into the hangar for coffee.

"Well, what d'ya think of the little bird?" asked Walker.

"I like it a lot. I've never been partial to biplanes, but this one could change my mind. It climbs like a homesick angel. Maybe after I've seen some of its tricky side, I might not like it so well, but so far, so good."

"Good. It's one of my favorites. We'll do a few more familiarization flights, and then we'll get you comfortable with that 'tricky side' with some spins and recoveries. After that, we'll move on to field carrier landings. See you at 1100."

Wednesday, March 12, 1941

Two weeks after beginning training in the F2F, Alan had decided that flying the F2F was as much fun as the SNJ—and aerobatics were even better—although sightseeing was not quite as good.

Finished with field carrier landing practice, Alan had moved on to gunnery a few days earlier. Luckily, Alan had learned something about marksmanship during his summers in West Virginia and Wyoming. At Pensacola, he had been learning deflection shooting, which was a technique that was unique to the US Navy. It was relatively easy to attack another airplane from behind, because the relative motion of the target was small. Deflection shooting was used to attack another airplane from the side or above, greatly increasing the flexibility of the attack, but making it necessary to "lead" the target—to shoot ahead of the other airplane, or to aim for where it would be when the bullets got there. The students fired at target sleeves towed by other airplanes. Each student had a different color of dye on his bullets so that it could be seen afterward which holes were made by whom.

It was 1330, and Alan was warming up his engine for his fourth session of gunnery practice. As he waited, he started watching the F3F on his right. The pilot was having trouble getting the engine started. Alan recognized the ground crewman cranking the inertia starter as Clay Hodge, whom he had gotten to know in the maintenance shops. Alan had developed a lot of respect for him, but he did not recognize the second ground crewman, who was manning the big fire extinguisher.

He noticed that the second man seemed to be bored by the long starting process. He was watching something out on the field rather than the engine being started. Clay pulled the starting crank out of the cowl and engaged the starter. Suddenly, the engine backfired, producing a flash and a bang loud enough that Alan heard it over the rumble of his own engine. Instantly, there was a large pool of flaming gasoline surrounding Clay on the concrete. He backed out of the pool, toward Alan's airplane, as the second man began fighting the fire. Clay was swatting at the flames on his clothes, paying no attention to where he was going. Alan quickly switched off the ignition to his engine, but was afraid it was too late. Clay kept backing up, focused on putting out the flames. Alan bellowed a warning, but it was lost on the busy tarmac. In a horrific moment, pieces of Clay's body were thrown in the air in front of him, cut to pieces by Alan's propeller, which had not had time to coast down.

Alan scrambled out of the cockpit as a wave of nausea hit him. His feet hit the concrete, as he vomited. He pulled himself together and ran around the front of his airplane. There was little he could do when he got there. Alan's stomach heaved again as he saw chunks of Clay's body scattered around.

Alan saw that the second ground crewman had extinguished the fire on the concrete, but the fire had gotten into the airplane. The pilot had jumped out, moved away from his airplane, and was also vomiting. As Alan tried to steady himself, several ground crewmen came running up, and he could hear a siren in the distance—presumably the fire crew on the way.

Alan helped the ground crewmen push his own airplane away so that there was no chance of the fire reaching it. The fire crew arrived and quickly extinguished the fire in the F3F. They began to gently pick up the pieces of Clay's body as Alan started walking back to the hangar to report the accident.

Thursday, March 13, 1941

After ground school in the morning, Alan went to see if he could talk to the Advanced Training skipper, Lieutenant Commander Lloyd Hall. Alan found Hall in his office and introduced himself. Hall was starchy and stiff, like Alan's vision of a naval officer of 1900.

"So, Ericsson, ready to get back to flying this afternoon?" Hall asked with a cordial smile.

"Yes, sir."

"Glad to hear it. These things happen, and we mustn't let them get us down. Now, what's on your mind?"

Hearing this casual dismissal of Hodge's death, Alan began to take a strong dislike to Hall, but he tried to suppress it. "Well, sir, the funeral for Hodge is going to be on Saturday, and I would be glad to represent the squadron there."

"That's nice of you to offer, Ericsson, but that won't be necessary. I'll send my exec."

Alan had been thinking of making the case that sending an officer acquainted with Hodge would be show more respect for him, but he got a feeling that Hall was the kind of officer who would take a dim view of Alan being acquainted with an enlisted man.

"Yes, sir. Has the inquiry into the accident been scheduled?"

"Yes. Tomorrow at 0800, here in Advanced Training Headquarters.

"Very good, sir."

"That will be all, Ericsson."

Friday, March 14, 1941

The inquiry went smoothly because there was no conflict of testimony. The other pilot confirmed Alan's description of what happened. The other ground crewman, who had been manning the fire extinguisher, seemed to Alan to be feeling true remorse for his negligence. Alan decided he had probably learned his lesson, so when he claimed he had only looked away for a moment, Alan did not dispute it.

Thursday, March 20, 1941

Alan had completed the difficult, but rewarding, gunnery phase of Advanced Training, receiving one of the highest scores on the test at the end of the phase. Ed Miller and Wade Buckner had done a little better, though.

Dive-bombing came next. This consisted of dropping small practice bombs on targets in clearings out in the forest. The US Navy had developed their own technique of dive-bombing. The dive angle was extremely steep—about seventy degrees, which made it feel like the plane was headed straight down. Due to the steep angle of descent, the bomb, when released, hit the point that the airplane had been aimed at when the bomb was released, provided the airplane was flying straight ahead, not slipping, or pitching up or down. This made it a much more accurate type of bombing than any other. By rolling the airplane during the dive, the steep angle also allowed the pilot to correct his path to some extent for the maneuvers of a ship target, rather than having to anticipate them at the start of the dive.

Alan was set to make his first practice dive-bombing run. His squadron would practice by diving one by one on a large target with a bull's-eye. They would each drop a practice bomb, which was a small smoke bomb.

He was told to enter his dive by starting a split-S maneuver, which started with a half roll to an inverted attitude. Once upside down, the nose was gently pulled down through the vertical into the seventy-degree dive. He would then continue the dive to 2,500 feet, drop the bomb, and pull out. While in the dive, he would line up the target in the bomb sight, which had a ball instrument in it that needed to remain centered as he dropped the bomb so that the airplane would not be in a skid when he released the bomb. At the same time, he would try to keep the stick steady with his right hand and not to pitch up or down as he pulled the bomb release handle with his left.

The initial practice runs were done from 8,000 feet. Alan's group of students got into line-astern formation, about 500 feet apart. He remembered to open the canopy and shift the propeller to high pitch for the dive. When his turn came, he rolled the F2F over, closed the throttle, and pulled the nose down with the stick. He felt himself become light in the seat. As he stopped the maneuver at around seventy degrees, he completely lost contact with the seat and fell against the seat belt. He jabbed his left arm out quickly to grasp the glare shield and stopped his upper body from falling, just missing banging his nose on the bomb sight. With the canopy open, the roar of the wind built up rapidly as his airspeed climbed.

Coming down at 400 feet per second, he did not have long to stabilize the dive. After his clumsy start, Alan struggled to keep the target centered in the sight and the plane flying straight. He was still wandering when he released the bomb at 2,500 feet. With the ground rushing up at him at a terrifying rate, he immediately pulled the nose up to start the pullout. He felt himself becoming heavy in the seat, and his vision began to narrow under the g-force. He leveled off at 800 feet, feeling harried and afraid his bomb could have gone anywhere in a large area. Evidently, dive-bombing was another skill that would take some time to learn, at best. He found out later that no one in the group had hit the target, and this was not unusual on the first run.

Saturday, March 22, 1941

Alan now looked forward to the regular arrival of Jennifer's letters on Saturday.

Washington, D. C.
March 16, 1941

Dear Alan,

I am glad you're having such a good time with the F2F. Field carrier landing practice sounds very difficult, but not as scary as the real thing. Gunnery should be interesting, maybe even fun.

ONI will be getting its new permanent director this week. He is Captain Kitt, fresh from duty as a naval attaché in London. He is reputed to be no shrinking violet, and we have high hopes that he may be able to get the CNO to rein in Admiral Turner. Otherwise, my work continues to go well. I feel like I am starting to make a real contribution, and that is very encouraging to me.

In another month I think it might be warm enough to use my balcony occasionally. It faces south, and it will be shaded by a big oak tree when the leaves come out.

I have been looking into eastern Pennsylvania as a place to go on our honeymoon. I have never been there, and there are lots of interesting things to see, like the historic center of Philadelphia and the Pennsylvania Dutch country. Also there are some nice little inns to stay at. What do you think?

Keep telling me all about your flying. Your training is changing more frequently and it sounds exciting.

Oodles of love,

Jennifer

Sunday, March 23, 1941

Alan wrote back on Sunday, as usual.

Pensacola Naval Air Station

March 23, 1941

Dear Jennifer,

I hope the new director of ONI is able to get the CNO to rein in Admiral Turner. It seems that this problem is partly the fault of the CNO, who chooses not to make the director of War Plans stay on his own turf. I was very glad to hear that your work is going well and you are feeling encouraged about it.

I like your idea of going to eastern Pennsylvania on our honeymoon. It should be pleasantly warm there. As you say, there are lots of things to see and nice places to stay. When I find out where I will be going afterward, we can start to work out the details.

I finished gunnery last Wednesday. I did quite well on the final test, close to the top of the class, but two of my friends did a little better.

Spring has been here for a while. It should get to Washington by April, pretty soon now.

On Thursday, I started dive-bombing, dropping a practice bomb on a target out in the forest. Flying nearly straight down was pretty scary at first, and I was not able to keep the crosshairs in the sight on the target, so my bomb went wild. The pullout back to level flight was also fairly scary. I spent some time with my instructor going over what went wrong and I got some additional hints. I made two drops on Friday and they were better. I think I will be able to do a lot better when I have enough experience to not be distracted by all the excitement. I will have to learn fast, because we move on to dogfighting in another week and a half.

Keep telling me as much as you can about the conflicts inside Main Navy. It is a world I have had little access to, so it is fascinating.

Tons of love,

Alan

CHAPTER FOURTEEN

Fighter Training

Wednesday, April 2, 1941

Alan arrived at the Advanced Training hangar at 0610. He had been looking forward to this phase of his training—dogfighting— for some time, and he was anxious to get started. In a month, he would be asked for his preference among fighters, dive-bombers, and torpedo bombers even though, as with his assignment to carrier planes after Squadron One, no one seemed to know how the selection process worked. He would find out which type he was assigned to when he received his squadron assignment right after graduation from Pensacola. At this point, Alan remained unsure about whether he would prefer fighters or dive-bombers.

He checked to see which plane he was assigned to, gathered his gear, and went out to the airplane. It was a sunny day with clear air and only a few clouds. The temperature at dawn was in the upper fifties.

The students changed instructors at the beginning of the dog-fighting phase, but continued to fly the F2F or F3F as before. Alan was scheduled with his new instructor, Lieutenant Lee Jackson, at 0630, and Jackson arrived at 0625. He was handsome, reminding Alan of the stars in Western movies. His clothes looked very neat and clean. *Sharp and meticulous*, thought Alan.

"You must be Lieutenant j.g. Alan Ericsson," he said, extending his hand and showing a thin smile. "Lieutenant Lee Jackson."

"Very pleased to meet you," Alan replied, smiling. Jackson's expression changed to a smirk.

"Well, you have quite a reputation to live up to: Sucking up to Admiral Powers—the 'golden boy' of Squadron Three. I guess you're used to being a wheeler-dealer, but as long as you're my student, you'll have to master each step and earn every advance." His accent was definitely Southern, maybe from Tennessee or Arkansas. *He sure has formed a poor impression of me, without waiting to meet me. Perhaps it's a bias against Yankees.*

Alan had not been subjected to a boot-camp style provocation like this since he'd left the Naval Academy, which seemed like a different lifetime. He felt entitled to be offended, but he quickly decided to take this as another test of his tact and discretion and remained patient.

"Well, it sounds like there's a lot of noise on your branch of the mountain telegraph," Alan replied. "In regard to earning my way through each step, that's exactly what I want and expect."

Jackson's smirk vanished and he looked sharply at Alan, evidently surprised. He started to speak, but paused. The next time he spoke, he sounded more like a teacher. "Today we're going to do a little exercise to introduce you to dogfighting. I'll let you get on my tail, and then you'll try to stay on my tail while I try to shake you off and get on your tail. We'll do it several times."

"Okay."

"We'll follow the tracks north to Molino and climb to 6,000 feet. I'll follow you out. Go ahead and do your preflight."

"Aye, Aye."

Alan completed the preflight inspection and got the engine started and warmed up. He glanced over at Jackson's airplane, and Jackson gave him a thumbs-up. They taxied out and took off on runway three one right. Alan turned right and headed north, and Jackson followed.

When they reached Molino at 6,000 feet, Jackson signaled Alan to get on his tail. Alan did so, and Jackson flew straight and level for about twenty seconds before suddenly rolling into a hard turn to the left. Alan rolled left and followed. He was falling behind, so he opened the throttle and turned tighter to cut inside. He was surprised that Jackson let him do that because he was close to being back on Jackson's tail again. Jackson suddenly rolled back horizontally and abruptly pulled up into the start of a loop. Alan tried to follow, but he did not have enough entry speed to make it to the top of the loop. He stalled and fell through. Somehow, Jackson had managed to preserve enough speed to get over the top of the loop, and he dove down on Alan. Alan climbed straight ahead, and Jackson passed behind him. Alan made a 180-degree turn to the right to keep Jackson in front of him, but as he came around, he could not see Jackson. Then he saw Jackson in the last place he'd wanted to see him. While he had been turning right, Jackson had also been turning right to stay behind him, pulling onto Alan's tail. Alan sighed as the adrenaline rush subsided. He'd expected this end result, but he was a bit discouraged by how quickly Jackson was able to accomplish it.

They repeated the exercise two more times. Alan found Jackson's maneuvers hard to predict, but he noticed that Jackson always ended up with an altitude advantage, which he used to maneuver onto Alan's tail. The third exercise took about three times as long as the first, so Alan felt like he was making progress. After that, Jackson signaled for him to return to the field. Alan was sweating and felt like he had been exercising hard. Jackson followed Alan back to Chevalier Field, and Alan went back into the hangar for coffee after shutting down. After a few minutes, Jackson appeared from the direction of the squadron office.

Jackson said, "The first exercise went about the way I expected, and it did not take very long. I guess you haven't been breaking the rules and dogfighting with the other students at every chance, the way some of them do . . . . Each time it took longer to get on your tail, so you're starting to learn." He paused.

Alan replied, "Obviously, I had trouble anticipating your moves, but I did notice that each time, you were able to get an altitude advantage. Is there some way to counter that tactic?"

Jackson looked sharply at Alan. "You're starting to catch on. Some people come here thinking that dogfighting is made up of tight horizontal turns, but you noticed that vertical motion had a lot to do with it. You studied kinetic and potential energy in school, so you know that your kinetic energy comes from your speed and your potential energy from your altitude. You can trade them back and forth to accomplish your goal. You want to keep your total energy—kinetic plus potential—as high as possible. That means that you want as much speed and altitude as possible, so you want to keep the throttle wide open most of the time. In the first exercise, I lured you into a tight turn, and you were bleeding away your energy with the induced drag. Meanwhile, I didn't turn as hard and preserved my energy, which is why I could make it through the top of the loop and you could not.

"One exception to the method of preserving energy may occur when you need to get someone off your tail, so you chop the throttle and skid to slow down suddenly, hoping he'll be caught going too fast and overshoot you. That's a desperate move, though, because if it doesn't work, you're a sitting duck.

"We're simulating a fight between two airplanes of the same make and model with the same performance. In real combat, that won't happen. Besides differences in the dogfighting skills of the pilots, the enemy airplane will be more capable in some ways and, hopefully, less capable in others. You may know something about the enemy airplane from intelligence or reports of previous dog-fights, but you may need to find out on the fly. Two of the most important characteristics for dogfights are power loading and wing loading. High power loading gives you better acceleration and energy, and therefore a better ability to use vertical maneuvers. Low wing loading gives better turning, either horizontally or vertically. Fighters have tended to evolve toward higher power loading, and *higher* wing loading, giving up some turning capability for better acceleration and higher energy.

"Another important characteristic is roll rate. The enemy might have a better turning capability and will be able to stick to your tail, but if you have the higher roll rate, you can flip into a turn the other way and get away. You might even be able to flip back and get on his tail.

"Later this morning, we'll go out and do it again. I'll show you more maneuvers that you haven't seen yet. After that, we'll see what your weak points are and start working on them. Right now, I need to get to base headquarters for some office business I just heard about. My wife needed the car today, so I need a ride. Do you happen to have a car here?"

"Yes. I usually walk from the BOQ, but I do have my car today."

The temperature had risen into the seventies, and it was becoming a pleasant day. They walked out of the back of the hangar to the parking area. As Alan walked up to the Buick, Jackson stopped and scowled.

"Is that your car?"

"It runs better than it looks."

Jackson opened the door and climbed gingerly onto the passenger's seat with a look suggesting that he was afraid of soiling his clothes. Alan was glad he had recently had the seat recovered. He stepped on the clutch, turned on the ignition, and moved the spark lever on the steering column smartly from retard to advance and back again. The engine sprang to life instantly and settled into a contented idle.

Jackson looked startled and said, "Hey, *that* was . . . cute. How the hell did you do *that*?"

"If you shut off the engine with the spark retarded and the mixture rich, the engine will sometimes stop with one cylinder past top dead-center and the spark plug about ready to fire. You have to have at least six cylinders, and the engine stops in the right place less than half the time, but it's easy to try it before a normal start." Alan started driving toward base headquarters.

"Hmm. You flip the spark lever, and that one cylinder fires and cranks the engine so the rest of the cylinders start. That's pretty slick. There are some real advantages to the manual controls that old cars have, I suppose. But I thought you'd be driving a Cadillac V-16 or a Lincoln V-12," said Jackson, with a derisive smile.

"I'd like something a lot more maneuverable than that. I got this car from another student to use while I'm here, and it's worked out fine."

"Well, I never thought a society boy from Boston would be caught dead in a rattletrap like this. Who keeps it running?"

"I do."

"Where did you learn how to work on cars?"

"I worked for a car dealer during the summer after seventh, eighth, and ninth grades, working my way up to mechanic before I was old enough to have a driver's license. I went to school with some society boys later, but most of them would hardly speak to me."

"I'll be damned. Maybe there's something to what you said about noise on the telegraph." Jackson fell silent as they continued on to base headquarters.

Saturday, April 26, 1941

Alan had not forgotten about the struggles of ONI. He suspected that the conflict might be having a discouraging effect on ONI—and Jennifer in particular—although she did not say so. He was wondering how the new director of ONI was getting along. Jennifer had not mentioned him in her last few letters, but maybe today he would have news.

Washington, D. C.
April 20, 1941

Dear Alan,

By now you are probably an expert at dogfighting. I wonder if now you would prefer fighters over dive-bombers. I want to hear all about it.

Well, the conflict between ONI and Admiral Turner finally came to a head. Admiral Turner has been putting out intelligence estimates with no reference to ONI. Captain Kitt brought the matter up before the Deputy CNO. Captain Kitt and Admiral Turner had a stormy session in the office of the Deputy CNO, who took them to see the CNO. From what I hear, the CNO hates fighting and has a great respect for Admiral Turner, so Captain Kitt was doomed from the start and was overruled. Nothing was put in writing, however, leaving plenty of room for further misunderstanding and conflict. As you might imagine, respect for the CNO has plunged in some quarters.

My boss, Captain McCollum, was disgusted, but he is managing to take it in stride. He said Admiral Turner has little experience with intelligence. Hopefully Admiral Turner will move on eventually, but he has been at War Plans less than six months. I continue to enjoy my work, but in ONI we all wonder what use our work will be put to now.

Enough bad news. I have been using my balcony, and it is delightful. The oak tree is about to leaf out, which will make the balcony habitable in really warm weather.

I have compiled a big list of things to do and places to stay in eastern Pennsylvania, probably enough for a month, so we can pick and choose. It will be so much fun to spend some time with you!

Write and tell me what you are doing now in your training. Also don't forget to tell me what train you are coming on when you come to Washington, as soon as you know. Only three more weeks before you graduate and I get to see you! I can't wait.

Oodles of love,

Jennifer

Sunday, April 27, 1941

Pensacola Naval Air Station

April 27, 1941

Dear Jennifer,

It sounds like the shootout at the OK Corral in the CNO's office. The result is quite disappointing. Basically Admiral Turner is using bully tactics to get his way, and since he has impressed the CNO, he gets away with it. As you say, he will move on eventually.

I'm glad you're enjoying warmer weather. It is starting to get hot here, not so pleasant as it was.

I just finished with the dogfighting phase of training. I developed a lot of respect for Lee Jackson and we have become friends. Although it was easy for him to get on my tail at the beginning, by the end, he couldn't do it anymore unless I made a mistake. You were reading my mind: I have decided that my preference is for fighters, rather than dive-bombers. Now it seems like it could have been a mistake to be first in the class in the test at the end of dive-bombing.

Coming up we get one week of training each on more aerobatics, night formation flying, and a checkout in the TBD, our current torpedo bomber. The aerobatics should be fun. The night formation work is likely to be scary.

Checking out in the TBD should be interesting, but not really fun. Torpedo bombers are inherently larger and less maneuverable than other carrier aircraft, because they have to carry the weight of the torpedo (about a ton). About ten years ago, the top aeronautical brass decided that dive-bombers were likely to be more effective than torpedo bombers, and torpedo bombing has been playing second fiddle ever since. As a result the TBD has been kept in the fleet until it is obsolescent, although a far superior replacement, the Grumman TBF, is now on the way. Torpedoes are so expensive that the torpedo pilots do not get to practice dropping them. Not only that, they almost never even carry one. The airplane can also be used as a horizontal bomber, and it even has a place for a third crewmember to crawl under the cockpit and look down through the bottom of the fuselage with a bomb sight. The TBD can carry twice the bomb load of the typical dive-bomber, but this type of bombing is much less accurate than dive-bombing.

Enough of the work talk. I am glad you are putting your Pennsylvania guidebooks to good use. Your list will be most helpful when we actually hit the road.

I can't wait to spend some time with you too! I am scheduled to leave here at 1320 on Sunday, May 18, and arrive in Washington at 1930 on May 19 on the Southern Railway train number 88 from Atlanta. See you then!

Tons of love,

Alan

CHAPTER FIFTEEN

Completion of Flight Training

Friday, May 16, 1941

Alan had his last flight in the TBD, which was his last flight in the Pensacola curriculum. He had completed his flight training.As he walked back up the rise to the BOQ from Chevalier Field for the last time, nostalgia had already overtaken him. His time at Pensacola had flown by. It had mostly been good, but it was tinged with sadness from the loss of two friends in accidents.

Saturday, May 17, 1941

A simple graduation ceremony for Alan's class was held in the morning. After the ceremony, all the graduating students received their orders to report to their new operating squadrons.

Alan was headed for Al's Castle Bar to celebrate and say goodbye to his friends on the warm, sunny evening. He realized that he might not see these friends again for a long time, if ever.

Alan was proud that he had made it through, and he was wearing his wings of gold on his chest. Unlike the dolphins pin worn by submarine officers, though, these gold wings did not signify that he was fully qualified for his assignment. He still needed to complete his carrier qualification, which consisted of making enough carrier landings to prove that he could do it consistently, and he looked forward to being welcomed into the close-knit fraternity of carrier aviators after that. By comparison, a submarine officer earned his dolphins roughly a year after completion of submarine school, when he had demonstrated proficiency to his captain in all duties required.

Alan was riding with Les Travis in his 1939 DeSoto that evening. Alan had sold the old Buick to a new student for sixty dollars. As the number of students at Pensacola was increasing, the local price of used cars was going up, and Alan was pleased with his small profit. Les pulled into the parking lot and they saw Rudi Fischer's big Indian parked next to Wade Buckner's 1938 LaSalle. They walked in and found Rudi, Wade, and Ed Miller holding a table. They sat down and listened to the music, which had a Benny Goodman ring to it.

June appeared and got Alan's and Les's requests for pints of Ace High, as usual. When she returned with the beer, she put Alan's in front of him and then put her arm around his neck and winked at Les. By now, everyone knew that she had become sweet on Les. He had been a little hesitant to jump into Frank's shoes, however. There had not been enough time before graduation for them to get serious, but they had enjoyed each other's company.

Les's eyebrows went up, and he blurted out, "Hey, June, where's my beer?"

"Coming, Les," June replied as she darted around the table to Les. She placed his beer in front of him and kissed him on the cheek.

Les blushed, smiled at her, and put his arm around her waist. "With service like that, I might have to have more than one," he said.

"Good," she said before heading to another table, where empty glasses were raised.

There was a pause in the conversation while each took a pull on his beer. The bands were changing places, and Alan was pleased to see that the new band on stage looked like a hillbilly group that he had not heard before. They had a vocalist who sang "I

Saw a Rainbow at Midnight," one of Alan's favorites, and was accompanied by banjo and guitar.

After the song, Ed said, "Well, I'd like to hear what orders each of you got. I got a lulu! My orders are to report to Fighting Six on the *Enterprise*. I'm real happy."

Rudi said, "You always wanted to be in fighters. I hear that's a good outfit, too. I got orders to join Torpedo Two on the *Lexington*, so I'm real happy, too—torpeckers being my first choice." He grinned widely.

Wade spoke up next. "Well, my orders are to report to Fighting Three on the *Saratoga*. I'm tickled pink."

"Fighting Three is commanded by Jimmie Thach, I think. I hear he's top notch," said Les. "I'll see you aboard *Sara*, because I'm going to Scouting Three," he said with a smile.

"Well, we have three different carriers so far," said Ed. "What about you, Stringy?"

"I got orders saying I'll be joining a bombing squadron," Alan replied, "which is a little disappointing, because my first choice was fighters, but I have to admit that dive-bombers were a very close second. The rub is that they didn't give me a squadron. I'm ordered to Norfolk, where I'll be notified of my squadron assignment, which seems damned odd to me."

"You were right up there with me and Ed in gunnery and grab-ass, so you could have gotten into fighters," Wade joked with a grin. "But you spoiled it by doing too well in dive-bombing, Mr. Top-of-the-Class."

"Yeah, that's right," said Ed. "The fact that you're reporting to Norfolk must mean you'll be on the *Wasp* or the *Ranger*, since the other carriers are in the Pacific, but getting no squadron assignment *is* queer. At least you're going to a bombing squadron. You're lucky they didn't snag you for an instructor after checking out in the back seat of the SNJ. But wait a minute. *Wasp* and

Ranger don't have bombing squadrons, only fighting and scouting, two of each. Maybe that's going to change."

Alan had already considered all of this, with mixed emotions. He knew that the *Wasp* and the *Ranger* were smaller carriers, designed to fit within tonnage limits specified in the arms-limitation treaties. They were considered slightly inferior assignments, but being an instructor was always the least desirable, so at least he hadn't ended up with that.

Alan replied, "Yeah, I talked to my friend Harry Tolman, and he said he'd nose around and see what he could find out for me."

There was a pause while they listened to the music. After June appeared and took an order for another round, Alan said, "I wish Frank were here. He deserved to make it through."

"Damn right," said Les. There were nods around the table, and they fell silent for awhile.

Rudi picked the conversation back up. "Are you gonna drive that ancient Buick back to Boston, Alan?"

"No, I planned to sell it when I was ready to leave, but it went the first day I posted it—last Wednesday," said Alan. "How about you? Are you headed for San Diego on your big Indian?"

"Yep, with a visit home to Wisconsin along the way," replied Rudi with a big grin. "Didn't you say you were going to get married as soon as you got through here?"

"That's right. A week from today is the big day, and Harry Tolman is going to be best man. It's lucky I'm headed for Norfolk, actually, since my fiancée is working for ONI. At least this way, I can see her on weekends."

"That is lucky. I'm also planning to go home on the way to San Diego," said Les, "I could give you a ride out to San Diego, Ed, if you wanted."

Ed replied, "Thanks for the offer, Les, but Wade already offered. We plan to stop by both our homes along the way. It sounds like we've all got our orders and made our plans, so it's all over, in the blink of an eye. I'm going to miss you guys."

"We've all had lots of ups and downs here, that's for sure. Overall, though, I think it's been a lot of fun, and it was great to get to know you guys. I hope our paths cross again," said Alan.

There were nods of agreement all around the table, as each man looked at all the others, trying to record the image forever.

CHAPTER SIXTEEN

Home and Marriage

Monday, May 19, 1941

Alan had departed Pensacola on the train at 1320 Central time on Sunday. He took the same series of trains north that he had taken for the southbound trip, only in reverse and getting off in Washington, DC, to see Jennifer, instead of going all the way up to Boston. After changing trains in Atlanta at 0100 Monday morning, he managed to recover the lost sleep on the train Monday afternoon, so he was refreshed when the train arrived on time in Washington at 1930.

As the train eased into the station, Alan began searching for Jennifer on the crowded platform. All of a sudden, there she was. He jumped up and waved furiously. She caught the movement and began to walk quickly to follow the train, which soon stopped. He came out, dropped his luggage, and rushed into her open arms. Alan was surprised to find that she was full of energy as well as joy. They danced around in circles, hugging and kissing while tears of joy ran down their cheeks. After a while, as passersby began to stare at them, they stopped and collected themselves.

When he'd had a moment to breathe, he said, "Oh, it's so good to be with you. I want to hold you for a week!"

She giggled and said, "I would like that."

"You look and feel wonderful, Jennifer. Washington must agree with you."

"You do too, Alan. The long train ride didn't tire you out, I see. Flying must be good for you. It *has* been a busy week for me, getting everything done so I could be gone for two weeks. I left the office at noon and took a nap this afternoon, which made me feel much better."

They walked to a nearby restaurant, where Jennifer had made a reservation for 2000. They got settled at their table and ordered a bottle of Cabernet Sauvignon, and then Jennifer turned to him and asked, "Well, let's hear the bad news. What far corner of the world are they going to send you to?"

He grinned as he replied, "You won't believe it. I'm going to Norfolk!"

She cried out, "Oh, Alan, that's marvelous! Yippee!" She grabbed his arm and squeezed it. People at nearby tables turned to look at them. "You couldn't get any closer to Washington!"

The waiter returned, served the wine, and took their food orders.

After the waiter left, Jennifer turned to Alan and asked, "Did you get your squadron assignment?"

"Well, not quite. There was a simple graduation ceremony last Saturday. Right after that, we got our orders. Mine were to report to Norfolk on June 2 for assignment to an unspecified bombing squadron. Everyone else was ordered to a particular squadron, and all my friends got their first choices."

"I'm sorry you didn't get your first choice, and no specific squadron sounds odd."

"It was a little disappointing to be assigned to dive-bombers, but they were always a very close second to fighters for me, so I'm not *un*happy. It's disconcerting not to be assigned to a squadron, though. I talked to Harry Tolman, and he did some nosing around to see if he could find out what happened. He did find out how I got assigned to dive-bombers, which is something. He said that Lee Jackson argued strongly for me to be assigned to fighters, and Earl Walker was pretty neutral. Lieutenant Commander Hall, the skipper of Advanced Training, said that I wasn't aggressive enough to be a good fighter pilot, which was strongly denied by both Jackson and Walker, but Hall had the last word. I have to admit that I have disliked Hall from the first time I met him. I guess the feeling was mutual. Of course, it didn't help that I did so well in dive-bombing. Harry couldn't find out why I wasn't assigned to a specific squadron, but he tried to reassure me that it will all work out."

The waiter served their food, and they started eating.

Jennifer brightened and said, "I just realized something . . . Yeah . . . That's it! I'm pretty sure I know which squadron you're assigned to. If I'm right, no one could tell you without revealing secrets, which is why you haven't been told yet, but they'll have to tell you soon after you report to Norfolk. Be patient. I don't think you'll be disappointed, Alan."

He smiled and said, "You're starting to sound like an intelligence person, you scalawag. Anyway, I've been given two weeks' leave. My orders say that I'm not expected before June 2, which I think implies that it wouldn't do any good to report in early. That gives us a week for the honeymoon. We could come back down here to Washington at the end of the honeymoon, instead of going back to Boston, and use the whole week."

"That's right. There's no need to go back to Boston, and we'll have more time for sightseeing. I can't wait!"

"Me either. Speaking of Washington, what's your news?"

"Well . . . It has been a nice spring for me. I love my apartment, and I'm enjoying my balcony. I like my job, but the atmosphere in the office is discouraging."

"From what you said in your letters, that's very understandable. It still must be an exciting place to work."

"It is. That's what makes it tolerable. And I'm working with good people. I'm certainly getting acquainted with bureaucratic infighting that has progressed to the point that it could cause real damage. Maybe if it finally does, then the situation will be repaired. It will be interesting to see what happens."

"That's terrible. It makes me angry to hear about it."

"Anyway, there's *good* news for us. We're going to be married, and you're going to Norfolk, and that's plenty good enough for me."

"For me, too. I'm excited about going to Pennsylvania for the honeymoon."

"It should be great fun." She paused and looked at him. "I think I'll have plenty of time this week to take care of any last-minute details. You're going to be a single man for only a few more days. Are you all set, Alan?"

"Ready for launch, ma'am," he said, saluting.

She laughed.

He paused and said, "Mom told me that Winnie and Jenny are so pleased to be part of it. It was sweet of you to include them. Thank you."

"It was all part of a dark plot cooked up by your mom and Gertrude," Jennifer said, grinning. "There's something about your mom—she's able to draw people out. I think Gertrude is more relaxed with her than she is with our mom."

"It's hard to imagine anyone not being relaxed with your mom when she's not asking pointed questions, but family relations are complicated. Is putting on a wedding getting your mom or dad into a tizzy?"

"No, thank goodness. I think they're really enjoying it."

"That's wonderful! My mom started to get a little overwrought at one point before Megan's wedding, but she recognized it. She hardly ever drinks beer, but I remember that, one day, she stopped what she was doing and had a beer in the middle of the day to help relax herself. She felt much better after that."

As they finished their meal, the conversation turned to their plan to travel together to Boston by train the next day.

Saturday, May 24, 1941

The wedding was a joyous occasion. Roger had arranged for the ceremony to be held at 1600 in the Warrens' regular church, which was the stately brick Church of the Redeemer on Meriam Street in Lexington Center. Discussion with the priest beforehand had prepared Alan for the fact that the ceremony would be quite elaborate. Jennifer had suggested that they not follow the asymmetrical tradition of only the bride receiving a wedding ring; instead, both would present rings to each other. Alan liked the idea, and they had decided to exchange simple silver bands.

Roger had also arranged for the reception to be held at the Belmont Hill School, from which David had graduated. It was a private boys' school with a pleasant campus in Belmont, about a fifteen-minute drive from the church. The school was still in session and it had some boarding students, but the school only offered a five-day boarding program, so the campus was quiet on weekends. A large tent was set up on one of the lawns for the reception, and there was plenty of parking since the faculty weren't on campus. Having worried about the weather—which could easily have been either cool and wet or hot and sticky at the end of May—they were fortunate that the weather was clear and dry and the temperature was about seventy degrees.

It was the first wedding put on by the Warrens, and Alan suspected that the event probably had its anxious moments for them, particularly for Marjorie. As the day wore on, he was glad to see that both Roger and Marjorie seemed to be pleased. Alan felt it went quite smoothly, and he thought it seemed that way for Jennifer, too.

Alan knew beforehand that Jennifer had been delighted with her dress, but he had not been allowed to see it until she came down the aisle. He gaped and beamed at her when he first saw it. It was not the traditional white, but a royal blue that matched her eyes. It was much less ornate than most, he thought. It was the most beautiful wedding dress he had ever seen, and Winnie and Jenny were her flower girls in matching dresses in a darker shade of blue. He was carefully attired in his full dress-white uniform, complete with sword. On his chest were his gold wings; below them were his submarine dolphins.

Both Victoria and Harry added charm and grace to the occasion. Victoria was maid of honor and Harry was the best man, also in his dress uniform. Victoria toasted the bride and told a charming anecdote about watching Jennifer and Alan as they had been surprised to find each other in her parents' front hall a year earlier. Harry toasted the groom and told the story of the Down-Checker with entertaining humor. After an early supper, David had arranged for a square dance to be put on by the musicians and caller from the square dance club he belonged to. They threw in a Virginia Reel contra-dance, as well. Most of the guests seemed to truly enjoy the reception. A beautiful young woman whom Alan did not know caught the bouquet. Later, Jennifer told him that she was someone David had met at his square dance group and had his eye on.

Jennifer and Alan, both properly covered with confetti, were driven away by Nat Steele a little after 2100 in his 1929 Franklin Speedster with the top down. He took them to Brookline, where they changed their clothes and took off on their honeymoon in the Tatra, pleased that they had successfully evaded the traditional markings and noisemakers on either car. They had a short drive on the Worcester Turnpike out to Framingham, where they had reserved a room at a motor hotel—a new experience for them. After checking in, they took one more drink of champagne and went to bed at about 2300, tired and happy.

CHAPTER SEVENTEEN

Joining Bombing Five

Monday, June 2, 1941

Monday dawned bright and beautiful in Norfolk, Virginia. Alan walked into the Norfolk Naval Air Station Headquarters at 0750 and spoke to the yeoman, who told him that he would have to wait to see the operations officer.

Alan thought back over the previous week while he waited. He and Jennifer had had some great times together in the past, but the honeymoon outshone them all. The intimacy and privacy of the trip added a new level of enjoyment for each of them. They spent the week visiting Philadelphia and other historic sites, such as Valley Forge and the site of Washington's crossing of the Delaware River. Perhaps their favorite place to visit was the Pennsylvania Dutch country around Lancaster. They stayed in a different place every night, finding several delightful small inns.

On Saturday, they continued south to Washington, DC, and spent the night in Jennifer's apartment. They decided that they would try spending Saturday night together every two or three weeks, alternating between Washington and Norfolk. They could also talk by telephone occasionally without spending a week's pay, so they decided to do that. They parted on Sunday morning, and Alan drove down to Norfolk and checked into the BOQ.

Alan's mind was brought back to the present when he was summoned to the office of the operations officer, Commander Ruel. After greeting Alan, the commander scanned Alan's orders and turned to his personnel folder. "So, you were a submariner. We don't get too many of those."

"Yes, sir, but I know that some of the famous early naval aviators, like Ellyson and Whiting, were submariners."

"You're right," said Ruel, smiling. "There's also Admiral King. Anyway, you came here straight from Pensacola, where you checked out in the back seat of the SNJ. Unusual."

"Yes, sir."

"You must be wondering why you were not given a specific squadron assignment in your orders."

"Yes, sir," Alan replied eagerly.

Ruel said as he smiled again, "The reason involves some secret operations. You're going to know about them soon enough, in any case, so I'm going to tell you now." Ruel's expression became grave. "You understand that you must not reveal what I'm going to tell you to anyone, including your wife, your parents, or even your best friend." He looked at Alan sharply.

"Yes, sir." Alan smiled inwardly at the irony of not letting Jennifer in on the secret.

"Your squadron assignment is Bombing Five."

Alan's mind pounced on this information. "Five" meant that his squadron was assigned to CV-5, the *Yorktown*! There was nothing wrong with that. She was a full-size, modern aircraft carrier—the first of her class. He felt a brief glow of satisfaction. *Wait a minute,* he realized, *the Yorktown is in the Pacific. Why would they send me here? There must be more to the story.* Alan smiled and said, "I have to admit that I was worried about not having a specific squadron assignment, sir. I'm relieved to be assigned to a frontline squadron like Bombing Five."

"I thought that might be the case."

Alan relaxed slightly.

Ruel went on. "Due to the rising tensions in the Atlantic, it was decided to transfer the *Yorktown* to the Atlantic, but to make every effort to keep the transfer secret as long possible. That's why you weren't told what your squadron assignment was. She passed through the Panama Canal at night with all identifying marks covered, and as far as we know, she wasn't identified. She left the canal on May 7, and arrived at Bermuda on May 12." Ruel paused, verifying details and deciding what Alan could know.

So I really am assigned to the Yorktown! The glow rekindled within Alan. He knew that the US Navy base at Bermuda had been given to the US by Britain as part of the destroyers-for-bases deal the previous September, and that it had quickly become an active US Navy base as tensions in the Atlantic rose. Now, a naval air station was being added.

Ruel continued, "Now, here's where things get more complicated. The *Yorktown* underwent maintenance while awaiting the arrival of the *Ranger*. On May 23, the *Yorktown* went out and met the *Ranger* off Bermuda and swapped fighting, scouting, and bombing squadrons before the *Ranger* came into anchor. For the time being, the *Ranger* isn't equipped to accommodate a torpedo squadron, so VT-5 stayed behind on the *Yorktown*. The *Ranger* is doing one more neutrality patrol before returning here on the eleventh. She is scheduled for a major overhaul from mid-July to mid-September, so Bombing Five will be shore based for that time, but it will be transitioning from the BT-1 to the SBD. In September, Bombing Five will go back aboard the *Yorktown*. So you can see you're joining a squadron that's about to make a number of transitions, and you may have the opportunity to fly off the *Ranger* before the *Yorktown*."

"I see, sir. Two airplane types and two carriers should make it exciting."

"Before the *Ranger* gets in here, we should be able to get you checked out in the BT-1. When the *Ranger* gets in, you'll be officially welcomed into the squadron. The squadron will then give you more training, leading to your carrier qualification."

"Very good, sir." Alan's smile kept growing.

A little later, Alan left Base Headquarters with orders to report to Lieutenant Reinhold Rodenheiser at East Field at 1300 to start his checkout in the BT-1.

While he was eating lunch in the cafeteria, he thought about how lucky he was to be assigned to the *Yorktown*. She and her sister, the *Enterprise*, CV-6, were his favorite carriers. He thought back over the history of the US Navy's fleet carriers. The first US Navy carrier, the *Langley*, CV-1, was a converted collier whose purpose was experimental: to develop carrier procedures and equipment. Alan thought the *Langley* was entitled to a proud reputation as a pioneer, but she had been retired from carrier duty and converted to a seaplane tender in 1936. The *Lexington*, CV-2, and the *Saratoga*, CV-3, were big, capable carriers that were commissioned in 1927. They were built on battle cruiser hulls, however, that were available because the battle cruisers they were originally meant to be could not be completed as such under the limitations of the Washington Treaty of 1922. That made them big, fast, and well armored, but much less maneuverable than the later carriers. The hulls also compromised the internal arrangements, when compared to the *Yorktown* class. Alan would never object to assignment on one of those two carriers, which had already established enviable traditions of their own by prominent participation in Fleet Problems, but the *Yorktown* class was the better.

The next carrier, the *Ranger*, CV-4, was the first American aircraft carrier that was designed from the start for that purpose. The *Ranger* and the *Wasp*, CV-7, which was the most recent carrier to enter service, were attempts to make an aircraft carrier that was smaller than the other fleet carriers in order to fit within treaty tonnage limits. Alan had read that compromises in armor and internal compartmentation were made to enable them to operate the same four squadrons as the larger carriers did. Alan thought that these carriers were more vulnerable than the *Yorktown* class. The top brass apparently agreed because these two were assigned to duty in the Atlantic, where the naval threat was thought to be less than in the Pacific. For this duty, the two smaller carriers were assigned two fighting and two scouting squadrons, although they usually operated only one fighting squadron.

The four larger carriers usually operated one squadron of each of the four types: fighting, scouting, bombing, and torpedo. Originally, each squadron type served a distinct purpose. During the 1930s, however, the distinction indicated by the scouting and bombing labels had gradually faded away, so both squadrons were equally proficient in both the scouting and dive-bombing functions, and now they were in the process of being equipped with the same airplane, the SBD.

After lunch, Alan found Rodenheiser's office in a hangar at East Field.

"Have a seat. Let's drop the formality—I go by Rye."

"Okay, sir—I mean, Rye. I go by Alan."

"Okay, Alan, tell me about your recent flying."

Alan sensed that Rye was a no-nonsense, get-things-done type of officer. He described his flying for the past four months.

Rye quickly digested Alan's recent flying experience, and then he explained, "As you can imagine, the BT-1 will feel more like the SNJ or TBD than the F2F. It also has some characteristics that can bite you if you aren't careful. As you get near stall speed, it becomes a pig—the rudder becomes ineffective. In the stall, it will drop a wing and you cannot pick it up with the rudder. If you apply power quickly at low speeds, the same thing will happen, so go-arounds have to be executed very carefully. Likewise with accelerated stalls. Several pilots were killed when the BT-1 first became operational due to these characteristics. We'll practice at altitude so you'll become familiar with how the airplane behaves,

but you'll have to remember to always be careful at low speeds."
He looked sharply at Alan.

"I'm looking forward to getting to know both its good and
bad sides," Alan replied. He had heard a little about the tricky
side of the BT-1 from Earl Walker, and thought that perhaps this
tricky side had something to do with the airplane receiving the
nickname "Borrowed Times."

"Good. Except for the characteristics I just described, it feels
kind of like an oversize SNJ or a scaled-down TBD, and you
shouldn't have any trouble with it." He handed Alan a booklet as
he continued. "Here's the pilot's manual. Take it and read it. The
airplane is right out in front of this hangar, so you can look her
over. We have good weather today, so I think we can get started
flying right away, say around 1600."

"Okay, will do."

Alan left Rye's office and got a Coke out of a machine in the
hangar and then sat down and read the manual. After an hour and
a half, he walked out to look over the BT-1. It was powered by a
slightly more powerful version of the same engine that was in the
SBU and F2F. The traditional, colorful carrier paint scheme had
been replaced by a new, less-visible scheme that Alan had heard
was coming. There was dull blue-gray on the upper surfaces and
light blue-gray on the lower surfaces.

Now that he was going to be flying dive-bombers, Alan recalled what he had learned about current examples from aviation
magazines and Earl Walker. Unlike the older biplane dive-bombers,
such as the SBU, the modern monoplane dive-bombers—which
had no external struts and wires—needed some way of adding drag
during the dive in order to make steep dives safely. Otherwise, they
would get going so fast that they would not be able to pull out at
the bottom without the wings giving way due to the g-force. A
reversible-pitch propeller was tried on the navy's first monoplane

dive-bomber, the Vought-Sikorsky SB2U, but it had operational problems and was not adopted. Because of this, the SB2U airplane could not make the steep dives the navy expected.

The navy had continued to seek a steep-diving monoplane dive-bomber and ordered the BT-1 in 1936. It offered a different drag device in the form of split flaps on the wings that opened at the trailing edge like a clamshell to provide panels that were at an angle around thirty degrees from the airstream both above and below the wing. When the flaps were first tried, they provided the necessary drag, but caused severe buffeting of the tail. This problem was eventually overcome by perforating the flaps with holes to weaken the vortices coming off the outer corners of the flaps.

From what Alan remembered, the BT-1 was designed by Jack Northrop, who was one of the pioneers of aluminum, semi-monocoque construction. The BT-1 used this more-efficient type of structure throughout, and so its empty weight was about twenty percent less than the SB2U.

The main landing gear retracted straight back, leaving the lower half of the wheels protruding, partially enclosed by large fairings. Alan thought that this version of retractable landing gear was overly conservative. It made the BT-1 slower than the older SB2U, as well. At least the main landing gear had a wide stance, like the SB2U, SNJ, and TBD.

The greenhouse sections over both seats in the cockpit were open, and Alan climbed up onto the left wing and looked at the rear seat area, where the radioman/gunner sat. It looked similar to that of the SBU. The seat was surrounded by a large horizontal ring to support the flexible machine gun and allow it to be swung around to either side. In spite of this hindrance, there were still flight and engine controls and a few instruments in the rear cockpit. Forward visibility from the rear seat appeared to be about the same as in the SNJ, which was pretty poor.

Alan envisioned what it would be like to be a gunner, sitting facing aft with the canopy opened up and manning the machine gun as fighters swooped in from the rear. It would take at least as much courage as being a pilot, he realized.

Alan went up to the front seat and, finding that a parachute had been left there, he climbed in and sat down. The BT-1 had a big tubular bombing and gun sight that was much like the ones in the SBU and F2F, easy to hit with your face in a crash. Below the glare shield, there was a narrow instrument panel containing the usual flight and engine instruments. To the right of the main panel was the rear end of the single forward-firing, fixed .50-caliber machine gun and its charging handle.

Alan opened the manual and methodically went over all the gauges, controls, and switches. He had looked over just about everything when he felt Rye jump on the wing. Rye put his parachute in the rear seat and came forward to the front cockpit.

"Did you figure it all out?" Rye asked as he handed Alan a leather helmet.

"No mysteries so far."

Rye coached Alan through the preflight inspection. Only a few details were new to Alan. After strapping in, Rye went over the starting procedure, which was similar to the SNJ and TBD. Soon Alan was listening to the familiar rumble of the Twin Wasp Junior engine.

They taxied out, did their run-up, and took off. They first went north, then east, and climbed up to 5,000 feet over Chesapeake Bay. Alan found it hard to refrain from sightseeing, now that he was in new territory. He could see the whole south end of the bay.

Alan noted that the handling was not quite as crisp as the SNJ, but was more responsive than the TBD. Rye had Alan do a series of stalls with the power both on and off. The airplane usually rolled to the left in the stall, and like most airplanes, the rudder was used to control roll motion when the wing was stalled. In spite of Rye's warning, Alan was surprised by how ineffective the rudder was. Accelerated stalls, which were done while the airplane was in a turn, were worse.

Next, they practiced slow flight. As long as the throttle was left alone, the airplane behaved fairly well. Rye told Alan that they would practice simulated go-arounds, or balked landings, and they established a descent simulating final approach to a carrier landing, which was about five knots above stall speed with the gear and flaps down. When Rye gave the signal, Alan was supposed to stop the descent as quickly as possible by pitching up and adding throttle. On the first one, Alan thought he was being reasonably gentle with the throttle, but the airplane rolled to the left past ninety degrees.

After he recovered, Alan said, "That *is* scary. It's going take a while to get used to that."

"Damn right. We'll keep working on it until you master it. In the meantime, if you need to do a real go-around, sing out, and I'll take it."

"Will do."

Alan tried three more simulated go-arounds. He was able to reduce, but not eliminate, the roll by being gentle with the throttle and using full-right rudder. By then, they had been up in the plane for over an hour. Alan was sweaty, in spite of the canopy being open, and frustrated. He was relieved when Rye told him to head back to the field. They landed, taxied in, shut down, and climbed out.

Rye started the discussion. "You did well. Maybe it helps that you've just come from Pensacola and have recent experience in several different planes. Lots of experienced pilots have more trouble with the BT-1 than you're having."

Alan was surprised to hear that Rye thought he had done well. "Thank you, but I'm feeling frustrated by not being able to do a go-around after four tries."

"It's nothing unusual in this airplane. Another session or two, and you'll start to get on top of it. After you master it thoroughly, we'll start working mostly on field carrier landings and steep dives, but we'll do one or two practice go-arounds on every flight."

Wednesday, June 11, 1941

Rye had told Alan two days earlier that the *Ranger*'s temporary air group, composed of three squadrons that were normally assigned to the *Yorktown*, would fly into Norfolk NAS from the carrier that day. The three squadrons were Fighting Five with F3F-3s, Scouting Five with SBC-3s, and Bombing Five with BT-1s. Later in the day, Alan heard that the *Ranger* herself had come into Norfolk and docked at Pier Seven. Pilots started streaming into the BOQ in the afternoon.

Alan found out that the navy had waited until that week to tell the wives of the married *Yorktown* men where their husbands had gone after the *Yorktown* left Hawaii on what was supposed to be a routine cruise. So most of their wives now had to pick up and move back to the east coast. Thus, BOQ was filled up with the married pilots until they found off-base housing for themselves and their families.

Thursday, June 12, 1941

Alan was formally welcomed into the squadron on Thursday morning, and introduced to all the pilots. Later, he was interviewed by the executive officer, Lieutenant John "Jack" Casey. Alan informed Casey that he had come to the base directly from his honeymoon, and that his new wife was planning to visit him and spend the coming Saturday night in Norfolk, going on to explain why Jennifer would not be coming to reside at Norfolk. Casey had taken all this in and had been very cordial and accepting, but Alan understood that an officer's wife also being employed by the navy and not able to leave her job to follow her husband was a situation that had not been anticipated in standard navy social etiquette.

Alan had long been aware that the navy encouraged—almost required—a strong social network among officers who worked together. He had been surprised, however, when Casey had apologized for not being able to put Alan and his wife up at his house on Saturday night because he didn't have one yet. He had offered instead to buy Alan and Jennifer dinner at the Officers' Club, and Alan had politely asked to be excused from dinner because his wife's visit would be so short. Casey accepted this excuse, which Alan sincerely appreciated, instead accepting an invitation for a drink before dinner.

Saturday, June 14, 1941

Jennifer drove down to Norfolk in the afternoon, meeting Alan at about 1600 at the hotel he had booked. She seemed tired, but happy. Alan just wanted to hold her in his arms and forget about social obligations, but they were due at the Officers' Club at 1800. After showering and changing for dinner, they took a drive around the air station on the way to their appointment with Casey.

The entire base, known as Norfolk Naval Operating Base, was the largest on the East Coast. It included piers for large ships and an extensive navy yard. The Naval Air Station on the base was big in itself, with two separate landing fields and a seaplane base. With war on the horizon, Norfolk NAS had been undergoing a major expansion. Both the BOQ and East Field had been recently completed. East Field had been added because Chambers Field had runways that were too short for newer or larger aircraft, and there was no room to lengthen them. There was a long taxiway leading northwest from East Field so that aircraft could taxi to Chambers Field, which was connected by another taxiway to the dock area on the west side, so that aircraft could be loaded aboard carriers.

Casey met them as they walked into the club, and Alan made the introductions. Casey bought a round of drinks, and they sat in the bar and chatted. Alan and Jennifer had just thanked Casey and had risen to depart for dinner at a restaurant in Norfolk when the skipper of Bombing Five, Lieutenant Commander Murray Arnham, walked into the bar. Casey made the introductions, and Arnham congratulated Alan and Jennifer on their recent marriage before they were able to depart for dinner.

They arrived at the restaurant at 1930. It was a place frequented mainly by local residents rather than navy people, and it had been recommended by Rye. Alan and Jennifer were shown to a booth in the back. They studied the menu and decided on their orders.

Not seeing the waiter, Jennifer turned to him and smiled. "Let's hear your news first."

"Well, let's see: I've gotten checked out in the BT-1, and I've completed field carrier landing practice, but haven't made any carrier landings yet. I've had a little dive-bombing practice, too. The BT-1 feels quite different from the F2F—much bigger and heavier. The dive flaps work well, but it's still an exciting experience for me to make a steep dive, let alone drop a bomb. The ailerons get heavy at high speed in the dive, so it's a little hard to keep on the target."

"I've heard the BT-1 can get nasty at low speeds, too."

"That's right. No secrets are safe from you intelligence scalawags, are they?" Alan laughed. "I've practiced slow flight and go-arounds a lot, and I think I'm able to handle the nastier characteristics. It's easy, however, to see how some pilots were ambushed by it when the airplane first went operational."

"You can never be too careful, Alan." She looked directly into his eyes with a firm expression on her face.

He looked back into her eyes and said, "I know."

The waiter appeared and took their orders for mint juleps and dinner.

Alan continued, "The air group I'm with has been at sea or anchored at Bermuda for almost two months, so everyone is catching up on shore time right now. I was included in the air group party last night, and the group seems like a very good bunch of guys. Last Monday, another pilot in the class behind me at Pensacola reported in for Bombing Five, so already I'm not the newest rookie. He had an intensive checkout in the BT-1 so he could join me for field carrier landing practice. Next week, we'll be doing our carrier qualifications aboard the *Ranger*."

"I know that you've been looking forward to that for a long time, but it gives me the willies."

"There will probably be scary moments, but it should be very satisfying in the end. I'm sure everything will be fine."

The waiter returned with their mint juleps.

Jennifer continued, "Carrier aviation must be very different from submarines."

"It is. In a fleet submarine, you're part of a team of seventy men, and you get to know them all. You all have to get along and work together or you may die together. Aviation—at least, carrier aviation—is much more individualistic. In carrier aviation, you're either alone or with one or two enlisted men in the airplane. The enlisted men are assigned by the squadron to your plane, so their assignments often change at the last minute. You may not know them at all, so you're on your own to a large extent. You have to work with the other pilots, but, with the possible exception of your wingman, your survival isn't so closely intertwined with theirs. Also, in submarines, the officers are nearly all Academy men. In aviation, I'm a 'Ringknocker,' and not always welcomed by the reservists. A lot of men who'd be happy in aviation would not be happy in submarines, and vice versa. Fortunately, I seem to be adaptable to both."

"You're lucky. I'm glad you like it. How is the BOQ?"

"It's actually pretty nice. Discipline seems a little lax among the pilots, though. This morning when I got up, there were several girls in the BOQ."

"Oh my! And they'd spent the night?"

Alan nodded. The waiter brought their dinners, and they ate in silence for a few minutes.

Alan resumed. "During the summer, both Scouting Five and Bombing Five will be transitioning to the SBD. Scouting Five's SBDs have already started arriving at Norfolk, so they'll get them right away. We'll get ours in late July or early August. I like everything I've heard about the SBD. It's really a completely revised version of the BT-1, with all of the bad characteristics gone and many big improvements. I've had a chance to see it up close now, and I can't wait to fly it."

"I've heard only good things about the SBD."

"Well, that's all my news. What has been happening in your life?"

"My apartment is a source of comfort, but things at the office keep going downhill. What I'm going to tell you next is not secret, but it shouldn't be spread around." She looked into his eyes.

"Okay, I understand," he said with a serious expression.

"About ten days ago, there was an uproar when CNO got an important piece of intelligence from CINCPAC that neither CNO nor ONI were aware of. It turned out that it was something that the Pacific Fleet Intelligence Officer, Layton, had picked up. We had missed it. I think that's because we're understaffed and distracted."

"I know Layton. I served with him during my surface tour in the *Pennsylvania*. He's a good officer, well suited to intelligence."

"I've heard that about Layton, too. As you can imagine, ONI was acutely embarrassed at having overlooked this intelligence, which depressed morale even further. Now, Alan, I love you dearly, and please don't get upset, but I've started to consider the possibility of asking for a transfer to Pearl Harbor, because I've heard that the intelligence group there was looking for people, particularly those who know Japanese, and I think morale would be much higher in that office."

Alan's heart sank. *No sooner do the two of us get sent to the same part of the country, so we have a chance to see each other, than we might be split apart again.*

Jennifer let her comment sink in before explaining further, "I've heard that Joe Rochefort recently took over that group, and he has a very good reputation among the intelligence people. The overseas intelligence groups are independent, not under ONI and subject to Main Navy's internal strife. But I know that it would be very hard for us to be apart again. Anyway, I think I owe it to ONI to stick it out for a while longer, so I'm not ready to make a decision yet."

"Wow, Pearl Harbor would be a big change for you—and for us. It's sad to think about you going away just when we're having a chance to see each other, but I can see why going to Pearl Harbor might be appealing to you. Rochefort is a sharp intelligence officer."

"Yes, and they have some of the navy's best cryptanalysts, men like Tom Dyer and Ham Wright."

"Layton, Rochefort, Dyer, *and* Wright—that's a remarkable coincidence! When I was on the *Pennsylvania* six years ago, I served in the number-four turret. The captain of number-four turret at the time was Layton, and the captain of the number-three turret was Dyer. When CINCPAC made the *Pennsylvania* his flagship and moved on board, he brought his assistant operations and intelligence officer, Rochefort. Before I left, Wright was assigned to the ship, as well. They all knew each other, and they allowed me to sit in on a few of their bull sessions. It was fascinating to hear about intelligence work. They didn't talk about code breaking in my presence, but I gathered that they knew a lot about it."

"Now it's my turn to be amazed. You're acquainted with all four of these intelligence guys?"

"Yeah. I had no idea that they're all together again at Pearl Harbor. They're good people." He paused. "If you go there, it would be my turn to tell *you* to be careful. Did your study at the War College include the three times that Pearl Harbor had been successfully attacked in the Fleet Problems?"

"Yes, and I remember that Roosevelt moved the fleet there last year and then relieved Admiral Richardson of command when he repeatedly pointed out the dangers of basing the fleet there. The politicians thought that basing the fleet there would deter Japan, but Richardson thought that its vulnerability would have the opposite effect."

"Exactly. I took a class at the Academy that covered War Plan Orange, which you must have studied at the War College. Even before the last war, many strategists thought that Japan would be likely to start a war suddenly with a surprise attack. Pearl Harbor would be a logical choice."

"I agree that the risk of an attack on Pearl Harbor is underrated, but our navy has only very recently developed the equipment for underway refueling and gotten good enough at it to undertake a long fleet voyage without stopping. The Japanese would need the same thing to get to Pearl Harbor, but not to get most anywhere else they might want to go. Our people think it is unlikely that they have bothered to develop underway refueling."

"Yeah, but I wouldn't count on it. I think the navy has a tendency to underestimate the Japanese." He paused and took a sip of his mint julep. "I imagine that the Japanese know just as well as we do that the best time for an attack is at dawn on a Sunday. Did you hear about the time that the navy had a practice attack early on a Sunday morning and the army was caught completely off guard? They said it was 'unfair' to attack on a Sunday," he said with a chuckle. "If you go, don't get drunk on Saturday nights."

"Yes, sir, you rascal," she said, laughing. Her smile faded suddenly and she became more serious. "At the War College, the topic of a two-ocean war and attempting to prevent or delay war in the Pacific received a lot of attention. There was a sense that Roosevelt wants to restrain Japan, but both army and navy leaders believe that we won't have the forces available for some time to back up any threats. If the Japanese keep making aggressive moves, Roosevelt may freeze their assets in the US and cut off their oil supply, which nearly all comes from us. In that case, the Japanese will have to either give in or fight, and if they fight, they'll have to attack before their oil supply is depleted. It's like lighting the fuse on a time bomb."

"That all makes a lot of sense to me. I've thought for some time that the administration doesn't seem to understand how weak our armed forces continue to be in spite of our rearmament so far. If Japan's oil supply is cut off, we're likely to have to fight before we're ready."

"That's right."

Alan thought of something that he hardly dared mention, but he felt obligated to say, anyway. "You know, in the long run, there's very likely going to be war with Japan. In that case, it seems that the *Yorktown* would almost certainly be sent back to the Pacific, and then we'd have many more chances to see each other if you were at Pearl Harbor. I would hate to have you leave, but if you go there, it just might be better for us in the end."

"I hadn't put all that together. I haven't been thinking about this idea for very long, but I can see what you're saying."

Their conversation turned back to what they would do the next day and during their next visit together. The Fourth of July holiday would be on a Friday, and they both thought they would be able to take that day off, making a three-day weekend possible. They decided to wait until then to get together, and to meet in Annapolis, instead of at Jennifer's apartment in Washington.

CHAPTER EIGHTEEN

Carrier Qualification

Monday, June 16, 1941

Alan had his last session of field carrier landing practice in the morning, which consisted of making landings on a runway that had the outline of an aircraft carrier deck marked on it with white stripes. As on a real carrier, a Landing Signal Officer (LSO) stood at the approach end of the landing area on the left side and used a pair of large paddles to coach the pilot with signals. For the last few sessions of this practice, he had been coached by the *Yorktown* air group's own LSO, Lieutenant Norwood "Soupy" Campbell, who would also coach him when he tried for his carrier qualification the following day, giving him the advantage of being familiar with his LSO's signals.

The technique for a carrier landing was similar to that for a very short runway on land. Most of the descent was accomplished before turning onto the final leg, approaching the stern straight in from directly aft. The final leg was flown with full flaps and a fair amount of power in a shallow descent just above stall speed. Alan used pitch attitude, controlled by his right hand on the stick, to adjust the airspeed. He used engine power, controlled by his left hand on the throttle, to adjust the descent angle. When the airplane was close to the approach end of the landing area, the LSO would give him one of two signals. If the LSO gave him the "cut" signal, he would close the throttle and land with very little flare, since he was already close to a stall. If the LSO gave him the "wave off" signal, he would immediately add power, pull up, and not land. This was the maneuver that was so difficult in the BT-1: the go-around.

Alan was acutely aware that real carrier landings would be different from field carrier landing practice. First, there was likely to be considerably more wind, but no crosswind, because the carrier steamed straight into the wind. Second, the carrier might pitch and roll some on the swell, if there was one. Third, the carrier had arresting gear. Last, but not least, Alan knew that going beyond the edge of the deck would be more than just embarrassing.

Joining Alan for the field carrier landing practice was the other new pilot in Bombing Five, Ensign Edward "Ned" Morris. He and Alan—the rookies—were naturally grouped together. As they waited for their instructor to appear, Alan found out that Ned was an AvCad from Arizona, and he had graduated from the University of Arizona. His family ran a cattle ranch in the high country south of Tucson, near the Mexican border. He looked like a cowboy, and Alan's summer on a cattle ranch in Wyoming gave them something in common. Ned seemed friendly, even though Alan was six years older than him—and a Ringknocker.

Like most prospective carrier pilots, Alan had never set foot on an aircraft carrier. Casey gave Ned and Alan a tour of the *Ranger*'s flight and hangar decks at the pier that afternoon, before their qualification. They boarded the *Ranger* and walked out onto the nearly deserted flight deck through a door in the island, the superstructure that protruded above the flight deck on the starboard edge. The *Ranger* had an unusually small island because it had been added as an afterthought during construction.

With a big drop-off on all sides, the flight deck seemed incredibly small to Alan. He noticed that the flight deck was made of wood, which he remembered was used on all US carriers. It was easily damaged, but it was also easily repaired—and lightweight. This was important, because having a lot of weight so far above the waterline would reduce the stability of the ship. Alan also knew that the British took the opposite view and armored their flight decks, which resulted in being able to carry fewer aircraft, but he wasn't sure which was better.

As he looked around, Alan remembered what he had been taught at Pensacola about the basic concepts of carrier flight operations. For takeoff, which was often called "launching" on a carrier, many aircraft were parked at the aft end. These parked aircraft used up as much as half the deck. The aircraft took off one by one from the front row, with the line progressing aft until all were launched. If more aircraft were to be launched, they would then be brought up on the elevators, parked aft, and the process would be repeated. For landing, also called "recovery," only about half the flight deck was used as the actual landing area. The forward end was used to park aircraft that had landed, just as the aft end was used to hold planes for take-off. The elevators were generally not used during flight operations, because the hole created by their use would disrupt operations on the flight deck.

Like the old *Langley*, the *Ranger* was originally designed without an island, so the funnels were located aft, beside the flight deck on both sides, instead of in the island like those of the other US carriers. Alan, Ned, and Casey walked aft to the three starboard funnels as Casey described how they could be swiveled down for flight operations to point sideways and not protrude above the flight deck. Now in the up position, the funnels came up through the gallery, a narrow catwalk along the sides of the flight deck and about four feet below it.

Casey showed them the nine aft arresting wires. There were also eight forward arresting wires, which could be used if there was a following wind and the situation made it awkward to turn the ship around, in which case the airplanes landed over the bow with the ship steaming in reverse. Alan saw that the arresting wires were stretched a couple of inches above the flight deck, crossing the entire deck, so that the arresting hook of an arriving airplane could easily catch one shortly after landing. Once a hook caught a wire, the plane would rock forward on its main wheels, raising the tail, and the hook would clear the wires further forward. The "wires" were actually sturdy steel cables that were supposed to be able to stand the strain of many arrested landings. The wire went over pulleys at the edge of the flight deck, which allowed it to pay out from below deck when a plane's arresting hook caught it. Below deck, the cables were connected to weights and hydraulic dampers that absorbed the energy of the landing airplane. The arresting gear kept the landing roll extremely short so that it would fit within the aft half of the flight deck. Alan had been forewarned about how he would be thrown forward in the cockpit by the sudden deceleration.

Casey also described what happened when an arresting wire broke. The weights would cause the wire to reel in at high speed, which would cause the two broken ends of the wire to whip around the deck. If one hit a man's leg, it could sever it. The best protection was to stay away from the wires in general. If the worst happened, the next best tactic was to keep your cool and attempt to jump up at the right moment so that the wire would pass under you. It was just one of the many dangers on the flight deck, which explained why pilots were discouraged from being on the deck unless it was necessary to get to or from their planes.

They walked forward, and Casey pointed out the six barriers amidships, which were now all folded down. When an arresting wire broke or the arresting hook on the plane bounced over the wires, the airplane would continue forward. In this case, the erected barriers acted like fences to protect the personnel and parked aircraft by stopping the landing plane. Two barriers were normally used, but the carriers had more than that so that the position of the barriers in use could be adjusted fore and aft. Each barrier consisted of double wires that gave only a little when hit. As soon as a plane had stopped after landing, both the arresting wires and the barriers were folded down so that the wires lay in grooves in the deck, so that they were easy to taxi over. Casey explained that all this gear had evolved during intensive experimental operations aboard the *Langley* in the 1920s, under the leadership of then Captain Reeves.

The three officers went below to see the hangar deck, which was also nearly empty. Although it was a big space, it was hard to imagine sixty or seventy airplanes packed into it. Casey noted that a large hangar deck had been emphasized during the *Ranger's* design. She had a twenty-five percent larger hangar than the *Lexington* and the *Saratoga*, even though she was considerably smaller. She was also the first US carrier to be designed with a hangar tall enough to store additional aircraft by securing them to the overhead. Unlike the earlier carriers, the *Ranger* had large openings in the side of the hangar deck for ventilation and for hangar-deck catapults. Curtains were provided, both to cover the openings so that the hangar deck could be lighted at night without giving away the location of the ship, and to close off the hangar deck in foul or cold weather.

Tuesday, June 17, 1941

Alan was more keyed up than he had been at any time since before his first flight with Admiral Powers. He was scheduled to attempt his carrier qualification by making landings aboard the *Ranger* in the practice area off Virginia Beach. The *Ranger* had been assigned to training activities in the Hampton Roads area for the remainder of June and early July.

A cold front had gone through the night before. The day dawned bright and clear, with a few cumulus clouds and a northwest wind. Alan arrived at 0650 at the Bombing Five hangar on East Field and reported with Ned to Jack Casey. Jack said that he would lead them out to the *Ranger* and that they would probably have time for four landings that day. Four was the minimum necessary for qualification, so if the landings were acceptable, they would be qualified by the end of the day. Jack told them they would launch at 0800 and showed them which aircraft they were assigned to. He mentioned that there would be some marine pilots from Quantico also qualifying on the *Ranger* that day, and that the marines would arrive over the *Ranger* later because they had to come from farther away.

Alan thought about Marine Corps officers in general as he went to the head before the flight. Many navy officers looked down on them as country bumpkins because they were not usually familiar with the sophisticated machinery of ships or blue water navigation. Alan thought that they easily made up for that with their rough and ready versatility and ability to make do with what they had, including worn out and obsolete equipment. For example, their aviators were expected to know how to land on a carrier even though they had few opportunities to practice because they were not assigned to carriers.

Alan was in the cockpit at 0745 and went through the engine-start procedure. He looked around and saw that Jack and Ned had their engines started also. A few minutes later they taxied out, did their run-ups, and took off on runway zero one. They easily formed up into a stepped down V-formation as they made a gradual right turn to head east toward Cape Henry. Jack led, with Alan on his left wing and Ned on his right. They climbed to 3,000 feet, and Alan could see Cape Henry in the distance ahead.

Their formation was typical of carrier operations. With the exception of fighter squadrons, carrier squadrons used three-plane sections consisting of a senior pilot leader and two wingmen, who normally flew on either side of the leader. Two sections constituted a division, and there were three divisions in the typical scouting or bombing squadron. The three divisions were normally led by the skipper, the exec, and the flight officer.

As they approached Cape Henry, Alan spotted the *Ranger* about twenty miles to the southeast. After passing the cape, they turned southeast toward the ship. As they approached, Alan could see that she was coming toward them, steaming into the northwest wind. Two destroyers trailed her, one on each side. He knew that these destroyers were on plane guard duty, in position to pick up aviators who went into the water. Alan was used to airport runways appearing small when seen from a passing airplane, but the carrier deck looked much smaller. Jack gave the hand signal for descent, and they started down. They leveled off at 1,000 feet and left the ship about two miles to starboard as they went past, staying well clear of the landing pattern on the port side of the ship. Jack checked in with the ship on the radio and received permission for their flight of three to land. Alan could see that the *Ranger* had her distinctive funnels turned out sideways for flight operations.

They made a gradual 180-degree turn to the right, lined up with the flight deck, and flew directly toward the stern of the ship in trail at cruise speed. They broke up the formation for landing in the standard military way. Jack turned left 180 degrees, and then at ten-second intervals, Alan and Ned each did the same. This procedure spaced them out for landing. As each pilot turned, he slowed down and lowered his landing gear. After the turn, Alan slid back the cockpit canopy and went methodically through the carrier landing checklist, being sure to lower the arresting hook and unlock the tail wheel. He felt the stress rising further. *This is it*, he thought, *I am going to make a carrier landing.*

He was relieved to see that the *Ranger* was not pitching much on the swell, probably because the shelter of Cape Henry kept the fetch small in the northwest wind. As he turned onto the final approach leg, he could see Jack's airplane taxiing forward over the first barrier, so his landing had gone well.

Behind Campbell, the LSO, was a cameraman with a movie camera. Alan had been told that there would often be a cameraman behind the LSO to film landings for training and evaluation purposes. The scuttlebutt was that the cameraman would only film landings that looked inauspicious. Therefore, if you saw the cameraman go into action, you knew you were in trouble.

Alan started making adjustments based on the signals from Campbell. He was so busy that he did not have time to think about being scared. He was aware that "RNGR" was painted in large white letters across the aft end of the deck and that two barriers were up amidships. Now he was close in, watching for the cut or wave-off signal, and Campbell gave him the cut. Alan pulled the throttle all the way back.

He came down hard beyond the first wire, bounced, and came down again near the third wire. The arresting hook bounced and caught on the fourth wire. He was thrown forward as the airplane was hauled down to a stop within about a hundred feet. He had practiced bracing himself with his left hand against the glare shield at the top of the instrument panel, but he still bumped his forehead lightly on the bomb sight. The tightened seat belt kept him from sliding off the seat, digging into his abdomen. Any fears were immediately overwhelmed by relief and delight about the fact that he had made a respectable landing. He was glad that he had not caught one of the further wires, which were adjusted to stop the airplane faster so that it would not hit the barriers, making the deceleration even more violent.

He let out a long breath and looked up to see a yellow-shirted deck control man signaling him to release the brakes so that the green-shirted arresting-gear men could move the plane back slightly and unhook the arresting hook from the wire. He quickly did so, and the yellow shirt signaled him to taxi forward. He knew he was expected to get out of the landing area immediately after his hook was disengaged in order to clear the landing area for the next arrival, which was thirty seconds behind. He straightened himself up and moved the lever that raised the hook. He grasped the throttle and hurriedly taxied forward over the arresting wires, folded barriers, and elevators to a parking spot forward of the forward elevator. Another yellow-shirted man gave him the throat-cut signal to shut down the engine. Two blue-shirted plane handlers converged on Alan's plane and placed chocks around the main wheels to prevent it from moving. Alan carefully went through the shutdown procedure. As the propeller came to a stop, he heard the noise of another airplane taxiing up from aft. He turned and saw that it was Ned Morris. He had made a satisfactory landing, too.

Alan climbed out and was immediately struck by the thirty-knot relative wind over the deck. The legs and sleeves of his khaki uniform were set flapping and his sweaty clothes suddenly felt cold. He glanced at his watch, which said 0827. He could hear a loudspeaker announcing something, but it was hard to understand in the wind. The yellow-shirted man was looking at Alan and pointing to the island. Alan started walking aft toward the island, glancing warily around to make sure that he was not going to be hit by anything. There were purple-shirted fuel men and red-shirted ordnance men waiting in the gallery forward. A loud horn sounded *gah-oogah*, and he saw a BT-1, which he realized was Jack's airplane, start down on the forward elevator. It was accompanied by a clanging bell. Alan went over to the starboard side of the deck to get out of the way and go past the forward elevator to the island.

He saw Jack standing forward of the island. As Alan came up, Jack smiled.

"Nice work, Alan. Which wire did you catch? The fourth? If they're all like that, you won't have any trouble," he said in a loud voice so that Alan could hear him over the wind.

Alan grinned. "Thanks, Jack. Yeah, I got the fourth wire. I suspect it won't turn out that well every time."

Jack glanced forward, and Alan turned as Ned walked up.

Jack said, "Great job, Ned! Fifth wire—you're off to a good start."

"Thanks, Jack." Ned beamed.

Jack said, "The marines are due to arrive before long. I know a reasonably safe place to watch from—the gallery aft of the island. Let's go back there and see how they do. After that, the deck crew is going to re-spot for takeoff. While they're doing that, we might as well go down to the wardroom and have a cup of coffee."

Jack led the way aft around the island and into the after gallery. They made their way aft past some anti-aircraft machine guns and to a position forward of the funnels and next to arresting wire number eight. "Here, we should be out of the way of the aft flight-deck crewmen, who mostly gather in the gallery above the funnels," said Jack. Alan could see that the gallery was kept free of guns and equipment in that area because the funnels were there when they were in the vertical position.

Alan glanced around the flight deck. Forward, blue shirts were tying down his and Ned's airplanes to the deck. A loudspeaker announced that the marine airplanes were expected in fifteen minutes. Men in blue and green shirts on the aft half of the flight deck headed toward the galleries on each side to wait. Yellow-shirted men gathered near the island. The flurry of activity on the flight deck gradually came to a stop. The arresting wires and barriers three and four rose up again, and Alan noticed that they were controlled by a petty officer in the gallery.

The three pilots turned and looked forward, to the right of the island, toward the north, where they expected to first see the approaching marine aircraft.

"There they are," Jack said and pointed.

Alan looked and saw them approaching. They were about four miles off, just to the right of the island, and heading southeast. As they came closer, he could see that there were two echelons, the leading one consisting of three low-wing monoplanes and the other consisting of three biplanes with retractable gear.

"Three SB2Us and three SBCs," Jack pointed out.

Alan remembered that the company nicknames for these airplanes were "Vindicator" and "Helldiver." The SB2U was also referred to as the "Wind Indicator" by those who were not so fond of it. The three watched as the marines followed the same pattern that their own flight had used.

"Nice formation work," Jack remarked as they passed over the ship.

The marines executed the same break sequence to space out for landing, and the Vought SB2Us led the Curtiss SBCs. One by one, landing gear came down and cockpit canopies were opened.

As the leader turned onto his base leg, the three navy pilots focused intently on him. He turned onto final and was coming almost straight at them. Alan felt himself tense as he watched the landing unfold. The airplane seemed to be in the groove, as the proper final flight path was known, and Campbell was giving him small corrections. When he was close, Campbell gave him the cut. He settled firmly near the fourth wire and caught the fifth.

"Well done," said Jack. Alan relaxed as the barriers and wires folded down. Three green shirts ran out from the gallery and disengaged the hook. The pilot retracted it, and the arresting wire reeled in. The pilot taxied forward over the wires and barriers as a yellow shirt directed him to a spot next to Ned's airplane.

The three pilots turned their attention to the second marine aircraft. Alan had the impression that this pilot was a little high and close-in as he turned onto his final leg, and he felt the tension rising again. Campbell was signaling that the plane was high. Alan saw the nose drop as the pilot attempted to correct, but this was the wrong technique, because it would add to his speed. The plane was close, and seemed to Alan to be in a good position, though fast.

"He's very fast," said Jack. Campbell gave the pilot the cut.

As the plane came over the stern, Alan could see for himself that the plane's speed was high. The plane thumped down near the sixth wire, bounced, and caught the eighth. There was a sudden loud bang as the arresting wire parted. The three navy pilots winced at the sound and stared for a second in fascination as the plane continued forward. The two broken ends of the arresting cable started to whip around the deck, and the three pilots quickly ducked below the flight deck to avoid the flying wire. Alan saw a green shirt take a hasty jump off the flight deck into the gallery near the funnels.

They heard another bang a second later. The noise of the number-eight wire reeling in fast had abruptly stopped. Then another bang. They cautiously rose until their eyes were an inch above the flight deck, and they saw that nothing was moving on the aft half of the deck. They stood up, and saw that the airplane had broken through both barriers, accounting for the bangs. Fortunately, the two barriers had absorbed most of the plane's energy. It had come to a stop before hitting the planes parked farther forward. The propeller blades were bent and there was a piece of cable wrapped around the propeller hub.

Alan looked aft. Two green shirts were kneeling over the man who had jumped off the flight deck. He was now stretched out on the gallery deck. One of the green shirts was calling aft for pharmacist's mates. Alan looked forward and could see two blue shirts lying on the deck where they had fallen in their haste to get out of the path of the plane. They sat up, and he could see that they had some cuts and scrapes, but looked okay otherwise. Two white-shirted pharmacist's mates rushed out from the forward gallery and toward the plane with a stretcher. They dropped the stretcher and leaped onto the left wing to check on the condition of the pilot.

From aft came the sudden growl of an airplane engine going to full power. The navy pilots quickly turned toward the sound. Alan saw the third marine SB2U approaching the stern. It roared overhead, its landing gear retracting rearward. With the deck fouled, Alan realized that Campbell had given the third marine an immediate wave-off. This airplane joined the three biplanes circling the carrier at about 1,000 feet. Alan turned to look forward again. The pilot of the second airplane had climbed out and appeared to be unharmed, and the pharmacist's mates were helping the two blue shirts toward the island. In the gallery aft, two pharmacist's mates were moving the injured green shirt onto a stretcher.

Jack told Alan and Ned, "They'll make temporary repairs to the barriers, but they'll probably leave the repair of the number-eight wire until after the other marines have landed."

Two repair parties were already temporarily splicing the cables in the two barriers. In about fifteen minutes, the repairs to the barriers had been completed.

The remaining four marine aircraft landed with no further mishaps. Each landing was different, and Alan was fascinated. Some bounced; some did not. No one got the number one or nine wires, but several of the others got exercised. Finally, the last airplane taxied forward over the barriers.

"I think we can head down to the wardroom now without missing any excitement," Jack said with a smile. He turned and led the way up the steps and through door into the aft end of the island. The time was 0954.

An hour later, the loudspeaker told the navy and marine pilots to man their planes. While they were below, the ship had turned around and steamed southeast and their airplanes had been re-spotted aft for takeoff. Jack and the captain leading the marines had plenty of recent carrier landing practice, so they would not be joining the practice. The marine first lieutenant who had crashed the barriers would also be sitting out the rest of the day's practice. When Alan emerged onto the flight deck, he noticed that there was hardly any wind over the deck because the carrier was headed downwind. The ship started to heel to port as it began to turn to the right and steam back into the northwest wind for flight operations. There were more cumulus clouds, and as the ship turned across the wind, Alan could feel that it had become gustier.

Apparently, the deck crew was taking the opportunity for some additional practice themselves, because they had reversed the order of parking as they moved the planes aft. Alan could see that his and Ned's BT-1s, whose wings could not fold, were in the last row of parked planes near the stern. He and Ned would takeoff last. The functioning marine SB2U was in the next row, its wings folded upward over the fuselage, with one of the SBCs. The other two SBCs were in the front row. The damaged SB2U had been struck below to join Jack's BT-1 and the marine captain's SB2U. As the three navy pilots started to walk aft, Jack shouted, "Good luck," and turned away to take his place in the gallery.

As Alan continued aft to his plane, he noticed that the number-eight arresting wire had been replaced. The Deck Signal Officer, called "Fly One," gave all the pilots the signal to start their engines after they were strapped in. Alan went through the warm start procedure, and the engine was soon rumbling again. He went through the carrier takeoff checklist, making sure the hook was raised and the wing flaps were lowered fifteen degrees for the shortest possible takeoff. Alan noticed that the marine SB2U started its engine with its wings folded, since there was not room enough to unfold the wings until it had taxied forward a few feet to clear the neighboring planes. Alan felt the excitement rising again.

He looked up to see Fly One swing his checkered flag down and send the first SBC on its way. With plenty of room for the takeoff roll, the first marine got off with no problem. The other four marine aircraft also got off, and soon Ned was on his way, too.

Fly One now stood to the right of Alan's plane. He unfurled his checkered flag over his head as Alan looked at him, which was the signal to hold the brakes and go to full power. Alan made sure the stick was fully back, stood hard on the toe brakes, and moved the throttle smoothly to full power. The airplane shook in the propeller wake at full power. He checked oil pressure, oil temperature, manifold pressure, and rpm. Fly One was holding his hand cupped to his ear, the signal that the engine sounded okay to him and he was asking if the pilot was ready to go. Alan thought it sounded all right, and he nodded. Fly One brought the flag smartly forward and down, and Alan released the brakes and eased the stick forward as the airplane accelerated rapidly. The tail came up as he was passing the seventh wire. He used the rudder to gently move over to the centerline of the flight deck and lifted off just forward of the mid-ship elevator.

Alan knew that he should not be complacent about the shortness of his takeoff roll, because his airplane was light compared to what it would be with a typical combat load. Also, in combat, it would be common to have a full-deck load launch in order to get a large number of aircraft launched quickly. In that case, the parked aircraft would cover the entire aft half of the flight deck, and he could be in the front row, about amidships.

Alan climbed to 1,000 feet and leveled off. He caught up with Ned, and they continued around the circuit to follow the marines as they approached the ship from astern. The two little formations flew over the ship and executed the break. By the time Alan had completed his break, he could see that the leading marine biplane was turning onto final approach. He wanted to watch the landing, but he had to devote himself to his own landing checklist. When he had finished that, he was about forty-five degrees off the ship's port bow. He saw that the marine biplanes had landed, apparently without difficulty, and that the SB2U was turning onto its final.

Alan felt his body starting to get tense again and then saw that he was creeping up on Ned, so he slowed more. As Ned neared the turn onto his base leg, Alan realized he was still creeping up on Ned. Apparently, Ned was slowing to keep his distance on the last marine. Alan decided to delay his turn to base leg to give more space. In a short while, Alan was turning onto his final approach and Ned had landed. Alan had been too busy to watch any of the landings. His apprehension continued to rise.

He started watching Campbell as he approached, and Campbell began signaling that Alan was low. Remembering the nasty tricks of the BT-1, he gently moved the throttle forward. The angle of descent decreased, but not enough. The cameraman was beginning to film, and a wave of fear hit Alan. Campbell was signaling vigorously that he was low, so Alan continued opening the throttle until he was back to the correct glide path, but then his angle of descent was too shallow. Campbell gave Alan the cut signal. He had just closed the throttle when a gust of wind hit his airplane and pushed it up well above the correct glide path as he went over the stern.

He quickly realized that he was so high that there was a danger of missing all the arresting wires. He had to try to go around, even though it would be nip-and-tuck. His adrenaline spiked. He began opening the throttle slowly. He glanced at the airspeed indicator, which remained close to sixty-five knots. To avoid having to fly over the aircraft that were parked forward, he began a very shallow turn to the left, since turning right would have taken him toward the island. In a quick movement that he had practiced during his checkout, he took his left hand off the throttle, shoved the tail hook lever that was beside the seat forward as fast as he could to raise the hook, and brought his hand back to the throttle to keep it moving forward.

He was in a tight spot and more adrenaline was pumping. He wanted to raise the landing gear, but he was too busy, just as he had been told he would be in this situation. He kept the throttle moving forward as fast as he dared and began to lift the nose. He leveled off as he went past the funnels. He cleared the first barrier that was up, which was number three. By then, he had the throttle fully open. He was about ten feet above the deck as he approached the port edge and saw that the men in the gallery had ducked down. A blue shirt was on his stomach on the flight deck. He glanced at the airspeed indicator again, and it was still at sixty-five knots. His right wing cleared barrier number four by about two feet. Then he was over the water and had another fifty feet of altitude to work with.

He put the nose down to gain a little more speed and turned to raising the landing gear, grasping the stick with his left hand. When that was finished, he put his right hand back on the stick and leveled off about ten feet above the water. He was still gaining speed slowly as the landing gear finished coming up. When the landing gear was up, he was doing eighty knots—twenty knots above stall speed. He brought the flaps up in steps to avoid losing any more altitude. Finally, he was doing 100 knots and starting a normal climb.

He glanced at the cylinder head temperature and saw that it was reading 260 degrees Centigrade, which was right at the red line that indicated the maximum temperature allowed. The BT-1 had cowl flaps that opened behind the engine to let more cooling air flow over the cylinders. He was glad that these were normally opened as the last item on the landing checklist to be prepared for a go-around. He pulled the power back to the climb setting and knew that the cylinder heads would start to cool down. He let out a long sigh, and his heart rate began to ease off. He realized he was soaking wet with sweat, even though there was a nice breeze in the cockpit with the canopy open. He felt drained, but he still had to go around the circuit again and land.

On the downwind leg, he pulled himself together and went through the landing checklist again methodically. The cylinder head temperature had come down to 220, so that was good. He had the landing circuit to himself. He turned base and throttled back. As he turned final, his speed was approaching five knots above stall, which was right where he wanted it. He started watching Campbell intently. Alan seemed to be in the groove this time, because he got only an occasional brief signal from Campbell. As he got close in, Campbell gave Alan the cut, so he closed the throttle and hit near the number-two wire. The hook caught the third. He was grateful to be thrown forward against his braced left arm and the seat belt this time. He let out another long sigh.

Green shirts released the hook and yellow shirts directed him to park. He shut down and climbed out. The wind made his sweaty clothes seem even colder than before. When he glanced at his watch, it said 1150. It seemed like hours since he had taken off, but it had only been about thirty minutes. He jumped down to the deck.

The nearest yellow shirt shouted, "I trust you're aware of the regulation, sir, that says you have to buy new skivvies for the whole deck crew?"

Alan had expected that they would be sullen at best, but he glanced around and they were all grinning.

"Welcome to carrier aviation," said the yellow shirt.

Alan smiled weakly and shouted back, "Thank you!" *Fine crew,* he thought, *to remain so cheerful after a bad scare.* He started walking aft toward the island and saw that Jack was standing in the same place he had been in earlier, forward of the island, talking to Ned and a marine captain and first lieutenant.

As he walked up, Jack introduced him to the marines.

The first marine grinned and said, "Glad you were able to turn and miss the planes that were parked forward. We figure that our wing loading is high enough without having our wings clipped."

"That was close," agreed the second marine.

"But only BT-1 pilots can fully appreciate how nice that was," Ned replied.

"Thanks, Ned," said Alan. "I don't know what else I could have done."

"Once you decided to go around, you did a fine job," Jack told Alan with a serious expression. "And you weren't so rattled that you couldn't make an excellent landing afterward. It isn't absolutely necessary to catch one of the first four wires, however." He broke into a wide grin.

"Thank you, sir," said Alan.

"I'm getting hungry," piped in the second marine.

They turned and walked toward the island. The two marines went through the door into the island, followed by Ned. Jack drew Alan aside and they walked over to the starboard side of the deck.

Jack leaned toward Alan so that he would not need to raise his voice over the wind. "You didn't have to go around. That gust of wind caused you to balloon up and increased your airspeed, making you think you were high and fast, but it didn't increase your speed over the deck. If you'd have chopped your throttle and kept coming, I think you'd have hit before the sixth wire."

Alan had not thought of this. "I see what you mean about my speed over the deck. You're probably right . . . . No, I'm *sure* you're right. I'm just a little too anxious to catch one of the first few wires, I suppose."

"Those further wires are there to be used. Of course, if you're really fast, like that marine lieutenant was, you'll have trouble."

"Yes, sir." Alan felt deflated, but he appreciated that Jack had taken him aside for the negative parts of his review.

Jack clapped him on the shoulder and said, "Let's get some lunch." They walked into the island and down to the wardroom.

It was a little before 1330 when they came back onto the flight deck. The weather remained fine, and had gotten a little warmer. The planes had been re-spotted aft again. Alan and Ned were in the front row, reversing the order once again. The ship was steaming southeast. Ned and Alan headed for their planes, and Jack turned away again to take his place in the gallery. As Alan came up to his plane, the deck began to cant to port as the ship started to turn back into the northwest wind.

Alan took off and Ned joined up on his right wing. In his landing, Alan caught a puff of wind just after he got the cut, much like the first approach his last time around. This time he closed the throttle and maintained his airspeed. He bounced near the fifth wire and caught the sixth. He found he could handle the extra deceleration of the further wire okay. Perhaps he was simply getting more used to the forces. His plane stopped well short of the first barrier that was up, but it still made him nervous. The time was 1403.

For the fourth round, the same pattern of operations continued. They started their engines and took off again, with Alan the "Tail-End Charlie" once more. Alan caught up with Ned and they flew their circuit as before.

On his base leg, he took one more glance at the flight deck to see that Ned was about to touch down. As he straightened up on final, he saw Ned taxiing forward. Although the wind was gustier, Alan stayed pretty well in the groove as he came in to land, and Campbell gave him the cut. As he approached the deck, a gust of wind lifted the right wing. He immediately put in the full right aileron and rudder, but the roll angle got bigger. He hit the deck hard on the left landing gear first. As the airplane began to rock to the right, there was a bang. Suddenly his left wing went down. The wing dragged on the deck as his hook, which had caught a wire, hauled down his speed and the airplane came to a grating stop. He knew that the left main landing gear had collapsed.

He was not going anywhere. He sat in the strangely canted cockpit and carefully shut down the engine and turned off the switches. He unstrapped and climbed out, nearly falling off the canted left wing. He jumped down and waved off the pharmacist's mates who came rushing up. Alan felt defeated and subdued, but he was physically fine. He didn't know what he could have done differently, but his carrier qualification had come to an abrupt end before the required four successful landings.

He looked around and saw blue shirts running toward his airplane from all over the flight deck. Alan walked around the left wing to look at the damage, and a yellow shirt told him to get off the flight deck, which Alan interpreted to mean "Get the hell out of the way." He went over to the starboard gallery and turned to watch how the flight deck crew would deal with the fouled deck.

Several yellow shirts were directing the converging blue shirts. Ten of the blue shirts climbed onto the right wing and crept out toward the tip. They seated themselves as far out as possible on top of the right wing, with their legs dangling over the leading edge. Twenty more blue shirts began to squeeze under the left wing. With their backs against the lower wing surface, they began pushing upward. Alan watched in fascination. He realized that those on the right wing were using the wing as a lever to lighten the load on the left wing. After a few minutes, all twenty blue shirts were under the left wing and had raised it to the normal, level position.

A mixture of blue and green shirts surrounded the collapsed landing gear and manhandled it into the down position. Two mechanics, who did not have colored shirts, came running up from the hangar deck and locked the gear into the down position. Alan was amazed that it took only about ten minutes to get his immobilized airplane ready to roll, without the use of cranes or jacks. *A lot of skilled and eager manpower can accomplish remarkable things quickly,* he realized. He also suspected that the structural engineers at Northrop had never analyzed the stresses caused by this particular maneuver. His BT-1 was pushed forward to the mid-ship elevator.

It was 1505. Jack and Ned came aft to the gallery. "The same thing happened to you as happened to Ned," Jack told him, "but he was luckier. The gust that hit your airplane was harder, and you tipped further. That's what collapsed the left landing gear."

"What should we be doing to prevent this?" Alan asked.

Jack said, "These gusts are pretty hard to handle. The ship is still heading into the northwest wind, but there are gusts from the north, and I think the island and funnels are adding to the turbulence. When the wind is this strong and gusty, you should carry five knots more on final. That might have kept you both out of trouble. Fortunately, we aren't scheduled for more carrier landings today. Congratulations, Ned, you are qualified. Alan will ride back with me and finish his qualification another day. Let's get a Coke while the deck crewmen are re-spotting the airplanes."

They had their Cokes and returned to the flight deck. They said good-bye to the marines and headed to their airplanes. This time, the order had not been reversed, so the marines were still in front. After they had taken off, it was Ned's turn. Jack took off last, and Alan rode as his passenger. During the flight back, Alan thought over the events of the day. He understood that his accident was really a matter of luck, and it could have happened just as easily to Ned, but that knowledge did not keep him from feeling glum. He was the pilot that didn't pass carrier qualification, and no amount of explaining would change that. They arrived back at Norfolk at 1625. It was not late, but Alan felt that he had had a long day.

Friday, June 20, 1941

By the time Jack Casey stood up to propose a toast during the squadron party at the Officers' Club, everyone had already had a fair amount to drink. Although the party had been scheduled for some time, Jack took the opportunity to celebrate Alan's and Ned's carrier qualifications. He gave a colorful description of all the ups and downs of Alan's and Ned's qualification landings on Tuesday, including the marine pilot's crash, Alan's last-minute go-around, and his landing gear collapse. Jack continued, "Ericsson took up his qualification again yesterday. Although he only needed to make one additional landing to qualify, he insisted on making four. They all worked out well. He may not be our luckiest pilot, but he does not lack determination." Jack raised his glass. "I propose a toast to the squadron's newest qualified pilots, Ned Morris and Alan Ericsson!" There was a roar of approval and all stood and toasted Ned and Alan.

Alan was moved. He still felt like the least-qualified rookie, but the gesture went a long way toward making him feel truly welcomed to the fraternity. It was something that he had looked forward to since he had applied for pilot training almost a year earlier.

CHAPTER NINETEEN

Jennifer's Plans

Friday, July 4, 1941

Alan and Jennifer met just after 1400 at their hotel in Annapolis, Maryland. Alan showed Jennifer around the Naval Academy before dinner, and then they ate at a nice restaurant on an outdoor terrace overlooking the water.

During dinner the conversation inevitably turned to the German invasion of Russia, which had started two weeks earlier.

Russia had begun to focus on Germany alone, and not Japan, removing one possible restraint on Japanese expansion. Jennifer reported that the navy director of War Plans thought that the Japanese would invade Russia's eastern territories, now that Russia was distracted in the west, but not many agreed with him. The idea that Japan would invade Russia made little sense to Jennifer or Alan, because it was well known that the Japanese coveted the resources of Southeast Asia and the East Indies much more than anything in Russia. Also, they realized that the Japanese Army would have to lead an invasion of Russia, and their army remained largely bogged down in China.

They talked about their plans for the rest of the weekend, as well. They had made a plan two weeks earlier to sail over to the eastern side of Chesapeake Bay and return on Sunday. In the meantime Alan had chartered a thirty-foot sailboat through a friend at the Academy.

Saturday, July 5, 1941

After spending a pleasant night in their hotel, Alan and Jennifer boarded the thirty-foot ketch that Alan had chartered. After looking over the boat and stowing their food and clothes, they took a leisurely sail across Chesapeake Bay, getting familiar with the boat along the way. In the late afternoon they rounded Willard Point and sailed into Eastern Bay, anchoring for the night. Being on the water was a relief from the heat on shore, but in the bay they were sheltered from the west wind, and they went for a swim off the boat. They kept their swim suits on and Jennifer warmed up supper on the little galley stove while Alan cleaned the cockpit and pumped out the bilge.

After supper, they sat in the cockpit and sipped gin and tonic. The boat had a platform that could be set up between the benches on the sides of the cockpit, forming a double bed. They sat close together at the after end, propped up with cushions, watching the sunset over the bow.

"The sunset reminds me that in another month it will be the anniversary of your proposal," said Jennifer.

Alan leaned over and gave her a kiss. "That's right. I wonder where we'll be a year from now."

"Good question. We could both be at Pearl Harbor."

"Wow. That's true. When you think about it that seems to be one of the more likely possibilities."

She leaned over and gave him a kiss. "Wherever it is, you rascal, I hope we can be together some of the time."

"Me too, you scalawag."

Saturday, July 26, 1941

Having met closer to Jennifer's home earlier in the month, Alan and Jennifer decided to go to the newly restored colonial village of Williamsburg, Virginia. Not relishing the long drive from Washington, Jennifer decided to try the ferry steamer. It went from Washington to Gloucester, on the west side of Chesapeake Bay, which was a short local ferry ride across the York River from

Yorktown, the site of the battle after which the carrier was named. Williamsburg was just a ten-mile drive from Yorktown.

To go north from Norfolk NAS toward Yorktown to meet Jennifer, the easy way was to take the ferry from Willoughby Spit north across the James River entrance to Old Point Comfort, a route Alan had used several times to get to Hampton. Jennifer was due to arrive in Yorktown on the ferry at about 1515. Alan had plenty of time get there and meet her, so he decided for variety to go around to the west and cross over the James River Bridge instead.

After a circuitous drive south and west from Norfolk NOB, Alan crossed the long bridge and approached South Newport News. He looked off to his right and saw the brand new aircraft carrier *Hornet*, CV-8, docked at the Newport News shipyard for fitting out. She looked big. She was almost identical to the *Yorktown* class carriers, but she had a few changes that the navy thought justified giving her a class of her own. Nearby, he recognized the recently commissioned *Long Island*, the first US Navy escort carrier, which had been converted from a cargo ship in just sixty-seven days. Alan understood that escort carriers could be churned out much faster and cheaper than the big fleet carriers, and they would be very useful where the US had control of the air, but she looked small and vulnerable.

Alan remembered hearing that, after the *Hornet* had slid down the ways into the James River the previous December, workmen had immediately started to lay the keel of the *Essex* in the same slip on the same day. It was a good indicator of the urgency of the carrier-building program. The *Essex*, CV-9, was planned to be the first of eleven in a new and larger class of carriers. They would be a tremendous addition to the fleet, but the *Essex* would probably not be ready for combat for at least two more years.

He continued north on US Route 17 for about twenty miles, until he reached Yorktown and made his way to the ferry terminal.

Jennifer arrived on schedule at 1515 after a pleasant ride down the Potomac and lower Chesapeake Bay. They drove to their hotel in Williamsburg and checked in, and then they walked around the village, stopping to tour some of the houses and shops. There were people in the houses dressed in period clothing, and trained in the spoken English of the time. Alan and Jennifer found themselves feeling like they had truly stepped back in time, and they were captivated. As the afternoon came to a close, they returned to their hotel, changed, and walked to a restaurant for dinner.

Jennifer was almost always cheerful and enthusiastic when they got together, but on this occasion Alan had noticed that she had seemed subdued since the moment she arrived. After they ordered drinks, Alan decided to ask about it.

"I have a feeling that you have something weighty on your mind. Does it have something to do with your work?"

"You read me like a book, don't you?" She smiled. "Yes, it does. Did you listen to the radio today? Did you hear about Roosevelt's announcement in response to the Japanese going into Indochina? Did you also hear that they announced today that they're bringing MacArthur out of retirement?"

"I heard both. Roosevelt said he'd frozen Japanese assets, but I didn't hear him say anything about an oil embargo."

"If there isn't a very quiet oil embargo already in place, it seems very likely that there soon will be. It all fits together. Roosevelt has been resisting an embargo because, as he himself put it, he doesn't have enough navy to go around. Now the Army has stepped into the gap. They've convinced both themselves and the president that they can defend the Philippines and block Japan's thrust to the south."

Alan exclaimed, "Oh boy, it sounds like a disaster in the making, reversing thirty years of planning in a few days. What made the army change their minds?"

"The B-17. The heavy bomber boys think it's unstoppable," Jennifer replied.

"That's even worse. You know, a year ago the British were showing the world what it takes to defend against a strong air attack. They have a lot of heavy bombers, but those didn't play much of a role in the defense."

"I agree. In any case, I think we're headed toward war, and I've been thinking more about going to Pearl Harbor. You know ONI has access to all of the current plans for naval units. I got confirmation that the plan is for Bombing Five to go back aboard the *Yorktown* in September and that the *Yorktown* is scheduled to be away from Norfolk on neutrality patrols for the whole fall. We wouldn't be seeing much of each other this fall in any case.

"I went out to lunch a couple of times with Mrs. Driscoll, the other professional woman who works for ONC, and I asked her for her advice. She said that, at Pearl Harbor, I would really be the lone woman. I would not have even her to talk to. She thinks I could handle it, though, and that, with my background, I might be happier working there."

Jennifer paused, grasped Alan's hand, and looked into his eyes. He looked back and saw that hers were shiny with tears. "I turned this all over in my mind pretty thoroughly on my ferry trip down here, Alan. I want to ask for your consent to let me apply for transfer to Pearl Harbor."

He had been bracing himself for this possibility since their first conversation about it in June, but it still hit him hard. Even so, he could not hold her back for a little extra time together. "Jennifer, I'll never stand in your way. It'll be hard to be away from you for a long time again, but, as you say, it seems inevitable that we will be apart for the whole fall, at least. After that, who knows?"

She began to sob. "Oh, Alan, you're such an understanding man. It makes it even harder to think about going away. I love you very much. I guess that you and I just aren't destined to lead a normal life together for the next few years." She leaned into him and buried her face in his shoulder, tears running down her cheeks.

He wrapped his arms around her as tears welled up in his eyes, as well. "You're right. Neither of us could shirk from doing our best for our country at a time like this, even if it means being apart. It makes me proud to be your husband. I love you, Jennifer."

She pushed back and looked him in the eyes again. "What a beautiful thing to say," she exclaimed before bursting into tears again and hugging him.

After a couple of minutes, they got out handkerchiefs and collected themselves. The waiter, who had been hovering discreetly out of sight with their drinks, finally appeared, served their drinks, and took their dinner orders.

Alan said, "I imagine the transfer process will take a while, so you won't miss Victoria's wedding, in any case. Right?"

"That's right. I think it'll take a couple of months, at least, so you're likely to go away before I do."

"Well, we should have some time together on the train going to and from Providence."

"I guess so. I've been thinking mostly about going to Pearl Harbor and not any other travel." She paused. "Now, let's hear about what has been happening in your life."

"Well, having gotten through my carrier qualification, I've hit the next big hurdle. We've been practicing dive-bombing on a moving target, which is a sled that they tow behind a destroyer off of Virginia Beach. I was the best in my class in dive-bombing at Pensacola, but that was bombing a fixed target on land. I knew that a moving target would be harder to hit, but I had no idea how much harder. I got the lowest score in the squadron the first time we tried. The tow ship does evasive maneuvers, usually turning in a tight circle. During the dive, you have to roll the airplane to follow the target, and you also want to keep your aiming point upwind of the target. Since you're looking nearly straight down and not at the horizon, it's hard to keep track of which direction you're going, relative to the wind."

"That sounds nearly impossible," she commiserated.

"Some of the pilots are good at it, so there must be a way to get the hang of it. I guess that it's just another thing I will have to keep working at."

"I'm sure you'll figure it out."

"I hope so. I'm continuing to get to know the pilots in the squadron. There's a lot of variety there. One fellow I particularly like is Lieutenant j.g. James Lowery. Some people call him Jim, but he got the nickname Jolly at the Academy—for good reason. He's a conscientious member of the squadron, and he gets good dive-bombing scores. He has a mind of his own, however, and an irrepressible, rebellious sense of humor, which is ready to spring out at any time.

"I've been appointed assistant engineering officer, which mainly means that I help supervise the enlisted men who maintain the airplanes, and it seems like a good place for me for the time being. My boss is the engineering officer, Lieutenant Angus MacAllester, known as Scottie, and I consider him a friend.

"The navigation officer, Lieutenant Chauncey Vang, is an interesting character. He was in the class of '30 at the Academy, so he left just as I started. He's tall, handsome, and sociable, but he puts on an air of superiority. He's a blue-blood from Boston. I've heard rumors that he is not well respected as a pilot in the squadron. Boom is his nickname, named after the sailboat term. He despises it, but it seems like a good antidote to his haughty manner."

The waiter appeared with their dinners.

Alan continued, "The big news in my life is that the squadron is about to make a really long flight. We just got our orders on

Thursday. We get leave starting next Wednesday, and we are to report to El Segundo, near Los Angeles, on August 6. The plan is that we'll spend a few days out there checking out in our SBDs and then fly them back here to Norfolk. This is the kind of thing I've been hoping might happen, because I've always looked forward to really going somewhere by air. We should see all sorts of scenery from the air. There may be some intriguing navigational problems and instrument flying, too."

"That sounds very exciting, Alan. I confess that I'm jealous, although I have only a vague idea what it would be like, really. When do you think you'll be back in Norfolk?"

"They told us that it would be roughly a week after we get to Los Angeles."

"So we could get together the weekend of August 16? It's your turn to come north, and I guess you might as well come to my apartment. It would be fun to go to Annapolis again, but probably not worth it for one day."

"You're right. Three weeks after that will be Victoria's wedding. I think I can wangle Friday off, so we won't have to take a sleeper. How about you?"

"I've already talked to my boss about it, and he said that I could make it up on a Saturday. I told him that the bride and groom were both navy people, and he smiled and said, 'That makes it tantamount to navy business, doesn't it?' He was very nice about it. I hope he doesn't turn sour when I tell him I want to go to Pearl. I think he already knows, though."

"I hope he doesn't sour, too. He sounds like a good guy. He must be really frustrated by the situation at ONI."

"Definitely."

Their conversation turned to what places in Williamsburg they would see the next day before he took her back to the ferry at Yorktown, finishing their meal. After dinner they took another stroll around the village on the way back to their hotel.

CHAPTER TWENTY

Switching to the Dauntless

Wednesday, August 6, 1941

Bombing Five's pilots were meeting in a conference room at the El Segundo plant of Douglas Aircraft Company. They had spent the morning and the first half of the afternoon being thoroughly introduced to the SBD in ground school. The pilots had been issued the pilot's manual back at Norfolk, but ground school brought up the important points in a more memorable way, and they were able to talk about a few more things that had not made it into the manual.

Alan had read that the prototype of the SBD had been planned to be just an improved version of the BT-1, and it was called the XBT-2. Somehow, the scope of work quietly expanded to include a switch to the larger and more powerful Wright R-1820 Cyclone engine, fully retractable main landing gear, and many other changes. It was really a new airplane, which normally required that the program be opened up to competition with other manufacturers, but in this case the navy preferred to keep the process short and simple. At the same time, the navy decided that any dive-bomber should also be able to be used for reconnaissance, known as scouting, so the letter "S" was added to the aircraft designation. The Northrop Company in El Segundo, which started the design as the XBT-2, was bought out by Douglas, leading to the change in the aircraft designation to SBD. Its company nickname was Dauntless, and many who knew the airplane also called it the "Slow But Deadly" or the "Speedy D."

Alan learned that Bombing Five was to receive the latest version, the SBD-3, which had gone into production the previous March. This version was equipped with a bulletproof windshield, armor protection for both crewmen, and self-sealing fuel tanks. Like the BT-1, it was able to carry either a 500-pound or 1,000-pound bomb externally under the fuselage. For defense, it had two fixed .50-caliber machine guns in the top of the fuselage in front of the cockpit that fired forward through the propeller, and, like the BT-1, one flexible .30-caliber machine gun in the rear cockpit.

As the pilots came back to the conference room after a short break, the Douglas public relations man announced, "Now, you're going to get to meet two men who were key in the development of the SBD. The first is Ed Heinemann, the man who designed the SBD. He also worked on the BT-1 that you've been flying. The second is Vance Breese, test pilot on both aircraft. Here's Ed." *Wow, Ed Heinemann himself!* thought Alan, suddenly excited. A tall, thin man with glasses and hair that was combed straight back strode to the front of the room. He did not look many years older than Alan.

"Gentlemen, I'm here to give you a brief description of what we did to the BT-1 to turn it into the SBD. Please feel free to ask questions either as we go along or after I've finished." He proceeded to describe the process of modifying the design of the BT-1 to become the XBT-2 and the SBD. He finished by saying, "In the end, about the only things we *didn't* change were the gunner's seat and the flaps. As you know, we put a lot of effort into developing those flaps on the BT-1, and we were pretty sure they didn't need any improvement." There was a murmur of agreement among the pilots and then a pause as Heinemann glanced around, evidently soliciting questions.

Scottie broke the ice. "When I look at drawings of the two airplanes, they look an awful lot alike. How can the SBD handle so much better when you cannot see much difference on paper?"

Heinemann smiled and said, "That's a very good question. Of course, the visible things like sizes, aspect ratios, and clean lines all make a big difference in performance, but the fact is that when it comes to the aerodynamics involved in handling qualities, little things can make a big difference also. That's why we did all that tinkering with the ailerons, wing slots, rudder, and elevators.

"Let me give you an example: Last year, Vance Breese was checking out one of our new SBD-2s, and he found that it stalled at a speed more than a few knots higher than it was supposed to. This was a complete surprise, and it left us scratching our heads for a couple of days. We started looking closely at the leading edges of the wings and we noticed that where the yellow paint on the top of the wings met the aluminum color on the bottom, the paint had formed a little ridge along the leading edge that was a little ways back from the stagnation point. After we smoothed that ridge off, Vance flew the airplane again, and it stalled at the normal speed."

There were smiles and another murmur of appreciation among the pilots.

The public relations man stood up and said, "Let's take a ten-minute break. Ed will stay here a few more minutes if you have any further questions."

Most of the pilots went outside into the California sunshine. Alan went up to the front of the conference room, feeling very deferential in the presence of this highly respected aircraft designer.

"Hello. Lieutenant j.g. Alan Ericsson," Alan introduced himself.

Heinemann smiled and said, "I'm pleased to meet you. What can I do for you?"

"Thank you very much for talking to us. It's a great pleasure to hear a real airplane designer discuss his work. I have a question: The BT-1 and the SBD both have fairly large fairings between the wings and the fuselage, and I've noticed that in some of the newer designs, like the SB2C and the F4F, there are minimal fairings. In the F4U, there are none. Is that the current trend, to get rid of them?"

"You're interested in aircraft design, I see. Yes, starting in the mid-'30s, wind tunnel tests have indicated that fairings aren't as helpful as we used to think. Vought jumped ahead and took it to the extreme with the F4U, but I think they were on the right track. If we were designing a completely new dive-bomber today, it would have minimal or no fairings."

"I imagine that, even when there's a project underway, you're always working on a few other designs that are tucked away in a drawer somewhere," Alan prodded.

"That's right," said Heinemann, his eyes twinkling.

"I'd love to see what's in that drawer," said Alan, smiling, "but obviously, I'm far from eligible for that privilege. Thanks very much."

"You're welcome. I'm always glad to meet a pilot who cares about aircraft design."

Alan had become aware that Vang was standing impatiently behind him and to his right. Vang shouldered Alan aside and moved in front.

"Lieutenant Chauncey Vang, sir. I was wondering if you could give us more range? It could be critical in a carrier versus carrier situation."

Alan felt like rolling his eyes, but he refrained. Over Vang's shoulder, Alan watched Heinemann, who seemed to be taking it in stride.

"We've been working on a drop tank for scouting, but we had to put it on the centerline attach point, and it would take a while to switch over to the bomb rack."

"I was thinking of putting another tank in the fuselage that we could use for any mission. There seems to be a lot of space under the cockpit."

Heinemann's benign expression faded, and he started to look bored. "That's where the main fuel tanks are," Heinemann explained.

"We were told this morning that the main tanks are in the wings," Vang responded.

Heinemann is having trouble hiding his impatience, Alan noticed.

"That's right, and the wing center section passes through the fuselage under the cockpit."

Vang was about to say something in response when the public relations man deftly interceded. "Thanks a lot, Ed. I'm sure the pilots appreciated what you had to say."

Heinemann turned and exited quickly.

Raising his voice, the public relations man announced to the whole room, "Please come back and sit down," and then he waited while the rest of the pilots took their seats. "I'd like to introduce Vance Breese, who did a lot of the test flying on both the BT-1 and the SBD. We aren't the only ones who think highly of Vance, either. Last October, when our friends up the street at North American needed a test pilot to make the first flight in their hot new fighter, they chose Vance."

Like most pilots, Alan had read about the hot new fighter that the British had ordered from North American. The British called it the Mustang, and the US Army called it the XP-51 Apache. He had also heard via the grapevine that a month into the flight test program, last November, the prototype had run a fuel tank dry and made a forced landing in a field, nosing over. The incident seemed amazingly similar to the XF4U forced landing Alan had witnessed four months before that, except that it occurred in good weather.

A balding, dark-haired man with a double chin and wearing a business suit came up to the front of the room. *He doesn't look like a superman test pilot*, Alan observed. The man proceeded to give a short talk on the various ways in which the SBD would feel different from the BT-1. When he was finished, Alan had no doubt that Breese was an expert test pilot. Breese asked if there were any questions, and there was an awkward pause.

"What was your most frightening moment during the test program?" asked Jack Casey.

Breese smiled and said, "You may be disappointed to hear that the most frightening moment for me occurred on the ground." He paused to let that sink in. "As you know, when we started the diving tests with the XBT-1, we had a bad tail buffet when we used the new split dive flaps. Ed Heinemann got in the back seat and went up with me over several flights, and he filmed the tail with a movie camera. When we came down, we got the film processed and sat down together to watch the movie. The movie showed how much the tail was moving; the tips of the horizontal stabilizer were going up and down about a foot either way. The structure was a very sturdy design to take that kind of abuse without coming apart, and it scared the hell out of me. Later, Ed admitted to me that it scared the hell out of him, too. As you probably know, a NACA expert suggested that we put a lot of holes in the flaps, and that got rid of the tail buffet."

There was a moment of stunned silence, followed by a murmur of appreciation from the pilots. *Both Breese and Heinemann would probably have been killed if the tail had come apart*, Alan realized.

The public relations man stood and said, "Well, that winds up the ground school part of your time here. It's almost five o'clock . . . excuse me, 1700, so I think we can call it a day. It has been a pleasure to meet all of you. I'll turn the floor over to Commander Arnham."

Arnham came up to the front. Alan remembered meeting him at the Officers' Club with Jack in the spring, and had since learned that Arnham was a dynamic and demanding officer who could bark out orders in spite of his short stature. He was highly respected by his wary pilots.

"Okay, the Douglas shuttle bus is on its way here to take us back to the hotel. Here's the plan: Tomorrow, the shuttle bus will pick us up at the hotel at 0710 and take us directly out to the Douglas hangar on Mines Field. We should be there by 0730. As you know, the exec, the flight officer, and I came out a couple of days early, and we've been checked out as pilots and checkout instructors by three Douglas pilots." Arnham continued, "Tomorrow morning, the three of us and the three Douglas pilots will each take three of you for a checkout flight of one hour. In the afternoon, you'll all have your own aircraft for solo practice for a couple of hours. We plan to have more solo practice Friday morning, as well. Friday afternoon, we'll make our final preparations for the trip back to Norfolk. We plan to depart Saturday morning. Any questions?"

"What's the weather forecast?" asked Jim Lowery.

Arnham replied, "Sunny and pleasant. Sometimes fog comes in off the ocean in the afternoon or at night and hangs around during the morning, but that isn't forecast for the next two days." He looked around the room for more questions, but none came. "Okay, get a good night's rest," he instructed with a grin.

Thursday, August 7, 1941

The Douglas shuttle bus was right on time, and the pilots of Bombing Five were on their way to Mines Field. Alan noted that one of the pilots, Ensign Sherwood "Slippery" Simpkin, had missed the shuttle bus for the second time. Another pilot, Lieutenant j.g. Jeremiah "Jerry" West, who was originally from Santa Monica, spent the ride telling some of the other pilots about the layout of the western side of Los Angeles and Mines Field. Alan was also somewhat familiar with the area, because during his surface tour, the *Pennsylvania* had been based in San Pedro, about twelve miles to the south. Ned Morris told Alan that he had been to Los Angeles once on a family trip from Tucson.

The bus went west past the north end of the Douglas plant and took a right onto Douglas Street. When they crossed Imperial Highway, they came to a gate with a guard. The guard boarded the bus, took some paperwork from the driver, and looked around the bus. He counted the number of passengers and checked it against his manifest.

"Somebody's missing," he grunted.

"One of our pilots missed the bus," Arnham replied. "Ensign Simpkin."

"Okay," the guard said. Seeing that they were all in uniform, he told the bus driver, "Okay, Buck, they all look legit."

After passing through the gate, they were on the airfield. Alan looked to his right and saw rows of parked airplanes in front of a large factory building.

"That's the North American plant," remarked one of the pilots.

"Shiny new SNJs," another noticed.

"Or army AT-6s. That must be about the last batch to be built here. They're transferring that production line to their new plant in Dallas," replied the first.

"Those big twin-tailed airplanes must be B-25s," another pilot chimed in.

"Yeah," answered the first.

Alan was looking at a single-engine airplane that stood by itself in front. It was a sleek, low-wing monoplane, a single-seater. The streamlined nose showed that it had an inline liquid-cooled engine. Alan had no doubt about what type of plane it was. The engine was the Allison V-1710, which was the same as the engine in the P-40, but the airplane was much cleaner than the P-40. "There it is, the XP-51," he announced.

"What? Where?" asked several pilots.

Alan noticed that Arnham and Casey glanced at him and then back at the XP-51. The bus driver spoke up.

"Two weeks ago last Sunday, North American had an event for their employees. A lot of Douglas employees heard about it and came to the field, too. North American demonstrated all their airplanes, but that Apache stole the show. It was really amazing. I've been around a lot of military aircraft, and I've never seen anything like it. That airplane is very fast—and maneuverable, too."

The bus turned left onto a road parallel to the main runway, and stopped at a large hangar. Two dozen SBDs were parked in front of it. The pilots got out of the bus and stretched. The sky was clear, though a little hazy, and the temperature was in the mid-sixties. *Typical beautiful Southern California weather*, Alan thought, enjoying it.

They went into the hangar. The usual large blackboard that showed the flight schedule was set up in front of rows of folding chairs. The pilots were divided into three groups, flying at 0800, 0930, and 1100. Alan saw that he was scheduled to fly at 0930 in aircraft number sixteen with Gordie Bellingham, the flight officer. He looked for Simpkin's name to see if he would miss his flight. Perhaps someone anticipated his late arrival, because he was scheduled at 1100. Coffee was laid out on a table to one side, and Alan took a cup.

The Douglas chief pilot stood next to the blackboard and called for the pilots to take their seats.

"Welcome to Mines Field. As you've probably already noticed, your flight schedule is on the blackboard here. The airplane you fly this morning will be yours for the trip back east unless we have a bad squawk and have to make a swap. You can pick up your parachutes in the back of the hangar. Also, this morning, our maintenance chief, Joe Pruitt," he said as he pointed to a stocky man with a crew cut, "will be conducting a walk-around with small groups to get you all familiar with the maintenance requirements of the SBD. When you aren't flying, you should join one of his groups. If you notice anything wrong with one of the airplanes, let him know and he'll get it taken care of. All of the airplanes have at least a few hours of flight test on them, but otherwise they're brand new. Take care, and have a good flight."

Alan decided to look over his airplane before his flight and join the maintenance session afterward. He finished his cup of coffee, picked up his parachute, and headed out to the flight line. He found number sixteen and began looking it over. As he got close, he could smell the new paint. There was something about the way the SBD looked that he really liked. The proportions just seemed right to him, like those of the SNJ. On the other hand, the BT-1's fuselage seemed long and skinny, in addition to its landing gear looking clumsy.

He had plenty of time before his checkout flight, so he climbed up and put his parachute in the pilot's seat and then jumped down and started to look over the exterior. The big perforated flaps at the trailing edge on both the upper and lower surfaces of the wings were similar to those on the BT-1. As he passed the right wing tip, though, he was pleased to see the three slots in the leading edge of the wing that were placed there to improve the stall behavior by preventing the outer part of the wing from stalling first. If the outer part of the wing remained unstalled as the rest of the wing approached a stall, there was much less tendency for one wing to fall off, as well as a chance of retaining aileron effectiveness.

Alan looked at the nose and realized that this would be the first plane that he would fly that had a three-bladed propeller. He smiled as he thought about how it must have irked the Curtiss-Wright Company to have the competition's Hamilton Standard propeller on their engine. On the other hand, it probably irked Pratt & Whitney, a division of United Aircraft like Hamilton

Standard, to have the competition's Curtiss electric propeller on the F4F. The nine-cylinder Wright Cyclone engine on the SBD was the largest single-row radial engine that Alan had heard of. It had been around for about ten years, so it had undergone considerable development and was quite reliable. It did not look too large for the fuselage, contrary to some rumors that he had heard about it. This version was rated at 1,000 horsepower.

The main landing gear looked very much like the gear on the SNJ, except that it was somewhat bigger. It seemed like a huge improvement over the arrangement on the BT-1, but not quite as clean as the fully enclosed main gear Alan had seen on the SB2U. The retractable gear and the more powerful engine made the airplane about twenty knots faster than the BT-1, or about the same speed as the SB2U. The designers at Vought deserved a lot of credit for the clean design of the SB2U, considering that it was three years older than the SBD and had a less powerful engine.

Alan climbed onto the wing walk next to the fuselage on the left side to get a look into the cockpit. He used the step in the fuselage to get up and lean easily into the rear cockpit, which was quite similar to that of the BT-1. Moving up to the front cockpit, he saw the muzzles of the two 0.50-caliber machine guns protruding from behind the top of the engine cowling, and noticed the grooves in the cowling which let the bullets pass. Once he was seated in the pilot's seat, the breeches of the two machine guns were prominent, sitting on either side of the main instrument panel, with the charging handles within easy reach. He imagined there would be impressive smoke and noise from twice the forward armament of the BT-1.

As he looked forward, he saw the outer windshield, which was made of curved plastic. Behind the outer windshield was a second windshield, which was flat glass that was about an inch thick. This second windshield was designed to be bullet resistant. He also noticed the armor plate behind the pilot's seat.

At 0900, the airplanes in the first group started returning to their parking spots. Alan climbed out of his airplane and went back into the hangar to use the head. When he came back out, he saw Bellingham having a cup of coffee.

"Are you ready to fly?" Bellingham asked.

"Yes, sir."

"Okay, Alan, let's get started then."

They walked out of the hangar to Alan's SBD, and Bellingham coached him through the preflight inspection and starting procedure. After that, they taxied out to the end of runway two five, did their run-up, called the tower, and got their clearance to take off. As the airplane accelerated down the runway, it felt to Alan somewhat like a BT-1 with more power.

After they took off, they turned left and headed south along the coast. There was some residual haze, but otherwise, the weather was nearly perfect. The light brown of the roads and hills, the green of the farm fields, the white of the beaches, and the turquoise of the ocean all combined to produce a very pleasant view.

After he had done the normal preliminary maneuvers, Alan realized how crisp the SBD's handling was, reminding him of the SNJ. Bellingham coached him on stalls and slow flight. Alan had been told repeatedly that the SBD had none of the nasty characteristics of the BT-1, so it could be flown much more aggressively when going slow and go-arounds were not a problem. The speed with which one opened the throttle was limited by the typical hesitant response of the large radial engine rather than by the airplane going into an uncontrollable roll. In spite of this repeated instruction, the habit of very tenderly using the throttle in slow flight was now so ingrained in Alan that at first he was unable to take advantage of the great improvement in the SBD.

After several tries, though, he began to get the feel of it.

Overall, the SBD proved to be pleasant to fly. It was much more responsive than the BT-1, although it did not have the snappy response of the F2F. Alan thought that it might be quick enough to give a good account of itself in a dogfight.

When they returned to Mines Field, Alan made two wheel landings and four full-stall landings. He felt that the ground handling was at least as good as that of the SNJ or the BT-1.

As they taxied in toward the Douglas hangar after the last landing, Alan thought that this airplane did not seem to have any kind of nasty streaks, unlike the BT-1, and perhaps even the F2F. He was very happy that this would be the type of airplane that he would fly for some time to come.

This had also been his first personal experience with Gordie Bellingham, the flight officer, who was the third-ranking officer in the squadron hierarchy. He took an immediate liking to the man. He was fairly quiet, but knowledgeable, diligent, and friendly.

Saturday, August 9, 1941

The squadron was ready to start out on the long trip back to Norfolk. The Douglas shuttle bus again brought the squadron from the hotel to Mines Field, arriving at 0730. Alan smiled as he noticed that "Slippery" Simpkin had made it a clean sweep, missing the bus for the fourth time.

Late the previous afternoon, a low overcast had suddenly rolled in off the ocean. He remembered from his time on the *Pennsylvania* that this was a common Southern California phenomenon and that it usually burned off in the morning. It was not associated with any stormy weather, in spite of its ominous look. Today low fog was still there in the morning, not burning off as it had the previous three mornings.

The pilots gathered in the hangar. In front of the rows of folding chairs, there were now three blackboards.

Arnham addressed the squadron. "We've divided the squadron into two flights, as shown on this board," he said, pointing to a blackboard on his right. "Whether or not this overcast has burned off, we plan to launch my group of eleven on schedule at 1000 and the second group of ten under the executive officer at 1015. We'll take off at thirty-second intervals, so you should be able to find the airplane in front of you when you break out. The top of the overcast is reported to be 1,500 feet, with clear above. We've been given a block of airspace by Air Traffic Control. Each flight will get on top of the overcast, and then cancel the instrument clearance. Follow the instructions on this board," he said, pointing to another blackboard on his left. "Write this down: You're to climb on runway heading to 1,000 feet, and then you will make a 180-degree climbing turn to the left. You should break out either by the time that turn is finished or shortly afterward. Keep climbing. When you break out, join up for the climb to 9,000 feet.

"We want a little realism in this trip, so you will maintain radio silence unless there's an emergency or you're authorized by your flight leader. We decided to make our first day of flying fairly short, to allow time to correct any problems that could come up." He paused to give the pilots, who were busily scribbling their notes, time to catch up. "Our first leg is from here directly to Flagstaff, Arizona. We'll overfly Flagstaff unless there's some problem. Our second leg will take us to Albuquerque, New Mexico, where we'll land. Now the navigation officer will give you the navigation dope." Arnham sat down in the front row.

Vang stood up and went to the front. "I've tabulated the magnetic courses, distances, times, and radio range frequencies, as shown here," he said, pointing to the third blackboard to his left. "We plan to cruise at 135 knots indicated, which should work out to around 150 knots true. We should have a small tailwind, but to be conservative, times for the two legs are shown here with no wind. We expect about four hours total time en route."

A door at the back of the hangar opened. The bright light silhouetted Simpkin as he tried to slink in inconspicuously.

Arnham stood up and boomed in his public-address voice, "Ah, Simpkin, nice of you to join us."

All the pilots glanced at each other and smiled, except for Simpkin's friend, Lieutenant j.g. Winfield "Pooh" Featherstone. Simpkin's uniform looked like he had slept in it. Vang sat down, looking disgusted.

Arnham turned and addressed the group again. "Remember that you will be taking off this time with full fuel, so your gross weight will be higher than in your practice flights. By the time you get to Albuquerque, you will be a lot lighter. The field elevation at Albuquerque is 5,335 feet. Remember that the thin air will mean that your true airspeed will be faster relative to your indicated airspeed. Use the same indicated airspeeds that you would normally use at sea level. You'll notice that you're going faster relative to the ground when you approach and land. Now the flight officer will give us a weather briefing." Arnham sat down again.

Bellingham walked up to the front, and announced, "Except for the fog here, which only extends about five miles inland, the weather is basically excellent all the way. The thermals in the desert may give us a bumpy ride, however." He went on to give details of what could be expected at several locations along their route.

When Bellingham was done, Arnham stood up once more. "Okay, that completes our briefing. Any questions?"

"What fuel reserve will we have when we arrive at Albuquerque?" asked Featherstone.

"It should be quite adequate, but each pilot should calculate that for himself to be sure," Arnham replied. He paused and looked over the group. "Okay, if there are no more questions, make sure that you have everything written down where you can find it, and then get your airplane loaded up and do the preflight. Come back here at 0930 for final instructions."

Alan had been busy writing. He had everything written on his briefing pad and was ready to go. As the other pilots were getting up and moving away, he scanned his notes. He noticed that the magnetic courses given by Vang did not look right. The course to Flagstaff was given as 095, which was slightly south of due east. From his surface-tour days, Alan knew that the magnetic variation at Los Angeles was thirteen degrees east, meaning that magnetic north was thirteen degrees east of true north. That meant that the magnetic course should be a smaller number than the true course. He suspected that Flagstaff was slightly further north than Los Angeles, so the true course should have been north of due east. He pulled out his chart and navigation plotter and checked the true course from Los Angeles to Flagstaff, which he worked out to be 082. He realized that Vang got 095 for the magnetic course because he had added the magnetic variation of thirteen degrees to the true course of eighty-two degrees, instead of subtracting it. *Some navigation officer*, Alan thought. Adding the magnetic variation was the correct procedure on the East Coast, where the magnetic variation was west. All of Vang's aviation duty had occurred on the East Coast, and he'd had no experience with West Coast navigation. But that was no excuse; a navigation officer should be thoroughly familiar with magnetic variation and how to correct for it. He decided to take the error up with Arnham in private, if possible, to avoid any appearance of wanting to publicly embarrass Vang.

He gathered up his briefing materials and charts and walked up near the blackboards, where Arnham was talking with Pruitt. Casey, Vang, and Bellingham were nearby. Alan waited for Arnham to finish, and then he stepped forward.

"May I have a word with you, sir?" Alan was slightly nervous about doing this, but fortunately, things had been going smoothly that morning and Arnham was in a good mood.

"Sure, Ericsson, what's on your mind?" he said with a smile.

"In private, sir?" Alan requested. Arnham's smile turned to a frown.

"Okay, Ericsson, come with me." Arnham led the way into an office at the back of the hangar and closed the door.

"Now, Ericsson, what the hell is this all about?"

"Sir, I think the magnetic courses for both legs are wrong. It looks like the magnetic variation was *added to* the true course instead of being subtracted from it."

"So you're saying that Lieutenant Vang, who's been flying a lot longer than you, screwed up. Is that correct?"

"Yes, sir."

"You'd better be right, Ericsson. Show me."

"Yes, sir." Alan pulled out his chart and plotter and put them on a desk. He laid the plotter on the chart and adjusted it as Arnham leaned over to watch closely. Alan said, "As you can see, the true course from here to Flagstaff is 082. The magnetic course, with the variation of thirteen degrees *east*, is 069."

Arnham pulled some notes out of a pocket of his flight suit. "Vang gave the magnetic course as 095."

"Yes, sir."

Arnham's gruffness melted. "Okay, Ericsson, have a seat," he offered as he took one himself. "I'm glad you picked this up, and I'm glad that you brought it up in private."

"Yes, sir."

Arnham leaned back in his chair with his hands behind his head, looking up at the ceiling. He was silent for a minute, obviously lost in thought. He suddenly leaned forward over the chart, looking down at it, and asked, "If we follow Vang's course, where will we end up?"

Alan leaned over the chart and adjusted his plotter again. "We'll go south of Phoenix, though probably not close enough to see it, and then we'll go right over Tucson, sir."

"And if we went to Albuquerque via Tucson, instead of via Flagstaff, how much farther is the whole flight?"

Alan pulled out his dividers and worked out the two distances as Arnham watched closely. "Four hundred nautical miles to Tucson, and 280 to Albuquerque from there. That would be a total of 680 miles, compared to the 590 it would take via Flagstaff, so . . . it's an additional ninety miles, sir. The terrain is higher between Tucson and Albuquerque than it is between Flagstaff and Albuquerque. If we go that way, we should probably climb to 11,000 feet."

"That shouldn't be any problem," Arnham remarked, almost to himself. "We can manage that without using oxygen, and we should still have an adequate fuel reserve." He turned back to Alan. "What landmarks will we pass early in the flight that will confirm that we're headed for Tucson?"

"Well, let's see . . . on the correct course, the mountains north of San Bernardino would be on our right and would appear early in the flight. On Vang's course, the mountains will come up a little bit later, and they will all be on our left, and San Bernardino will be a ways off on our left. Probably the best landmark is the Salton Sea, though. If we're on course for Flagstaff, we will pass about fifty miles north of the north end of it, and we may not even see it. If we're on course for Tucson, we should pass right over the north end, and I'd expect the visibility to be good in the desert."

"You're right. The navy has a little seaplane base at the north end of the Salton Sea, and if there are any planes there, they should be obvious. It all sounds good for what I have in mind." Arnham was quiet again for a while.

After a short pause, he looked Alan in the eye and informed him, "Here's what I'm going to do: I want Lieutenant Vang to find the mistake himself, so I'm not going to say anything about this. I don't want you to say anything about it, either. At some point, Vang should figure out that we're off course, and I'll let him recommend a new course to take up. If some of the other pilots notice the error before we take off, I'll tell them to keep mum. If they notice it in flight, I'll ask Vang about it and do what he suggests. If Vang hasn't figured it out by the time we get to Tucson, we will take up the correct course for Albuquerque that you have laid out. We'll juggle the formation. I want you to fly wing on me so that we can use hand signals. I'm appointing you temporary backup navigation officer, and I want you to double-check everything we've been given so far and everything that Vang suggests in the air. I'll tell Casey and Bellingham what is afoot and get the weather at Tucson.

"Yes, sir. Thank you, sir."

"Okay, go get your airplane ready."

"Yes, sir." Alan had been looking forward to the long trip across the country for weeks, and he was excited about it. Now, he, the rookie, had been given an important additional responsibility. He felt flattered and humbled at the same time.

Alan gathered up his materials and went back out into the hangar, followed by Arnham. He picked up his small bag with his clothes, put on his parachute, and started for his airplane. Alan noticed that Arnham was already engaged in a discussion with Casey and another pilot from Casey's flight, and he wondered if that pilot had also noticed the mistake. Finding his airplane, Alan stowed the parachute in the pilot's seat. When he opened the door to the small baggage compartment behind the rear cockpit, he found that it was filled with spare parts and gallon cans of engine oil, so he strapped his bag into the gunner's seat with the seat belt. He did the preflight inspection meticulously, conscious of the long trip ahead. The Douglas mechanics seemed to have checked everything over thoroughly, and he was pleased with the readiness of his airplane. When he had finished, it was only 0855. He decided to go back to the hangar before 0930, in case Arnham wanted to speak to him.

He went to the back of the hangar and found a table and chair. He opened his chart and carefully checked the rest of the numbers that Vang had provided, finding that everything but the courses checked out. As he finished, he looked up to see Arnham coming over to speak to him.

Arnham said in a low voice, "Two of Casey's pilots noticed the error, so Casey decided to take the correct course and go by Flagstaff. In the formation, you'll change places with West and fly wing on me. Are you ready?"

"Yes, sir. I double-checked everything as you requested, and except for the magnetic courses, the numbers check out."

"Good."

The final briefing was short, and the pilots manned their planes afterward. The first flight started up and taxied out in their order of takeoff. The first section of three airplanes consisted of Arnham and his wingmen, Alan and Ned Morris. The rest of the flight consisted of two more sections of three and a section of two. Vang would lead the last section of three, and the section of two airplanes would be Featherstone with Simpkin on his wing. The Douglas chief pilot had driven out to the end of runway two five to flag the planes off at thirty-second intervals. The pilots did their run-ups while waiting in line at the end of the runway.

Arnham got the flag and took off. He disappeared into the overcast as Alan taxied into position on the runway. The chief pilot pointed his flag at Alan, waved it over his head as he looked at his watch, and then brought it sharply down, signaling Alan to take off. Alan opened the throttle and rolled down the runway, scanning the engine instruments, which were all in the green. The engine felt like it was running smoothly. He took off and retracted the landing gear. A few seconds later, he was in the clouds, so he focused on his instruments. Luckily, the air was smooth, so the airplane did not bounce around and change heading on its own. This made it easier to fly the airplane on instruments. He pulled the power back to climb and climbed to 1,000 feet on a heading of 250. Then he began a standard rate turn to the left.

After about a minute, the sky above got brighter as he neared the top of the clouds. He rolled out on a heading of 070, and then suddenly he was in the clear above the clouds. Up there, it was a beautiful, bright, sunny morning. The top of the overcast was a dazzling white below. Alan looked around and saw Arnham ahead, noticing that Arnham had slowed to make it easier for the others to join up. As Alan eased in on Arnham's right, he looked around to the eight o'clock position and saw Ned coming up on Arnham's left. He smiled as he thought, *This is the start of a real adventure.*

Arnham continued climbing slowly on a heading of 070. More planes joined up, and after another few minutes, Alan noticed that they were a flight of nine. There were no more planes in sight. Arnham gave the signal to reduce speed, and they slowed down about twenty more knots. Alan understood that Arnham did this to give the stragglers a better chance to catch up.

After another few minutes, Arnham came on the radio. "Featherstone, where are you?"

There was a pause, and then Featherstone came back. "I lost the airplane ahead of me in the clouds. Simpkin is on my wing, but I don't see anyone else."

Arnham came on again. "Which way did you turn, and what's your heading?"

"We're on a heading of 070. We followed the briefing. We climbed to 1,000 feet and then made a 180-degree turn to the right."

They turned right instead of left, Alan realized. *That's a serious screw-up. Featherstone will probably catch hell from Arnham after the flight. And wouldn't you know it, Simpkin turned the wrong way, too.*

"Briefing called for a 180-degree turn to the *left,*" Arnham replied in a strong voice. "Try heading 085 and see if you see us. We've slowed down to ninety knots. We're approaching the east side of the city at 5,000 feet."

Featherstone's section appeared in the distance at eight o'clock not long after the exchange, and they joined up with the rest of the group.

Arnham gave the signal for a right turn and took up a heading of 095. They continued the climb and leveled off at 9,000 feet. He gave the signal to open up the formation for cruising, which allowed all the pilots to use their autopilots. It was a little hazy around San Bernardino, but Alan could clearly see the mountains north and south of Banning Pass. The long join-up process on a heading of 070 had carried them a little north of their course, but they were leaving all the high mountains to their left, as he had predicted. On this course, they would pass only about ten miles southwest of Mount San Jacinto, whose summit would be well above them at 10,800 feet.

As they passed Mount San Jacinto, Alan could see the Salton Sea ahead. There was no haze in the desert, which made it prettier in Alan's eyes. He was gratified to see that they would pass over the north end of the Salton Sea, as he'd told Arnham they would. At 1054, they were over the north end of the Salton Sea, and Arnham pointed down and gave Alan a thumbs-up signal. Alan could see two float planes at a pier, which must be the little navy base that Arnham mentioned.

Arnham came on the radio. "Navigation officer, are we on course?"

There was a fairly long pause, and then Vang replied, "Yes, sir."

Arnham came back on the radio. "What body of water is that below us?"

Vang replied, "I don't know, sir." Alan realized that Arnham was giving Vang every chance to notice the mistake. The radio went silent.

A few minutes later, Alan noticed West drop out of the formation and approach Arnham. West was another experienced pilot in the squadron. He could see West hand signaling and pointing to the northeast.

Arnham replied with hand signals and continued flying steadily on the same course. West dropped back and resumed his place in the formation. Alan understood that West had figured out that they were off course; he was trying to tell the skipper. Vang had just confirmed that they were on course, though, and Arnham was going to play the game out just like he said he would. *All of the pilots must have seen what happened*, Alan thought. He was sure that some of them would soon begin to question the navigation.

The desert scenery was tan and stark, but small ridges of jagged mountains were always in view. Alan thought that the desert had a mysterious allure, probably because it was so different from the landscape of the eastern United States. It would be too hot to explore at this time of year, he realized, but in the spring or fall coming back and exploring the desert might be fun. It was one of a number of places in the southwest that he should mention to Jennifer. A band of sand dunes came into view ahead, reminding Alan of pictures he had seen of the Sahara Desert.

Beyond the dunes was a narrow ribbon of water—a river—looking incongruous in the desert. Alan thought that it was the Colorado River. They were over it at 1123. Alan calculated that they had about five knots of tailwind. Twenty miles to the right, there was a town on the river. Alan could make out an airport southeast of the town. *Yuma, Arizona*, he decided. Further away to his right, Alan could make out a large body of water extending to the horizon. That was the Gulf of California. Everything checked out.

Arnham came on the radio again. "Navigation officer, are we still on course?"

Vang came back, "Yes, sir."

Arnham inquired, "What's the river below?"

Vang replied quickly, with a hint of triumph, "The Colorado River, sir."

Arnham then asked, "What's that large body of water far off to the right?"

There was a long pause, and Vang replied, "I don't know, sir." The radio went silent again.

Alan was astonished that Vang still clung obstinately to his course when there were obvious landmarks to show that he was wrong. West had figured it out right away, but West was probably familiar with the major landmarks to some degree, being from the Los Angeles area. Certainly the other pilots would think that something was wrong when the navigation officer could not identify major landmarks. Perhaps some of them had known for a while that they were way off course, but they had seen that West was not able to get the skipper to change course, so they did not speak up. As Alan turned it over in his mind, he understood that this would be a lesson that the pilots would not soon forget, and he admired Arnham's teaching technique. Arnham knew what he was doing, taking full advantage of the opportunity for some valuable training.

They continued on, crossing a small river that was coming from the east-northeast with a little water in it. A road paralleled it on the south side. Alan pulled out the chart board from under the instrument panel and checked the chart. It was the Gila River. After that, there were few landmarks. There were low, jagged ridges running north-northwest, and the emptiness beckoned to Alan.

It looked like Vang might never figure it out and that they would go all the way to Tucson before heading for Albuquerque. Alan decided to work out the course and time en route from Tucson to Albuquerque. He pulled out his E6B calculator and began plotting and calculating, looking up frequently to make sure that he was still in position relative to Arnham. Soon, he had the numbers.

At 1158, Alan noticed a small town off to the right. He could see signs of excavation and a tall smokestack with dense smoke coming out of it. He studied his chart, and narrowed the options down to Ajo. He looked to the left, but he could not see Phoenix.

They continued on over ranges of larger mountains. Alan looked ahead, hoping to pick up the first signs of Tucson. Around 1230, he thought he saw something definite. Shortly after that, Tucson came into view. Alan hand signaled to Arnham that Tucson was ahead, and Arnham gave him a thumbs-up signal.

Arnham came on the radio again. "Navigation officer, what's the city ahead?"

Vang replied fairly quickly, "Flagstaff, sir."

"By my calculation, we're about twenty-five minutes late getting here," said Arnham.

"Apparently we had a headwind instead of a tailwind, sir," came Vang's reply.

"The highway and the railroad run east and west near Flagstaff, but here, they're running northwest and southeast. Something is very fishy," Arnham replied, giving Vang another chance to correct himself. There was a considerable pause, and Vang did not reply. Finally, Arnham came on again. "Anyone else have an idea about where we are?" Alan thought, *I doubt he wants me to speak up and cut short the lesson. If no one else does, Ned Morris should recognize Tucson, since he's from the area.* By now, they were over the west side of the city and it was 1239.

After a pause, Ned Morris spoke up. "Morris, here, sir. We're over Tucson, Arizona."

Arnham replied, "What makes you think that, Morris?"

Morris replied, "I graduated from the University of Arizona, and I can see the campus, sir."

Arnham replied, "Very good, Morris. We're twenty-six degrees off course to the right, as Ericsson pointed out to me before we took off. We went to Tucson instead of Flagstaff. West figured it out pretty quickly, and some of the rest of you may have noticed after that, as well, but the navigation officer never did. Let this be a lesson: All of you should be checking both the navigation and any landmarks that are available. On a scouting mission over the ocean, you'll be alone or with one other aircraft. You'll need to navigate accurately, or you'll never make it back to the carrier. I want each of you to figure out exactly why this happened." He paused. "I'm appointing Ericsson temporary navigation officer for the rest of this flight and relieving Vang. We're going to go on to Albuquerque directly from here. We'll climb to 11,000 feet to clear the terrain en route. Ericsson, what are the magnetic course and the time en route to Albuquerque?"

Alan replied, "The course is 043 and the time is one hour and fifty-two minutes, sir."

"Okay. We'll turn to a heading of 043 and climb to 11,000 feet. We expect to arrive at Albuquerque around 1435." Arnham made a gentle left turn to the northeast, slowing as he began the climb, and the rest of the flight followed. The flight cleared the high ridge of mountains northeast of Tucson, and Alan could see 9,200-foot-high Mount Lemmon to the left. Alan thought the scene of the SBDs climbing against the background of nearby forested mountaintops was a spectacular sight.

They leveled off at 11,000 feet. Alan noticed that his breathing seemed more rapid, especially if he heaved himself around in the cockpit. As he tried to sit still to conserve oxygen, his thoughts went back to Vang. Alan knew that it would be hard for Vang to overcome the bad impression he'd made and advance within the squadron. Alan guessed that Vang did not have the patience to attempt it, either. He wondered if Vang was reconsidering his future in the squadron.

They passed over two more high ridges and across a broad valley. Eight miles to the right, Alan could see a town with more smokestacks, which he decided was Safford, Arizona. They passed over a large area of high, rugged terrain.

The terrain began to gradually drop after a while, and the forest petered out. At 1400, Alan could see that they were coming into a large valley that ran north and south—the Rio Grande valley. They went over a narrow, high ridge, and the bottom of the big valley came into view on the right as they converged with it. He signaled Arnham, recommending the start of their descent. Arnham gently started down, and the squadron followed.

At 1420, Alan could see Albuquerque ahead of them. Arnham came on the radio. "That's Albuquerque, ahead. I'm going to report our arrival to Albuquerque Radio and get the wind and runway." A couple of minutes passed, and he came back on. "At Albuquerque, the wind is 290 at 10, and they're using runway three zero. We'll make a standard overhead approach at 6,300 feet." Arnham handled the radio with the control tower and led the flight through the approach, and they landed in good order.

As they taxied into the ramp, Alan could see the ten SBDs of Casey's flight neatly parked. The pilots were gathered in a group next to the airplanes to watch Arnham's flight come in. Two ground crewmen appeared and directed them to their parking spaces next to Casey's group. Arnham's section was naturally the first to shut down and climb out. The air was clear and dry, and the temperature was around eighty degrees, Alan guessed.

Arnham walked over to Alan, smiled, and shook his hand. He looked Alan in the eye and said, "Nice work, Ericsson. You could probably handle being navigation officer right now, but I have to give the job to someone who is more senior. Keep up the good work in engineering, though, and your chance will come."

"Thank you, sir." Alan was pleased that he had impressed the skipper, but he still felt very much the rookie. Jack Casey was approaching, and Arnham walked toward him so that they could have a private conversation. Alan turned back toward his airplane and started his post-flight inspection, but he heard every word.

Arnham said, "We went all the way to Tucson, and Vang never did catch on. He told us that Tucson was Flagstaff and that we had a headwind."

"Jesus, I never thought he'd go that far off," Casey admitted. "I didn't tell my flight that your flight took the wrong heading. I was not sure about how far off you'd go before he caught on, so I thought we might see you as you came back on course. When we got here and you weren't here, I had to explain it to them. We landed about twenty minutes ago."

"Glad everything went smoothly, Jack. Vang's original error is possibly excusable, because he has never been west, but either he really never figured it out or he couldn't admit it. Either way, he doesn't belong in a carrier squadron, or even in aviation. I'll have to bilge him when we get back."

"Yes, sir," Casey replied.

Alan realized that one big mistake could finish you in this business, but then the thought occurred to him that perhaps

Arnham had been harboring doubts about Vang for a long time and that this was simply the last straw.

Arnham told Casey, "I want each pilot to do a thorough post-flight inspection so that we have time to deal with any squawks before departure tomorrow. After that, I want you to debrief your pilots individually, and I'll debrief mine, and then we can head for the hotel. You and I can talk more after we get there."

"Yes, sir. We can use this hangar here for debriefing," Casey said, pointing to the nearest one. "The head mechanic came out and introduced himself to me when we'd all landed, so I can get him out here if there are any squawks."

"Good." Arnham and Casey parted to pass the word to their pilots.

Alan became aware of background chatter as Casey's pilots questioned the pilots in Arnham's flight about why they were late arriving. "Where have you guys been, taking a break in Tijuana?" he heard one of Casey's pilots ask. This was greeted with loud laughter.

Vang set us up for that, Alan thought.

CHAPTER TWENTY-ONE

Jennifer's Departure

Tuesday, August 12, 1941

It was a hot, sticky late afternoon in Norfolk. Thunder was rumbling in the distance. Bombing Five had arrived back at Norfolk NAS in the early afternoon, ahead of an approaching cold front. When Alan got to the BOQ in the late afternoon, he was found a telegram that had arrived that day. Telegrams usually meant important news, and he nervously opened the familiar yellow envelope. The message read:

```
TRANSFER APPROVED EARLY DEPARTURE STOP
PLEASE CALL STOP

JENNIFER
```

His heart sank. He had looked forward to a having more time with her. He'd thought he would have at least until September, but now it looked doubtful. He waited until 1800 to call, giving her the chance to get home from work. At 1800, he headed for one of the phone booths in the lobby of the BOQ. She answered right away.

"Hello?"

"Hello, Jennifer, sweetheart, this is Alan. I'm back in Norfolk and got your telegram."

"Oh, Alan, darling, I'm sorry. I know this is bad news. I got notice yesterday that my transfer to Pearl Harbor was approved, and it was much sooner than I'd thought. They've booked passage for me leaving San Francisco on September 3. That means we can get together this weekend, as we planned, but I think it will get too tight if I stay another week in Washington. I am planning to move out next week and drive to Boston, and then I'll take the train to San Francisco the following week."

"You will miss Victoria's wedding."

"I know. I was looking forward to it so much." She sighed. "I wish they weren't in such a hurry. You'll just have to make excuses for me."

"I'm glad you let me know as soon as possible. It *is* bad news, but we would only have a little more time together, anyway. The word is out that Bombing Five will go aboard the *Yorktown* in the middle of September, just as you said."

"I still think I'm doing the right thing by going to Pearl. There are more signs that the fuse on the time bomb is burning. You know, it's been just over a year since you told me that you would be leaving for flight training. I thought you were doing the right thing at the time, too, as much as I wished I could be with you more."

"You're right, and now I feel the same way you did then. When you think about it, the fact that they're in a hurry to get you there is a good sign."

"I think so, too. My boss was disappointed when I asked for the transfer, but he understood why I was doing it. He said that he hoped I might come back in the future, which I thought was very nice of him."

"Yes, it was."

"You've been having an exciting time, too, haven't you? How are you? How did your trip out west and the flight back go?"

"I'm fine. The whole trip was great. There are a lot of beautiful places out west that I think we need to visit together. I got to see the Grand Canyon on the way out, and it is so spectacular that I felt like it was an illusion. I can tell you all about the trip this weekend, though. I think I could get up there late Friday night, and then I could stay until late Sunday afternoon. Would that be okay?"

"That sounds good. The longer you can be here, the better. Let's not plan anything. That way, we'll have more time to talk and be with each other. I love you, Alan."

"I love you, Jennifer. Good-bye."

"Good-bye, you rascal," Jennifer replied, trying her best to end the call with a smile.

Alan showered and changed, then headed for the Officers' Club for dinner and a party with the squadron. There was no flying scheduled for the next day, so it was decided that they should have a squadron party to celebrate the move up to the SBD and the successful completion of the ferry flight.

Alan had supper early and walked into the bar in the Officers' Club at 2003. Most of the squadron officers were already there, seated around four tables. Three of the guys had formed an improvised jazz band and were playing for everyone. He saw an empty seat at a table where several of his friends were. They all had beers in front of them, and there were chips and peanuts on the table.

"There he is! Stringy the Navigator," boomed Lieutenant j.g. Einar "Teeth" Jensen with a big grin.

Alan grinned back. "Thanks, Einar. Good evening, gentlemen."

Einar had gotten his nickname because his grin revealed a mouthful of large, crooked teeth. He was big guy from Minnesota, an Academy man, class of '35, and had spent two years as an enlisted man before attending the Academy. He had only been in the squadron for six months.

The others at the table greeted Alan, and then he turned and went to the bar, returning with a mug of National Premium. At the table were Einar, Jim Lowery, Ned Morris, Ensign Cedric "Slick" Davis, and Ensign Michael Burke. Cedric was also a Ringknocker, class of '37, from Arkansas. He had gone straight into aviation after his surface tour, and he had been in the squadron for over a year. Mike Burke was an AvCad from Chicago, and he had also been in the squadron for about a year.

"Why the long face, Alan?" Jim queried.

"My wife's transfer to Pearl Harbor was approved, and she's leaving much sooner than we'd expected. This weekend will probably be my last time with her for a long time."

Jim and Einar were in the reverse situation, having recently welcomed their wives to Norfolk after they'd moved from Honolulu.

Jim replied, "Oh, very sorry to hear that, but in the long run, war with Japan is likely. If that happens, the *Yorktown* is likely to go back to the Pacific and any dependents in Hawaii are likely to get sent home to the mainland. In that case, you'll be the only one in the fleet who gets to see his wife occasionally."

"I've thought of that possibility, and it could happen. Thanks for mentioning it."

"Stringy, is it really true that Boom Vang never had a clue that he was off-course on that first leg of the ferry flight?" asked Einar. Jim, Einar, and Mike had been in Casey's flight the day they left California.

"Nobody knows exactly what Vang was thinking, but you couldn't tell from his radio calls that there was any doubt in his mind," answered Alan.

Jim chuckled, and Einar grimaced and shook his head.

Alan looked at Cedric and Ned. "When did you guys realize what was going on?"

Cedric answered, "I thought it was damned peculiar when we flew over a big lake and it wasn't on the chart. There ain't a lot of big lakes in Southern California. At first, I didn't look far enough off-course on the charts to find the Salton Sea. I was sort of busy right then, because I was flying wing on West. He suddenly moved over next to the skipper, and I couldn't stay on his wing, so I dropped back a bit to wait and see what would happen. Pretty soon, he came back and I joined up on him again. When we got to the Colorado River, I saw that it ran into a bay to the south on the horizon. I recalled that the Colorado runs into the Gulf of California, and then I knew right where we were, and I realized that West had been trying to clue in the skipper."

Ned said, "I picked it up pretty early because I knew the landmarks from a car trip I'd taken with my family from Tucson to Los Angeles and back. I noticed that all the mountains around San Bernardino were on the left instead of the right, and then I saw the Salton Sea and knew exactly where we were. Being the newest man in the squadron, I wasn't going to be the first to rock the boat, though. West did it for me."

"Sounds like Vang was lost in more ways than one," Mike commented.

"I think he may have had doubts, but he couldn't bring himself to admit that he had made a mistake. But it's possible that he never figured it out, and he couldn't tell us how to get back on course," Alan replied.

Mike agreed, "That seems to fit. Nobody in the squadron respects him, but he doesn't seem to even notice."

Their glasses were empty, and the six of them went up to the bar for another round. Alan, Jim, and Einar stuck with National Premium, and the other three got National Bohemian or Gunther's, which were all brewed in Baltimore. They sat back down and each took a drink before continuing with their conversation. Alan glanced back toward the bar and noticed that Vang was there. The bartender was handing a drink to Vang, who then turned around and looked out over the tables.

"Gentlemen, may I have your attention, please?" he shouted, raising his voice over the general noise. He paused as the noise slowly died down, and he put on a big smile as he said, "You all know that I'll be leaving the squadron soon. I'm proud to have been a member." He raised his glass and said in a louder voice, "I offer a toast to Bombing Squadron Five."

There was total silence. No one stirred, but everyone's eyes glanced around to see what others would do as the color gradually rose in Vang's face. It was a long, embarrassing moment before Arnham and Casey, who had been looking at each other, stood up.

Arnham smiled, raised his glass, and called out, "To Bombing Squadron Five!"

Everyone else raised their glasses. Arnham took a drink, and everyone followed. Vang went back to his table, and conversation quickly resumed as everyone sat down.

"I don't think I've ever seen anything quite like that—refusing a toast. Good thing the skipper broke the ice," Cedric said softly.

"I might feel sorry for him, if he wasn't such a jerk," Mike observed.

"He'll probably make out fine. He just needs to stay away from anything technical," said Jim.

There were murmurs of agreement around the table, and they all took a pull on their beers and sat back.

"How do you guys feel about the possibility that we're cutting off the Japs' oil?" Einar asked.

"It's about time we called their bluff," Cedric answered.

Alan strongly disagreed, but being very junior, he thought he'd better put his answer mildly. He countered with, "If we cut off their oil, they're eventually going to run low. Before that happens, they have to either give in or attack us. Their government has gotten pretty fanatical, so I think they might attack. A two-ocean war could get pretty bad before we get up to speed."

"They could just back off a bit and get their oil from us again," said Mike.

Jim replied, "They'd have to back off a lot, and it would be a big public humiliation. They've been industrializing for sixty years so that they won't have to submit to us or to any western country."

"Couldn't they just go after the oil in the East Indies, get what they want, and leave us alone?" asked Ned.

Einar replied, "They could if we didn't have the Philippines, but their navy has to go right past the Philippines to get to the East Indies, so they'd have to take them."

"Pretty gloomy. So, what do you think we should be doing differently?" asked Cedric.

Alan replied, "Well, holding off on the oil embargo might help us. I suspect that we're arming faster than they are now, so time is on our side. We should also stick to our well-thought-out plans for a rapid evacuation of the Philippines and not try to defend them, especially if we go ahead with the embargo."

"You might be right, but it's hard to believe that this big country can't do better than that," countered Cedric.

The band was working itself into a crescendo, and they paused to listen until the band finished the number.

"What do you hear about us going back aboard the *Yorktown*?" asked Jim.

Cedric replied, "I heard that it'll be somewhere around the middle of next month. She'll probably be in Norfolk for a week or so before we go aboard. I think they'll want to re-qualify all of us since we've had three months on the beach. Stringy and Ned will need the practice more, since they haven't had much experience. Then I expect we'll go out on another neutrality patrol."

"Bunking aboard a carrier will be a brand-new experience for me. I haven't been to sea yet on any ship. What's it like?" asked Ned.

Cedric replied, "Well, you'll get used to it. The ship is so big that even old-timers can get lost. You can find all the services of a small city onboard. Aboard a big ship like the *Yorktown*, you shouldn't get seasick unless it's in a big storm. Your cabin will be small and crowded, but you can go to the wardroom or up to the gallery when you're off duty."

Mike said, "The SBD should be nice to land aboard, with its better ailerons and no low-speed quirks. No more sweat baths if you get a wave-off close in."

"Stringy knows all about that," Ned said with a smile.

"I won't soon forget it, either," said Alan. They all grinned.

About 2200, the pilots at Alan's table had had their fill, and they stood up to leave. As they headed off to their quarters, Alan noticed that Vang had disappeared.

Thursday, August 14, 1941

Alan heard on the news that while President Roosevelt had supposedly been on a fishing vacation off the New England coast, he had actually met with Prime Minister Churchill at an undisclosed location. They'd both signed the Atlantic Charter, and it upheld Roosevelt's Four Principles of Freedom. Alan suspected that there was a lot more to the conference than that, though. It would be typical of Roosevelt to make a verbal agreement with Churchill containing commitments that he was not prepared to reveal in case Congress should disagree.

Saturday, August 16, 1941

Jennifer and Alan had a poignant final visit together at her apartment in Washington. They spent most of the time lounging and talking in her apartment, taking full advantage of the balcony. They tried to talk about everything: his western trip, her expectations about life in Honolulu and working at Pearl Harbor, the war in Europe, the submarine war in the Atlantic, and the situation in the Pacific. Jennifer hinted at confirmation that, during the meeting between Roosevelt and Churchill, there were major commitments made by both sides that were not revealed, as Alan suspected.

By suppertime they were feeling like a change of venue and they decided to see the movie *Dive Bomber*, which was playing at a theatre about ten blocks away. The theatre was half empty and they bought large loge seats in the back. Early on, Jennifer moved into Alan's lap. They both paid attention to the flying and carrier scenes, she because it was a small window on Alan's professional life, and he to check on the realism. Since actual navy aircraft, and the *Yorktown's* sister , the carrier *Enterprise*, were used, these scenes were fairly realistic. They did not pay close attention to the rest of the movie, but enjoyed each other's company.

Sunday, August 17, 1941

As the time came to part, Alan found that he was torn between his own grief and trying to make things easier for Jennifer by not showing it. He couldn't cry on her shoulder, but he couldn't fake gaiety, either. He found himself becoming stiff and wooden.

She sensed his conflict, and said, "You're turning into a sphinx, Alan, and I think I know why. Loosen up, and tell me what's on your mind."

"This is a sad moment for me, but I don't want to dampen the start of your trip, you scalawag."

"I thought so. It's a hard moment for me, too. I would do almost anything not to be leaving you, but this has happened before, and it will probably happen again, you know. We will just have to learn to live with it. The nice thing is that there should be some glorious reunions for us in between."

"That's a very nice thought, Jennifer," Alan responded. They stood and kissed for a long time, and then he picked up his bag and strode determinedly out of her apartment.

Wednesday, September 3, 1941

As Alan awoke, he remembered that Jennifer would depart that day from San Francisco for Honolulu. It had been two and half weeks since they parted in Washington, and he missed her badly already. He had gotten one letter from her when she arrived at her parents' home in Lexington, and he had sent one to her that should have arrived there before she had to get on the train to San Francisco. They thought they would resume writing to each other about once a week, once she arrived in Honolulu, but he hoped she would send a letter or postcard to him before she left San Francisco.

It was a long trip she was making, across the country and then a comparable distance out into the Pacific. It was no easier being parted from her now than it had been at Pensacola, and this time there was no definite end point where they would see each other, even if only briefly. He fervently hoped that the *Yorktown* would be sent to the Pacific—the sooner the better.

It was another day of dive-bombing practice. There had been two others since they had gotten their SBDs, and Alan was a little surprised to find that the improved aileron response of the SBD helped in dive-bombing, as well as aerobatics and low-speed flight. It was easier to roll the airplane to follow the target's maneuvers in the SBD, and his scores began to slowly improve.

Two weeks earlier, Vang had left the squadron. Officially, he had requested a transfer, and he had been ordered to the staff of the admiral commanding the cruisers in the Atlantic—who was referred to as "COMCRULANT"—to be his flag lieutenant. Alan thought that Vang would fit in much better in that position. Vang's departure left a vacancy in the squadron, so two new pilots reported in, meaning that Alan and Ned and were no longer the new guys. One of the new pilots was a rookie straight out of Pensacola, an

AvCad ensign named Alvis Monroe from Lewiston, Maine. The new rookie had little trouble checking out in the SBD, but his dive-bombing scores were the squadron's lowest. Since Alan's scores were now better than Simpkin's, Alan moved up to third from the bottom in that department.

The other new pilot in Bombing Five was a lieutenant named Kelly Durham from Indiana, who was an experienced carrier pilot from Scouting Seventy-Two. Why he'd transferred out of that squadron was a mystery. He seemed competent and hard-working, but short on humor. The skipper appointed him gunnery officer because of his experience. He checked out quickly in the SBD and scored in the middle of the squadron in his first dive-bombing practice, having no difficulty making the transition from the SBC-3. As far as Alan could tell, both new men appeared to be good additions to the squadron.

Friday, September 5, 1941

Morning radio news reported that the US Navy destroyer *Greer* had dodged a couple of German torpedoes out in the middle of the North Atlantic the previous day, and the *Greer* had counterattacked with depth charges. Alan expected a strong response from Roosevelt, which would serve to push the country closer to war.

It was a beautiful late-summer day with fair-weather clouds. After an early lunch, Alan met Ned and they headed for East Field. Alan had gotten permission from Arnham to fly an SBD up to the big, new Naval Air Station at Quonset Point in Rhode Island, to attend Victoria Peckham's wedding, instead of taking the train. Arnham told him to take Ned along in another SBD for the cross country experience. They took off at 1300 and flew up the coast, right over New York City, to Quonset Point. They caught a navy shuttle from there to Newport, and arrived in time to have a delicious dinner at the Peckhams'.

Saturday, September 6, 1941

Ned spent the day seeing the sights of Newport. Alan visited a few friends from the Torpedo Station and then got into his dress uniform for the wedding at 1600. It was large and formal, in the big Congregational church at Pelham and Spring Streets. Alan met his family outside the church and sat with them toward the front. Victoria looked beautiful in her mother's dress, a traditional white dress with a train. Seth was polished and handsome in his dress uniform.

The reception, under a large tent on the Peckhams' lawn, started about 1700. In the receiving line, the Peckhams stopped the line for a minute until they had gotten a brief summary of Alan and Jennifer's recent activities. Alan kissed Victoria and got a firm handshake from Seth. Alan sat with his family during the sit-down buffet supper and had a chance to get all caught up on their news. After the traditional toasts, an admiral, whom Alan had noticed earlier but did not recognize, stood up. It turned out he was Rear Admiral Kalbfus, the president of the War College. His toast was a special honor for both bride and groom. After supper, there was dancing with live music on a wooden floor set up in the tent. Alan danced with Victoria, who was tired but euphoric.

"Remember when you razzed me about falling in love with Jennifer without checking with you first?" Alan asked with a smile.

"Yes," she said with a giggle.

"Well, I don't remember you checking with me when you fell in love with Seth," he said as his smile grew.

She laughed and said, "But that was different. I needed to get to know him before I presented him for your approval, and things went a little faster than I thought they would."

He laughed and said, "Okay, we'll let it pass just this once."

Her smile faded and she said, "I hear you are headed out into the Atlantic on the *Yorktown*. Be careful, Alan, and come back in one piece."

"I get a lot of that sort of advice from Jennifer."

"Good for her. Have you heard from her since she left?"

"No. Even if she sent something from San Francisco, it probably wouldn't have had time to get here yet. She was sad to miss the wedding, though, and she sends her greetings to you." The dance ended and Victoria gave him a quick squeeze before moving on to other guests.

Altogether, it was a very nice occasion, with no awkward moments as far as Alan noticed, unlike many weddings.

Sunday, September 7, 1941

The pleasant weather had held for Alan and Ned on their flight back to Norfolk, as well. As they approached the naval air station, Alan noticed the *Yorktown* at Pier Seven, at which she had arrived on Saturday. Bombing Five had been told that they would be embarking on the *Yorktown* on the following Saturday, and departing on a neutrality patrol the next day, which would be a big change after the summer on the beach.

On his way back to his room, Alan went by his mailbox, in case something from Jennifer had arrived. He was elated to find an airmail letter from her. As he sat down to read it in his room, he realized it was the first airmail letter he had ever gotten from her. Both the letter and the envelope used the special light crinkly airmail paper. As he pulled out the letter, he smelled her perfume, and once again it felt like she was there beside him, watching him read the letter.

San Francisco, Cal.
September 2, 1941

Dear Alan,

I am fine, except I miss you badly, you rascal. I got here yesterday. The train ride across the country was long. However, we happened to go through the Rockies west of Denver in daylight. It was very majestic, with snow still on the mountain tops. It was night when we crossed Utah, so I am still curious about that part. It was daytime again by the time we left Reno and crossed the Sierras. They were also majestic, but after the Rockies, the Sierras did not seem as impressive. I would love to see the beautiful areas of the west with you.

San Francisco is pleasant but quite chilly. I don't have much in the way of warm clothing, because I did not expect to need any. I am staying with friends of my parents who will put me on the Monterey tomorrow.

The voyage to Honolulu should be relaxing. Then I will be very busy, finding an apartment and getting settled.

By the time you get this, you will probably have been to Victoria's wedding. Remember to give me a complete description, you rascal: who was there, what they wore, everything.

Is your ship still going to leave soon, as we thought? I am feeling completely out of touch since I left the office. Good luck with your flying, especially off the carrier. Don't take chances. I want you to be still on board when your ship comes west.

Write soon again and tell me about your voyage.

Oodles of love,

Jennifer

Alan liked her optimism: "when," not "if," his ship goes west. He remembered that tomorrow was the day she would arrive in Honolulu. He was ready to write her a reply, giving her the "complete description" of the wedding. He reminded her to use his navy shipboard mailing address, which was USS *Yorktown*, then care of the Fleet Post Office in New York. With this kind of addressing, the location of ships was not revealed. When he had finished the letter to her, it was time to turn in.

CHAPTER TWENTY-TWO

The Yorktown Goes to Newfoundland

Saturday, September 13, 1941

It was a quiet evening in the BOQ. The *Yorktown* would be departing the next day for some sort of neutrality patrol of unspecified duration in the North Atlantic. The scuttlebutt had it they would not be going to Bermuda, but would be based somewhere farther north. The prospect of flying off the carrier in the cold North Atlantic and the increasing tension of the submarine war left the pilots feeling a little subdued. Alan decided to take advantage of the last opportunity to send mail before the ship sailed.

Norfolk Naval Air Station
September 13, 1941

Dear Jennifer,

I miss you very much. I liked your assumption that the ship will go west.

By now, you have been in Honolulu almost a week. I hope the pickings have not been too slim in apartments and you have found one. How do you like it there? I hope you can also tell me a little about your work and the atmosphere in the office.

That was quite a speech Roosevelt made on the radio two days ago. I thought he would react to the Greer incident, but he really came out fighting. In the western Atlantic, German and Italian ships to be attacked on sight, and convoy escort by US ships, those changes really amount to a declaration of limited war, with all the ramifications, but no acknowledgement. It now seems to me inevitable that we will start taking casualties.

Eventually that will stir up the general public and they will realize we are in a war. Fortunately we are somewhat prepared for convoy escort, since the British have been asking for some time. Since that speech a new, more-determined atmosphere has pervaded the Norfolk NOB.

At least now there will no longer be any question of what action to take if one of our ships or planes finds a German sub. As you know, I thought the previous lack of authorization to attack was unfair to our sailors and pilots.

As you may know, we depart tomorrow. You also may know where we're going, you scalawag, but we don't. I will soon be personally facing unrestricted submarine warfare, but my opinion that is not immoral has not changed.

I love you very much. Write soon.

Tons of love,

Alan

Sunday, September 14, 1941

In the afternoon, the *Yorktown* departed from the Norfolk NOB. The previous day, the aircraft and equipment of Bombing Five, along with those of Fighting Forty-Two and Torpedo Five, had been taken on board the *Yorktown* at Pier Seven. Their aircraft had been taxied over to the pier and hoisted aboard. VF-42 and VT-5 had had only a week ashore because those squadrons had been operating aboard the *Yorktown* most of the summer. Once at sea, it was announced that the ship was headed for the US Navy base at Argentia, Newfoundland.

Scouting Five was left behind. They, along with other navy and marine dive-bomber squadrons, were to be sent off to help the army with some big exercise in the southern states. Alan had heard that General Marshall wanted the army to develop its own dive-bombing capability. Alan thought that this was a good idea, but it would probably be greeted with little enthusiasm in the Army Air Force, which was dominated by heavy-bomber people.

Alan noticed the absence of a few of the pilots, although none that he knew well. They had decided to leave the navy for the time being and join the American Volunteer Group that was going to fight the Japanese in China under Captain Chennault. The army, navy, and marines had recently announced that they were allowing their pilots to make the transfer with no loss of seniority if they returned. The pay was high and fat bonuses were offered. Although the operation was led by a former army officer and used army aircraft, Alan had heard that more pilots were going from the navy and marines than from the army. As a rookie still learning the ropes, Alan was not itching to get into action in China, especially since it would take him farther from Jennifer.

Thursday, September 18, 1941

Bombing Five had been busy with carrier re-qualification since the *Yorktown*'s departure from Norfolk. This task was given top priority during the voyage northward, and had been completed in relatively benign weather off the Jersey Shore and Long Island. The new rookie, Monroe, qualified for the first time, and then he, Alan, and Ned were given extra practice due to their minimal carrier experience. The experienced pilot from Scouting Seventy-Two, Durham, demonstrated his expertise, as well.

The rest of the Bombing Five pilots, including Alan, were pleased to be flying the SBD instead of the BT-1. The improved low-speed handling characteristics of the SBD had made carrier operations a lot safer, but carrier landings were still a daunting experience for Alan, who couldn't help but think of his less-than-perfect first landing attempts during every approach. He did not look forward to landing aboard in the rougher seas of the North Atlantic.

As Alan got to know the *Yorktown*, he naturally compared her with the *Ranger*, the first carrier he'd been acquainted with. The *Yorktown* was bigger, but also faster. The flight deck was about 800 feet long, compared to the *Ranger*'s 700-foot-long deck. The nominal width of the flight deck was about the same, but the *Yorktown* had more beam to accommodate a wider island. The funnels were incorporated in the island, as on the *Lexington* and the *Saratoga*.

The *Yorktown* had three elevators for moving aircraft: one near the bow, one near the stern, and one just aft of the island, which could be accessed by the aircraft crane abaft the island. She had nine arresting wires aft of the mid-ship elevator, and thirteen forward. She also had nine folding barriers amidships to accommodate a variety of space allocations on the flight deck. Like the *Ranger*, the *Yorktown* had a gallery on both sides and large openings on the sides of the hangar deck that could be closed with curtains, *Yorktown*'s being steel.

The ensigns and j.g.s normally shared their staterooms with another officer of the same rank from their squadron, and the j.g.s' cabins were usually a little larger. The squadron skippers and some of the lieutenants had individual staterooms. The squadron skipper made the room assignments, and Alan was delighted with his assignment to room with Jim Lowery, having come to respect Jim's diligence and competence, as well as his sense of humor.

Alan had to become reacquainted with life on a surface ship, since he had not served on one for five years. On the plus side, it was much more luxurious than a fleet submarine. There was more room, and you could always get fresh air when off duty. Dining was remarkably formal unless the ship was in a state of alert. The officers dressed for dinner, they were seated in the wardroom at tables with linen tablecloths, and they ate with silver marked with the ship's monogram. The food was good. It was carefully prepared, then served by diligent, African-American and Filipino mess attendants.

That evening, Kelly Durham happened to sit across from Alan at dinner. In the middle of dinner Alan heard him say to his neighbor, "These niggers do a fine job, don't they? The navy is smart to give them a job they can understand."

Although Alan had had hardly any interaction with African-Americans, he had been taught that "nigger" was a strong and insulting word. He had heard it so often in the navy, however, that he no longer winced. He continued eating and was careful not to look across the table, to avoid getting involved in Durham's conversation.

Alan had already become somewhat acquainted with Durham. He was an extremely intense officer, competent and hard working. He rarely smiled and had little sense of humor, however, and he tended to be abusive toward everyone he outranked, although he tried to hold back when dealing with the other pilots in the squadron. He told everyone that his nickname was "Eagle," but word came over the mountain telegraph that his Academy nickname had been "Bull," although nobody dared to use it to his face. Because Bull Durham was the name of a well-known brand of tobacco, "Durham" had become associated with "bull"—bullshit and nonsense in popular slang. Having gotten to know Durham, Alan recognized that Durham's classmates had picked a good nickname. Jim, with nearly the opposite personality to Durham, thought Durham was amusing, and could barely keep a straight face in his presence.

A short time later, Alan heard Durham say, "Teddy Roosevelt had it right. God made the Anglo-Saxon race superior so they could dominate the more primitive races until they learn how to manage themselves. That is why they went out from Britain, found

North America, and took it over from the Indians. My ancestors were among the fine people that did that."

Alan was quite surprised to hear this—he thought that this kind of narrow-minded and self-serving view of the world had died out decades earlier. He glanced at Durham and, unfortunately, Durham caught his look.

"Say, Ericsson, where did your ancestors come from?"

"Iceland, Ireland, Italy, and Portugal," Alan replied calmly.

"No Anglo-Saxons there, but at least Iceland is Teutonic. I thought your skin looked pretty dark," said Durham with a smirk. The other officers at the table were glancing around apprehensively.

"Actually, the earliest explorers of the North Atlantic ocean, the ones before 1500, came from those four countries, and no others, so they were not Anglo-Saxons," Alan calmly explained. The apprehensive expressions vanished, and a few smirks appeared momentarily.

Durham hotly shot back, "What about John Cabot? He discovered North America."

Alan replied, still calmly, "In the first place, although few people were aware of it in John Cabot's time, the Norse had visited and lived in North America about five hundred years earlier, so Cabot was not the first European to discover it. In the second place, Cabot was an Italian living in Venice, who was hired by the King of England to explore for Britain." Alan saw more smirks and heard a chuckle from the far end of the table, near where Jim Lowry was sitting.

Durham was growing red in the face and was about to speak when Jerry West interjected, "That's right. I remember studying that in high school."

Durham cast a withering look at Jerry, got up and withdrew.

Monday, September 22, 1941

As they had continued north and east, the weather had gotten gradually worse, which did not surprise Alan. Although he had never had a chance to go to the Maritime Provinces of Canada or to Newfoundland, he was curious about both—particularly Newfoundland. He had heard many times about the foul weather there, particularly in the colder half of the year. There had already been several days when the air group had been unable to fly due to low ceilings and visibility. It had gotten steadily colder, as well, and the average swell had increased, especially after they had swung farther offshore north of Cape Cod.

Alan thought Newfoundland was a wild and intriguing place, even though it had been the first place in North America to have a settlement of Europeans. The climate was poor for farming and the interior was largely a wilderness, with most of the population outside the capital living in small fishing villages accessible only by boat. It seemed odd that it was not part of Canada, but apparently the inhabitants preferred it that way. It was a Dominion of the British Commonwealth that had been self-governing until 1934, when, in financial straits at the bottom of the Depression, their parliament took the unusual step of relinquishing self-government, and control reverted back to London. It was also odd that there were islands that were part of France right off the southern coast. It was not surprising to Alan that smuggling was a lively business, and the famous gangster Al Capone had been able to take advantage of the situation in his liquor smuggling business.

The US Navy base at Argentia was on the east side of Placentia Bay, a large indentation on the south coast. It was another American base on British Commonwealth territory that had been made possible by the destroyers-for-bases deal with the British that had been announced in September of 1940. The scuttlebutt had it that this was also where Roosevelt and Churchill had met in mid-summer, aboard American and British naval ships which converged there. *It was a good choice*, Alan thought. *The frequent fogs and lack of telephone service on shore would make it unlikely that their presence would become known to the outside world during their short stay.*

The *Yorktown* reached Argentia under a dark, overcast sky. As the ship dropped anchor, Alan looked forward to going ashore that evening to the Officers' Club on the base. Bombing Five had been selected to be the first squadron to go there; their departure was scheduled for 2000, after dinner. Just after dinner, Ardmore had called a meeting with Casey, Bellingham, MacAllester, and Durham, but the rest of the squadron officers left for shore on time.

It took almost forty minutes for the motor launch to reach the pier from the anchored *Yorktown*. It was humid and windy, and occasionally spray came up into the boat from the choppy water. With temperature in the lower fifties, most of the pilots were cold, wet, and a little grumpy by the time they reached the pier.

Leaving the pier, the pilots were told that it was about a thirty-minute walk north to the Officers' Club. *At least that will give us a chance to warm up if we walk briskly*, Alan thought. The sun had set around 1900. It was a cloudy night during the dark of the moon, so it could not have been much darker outside. Several of the pilots, including Alan, had brought flashlights, and they turned them on to see that the road led through the forest and past occasional clearings of varying sizes. The base had been under construction for about six months, and it soon became clear that it remained unfinished. Construction materials lay all around, and the road had no pavement. As the pilots' shoes became muddy, some of them became grumpier, but Alan became more cheerful as he warmed up.

As they walked along, Alan noticed that Pooh Featherstone and Slippery Simpkin seemed more relaxed and cheerful than the others. He guessed that they had had a nip or two from private stores before leaving the ship. Alan's growing impression was that these two were a cut below the other pilots. Their flying was okay, but their attitudes left a lot to be desired. Featherstone seemed to think bluster and bravado would get him through anything, and Simpkin was casual about everything but his flying; nothing seemed to perturb him.

As they passed a clearing and reentered the forest, Jim Lowery spoke up. "Do you suppose they have bears and wolves here?" he asked with a look of worry that Alan had come to recognize as contrived.

"No question about it," said Einar Jensen, glancing around furtively and picking up his pace.

Alan realized that Einar's Minnesota origins gave him an air of authority on wild animals in the northern forest, and a number of the pilots began following Einar's example. Featherstone and Simpkin appeared to be alarmed; their relaxed demeanor had vanished. He remembered that Featherstone and Simpkin were city boys, from Houston and Miami, respectively, so he decided to relax and enjoy the entertainment.

Featherstone announced loudly, "In Texas, where I come from, we're used to bears and wolves—and jaguars, too."

"They say that, in Houston, you can hear the wolves howling every night," Jim added.

There was a spluttering sound from Cedric Davis and a guffaw from Ned Morris.

"Okay, so they're outside the city," explained Featherstone.

"At least 300 miles out," chuckled Cedric.

The rest of the pilots cackled. Alan realized that Cedric's Arkansas home could actually be closer than 300 miles to Houston.

They continued walking for a few minutes, passing another small clearing, and then Alan noticed Jim and Einar very casually slowing their pace to drop back. Soon, they were well back from the others, and their footsteps could not be heard.

A few more minutes went by before twigs snapped in the woods to the right.

"What was that?" exclaimed Simpkin.

Everyone froze, and flashlights were pointed toward the noise, revealing a small shed. Nothing moved. The flashlights were turned back to the road ahead and the group resumed walking.

A minute later, more twigs snapped and the group heard running footsteps and a great bass roar. All the pilots turned toward the noise. Suddenly, two dark, hump-backed shapes came rushing out of the woods toward Featherstone and Simpkin, who backpedaled, staggered, and fell backward into the mud. When the shapes were revealed to be Jim and Einar, crouched with their coats drawn over their heads, many of the pilots convulsed with laughter. The other pilots, who had shown signs of fear, slowly joined in. They evidently realized that if it was necessary to fake wild animals, real ones were probably rare.

The laughter slowly subsided, Featherstone and Simpkin sheepishly picked themselves up, and the pilots resumed their walk.

They found the Officers' Club in a building that resembled a garage or warehouse. The pilots walked into the club and took off their damp raincoats. Featherstone and Simpkin looked a little better once their coats were removed—mud was now only on their pants and shoes.

A marine major was standing at one end of the bar, finishing a drink, and a marine sergeant was tending bar. Nearby, marine officers were sitting at two tables. The major eyed them, put down his drink, and said, "You gentlemen are from the *Yorktown*, I gather. Welcome to our club. It may be *called* a navy base, but we're mostly marines here, and we got the club built."

Alan realized that although he was fairly new in the squadron, he was the senior navy officer present. No lieutenants were present, and he had been promoted to lieutenant j.g. before any of the other j.g.s, including West. "Thank you, sir. We're glad to be here," he said with a smile, "We're from Bombing Five." While the pilots were getting their drinks at the bar, the major got his coat and left the club.

A marine first lieutenant got up from the table and approached the pilots, swaying a bit as he came. Alan noted that the marine did not have an Academy ring, and he steeled himself for whatever might come next. With a sneer, the marine said in a loud voice so that all could hear, "Straight from your dinner, served with silver on white linen, huh? This is probably the first time you navy boys have ever gotten your shoes muddy."

Jim chuckled, but Alan felt that most of the pilots were getting riled up. Pretty soon, they would start calling the marines "jarheads." Increasingly provocative insults would be lobbed back and forth until a fight started. The marines at the tables stood up at Jim's chuckle. Alan felt that he had to try to diffuse the situation.

The marine lieutenant snickered and continued. "Have you boys ever been outdoors at night before? Did you see any big, nasty bears, or wolves?"

Alan saw an opening, and he took it. "Sure thing! Two bears came charging full-steam out of the woods and attacked us. They knocked down two of us," he said, pointing to Featherstone and Simpkin.

The marines' frowns were replaced by smiles when they saw that Featherstone and Simpkin had mud on their clothes.

Jim picked up the thread. "We asked the bears what the hell they were doing, whose side they were on, and if the Germans were paying them, and they turned tail and slunk away."

The pilots laughed, but the marine lieutenant looked dumb-founded. He turned around and went back to his table. The other marines sat back down.

As the navy pilots sat down, West leaned over to Alan and said softly, "Well done."

The pilots enjoyed an hour at the club, and by the time they started back to the pier, they were warm, dry, and well lubricated, so the walk passed quickly. They were back on board before the effect wore off.

Wednesday, September 24, 1941

Alan was a little surprised to get mail only two days after arriving in Argentia. Apparently the ongoing construction of the base brought continual shipping traffic to and from the US, and the navy mail system using his shipboard address seemed to be efficient. He guessed this would be Jennifer's first letter sent from the Territory of Hawaii.

Honolulu, T. H.
September 15, 1941

Dear Alan,

I hope you are doing well and have not had any flying scares. I imagine the flying and everything else is not so hot now. I got your letter of the seventh. Thank you so much for telling me all about the wedding. You did a good job on the description, you rascal.

The five days getting here on the Monterey were nice and relaxing, a most pleasant break between hectic train travel and getting settled here. Swede Momsen was on the ship, so I got to know him a little and told him what you were doing. He sends his greetings. He is now on the staff of the Fourteenth Naval District in Hawaii.

I have been here a week and I am starting to feel more at home. The warmth and lack of rainy days is quite pleasant, but I think I would prefer it a little cooler. The presence of so many native Hawaiians and Japanese makes for a very different atmosphere than in the eastern US, but everybody seems to get along fairly well together. My spoken Japanese is pretty rusty, so hearing it and even speaking it occasionally is a welcome change. Hearing Japanese coming out of my mouth is quite a shock for the Japanese here, and makes for amusing situations.

I was lucky to find an apartment in Honolulu two days ago. As you and I expected, the influx of new people to help build up our military presence here has started to strain the local resources, especially housing. I had to settle for a small fourth-floor walk-up, but it is sunny and cheerful. It even has a little porch facing southwest, and a view of Waikiki Beach. I can't wait until you visit, you rascal.

Today I reported to Rochefort's Combat Intelligence Unit for the first time. It is housed in an amazingly inconspicuous basement office, to which the unit moved about two months ago. It is known to its inhabitants as "The Dungeon," partly because the ventilation system brings in very little fresh air and almost everyone smokes. The other problem is that the air conditioning is cranky, and it is often too cool. There is always a man sitting at a desk near the door, who acts as a "bouncer." If you can get past the bouncer, the atmosphere is friendly and exceedingly informal: nearly all military protocol is optional, including uniforms and saying "sir." First names are used most of the time, even by enlisted men. The pecking order seems to be determined by ability, rather than rank. I can't tell you much more until I have been there a while.

I looked up Mark Gallagher when I arrived and had dinner with him. Mark's big news is that his ship and several others are going to be heading out for a long time. Sorry I can't be more specific.

I am starting to think about buying a car. It would be quite handy at times, and I miss my Chevy. Dad's car is fairly old and worn, so he is driving the Chevy now. I would like to find another one just like it here, but may not be able to afford it because prices are so high, apparently due to shipping costs.

I miss you very much, and I think I am starting to be a little homesick already. But I still think I did the right thing.

Oodles of love,

Jennifer

Alan could tell she was homesick, but he couldn't blame her. She seemed to be doing well anyway. Her mention of "not so hot" told him that she knew where he was, as he thought she would. It was interesting news about Mark Gallagher: she was almost certainly saying that he was headed to the Philippines to join the Asiatic Fleet. If trouble started, he would surely be on the front lines there. Her careful phrasing made him realize that, from now on, their letters would have to be discreet, whether or not they were actually censored.

CHAPTER TWENTY-THREE

Search Mission

Wednesday, October 1, 1941

The *Yorktown* was steaming southwest, toward Newfoundland, and planning to be back in Argentia the next day. She, along with her escorting cruisers and destroyers, had departed Argentia on September 26 for a six-day routine patrol northeast out into the North Atlantic toward Greenland and Iceland.

The area was frequented by convoys going between Britain and her big suppliers in North America, the US and Canada. Everyone had known for some time that these convoys were essential to Britain's survival, and that losses to German submarines had risen to alarming levels. Long-range aircraft based in Britain had proven to be fairly effective in forcing the submarines to submerge— where they could only move slowly and not very far—and even occasionally in sinking the submarines. These aircraft did not have enough range to reach out to the middle of the Atlantic, however. The presence of the *Yorktown* was intended to temporarily fill in the gap with carrier aircraft.

The previous afternoon, the pilots of Bombing Five were told they would be making a morning search to the south, preceded by a briefing at 0700. Searches from carriers were generally done by the scouting or bombing squadrons, whose SBDs had more range than the F4F-3 or the TBD. For scouting missions in the Atlantic, each SBD was armed with one 325-pound depth charge—the normal anti-submarine armament—carried in the bomb crutch under the fuselage. With Scouting Five absent, Bombing Five had been busy, making a search most every day during this patrol, but usually with only part of the squadron. Although the missions were boring, Alan enjoyed the role of being the eyes of the fleet and was looking forward to another flight.

Alan had learned in ground school at Pensacola that typical scouting and bombing squadrons were capable of searches out beyond 300 miles. Even if the pilots were skilled and careful, however, they would be expected to accumulate a navigation error of two to four miles for every 100 miles flown. This would mean that they might be twelve to twenty-four miles off from their estimated position at the end of such a mission. In this case, even in fair visibility, they might not be able to see the carrier when they returned. They would then have to fly a standard search pattern to find the carrier, and scouting doctrine required a three-hour fuel reserve in this case, cutting the search range in half. The problem of finding the ship at the end of a mission weighed on Alan's mind every time he went out, whether it was a scouting or a bombing mission.

Fortunately, the Fleet Problems had uncovered this problem years earlier, and the Naval Research Laboratory had started working on the problem in the mid-'30s. The solution was to place a homing transmitter on the carrier, designated model YE (Yoke Easy in the US military phonetic alphabet), and a homing receiver in each aircraft, designated model ZB (Zed Baker). Deliveries of the YE began in late 1940, and Alan knew that all the fleet carriers now had them. Deliveries of the ZB had been delayed, but, fortunately, Bombing Five had received theirs at the last minute before departing Norfolk. The pilots had been briefed on this system while in transit, and Alan thought that it was a wonderful breakthrough.

Mechanics and radiomen had labored diligently and gotten them installed in all the Bombing Five aircraft just before the ship had departed Argentia for the current patrol. Since Bombing Five was still just learning to use the device, the *Yorktown* air group commander had decided to limit the searches in good weather to 150 miles during this patrol, as they had been before the ZB was installed. In a real war situation, single aircraft would likely be used for scouting missions to allow aircraft to be kept ready for a strike, but for this patrol, searches were to be performed in pairs for greater safety.

Alan was starting to feel quite at home on the ship. He knew his way around most of it, and he'd found that the pilots spent a lot of time in their squadron ready rooms. Fighting Forty-Two had its ready room high up in the island, but those for Bombing Five and Torpedo Five were below the flight deck and above the hangar deck. Most of the pilots did not like this location because it was down below the action. Alan felt a bit vulnerable right under the easily penetrated flight deck, even though the threat of a bombing attack on the carrier was remote in the North Atlantic.

Bombing Five's ready room was a typical naval ship compartment, painted white. Under the overhead, there was the usual assortment of pipes, ducts, wires, lights, loudspeakers, and other paraphernalia. The deck was covered with red linoleum. On the surrounding bulkheads, there were hooks for flight gear, life vests, and clipboards; and shelves for manuals. The compartment was pretty well filled with the chairs needed for twenty pilots, five rows of four, with a center aisle running through the middle. There was a little extra space at the back, where the gunners could stand when they were to be included in briefings.

The chairs were sturdy metal ones that were fixed to the deck, each with a folding arm that created a writing surface in front of the chair. They were well upholstered and comfortable, and they could even recline a little and had space underneath for personal gear. On the wall in front, there were large blackboards. Several sections of the boards had been ruled off, with space for flight information. Also in front, there was a small lectern and a teletype machine.

A little before 0700, Bombing Five gathered in their ready room for the briefing. The mission information was already written on the blackboards. Bombing Five's mission for the day was to launch at 0800 on a search out to 150 miles in an arc from 120 to 210 degrees true, or 140 to 230 degrees magnetic. As the ship moved, it was possible for the magnetic variation to be different every day, but during the last few days the ship had happened to steam along a line of constant variation, called an isogonic line. Nine pairs of aircraft would go out, so the whole squadron was going. Each pair would cover a ten-degree sector that was shaped like a very narrow pie slice. The pilots for each sector were listed in the ruled section of the blackboard.

Alan settled into his seat, swung the arm up to make a writing surface, and began writing down the information from the blackboard. This would be his third search mission on this particular patrol, and he was becoming more confident in his abilities. He was assigned one of the middle sectors, 180 degrees magnetic, with Jerry West. Bellingham appeared at the front of the room and went over the weather forecast: 1,500-foot overcast all day, visibility ten miles or better, except occasional visibility of one to three miles in widely scattered rain showers, wind 300 at twenty-five. After the weather report, Arnham came to the front and went over the details of the mission. Radio silence was to be observed except in an emergency. He emphasized careful navigation and use of the ZB receiver. When he finished, he told the pilots to double-check their numbers before leaving the room because they would be called on deck soon.

Alan used his E6B calculator to estimate heading and ground speed adjustments for wind. A few minutes after he was finished,

the loudspeaker announced, "Bombing Five, man your planes."
They all rose, gathered their gear, and filed quickly out and up to
the flight deck. Bombing Five's SBDs were spotted for takeoff on
the aft end of the flight deck. Arnham would be first off, so his
airplane was spotted in the front row. Alan's SBD was spotted in
the middle of the group, next to West's aircraft, so Alan would
follow West in the takeoff sequence.

As he walked down the flight deck, Alan glanced up and saw
two F4Fs overhead, flying just under the cloud cover. They were
on Combat Air Patrol (CAP), which was maintained over the
carrier when there was the possibility of an air attack. In this case,
it was more of a drill, since the Germans had only very rarely
flown this far west.

Alan usually flew aircraft number 5-B-12, but today he had
been assigned to 5-B-7. As he walked up to the left side of the
airplane, he saw his rear-seat man approaching. He greeted Aviation
Radioman Second Class Wayne Parker, who had been with Alan
on his last two missions. Alan had made it a point to try to get
to know Parker by arranging to meet him occasionally in those
places in the ship where neither was out of place, such as the
hangar deck. Parker was a small, wiry, twenty-year-old Missouri
native. He seemed to be serious about his work, and Alan had
developed a respect for him.

"Good morning, Parker. All set for the search?" asked Alan.

"Good morning, sir. Yes, sir."

"All aboard," said Alan.

They both climbed in and fastened their straps, and Alan got his
engine started. He glanced around and soon saw that all the propellers were turning. The standard interval between launches on the
Yorktown was thirty seconds. Alan could see Fly One getting ready
to send Arnham off, and soon Arnham was gone and the launch
was underway. A few minutes later, West took off. Alan followed,

getting off smartly in the stiff northwest wind, although he and
Parker were rocked around in the turbulence as they climbed away.

Alan started a gentle left turn, following West, and they rolled
out on heading 189 and leveled off at 1,000 feet. Alan took up
a position about 200 feet away from West, which was a good
cruising distance, since Alan was expected to spend most of his
time scanning the ocean and not working to stay in close formation
with West. Alan pulled back the power to the long-range cruise
setting and set the mixture to automatic lean. He began making
notes of times, headings, and speeds on a flight log form. When
the plane had settled into its cruise speed and was all trimmed
out, he engaged the autopilot, which was welcome on this day as
the gusty wind bounced them around.

The flight continued uneventfully to the turning point, and
Alan and Parker did their best to maintain a search. All they
saw were endless gray waves flecked with white under the lighter
gray, overcast sky. He announced over the intercom to Parker
when he was switching fuel tanks just to break up the monotony
and to make Parker feel like he was part of what was going on.
Finally, West made the left turn to end their outbound leg and
start the short cross leg before the turn inbound. Just as Alan
was about to turn to follow, he saw the dim outline of ships
dead ahead. It was an eastbound convoy that had just become
visible in the mist.

"Convoy dead ahead, about ten miles—about twenty ships
eastbound," he said to Parker over the intercom. He noted the
time and bearing of the convoy, and then he made the ninety-
degree left turn and noted the time. Since they were under radio
silence, he wanted to make sure he had all of the information
written down for his post-flight debriefing.

After he made the turn, Parker came on the intercom, "Convoy
sighting confirmed."

Alan appreciated that Parker's calls on the intercom were businesslike, brief and to the point.

After a few more minutes, West made the ninety-degree left turn to start the inbound leg and Alan followed, steadying out on a heading of 346, which would take them back to the launch position. Before they reached that position, though, they expected the Zed Baker to point the way back to the ship, which would have moved from the launch position. The *Yorktown* should have turned southwest after the launch was completed and gone about fifteen miles in that direction.

"Might as well turn on the Zed Baker," Alan said over the intercom.

"Zed Baker warming up," reported Parker after he turned on the homing receiver.

They continued on the return leg, scanning the ocean for ships and listening carefully for the first signal from the Yoke Easy. Roughly twenty minutes went by before they first heard the faint signal. After another few minutes, Alan was certain that it was *dash-dot*, the Morse code for N that indicated that they were in the 150- to 180-degree sector from the carrier, as expected. Then the Zed Baker suddenly went silent.

"Zed Baker has quit," Parker reported over the intercom. "Checking it out."

Alan was glad at that moment that Parker was a radioman and not a machinist.

A few minutes later, Parker announced, "Power wire too short, broke off. Will attempt temporary repair."

Alan thought angrily that it would not be easy to forgive the man who installed a power wire that was too short on a critical piece of equipment. He knew that he could always follow West and hope that West's Zed Baker was working, but Alan knew that single airplanes would be used for searches eventually, and it rattled him that this marvelous device was not working when needed.

Some time ago, Alan had thought through the consequences of having difficulty finding the carrier. He concluded that, in these northern waters, he and Parker would probably not survive if they could not find the carrier before their fuel ran low. If they ditched the airplane, they would only last a few minutes in the cold water. They had to either be in sight of a patrol vessel that could pick them up, or quickly retrieve the life raft from the sinking airplane, get into it, and get warm again before hypothermia set in. Even then, the chances of being found seemed slim. As long as the YE-ZB system was working, he'd felt reasonably confident that he wouldn't have to worry about this. Now that it had failed, he was on edge.

Alan continued to follow West on a heading of 346. They flew on for another fifteen minutes, during which time Alan kept up his scan of the ocean, knowing that Parker was busy repairing the wiring.

"Zed Baker back on again," reported Parker. Alan could hear the signal, still N, loud and clear. "I took some wire from one of the panel lights and made twisted connections, so it could fail again," Parker said.

"Very good, Parker, nice work," Alan complimented him, genuinely relieved.

They flew on for another ten minutes. A steady tone was coming into the background of the N signal being emitted by the Zed Baker. Alan knew that the tone had come in because they were approaching the 120- to 150-degree sector, designated by the *dot-dash* A signal. As it was with the radio range system on land, since the A signal was the opposite of the N signal, it filled in the gaps in the N signal to make a steady tone. As they reached the boundary between the sectors, the tone became completely steady.

West wiggled his wings and turned left to a heading of 330 to follow the sector boundary back to the ship, which happened to be the direction the ship would move in during flight operations. The ship would soon be recovering the first airplanes returning from the search. A short time later, Alan spotted her right where she was supposed to be, surrounded by her escort and steaming northwest into the wind to recover the search aircraft.

West flew straight ahead toward the stern of the ship for an overhead approach. Alan followed, closing up on West. He could see another SBD, one of the earlier search planes, flying up the groove to land. Again, there were a couple of Wildcats overhead, just under the cloud cover. The two SBDs flown by him and West stayed at 1,000 feet and overflew the ship from stern to bow. Alan could see that the ship was pitching heavily in the long westerly swells. They executed the break, and Alan followed West in the landing circuit. The usual nervousness he felt when landing on a carrier was coming on fast as he completed his landing checklist. He thought that the *Yorktown* might be pitching a little more than he had seen in any of his previous carrier landings, which caused his tension to rise even more. As he turned onto his final leg, he could see West taxiing forward after a successful landing.

Alan began watching LSO Campbell and adjusting his approach as needed. He thought that he would arrive over the stern just as it was nearly stationary at the bottom of its up-and-down motion in the swell. Soon he was close, and Campbell was telling him he was low. A strong gust of wind hit his airplane, slowing him down and throwing off his timing. The stern started to come up, and Campbell gave him the wave off. Alan saw the cameraman behind Campbell go into action once again. A wave of fear gripped him. He quickly added a lot of power and pulled up the nose, but it was too late. The fuselage barely cleared the deck, and the propeller and landing gear struck the aft edge of the deck with a loud bang.

The SBD skidded forward along the deck on its belly, emitting a horrible screeching noise. The plane was completely out of Alan's control, so he and Parker were nothing but terrified passengers. Something caught under the left wing, and the plane began to turn to the left. Deck crewmen jumped into the gallery. A cold sweat overtook Alan, and his heart raced as the airplane slid toward the port side of the deck. The airplane still had some momentum, so it went straight over the side, nose first. The screeching stopped.

Terror gripped Alan more strongly as he saw the sea rushing to meet him. He barely had time to get his left hand on the glare shield over the instrument panel, bracing himself for impact, before the plane hit the water at a steep angle. He felt a jab of pain as his forehead hit hard on the gun sight, and the severe yank of the seat belt took his breath away. At least he was still conscious. Water came over the windshield and splashed his face. The water was freezing, numbing him quickly, but Alan was slightly relieved that everything had come to a stop. The plane stopped sinking and rose until the wing was near the surface.

The airplane bobbed in the swell with the tail pointing up at about ten degrees. Alan's heart was still racing as he quickly unbuckled his seat belt and parachute and stepped out onto the left wing, holding onto the canopy. Parker was climbing out, and Alan could see that he had a cut on his forehead.

"You okay?" shouted Alan.

"Think so," answered Parker.

Thank goodness that Parker was not seriously injured. The plane was sinking fairly quickly. Alan began to shiver. He took a quick look around as the water rose to his waist, and he saw the carrier steaming on, already about 1,000 feet away, leaving them isolated and helpless. When he turned to the south, he was relieved to see the port plane guard destroyer easing toward them slowly, rolling heavily in the swell. He made out *409* in big white numerals on her bow, so she was the *Sims*. He could see that she was maneuvering to pick them up on the starboard side, which was facing southeast, offering shelter from the northwest wind. They both pulled the tabs to inflate their life vests and eased off the wing into the icy water.

A few minutes later, they were being helped by the *Sims*' sailors to climb up the cargo net that had been thrown over the side. Two sailors had gotten into the water to help them. When they reached the deck, they were both weak from the cold and could barely stand up. For the first time, things had slowed down enough for the shock to register in Alan's mind. Now that he was out of the frigid water, relief flooded through him. They were immediately wrapped in blankets and hustled below deck to the destroyer's sick bay.

In the sick bay, they were helped to undress and rewrapped in warm towels, during which Alan had time to reflect on the cause of the crash. It had happened so fast that there was no time to think while it was happening. The relief of being rescued quickly and being treated well aboard the *Sims* faded, to be replaced by feelings of guilt. He realized once again that he still had a tendency to try to touch down too near the stern, which was why he'd crashed. This time he got caught, perfectly illustrating why that was bad technique. He realized that it was particularly bad technique to land near the stern when timing for the lowest point in the pitch motion, leaving no way to adjust if his timing was off. He had endangered his gunner and the deck crewmen and had wrecked a perfectly good SBD. The only thing he could think to do to try and make up for this failure was to make sure it never happened again.

Alan reflected on his reputation in the squadron, now that he had added a crash landing to his other failures. Doubts about his standing in the squadron and his ability as a carrier pilot grew steadily within him, even as he could hear Parker chatting and laughing with the sick bay pharmacists mates. Warm dry clothes were brought for them both and Alan moved into a corner to be alone with his gloomy thoughts while he dressed. After a while, he got a grip on himself. He knew from experience that emotional swings were not uncommon after a traumatic experience, and he was reminded of his rapidly changing feelings after he had been rescued from the *Squalus*.

Two hours after they had been taken to sick bay, Alan and Parker came back up on deck, warm, dry and fed. Their cuts and bruises had been treated, and, although they both had bandages on their foreheads, no other injuries had been found. They were grateful for the warmth and good humor of the *Sims*'s men, who seemed to take the weather and the destroyer's extensive motion in the swell all in stride. Nevertheless, Alan was anxious to get back aboard the *Yorktown* and face whatever ill-will and discipline he had earned.

Thursday, October 2, 1941

Casey chaired the trouble board of senior officers in the squadron to review Alan's crash. The others on the board were Bellingham and MacAllester. Alan's explanation seemed to impress the board; especially because he understood the cause and accepted the blame. They decided not to impose any penalty on Alan and simply to watch his progress. He vowed to himself that afternoon to break his habit of landing too close to the stern and prove to them that their trust in him was not misplaced.

After the board was finished, he wondered whether he was an inch or a mile from being bilged. He thought that if the answer was an inch, the trouble board would owe it to him to give him a warning, which they did not. But his doubts remained, so he decided to talk it over with his roommate. He found him in their stateroom, and Jim was in his usual cheerful mood.

"How do you think I stand in the squadron?" Alan asked

"Why? Do you think your status in the squadron might be in doubt?" Jim asked.

"Well, I was slow to qualify, my bombing scores are low, and now I've made a crash landing."

"Stringy, let's put this in perspective. You were not unusually slow to qualify, your bombing scores are not low for someone with only a few chances to practice, and lots of pilots crash on landing at some point. I crashed on landing last spring in the Pacific, and the weather was a lot nicer than yesterday. Several other pilots in the squadron have crashed on landing. You know, some say it's a fairly tricky exercise to land on an aircraft carrier," Jim said, ending with a smile.

"I never heard that you had crashed." Alan paused. "That makes it sound a lot better," he said, relieved. "Thanks, Jolly."

"Nobody said being a carrier pilot is easy. You have to work hard at it. If you start feeling downcast, you're finished."

"Yes, sir, coach," quipped Alan with a smile.

Jim laughed and clapped Alan on the shoulder. "Let's get some supper."

Friday, October 3, 1941

With the ship back at anchor in Argentia, it was time to write Jennifer. Alan knew she would be horrified to hear about his crash, but he had to be honest with her.

USS Yorktown
c/o Fleet Post Office
New York, NY
October 3, 1941

Dear Jennifer,

I hope you are enjoying your work, now that you have been there a few weeks. It must be a very interesting place to work, like ONI. Your apartment sounds very nice, and should give you some exercise. I can't wait to see it. You know I am a car nut. So, if you decide to get a car, please tell me ALL about it. We can afford a car like you had, if that is what you want. Remember you will get some of the higher price back when you sell it.

I am feeling humble, because I have had a crash, while landing on the carrier. I can't give you the details due to secrecy. Neither my gunner nor I had more than very minor injuries. We did get wet and extremely cold in the sea, in the short interval before being picked up by a destroyer. Once on board, we were very well treated. However, a perfectly good airplane went to the bottom. I respect this gunner, who has flown with me several times. Apparently this is mutual, because he volunteered to fly with me again, even after the crash.

I think I understand fully why it happened, and it was my fault. There's one part of the landing technique in which I have consistently had a bias to do it near one edge of the safe range, and it finally caught me. I have vowed to change that. After discussing it with the skipper and exec, they were remarkably understanding, and did not discipline me. I hope to prove that their trust in me is justified. The rest of the squadron seemed to take it in stride, for which I was grateful.

Aside from that, you are right that things are "not so hot" here. The base is under construction and remains primitive. It takes about an hour to get to the officers' club, which is in a building like a warehouse. There is nothing larger than a small village nearby. I get exercise by jogging around the flight or hangar decks.

Many of the navy ships here are operating in worse conditions than we are, and under greater threat. Yet the average American hears little, if anything, about the effort here. Maybe that will change. We now have a reporter from the Saturday Evening Post on board.

I still miss you very much. Write soon and send some warm sun, you scalawag.

Tons of love,

Alan

CHAPTER TWENTY-FOUR

The Yorktown Goes to Casco Bay

Tuesday, October 14, 1941

The *Yorktown* had departed Argentia, Newfoundland, on October 10 and had arrived in Casco Bay, Maine, on October 13. She had sailed back to Maine in company with the battleship *New Mexico*, the heavy cruiser *Quincy*, the light cruiser *Savannah*, and two divisions of destroyers. On this voyage, the flotilla had encountered unusually heavy weather, and most of the ships, including the *Yorktown*, had sustained damage.

Alan enjoyed the spectacle of foul weather—as long as there was no immediate threat to him or the ship. He found a few semi-sheltered places between the hangar deck and the bow from which he could watch in relative safety as the ship plowed into the waves and then rose above them. He found that Jim shared a taste for this kind of excitement, too.

For this voyage only, COMCRULANT had been embarked in the *Yorktown*. Everyone in Bombing Five knew that his flag lieutenant, Lieutenant Vang, was on board as well. Alan had run into him twice, and both times Vang had seemed anxious to forget that he had ever been part of Bombing Five.

Aboard the *Yorktown*, most everyone had felt that the heavy weather was worth getting through to get back to civilization. The ship would be based in Casco Bay for the next few weeks, at least, and all hands were pleased to have access to Portland, Maine, which was considered a "real" city, after the primitive situation at Argentia. Many wives of the *Yorktown* personnel were even

CHAPTER TWENTY-FOUR ~ THE YORKTOWN GOES TO CASCO BAY

planning to come to Portland from Norfolk and elsewhere and rent houses while the carrier was based there.

Wednesday, October 15, 1941

While in Casco Bay, the captain of the *Yorktown* appointed Lieutenant Commander Arnham to be assistant air officer, and Lieutenant Commander Richard Armiston came aboard as the new skipper of Bombing Five. He came from duty as a senior instructor at Pensacola. The Bombing Five exec, Lieutenant Jack Casey, was sent to command a new squadron, Scouting Eight, which was forming at Norfolk to go on board the new carrier *Hornet*. The former flight officer, Lieutenant Gordon Bellingham, fleeted up to be squadron exec, and Armiston appointed the experienced Lieutenant Kelly Durham flight officer. He kept MacAllester as engineering officer and appointed Jerry West to be gunnery officer. Jim Lowery became navigation officer.

Saturday, October 18, 1941

The word had circulated around the *Yorktown* that US Navy ships were starting to take casualties in the Atlantic war. The previous day, the modern destroyer *Kearny* had been torpedoed, and there had been fatalities. She had been able to limp into Hvalfjordhur, Iceland, bypassing Reykjavik, and was escorted by the now-famous *Greer*. From what Alan had heard, those two harbors in Iceland were now visited frequently by US Navy ships, and they were known to American sailors as Valley Forge and Rinkydink, respectively.

Monday, October 20, 1941

It was around 0900 on a cold, foggy morning in Casco Bay, with the *Yorktown* at anchor. Scottie MacAllester was sick with a bad stomachache, so Alan was the acting engineering officer.

He was supervising Bombing Five's maintenance activity on the hangar deck.

The pilots on the regular flying roster each had an airplane assigned to them, and the name of the pilot was stenciled below the forward sliding canopy. Airplane number 5-B-12 had become Alan's airplane. For efficient use of airplanes, though, pilots were expected to always be ready to fly any airplane of the same type. They were discouraged from becoming too attached to any one airplane. Alan had learned that Durham had become possessive about "his" 5-B-5, and the plane captain, who was in charge of the condition of 5-B-5, Aviation Machinists Mate First Class Carlo Conti, confirmed this.

Alan remembered that, the previous day, Durham's gunner had noticed that there was a strange vibration at run-up in 5-B-5. The gunner had told Durham about the vibration at the time, but Durham apparently thought it was not significant, because he paid no attention. The gunner then told Parker, who had quietly passed this on to Alan. Alan talked it over with Scottie at the end of day, and Scottie had entered it on the squawk sheet for the airplane so that the gunner would not be put on the spot. Alan decided a run-up on the airplane was needed to see if the vibration could be detected. Alan drew Conti aside and asked, "Have you noticed a vibration at run-up on this airplane?"

"No, sir," Conti replied. "I saw it on the squawk sheet, but I haven't had a chance to do a run-up. I was going to ask you about it."

"Lieutenant MacAllester entered it on the squawk sheet," Alan informed him. "How about if you run her up and see what you think?"

"Beg pardon, sir, but I'd much rather that you did it."

"Why is that, Conti?"

"Lieutenant Durham is so damned particular, sir. I don't want to get on his bad side, or he'll have me thrown off being plane captain."

"I see," Alan replied. He paused and thought for a moment, then said, "Okay, I'll do it."

"I much appreciate it, sir," Conti said, obviously relieved.

Alan had 5-B-5 spotted forward near one of the openings in the steel curtains on the side of the hangar deck. The steel curtains were closed over most of the openings because of the cool weather, but they were open at the forward end so engines could be tested. He found a helmet to protect his ears from the noise and climbed into the front cockpit. He got the engine started and warmed it up at 1,000 rpm with the propeller in high pitch to put a load on the engine so that it would warm up quickly, but did not feel anything unusual. He put the propeller into low pitch and brought the engine up to the run-up speed of 1,900 rpm, at which point he heard a deep rumble and a corresponding vibration through the foot rails that his feet were resting on, neither of which was normal. He pulled the throttle back to idle and noticed that Durham was walking forward through the hangar. Alan went through the shutdown procedure and climbed out of the airplane.

Durham was waiting for him, coming up and standing directly in front of Alan when he had exited the plane. Durham was at least two inches taller than Alan—and not thin. Alan had noticed before that Durham deliberately used his size to make himself more intimidating, which was now coupled with a scowl on his face.

"What do you think you're doing?" Durham snarled.

"Checking out a vibration squawk on this airplane," Alan replied, keeping an even tone and expression.

"Did Scottie tell you to do that? Where's Conti?" The snarl continued.

"No, Scottie's in sick bay. I'm acting engineering officer," Alan informed him, hoping not to draw Conti into it.

"Who put in the squawk? *I* sure as hell didn't!"

"Scottie put it on the squawk sheet yesterday," Alan replied calmly.

"What are you going to do about it?" The color was rising in Durham's face, and there was spittle on his lips.

"There's definitely a strange noise and vibration, so I'm grounding the airplane until we can do a thorough examination of the engine and propeller."

"The hell you are!" Durham exploded. He grabbed Alan's collar. "Goddamn you, Ericsson, you put that airplane back on the line right now!"

The spittle landed on Alan's face and all nearby work ceased as the men paused to watch the show.

Alan controlled himself, with difficulty. His expression became very firm, and he looked Durham directly in the eye. He said in an even voice, "Sir, that airplane is not going anywhere before we find out what's causing that noise and vibration."

"We'll see about that," Durham yelled. He shoved Alan away, turned, and stalked out of the hangar.

Alan thought, *As if I'm not under a cloud already, now I've crossed the flight officer.* Alan was certain that he had done the right thing, though, so he did not have any second thoughts.

A half-hour later, a space in the workshop area of the hangar had opened up. Men were getting ready to move 5-B-5 back there from the forward end of the hangar when Lieutenant Commander Armiston strode into the hangar and drew Alan aside. Armiston had only been on board for a week, and Alan did not know what to expect. He could see right away that Armiston was in a bad mood, though. Alan was surprised that Armiston had not delegated the task of looking into Durham's complaint to Bellingham. Alan thought that Bellingham—if given the chance—would turn out to be a good exec, adept at shielding his skipper from this kind of petty discord.

"It turns out that Lieutenant Durham is senior to Lieutenant Bellingham, so I had to deal with this myself, goddammit," Armiston began, disgust written all over his face.

Durham's career must have had some setbacks for him to be so senior but not have gotten higher in the Scouting Seventy-Two hierarchy, Alan realized.

Armiston continued, "He came to me complaining that you'd grounded his airplane. I explained to him that *his* airplane actually belonged to the squadron, and was maintained by the squadron, but he insisted that the airplane was in fine shape when he flew it yesterday, and that you had no reason to ground it. Let me see if I can detect this vibration."

"Yes, sir. I'll be surprised if you don't notice it at 1,900 rpm," Alan replied.

Alan told the men who were about to move the airplane to tie it back down where it was, and then Alan went about his business while Armiston climbed in and went through the same procedure that Alan had.

Alan was deep into a conversation with some mechanics about another airplane when Armiston came up to him and drew him aside again.

"Jesus, Ericsson, there has to be something seriously wrong with that airplane," he confirmed. "Even if Durham didn't notice, I'm surprised that his gunner didn't bring it to his attention. Dig into it right away—and I'm glad you didn't let Durham sway your judgment. He seems to be a fine pilot, but he was out of line in this case."

"Yes, sir," said Alan, having already decided to not reveal the gunner's role in bringing up the squawk unless he had to.

Alan found Conti and told him to get the inspection started right away, and then he went back to checking on the progress of other maintenance activities.

At around 1500, Conti sought Alan out and asked him to take a look at what he had found. Alan walked with him back over to 5-B-5 and saw that the ring cowl that surrounded the engine and the panels that enclosed the accessory section behind the engine had all been removed. Conti was looking at the engine mount, a roughly cylindrical framework made of steel tubes that surrounded the accessory section behind the engine. The tubes were welded together at their ends. The forward end of the mount was bolted to the engine, and the aft end was bolted to the forward end of the fuselage. Conti pointed to the aft end of one of the steel tubes.

Alan looked closely and saw a large crack through the tube, right next to the weld. Alan grabbed the tube with both hands and tried to move it up and down. He was able to move it enough to see the crack open and close slightly. As the engine mount was carefully designed to minimize vibration coming from the engine, he thought that the new vibration was probably occurring because the severed tube upset the tuning. The rumble probably came from the two sides of the crack bumping each other.

"I think you found the source of the problem, all right. Glad we dug into this before it got worse. Do we have any spare engine mounts?" asked Alan.

"I doubt it, sir, but we have the jig to repair it, I think. I'll check right away."

"That sounds good, Conti. Let me know how it's going. I'll tell the skipper what you found. Oh, and I'd also like to take a look at the log book for this airplane."

"Yes, sir. Follow me." Conti went into a storage compartment, and Alan followed. Conti opened a steel cabinet full of log books and pulled out the one for 5-B-5, handing it to Alan. "There's something else for you here, sir," said Conti, reaching far into another cabinet. He pulled out a small, clear bottle containing about a pint of amber liquid. "That's pretty nice whiskey, sir—bourbon to you, perhaps. It's yours for helping me out and putting up with that shit this morning, sir."

"Much appreciated, Conti," Alan said with a smile, slipping the bottle into his pants pocket. Alan felt that he was being over-compensated, but it would never do to refuse the gift.

Alan took the log book to a desk and sat down. He began at the last entry and worked back, looking for anything that would suggest that the airplane had been subject to unusual stress. He found an entry on August 28, 1941 that read, "Airframe inspection following several hard landings. No discrepancies found." Alan remembered that Monroe had made several hard landings during his initial field carrier landing practice late in August, just before Durham joined the squadron. He went to the squadron office and asked the yeoman to pull the records on who flew which aircraft during the last two weeks of August, and he returned a half-hour later to study the records. He found that Monroe was flying 5-B-5 on August 25, 26, and 27. It seemed to fit together and helped to explain the cracked engine mount.

Alan went to Armiston's office. Finding him there, he told him about the crack and what he had found in the records.

"Good work, Ericsson. We're probably never going to know for sure why the tube cracked, but the hard landings seem like a likely contributor. Put everything in the log book in case there's more trouble. Also, try and get the airplane returned to service as soon as possible so that certain officers will have nothing to complain about," he said with a faint smile. "I'll tell Lieutenant Durham. Carry on."

"Yes, sir." Alan was pleased that the skipper also felt he had done the right thing. One way or another, the whole squadron would soon know that Alan was right and Durham was wrong. Unfortunately, Alan was pretty sure that Durham was the sort of person who would never admit it—or forgive him.

CHAPTER TWENTY-FIVE

A Buzz Job

Thursday, October 23, 1941

As Alan shaved and dressed, he felt the motion of the ship and the faint vibration of the propellers. The ship was underway. The previous day, there had been an announcement that the ship would weigh anchor and get underway early for a day of air exercises. Those who had taken up residence ashore with their families had to leave home well before dawn to get aboard before the ship weighed anchor. All air group pilots were ordered to report to their ready rooms at 0800. Alan decided on his way to breakfast to make his customary underway visit to the bow to take a look around. It was cool as he stood on the port side to look back at the coast and the northwest wind swirled around from the port side of the ship. He saw that the ship was well away from the islands on the edge of Casco Bay, heading east-southeast into the open water. The air office had picked a nice fall day for the exercises, with great visibility and a few small clouds.

After breakfast, as Alan approached the ready room at about 0745, he became aware of a loud conversation inside. Alan stopped in the hallway to avoid interrupting.

Alan recognized Durham's voice. ". . . and his bombing scores stink. I think we should give Furlong a chance to practice, sir."

"No. Put him back in place of Furlong. That will be ALL, Durham," Armiston's voice rang out with a no-nonsense tone, apparently terminating the conversation.

Alan resumed walking toward the ready room. As he entered, Durham was writing something on the blackboard at the front of the room. Armiston was at the lectern, and he nodded to Alan. None of the other pilots were there, so Alan took his seat and quickly scanned the blackboards. There was a large chart of Portland Harbor and its vicinity hung over the blackboards on the left. Durham stopped writing and took his seat.

Alan looked over the flight roster on the right-side blackboard to see where he was assigned. At first, he did not see his name, but then he spotted it in the middle of the order, in Bellingham's division. Alan's name was hard to read because it had been written over a hasty erasure, and no other erasures were apparent. He was assigned to 5-B-12, his usual airplane.

It looked like there had been some question about his participation in these exercises. Doubts about his standing in the squadron came flooding back. He stopped and realized something: *The flight officer sets the roster, and I got athwart his hawse a few days ago. If Durham took me out of the mission for personal reasons, Armiston would not be pleased, and maybe that's what the conversation I just overheard was about.*

Durham had assigned Aviation Ordnance Man Second Class Silas Schofield to be the gunner in 5-B-12. Alan did not know Schofield well because he worked for the gunnery officer, but Alan did know that Schofield was an experienced gunner. The other pilots streamed in, obscuring the blackboards, and Jim took his seat next to Alan.

Armiston began the briefing. "Today the air group has been assigned to make a mock attack on the Army coastal defense installations around Portland Harbor as an exercise for us and for the army. No ordnance or ammunition will be carried, and this will not be a surprise; the army will be waiting for us, although they won't know the exact time of our arrival. Bombing Five will take off at 0930 and attack first at 1000. We will clear the area, and Fighting Forty-Two and Torpedo Five will make their attacks.

"We will make a dive-bombing attack from 15,000 feet on the various forts, and then strafe. Each division will be assigned a certain area containing forts to be attacked, and they will not stray into the other areas so we can avoid interference and the chance of a collision. Division leaders will assign pilots to individual forts."

Alan and Jim turned and looked at each other with growing smiles, hardly daring to believe what they had just heard. Basically, they had been assigned to "buzz," or "flat hat"—fly terrifyingly low over—the army defenses. This was an opportunity that navy pilots normally could only dream about. The dive-bombing runs at the beginning would be easy, and they could not be scored if nothing was dropped. *I can see why Bull was so anxious to keep me out of this mission.*

Armiston moved over to the large chart that had the locations of the forts circled and labeled. "My division will take these two forts at the north end of the harbor; the exec's division will take these three forts in the center, nearest to the city; and the flight officer's division will take these two forts at the south end. This line here," he said, pointing to a thick black line that ran between two islands, "marks the division between the exec's territory and the flight officer's." Raising his voice, he commanded, "After the initial dive, do *not* cross this line!" Having driven home his point, he resumed a normal tone, continuing, "Each pilot is to sketch a map of his area, label the forts, and put in this line. Take your time and get it right. Stay within your area!" He paused, and then continued, "We will return to the carrier by divisions and not try to rendezvous with the whole squadron."

Durham described the weather, which was excellent. As navigation officer, Jim gave the course and distance to the target area, which was straight into the northwest wind. The pilots then collected around their division leaders in different corners of the room. Durham and Bellingham had smaller versions of the harbor chart, each attached to a stiff backing, which they laid against the backs of some chairs and pointed to while they described their territories and how they wanted to have the attack conducted.

Alan's mind had been racing, and he had an idea of how to make the strafing more effective. *Maybe Bellingham has already thought of it*, he supposed.

Bellingham began his briefing, pointing to items on the chart occasionally. "Today we have three targets and six airplanes, so we will have three two-plane sections. The dive and the immediate pullout should be made into the wind, which is northwest. Except for that, all operations are to be in a northeast-southwest direction to avoid cross-traffic. We'll each make three strafing runs. After that, we would probably be low on ammunition in a real mission, so we'll make no more. Morris and I will take Fort Preble, here on the mainland, strafing toward the southwest and making a hard right 180 to the northeast to go back for another run—"

Alan decided to take the chance. "May I make a suggestion, sir?" A fleeting trace of annoyance crossed Bellingham's face.

"Okay, Ericsson, shoot."

"We've gotten a look at some of the forts in our boat rides from the anchorage into the city, and they were built for defense against surface ships. Except for Fort Gorges, they all seem similar, all built on promontories with walls on the sea side only. In our strafing runs, we *could* stay lower if we approach from seaward, but the forts are well protected on that side. Could we approach from the unprotected land side?" Bellingham looked thoughtful, any hint of annoyance gone from his face. The other pilots glanced at each other, and some eyebrows went up. Alan thought, *They seem to be curious, at least.*

"Hmm . . . I see what you're getting at." A grin began to appear on Bellingham's face. "It would be a nice surprise for the army. Once we get past and over the water, we could duck down, so we'll probably be below where at least their 75-millimeter guns can depress. Okay, we'll do it. Morris and I will strafe northeast and turn left to go back southwest for another run." He was pointing at the map again. "Lowery and Becker, you take Fort Gorges, here in the middle of the harbor. Fort Gorges is built on a tiny island with walls all around, so you can strafe either way. Ericsson and Monroe, you take Fort Scammel, here on the south end of House Island, strafing toward the southwest then making a hard right 180 around to the northeast to go back for another run. If you don't go southeast of House Island, you will be well to the northwest of the black line here, far from Durham's area. After the strafing runs, sections will stick together and rendezvous here at 5,000 feet, five miles east of Peaks Island."

Alan realized that many officers were incapable of changing their plans on short notice based on advice from a junior officer. He had already formed a favorable opinion of Bellingham, but now he realized how lucky he was to have such a good-natured and self-confident officer as exec.

All the pilots got busy drawing their maps. Alan had drawn a lot of maps for geography classes, and he came up with a passable map fairly quickly. Jim did as well, and they were among the first to go back to their regular seats.

Jim turned to Alan and said with a grin, "Bull has already decided that you are going to violate his airspace. I heard him ask Becker who was assigned to Fort Scammel."

"I suppose that might be true. I wonder if Bellingham put me next to Bull's area on purpose to see what would happen."

Bombing Five was called to man their planes at 0915. Launch started on schedule at 0930, and Alan launched after Morris. Shortly, Monroe joined up on his right wing. After forming up, the squadron started for the target, climbing to 15,000 feet, passing through a layer of scattered cumulus at 5,000 feet. The sight of the whole squadron, as it climbed above the white background, was magnificent. It was a classic fall day, with visibility over 100 miles. Long before reaching the assigned altitude, Alan saw that the White Mountains, including the already snow-capped summit of Mount Washington, were clearly visible in the distance. Days like this lifted Alan's spirits.

The prospect of authorized low-level flying lifted Alan's spirits, too. Alan had always thought that driving a car at high speed was exciting and fun. Although most of his navy flying was at speeds two to three times as fast as it was practical to go in a car, the sensation of speed was usually much less. Alan found that to fully appreciate the speed of a plane, the plane had to pass close to something, either clouds or the ground. Clouds were often too vaguely defined or too far away to really fill a pilot with excitement, while the ground was usually too far away, which is what made low-level flying so exciting.

Unfortunately, that excitement also led many pilots to overdo it and get killed. Alan had heard about many accidents of that type even before he joined naval aviation. It was easy to get wrapped up in the fun and either fly too close to the ground or fail to see something ahead, like a tower or sharp hill, until it was too late. Alan was pretty sure from his experience with low-level flying that he could avoid that trap.

Approaching the Portland area at 15,000 feet, Alan soon spotted Cushing Island and House Island beyond it. Alan hand-signaled to Monroe to prepare for the dive, and then he slowed down and opened the canopy. He could hear Schofield, his gunner, behind him opening his canopy and swiveling his seat to face aft. It was bitterly cold at 15,000 feet, but they would not be there for long. Monroe slowed down and moved over to follow in a trail behind Alan.

Cushing Island disappeared under the plane's nose, and Alan kept the southwest end of House Island in view on the left side of the cowling, looking for Fort Scammel until he could see it. When he was nearly directly overhead, he rolled into the dive. He aimed for a point upwind on the northwest side of the island in order to compensate for his drift in the wind. Passing through 5,000 feet, he moved his aiming point to the northwest side of the fort itself. He went through the motions of releasing his bomb at 2,000 feet and then started his pullout, rolling to the right to end up going northeast.

As soon as the g-load eased off in the later part of the pullout, he glanced back at the fort over his right shoulder. He could make out several large-caliber anti-aircraft guns, and he was quite surprised to see that their barrels were far from vertical. Apparently, either his near vertical dive had not been anticipated or they were late in their preparations. If it had been a real attack, there would have been no heavy anti-aircraft opposition to the dive-bombing run. He leveled off at 500 feet. A few seconds later, Alan glanced back again and saw Monroe beginning his pullout.

Alan continued northeast past the northeast end of House Island and then began a fairly tight right turn back to the southwest, staying at 500 feet. Monroe joined on his right wing, stepped up. Alan looked ahead to the right toward Fort Preble. He spotted Bellingham turning southwest after his dive; Morris was in the pullout from his dive. Alan quickly looked straight ahead at Fort Scammel. The barrels of the large anti-aircraft guns had now been elevated to near vertical. *Just in time to be unprepared for our low-level strafing run*, he thought. *I wonder how fast they can depress.*

Alan dove to about 100 feet above the trees and pushed his speed up to 180 knots. Rushing toward the fort, he saw the guns had traversed to aim in his direction and were rapidly depressing down toward a horizontal position. He dropped down to fifty feet above the trees, which were streaming by in a blur. As he roared over the fort, the big guns were still not depressed enough, and men were dropping down behind guns and equipment to avoid being hit. Past the wall, he dropped down to fifty feet over the water. A mile away, he climbed to 100 feet and started a right 180-degree turn to go back for his second run, happy to see that Monroe was doing a good job holding formation.

Alan's second run was similar to his first. The big guns might have been depressed further, but they were still not far enough down to be effective. The third run was similar to his first two. He made one more 180-degree turn to the northeast. Passing the northeast end of House Island, he turned east and began climbing as he crossed Peaks Island. *What a fun mission!*

He and Monroe arrived first at the rendezvous, but Bellingham's and Lowery's sections appeared shortly after them. On the way back to the ship, they saw Fighting Forty-Two pass overhead, much higher, on their way to the target. Torpedo Five flew under them at 2,000 feet.

Back aboard ship, the Bombing Five pilots reported to the ready room. By 1100, everyone was there and Armiston announced individual debriefing in his office in order of takeoff.

It was Alan's turn at 1155. Armiston started in, "Lieutenant Bellingham tells me that it was your idea to strafe from the landward side, which was an excellent suggestion. In my division, we had not seen the layout of the forts ahead of time, but I decided to do the same thing once I had gotten a good look at the forts from the air. There is a general agreement among those I have debriefed so far that the 75-millimeter guns had not been elevated enough to fire on us in the dive, and they could not depress far enough to be effective against low-level strafing. Any other observations?"

Alan thought for a brief moment. "No, sir."

"So, you strafed Fort Scammel on House Island from the northeast. Which way did you turn to go back for another run?"

"I turned right to stay northwest of House Island."

"So you never went southeast of House Island, staying well away from Durham's area?"

"Yes, sir." Alan had forgotten about Jim Lowery's prediction until that moment.

"How low did you get over House Island?"

"About fifty feet above the trees, sir."

"Pretty low, but still fairly safe. Keep up the good work, Ericsson. That will be all."

"Thank you, sir," Alan said. He got up and left Armiston's office.

Alan had lunch in the wardroom and had started for the hangar deck to see what was happening when a voice behind him called his name. He turned around to see Armiston catching up with him.

"I just finished the debriefing. Durham says you came across the black line into his area more than once. I am convening a trouble board about this at 1500 in the ready room. That is all."

"Yes, sir. I'll be there." As Alan watched Armiston return the way he had come, he thought, *Just like Jolly predicted. That much fun was too good to be true.* Alan wanted to clear the matter up, but if Durham lied, the truth might never be clear to Armiston. He wished that Bellingham had not put him next to Durham's area. He began to worry again about his position in the squadron, and then he felt himself getting angry. *Why is Bull such a jerk?* On the other hand, maybe Bellingham thought that this was a chance to test both Alan's and Durham's reliability. *Maybe if I keep calm and stick to my guns, I'll end up improving my position in the squadron.*

Alan walked into the ready room at 1455. Armiston, Bellingham, and Durham were already there. Alan sat down, and then MacAllester and Monroe came in. Armiston asked Monroe to close the rear door as he closed the side door. These doors normally remained open, but this was a private matter. The group gathered in front of the large chart of the harbor.

Armiston announced the purpose of the board and had Durham give his testimony first. Durham said that he saw Alan flying southwest with his wingman on the southeast side of House Island three times on his return legs between strafing runs, and that Alan had come at least half a mile into Durham's area. He claimed that when he saw Alan, Durham was also flying southwest on the northwest side of Cushing Island. Durham claimed that he had to stay well within his area to avoid colliding with Alan, but he was plenty close enough to read Alan's plane number: 5-B-12. As Durham talked, Alan felt his anger rising.

Durham's description of events was a complete lie. Although this was not a surprise, it still made Alan furious. He realized that maybe that was exactly Durham's intention—to get him to have an outburst. Among other things, Durham had the directions of Alan's flying reversed, because he had assumed that Alan strafed from seaward, which made it more likely that the truth would come out. Alan glanced at Bellingham, who made eye contact and gave a faint smile. Alan was surprised, but definitely felt more confident.

By the time Armiston asked Alan for his testimony, Alan had put aside his anger in favor of a cool determination. Armiston had already heard Alan's story in the debriefing, but Alan figured that he wanted the others to hear it. Armiston then asked Monroe for his testimony, which agreed with Alan's entirely.

Armiston followed up by asking Monroe, "You are sure that you were never on the southeast side of House Island?"

"Yes, sir."

"If you were flying wing on Ericsson, you would not be able to navigate at the same time, so how are you so sure where you went?"

"Sir, I'm from Lewiston, Maine, and my dad was a school teacher. I spent a lot of summers around Portland harbor when I was growing up, because my dad had a job in a restaurant during the tourist season," Monroe said. "I did a lot of boating and I got to know the harbor like the back of my hand. On a clear day like today, I can tell where I am every second without having to look around."

"Okay, Monroe, very good."

Alan thought, *Monroe will have to make a lot more hard landings to undo the good work that he has just done with his testimony.* Alan stole a glance at Durham, and he saw that Durham's face was red and he looked a bit nervous.

Armiston next asked Bellingham what he had been able to see of Ericsson's section from where he was, and Bellingham described the plan of operations that he had specified in his briefing. He then said that he occasionally saw all of the planes in his division during their strafing runs, and they all appeared to be following the briefing plan. Specifically, he saw Alan and Monroe strafing to the southwest and returning northeast for the next run on the northwest side of House Island.

Armiston asked, "So your briefing included strafing the forts from the landward side?"

"Yes, sir," Bellingham replied.

"Why did you decide on that?"

"The forts were built for defense against surface ships, and had no protection on the landward side—except for Fort Gorges, that is, because it doesn't have a landward side."

"Okay. That agrees with my reasoning for the northern forts, which is why we also strafed from the landward side. Is there any reason that Ericsson would want to strafe from the seaward side? Did he say anything about that during the briefing?"

"No, sir. He was all for strafing from the landward side at the briefing."

He doesn't want to say it was my idea, which is just as well.

Armiston continued, speaking to Bellingham, "Everyone is in agreement about what happened except Durham. There is one thing that is still bothering me, though. If Ericsson was never close to Durham, how did Durham even know that Ericsson was assigned to Fort Scammel?"

Bellingham replied, "Sir, I recall overhearing Durham ask Becker who was assigned to Fort Scammel at the end of the briefing."

"Okay, that settles it in my mind. Gordie, Scottie, any questions?"

They both shook their heads.

"Durham, I want to see you in my office in five minutes. The rest of you, keep up the good work. This trouble board is dismissed."

Phew! If I had showed my anger, it could have spoiled everything. I think I came out of this at least okay—maybe better than that. Except for Bull, and maybe Featherstone and Simpkin, this is a good bunch of guys to work with.

Around 1730, Alan returned to his stateroom to change for dinner and found Jim there.

"Well," Jim commented, "I told you that Bull would say that you violated his airspace. What happened at the trouble board?"

"Bull told a total lie. He didn't know that we were strafing from the landward side, so he had it all wrong, and the board didn't believe him."

"Ah, that explains why Durham looked so downtrodden when I saw him coming out of Armiston's office just now. Poor thing, Armiston must have given him a good reaming out," Jim said with a chuckle.

Friday, October 24, 1941

Alan had now gotten six letters from Jennifer in Hawaii and he savored each one.

Honolulu, T. H.
October 17, 1941

Dear Alan,

I hear you are based in more hospitable surroundings now. No more scares or crashes I fervently hope. As I think about it, an aircraft carrier seems particularly vulnerable to cold weather, with so many people working in an exposed, windy situation.

I have now been in the office for five weeks. I am impressed every day that I made the right move. There are some unusually talented people here also, as we talked about last summer.

The atmosphere in the office is amazingly friendly, but there is also a strong sense of urgency here, that was often missing in Washington. This leads to strong teamwork. There are eight sections in the office, each of which works six days, then gets two days off, so there are people working every day of the week. The problem with the ventilation system was found and fixed, so the physical atmosphere in the office is much improved. I miss having windows, but otherwise it is a great place to work.

The steady stream of B-17s passing through westbound has attracted the attention of everyone on Oahu. The army will not say where they are going, but everyone knows. I think the fuse on the time bomb that we talked about last summer might be burning faster.

My big news is that I went shopping for a car, and I ended up buying one. I actually picked it up yesterday. Jasper Holmes, the former submariner and novelist from our office that I mentioned, came along to help me. He has lived here for years, and knows the car dealers. Thanks for confirming that we could afford a Chevy like mine at home, because that is what I really wanted and got, sort of. I would have never thought of a four-door sedan, because they seem huge. Actually they are no bigger on the outside and Jasper mentioned that coupes and even convertibles get pretty hot after they have been parked in the hot sun here. With a four-door, you can open all four doors and it cools off pretty fast, and there are a lot of windows to open while driving. So we looked at several '37 Chevy four-doors, and Jasper helped with looking them over and with the bargaining. We got a Master De Luxe Sport Sedan, in a pale sea green color, light colors being much preferred here. It has 40,000 miles on it and is in very good condition. I paid $199.

I miss you very much. I hope your flying goes well and you go to a warmer place for the winter.

Oodles of love,

Jennifer

Alan thought what she said about the B-17s was fascinating. No doubt the Japanese consulate in Honolulu was also taking note. Alan suspected those B-17s had been planned for use in England, to begin an offensive against Germany, which would now be delayed.

CHAPTER TWENTY-SIX

Anti-Submarine Patrol

Sunday, October 26, 1941

The scuttlebutt had it that the next patrol was going to be more than a routine patrol. After lunch, Alan went up to the gallery to watch all the ships get underway. The *Yorktown* stood out of Casco Bay in company with the battleship *New Mexico*, the light cruisers *Philadelphia* and *Savannah*, and nine modern destroyers. It was an impressive sight. Most of the ships had accompanied the *Yorktown* on the voyage down from Argentia.

Once the *Yorktown* was at sea, the pilots were called to their ready rooms and briefed on the overall mission. This protective force was headed for a rendezvous off Halifax. It had been assigned, in addition to the regular escort, to protect a valuable eastbound convoy of six cargo ships that had recently been transferred from the US merchant marine to the British at Halifax. COMCRULANT had been put in charge of this protective force, but this time he flew his flag in the *Philadelphia*.

Thursday, October 30, 1941

Lowery crashed on landing in an accident that was similar to Alan's crash at the beginning of the month. The destroyer *Hammann* picked up Jim and his gunner, both of whom were unhurt. Bombing Five now had only one spare SBD. Afterward, Alan talked to Jim, and Jim did not feel that his standing in the squadron had suffered very much, which helped Alan feel a little better about his own crash. Even so, they knew that other squadron pilots had begun to mumble about a bad landing disease in Alan and Jim's stateroom.

Throughout the voyage of the protective force, nearby submarine activity was intense. News about the things that were happening within scouting range was announced to everyone on the ship's loudspeaker. A westbound convoy had been attacked. Two torpedoes had hit the US Navy tanker *Salinas*, but she did not sink. She kept on with the convoy. And, later, Alan heard that she was returning empty. The flooding was in her empty cargo tanks, and her engineers were able to stop the flooding at a point that was within the normal range of her cargo.

Friday, October 31, 1941

A submarine attacked an eastbound convoy a little farther away and sank the *Reuben James*, a four-stacker destroyer. She was the first US Navy ship lost in the Atlantic war, and three quarters of her crew were killed.

Alan had known since his Academy days about the significant differences between the modern destroyers of the *Farragut* and later classes that had been built in the 1930s and the WWI-era destroyers, known as four-stackers or flush-deckers. The older destroyers lacked range, firepower, damage protection, and most everything else compared with the newer ships. This sinking made the difference starkly evident, when compared with the torpedoing of the *Kearny* two weeks earlier near Iceland. If the *Reuben James* had been one of the modern destroyers, she might well have survived and had many fewer casualties, like the *Kearny*. Nevertheless, the older ships were pressed into service at this time and sometimes wrongly seen as interchangeable with their more modern sisters. Alan felt that their crews should get hazardous-duty pay, sort of like flight pay for aviators.

Saturday, November 1, 1941

The *Yorktown* was steaming east, approaching the MOMP—the Mid-Ocean Meeting Point—where the high-value convoy she was shadowing would be turned over by the American escort to a British escort. The American escort would then take over a westbound convoy from the British. This westbound convoy was also of high value. It consisted primarily of troopships loaded with Canadian soldiers, and it would also be shadowed by the protective force of heavy American warships. So far, the protective force had not seen action, but there had been a lot going on nearby.

It was 0630 when Alan finished breakfast and headed for the Bombing Five ready room—and it was pitch black outside. Bombing Five had been assigned two anti-submarine patrols, one at dawn and one in the afternoon, with nine airplanes in each search. Launch for the dawn search was scheduled for thirty minutes before sunrise, but sunrise would not be for another hour and a half, coming late at this high latitude in November. In clear weather, there might have been some light this early because the sun's path was at a shallow angle to the horizon, but it was overcast, as usual.

The mission briefing followed the usual routine. Alan noticed that he was in the middle of the roster for the morning search, and that Durham and Jim were in the afternoon search. Durham went over the weather: ceiling 1,000 feet overcast, visibility twenty miles, wind 250 at twenty-five, temperature thirty-four, dew point thirty. Alan thought that Durham's manner had been more subdued since his visit to Armiston's office a week earlier. Lowery had probably been right that Armiston must have read Durham the riot act after the Portland exercise.

Armiston went over the plan for the mission: Bombing Five would search thirty-six degrees on either side of the carrier's base course out to 150 miles. Nine single aircraft would conduct the search on four-degree intervals in each search. Alan knew better than the other pilots that there was little chance of catching a submarine on the surface because any reasonably alert submarine would probably see or hear an airplane in time to submerge. However, seeing a single-engine airplane in mid-ocean would alert any lurking submarines to the fact that there was an aircraft carrier in the vicinity. That might make them more cautious—and less effective.

The protective force and the convoy were on the same base course. The convoy was about thirty miles to the south, but each was zigzagging independently. The *Yorktown* was headed east at twenty-five knots to get ahead of the convoy. Alan could feel the throb from the propellers, which was transmitted throughout the ship when she was going at high speed. The ship needed to get ahead of the convoy, because she would have to turn around and head west into the wind for the launch. After this, the ship would turn around again and continue east at high speed to be northeast of the convoy again for the recovery. If the carrier made an unplanned turn, as sometimes happened, the airplanes would have to use the Zed Baker to get back to her.

Alan was assigned to the middle sector, on the base course of 070 true, 087 magnetic. He was in aircraft 5-B-12, but he had another new gunner, AOM3c Eric Mueller. Like Schofield, Mueller worked for the gunnery officer, so Alan did not know him very well. Apparently, Durham wanted to see that Alan never again had the same gunner twice.

The briefing was completed by 0700. A few minutes later, Alan had everything he needed copied down. According to the reports, the wind would be a tailwind going out and a headwind coming back, making navigation simpler. Finished with his calculations, he waited for everyone else. The loudspeaker ordered Bombing Five to man their planes at 0710. He and Mueller exchanged greetings at the airplane, and Mueller seemed businesslike, at least.

Bombing Five's launch went off on schedule and Alan launched fifth at 0733. There was a pale gray light, which was just enough to see the ocean and nearby aircraft. Alan climbed to 900 feet, which was barely under the cloud layer, while making a right turn around to his assigned heading of 087. He settled into cruise, leaned the mixture, and turned on the autopilot. Visibility was unusually good under the broken layer, and the ocean ahead was becoming much brighter. The bottoms of the clouds far ahead were lit in patches by the sun over the horizon, so evidently there was some clear weather to the east.

About twenty minutes later, the sun peeked up about ten degrees off to the right of the nose under the overcast. Alan quickly scanned the horizon to the east, where any vessel would be silhouetted. Suddenly, he locked onto an unmistakable silhouette close to the sun's direction—a submarine on the surface about five miles away. Even though it was nearly end on, he was sure of what it was. He felt a rush of excitement as he shut off the autopilot, pulled the stick back abruptly and felt himself pressed down into his seat as the plane zoomed into the cloud layer above.

"Submarine on the surface silhouetted in the sun, about five miles ahead," he told Mueller over the intercom as they slipped into the overcast. Alan's mind raced as he tried to think of how to get into an attack position without the submarine's lookouts becoming aware of his presence, resulting in a crash dive by the submarine. He had to assume that the submarine was using its diesel engines, so their engine noise would mask the noise of his engine. If not, the lookouts would be able to hear him and he would never get close enough to attack. Also, if the lookouts could not hear him, they might not have seen him, either, before he pulled into the overcast.

He turned right to 097 to fly toward the sun, and leveled off at 1,500 feet, flying on instruments in the clouds. He wanted to attack out of the sun, the classic tactic used to make an approach difficult to see. He started picking up ice on the windshield and elsewhere from the moisture in the clouds. Travelling at about two and a half miles a minute, he would fly four minutes to go ten miles, which would be about five miles beyond the sub, and then he would reverse course and drop down for a brief look under the overcast.

He flew four minutes and made a 180-degree left turn to 277, and then he dove down and popped out of the overcast at 1,100 feet. He scanned ahead quickly, looking around the ice on his windshield. *There she is,* he noted, *about five miles ahead and five degrees to the right.* He quickly pulled back up to 1,200 feet in the clouds. *She hasn't picked us up yet,* he thought, his excitement rising further. He flew on for a minute and a half, checking that the depth charge was armed and ready to drop.

He abruptly dove out of the clouds. *There she is!* The sub was slightly to the left and was close enough that he got another adrenaline rush. There was some ice on the windshield, but he could look around it to see that the bow of the submarine was going under. *She is in a crash dive! Somehow, they detected us.* He swooped down and dropped the depth charge. He leveled off fifty feet above the water, and then he did a climbing turn to the right to get a view of the depth charge explosion. The ocean erupted above the explosion, which was about thirty feet away from the sub on the port-side aft. The sub had submerged, but the periscopes were still cutting the water.

"That ought to rattle their teeth, at least!" Mueller exclaimed over the intercom.

"I hope so!"

Alan thought that the submarine had to have been damaged by a depth charge exploding that close, so he continued to circle the spot. The wake of the sub and the waves caused by the depth charge faded away, and they were replaced by the same windswept swells that covered the ocean everywhere. As he circled, he came around so that he was looking east. He saw an oil slick.

"I see an oil slick in the refection of the sunlight," he shouted jubilantly over the intercom.

"I missed it, sir. Circle around once more so that I can look again."

Alan circled, and he saw the oil slick again. He could see that it was suppressing the white caps on the waves.

"I see it, sir! No doubt about it," shouted Mueller.

"Glad you saw it, Mueller. It's more believable if we both saw it."

"Yes, sir."

The adrenaline rush subsided. If debris came to the surface, it was not visible to Alan. He felt the same frustration as many others had who had attacked submarines in the North Atlantic, because the results were not conclusive. At least the oil slick meant there was probable damage.

He remembered that the search plan called for any airplane that encountered a submarine to return to the carrier and drop a message, which was the only means of reporting back under radio silence, since the carrier did not want to reverse course into the wind to recover individual aircraft. Alan thought that he should be close to his outbound bearing of 087, so he took up the reverse heading of 267 to go back to the *Yorktown*.

"We're heading back to the ship to report the sub. Turn on the Zed Baker," he called to Mueller.

"Zed Baker warming up," replied Mueller.

Soon Alan heard the Zed Baker giving the Morse *dot-dash-dot*, or R, indicating that he was in the 60- to 90-degree magnetic sector, as expected. While he immediately had a pretty good idea of the direction to the *Yorktown*, he was less certain of how far away she was. The problem was simplified because he and the carrier had been moving nearly directly toward or away from each other the entire time, but they had been going east and west at different times. Making reasonable estimates of the carrier's movements and his own, he estimated that he should be back at the carrier twenty-two minutes after he turned west.

"Prepare message for drop on the carrier," Alan told Mueller over the intercom.

There was a brief pause. "Ready to copy message," Mueller informed him.

Alan called, "Message to read, 'Five Baker Twelve dropped depth charge on submerging sub bearing 087, sixty miles from launch, time 0806. Probable damage."

There was another pause as Mueller got the message written down, and then he read it back.

"Message correct," Alan confirmed.

After ten minutes, Alan began to hear a continuous tone in the background from the Zed Baker. The next sector in the Yoke Easy pattern, covering 90- to 120-degrees bearing from the carrier, was designated by *dash-dot-dash*, the letter K, which was the opposite of the letter R. Alan turned to a heading of 270 to follow that heading back to the carrier. He began to scan ahead for the *Yorktown* and the rest of the protective force. Shortly, ships of the protective force appeared ahead, occasionally lit by flashes of sunlight coming through the broken cloud cover.

Alan found the *Yorktown* and jogged to the right to pass down on the port side in the downwind leg of the landing pattern, even though it was upwind at the moment. Since there was little relative wind on the carrier, it did not make much difference which way he flew along the deck, but he thought the conventional stern-to-bow movement would cause less confusion. He kept the landing gear and arresting hook up to indicate that he was not landing, but did the rest of the landing checklist. A cold wind entered the cockpit as they both opened their canopies. Two Wildcats were spotted on deck aft, and there were two Wildcats flying overhead.

"Ready for message drop?" he inquired over the intercom.

"Ready," answered Mueller.

Alan turned onto base and then onto final, heading toward the stern. He descended to about fifty feet above the deck and leveled off. As he went over the two Wildcats, he called, "Drop now!"

"Message dropped," Mueller replied as they were about amidships.

Alan continued to circle in the pattern at about 500 feet to be able to see any messages for him in the form of hoists of shapes, flags, or blinker-light messages. After several orbits, the shape went up for flight operations, recovery of aircraft.

"Looks like they want us back aboard," he said to Mueller. "They might want more details."

"Yes, sir," replied Mueller.

The escorts to the starboard of the *Yorktown* were maneuvering away, and she was starting a right turn as deck crew members were filing into the galleries. The two Wildcats on deck were being pushed forward to make room for the recovery operation. Alan adjusted his orbit to follow the *Yorktown* in her turn. Finally, she steadied out on a westerly heading of 250. Soon after that, he got a green light from the air office as he started his next downwind leg.

Alan went through the landing checklist again, lowering the gear and the arresting hook this time. The *Yorktown* was pitching as much as he had ever seen it during flight operations, and although he had made eight carrier landings since his crash, he was still nervous. He had decided some time ago that the middle of the stern's upward motion was the best point in the pitching motion. He succeeded in timing his arrival to that, and the LSO gave Alan the cut. He closed the throttle, and the pitching deck came up to meet him. He caught the sixth wire and felt the sudden deceleration. Relief flooded into him as he raised the hook, taxied forward, and parked near the mid-ship elevator, as directed. He shut the engine down, and then he and Mueller climbed out. It was only 0910. As he approached the island, a door in it opened and an orderly popped out. Alan was told to report to the air officer.

Alan had been to the air office a few times, and he remembered the way. The air office was a compartment high on the port side of the island behind the bridge. Its large windows projected out from the island to provide a complete view of the flight deck. The air office was where flight operations were controlled in a manner roughly analogous to a control tower on land. He felt the propeller vibration from high-speed operations go away as the ship slowed down. Flight operations were again suspended. As he came through the door of the air office, the *Yorktown*'s air officer was speaking into a telephone. Arnham, Alan's previous skipper who was now assistant air officer, was seated nearby and nodded to Alan. Alan looked out and noticed that his SBD was already on its way to the hangar on the mid-ship elevator.

"Launch the two ready fighters to relieve the CAP. After that, recover the two fighters now on CAP." The air officer hung up the telephone after he barked those orders, then turned and greeted Alan.

"There you are, Ericsson."

"Reporting as ordered, sir."

Just then, a door at the forward end of the compartment opened and two men came in. One was a tall, gray-haired officer with captain's stripes. Alan recognized him as The *Yorktown*'s captain. The other was the ship's first lieutenant, who was the captain's right-hand man. Alan had not had an opportunity to meet the captain, but he had met the first lieutenant, once. He felt the ship speeding up again in response to the air officer's orders.

The air officer made the introductions. "Captain, this is Lieutenant j.g. Ericsson, the pilot that just landed after dropping the message."

"Pleased to meet you, Lieutenant," said the captain, extending his hand.

"Very pleased to meet you, sir," replied Alan.

"What do you estimate to be the accuracy of your report of the submarine's position?" inquired the captain.

"Could be off by about two miles in any direction, sir," replied Alan.

"Okay, pretty accurate, then. We'll have to turn, or we'll run right over him. If we and the convoy turn to northeast course, though, the convoy will likely run right over him."

Turning to the first lieutenant, he said, "Get an urgent message in my name to COMCRULANT giving the sub's position and recommending a turn to the southeast."

"Aye aye, sir," said the first lieutenant, turning and disappearing forward.

"Now, Ericsson, tell us about how you found the sub and how you attacked."

Alan proceeded to describe his approach and attack, noting in his retelling that there were several fortuitous circumstances.

"Good work, Lieutenant. Keep it up. As you say, you had luck on your side, but you took full advantage of it. Be sure to debrief with Commander Armiston when he gets back from the search. That will be all," said the captain.

Alan noticed that Arnham, who was behind the captain, was looking his way, smiling, and giving the thumbs-up sign.

"Yes, sir. Thank you, sir." Alan was feeling pleased, even though neither he nor the captain could be sure that the damage to the submarine was significant. He was aware of the irony in the fact that, as a qualified submariner, his first taste of combat was to attack a submarine with an airplane.

Alan's watch said 0929 as he left the air office, and it was about time for the first of the search airplanes to return. He stepped out of the island and saw an SBD approaching the stern for an overhead approach. He knew that there was sure to be a debriefing soon, so he decided to get a cup of coffee in the wardroom and go to the ready room to wait for that.

As he came into the ready room, he saw that the afternoon search pilots were already there. Alan greeted Jim, who was in the next seat, as he sat down. Gradually, all the morning search pilots arrived, except Armiston. Alan gathered from the conversation around the room that the skipper was debriefing with the air group commander and the air officer. None of the other pilots had seen anything, and Alan didn't feel like tooting his own horn by talking about his flight. Apparently, Jim assumed that Alan had not seen anything, either, because he didn't ask.

"As you were," Armiston declared as he strode in with a satisfied expression on his face. His eyes swept over the pilots, stopping and winking at Alan. He looked up and addressed the pilots with a growing smile. "It was a good search mission, particularly since one of our pilots dropped a depth charge on a German sub."

He paused as the pilots started mumbling and looking around at each other.

"Ericsson, front and center," the skipper barked.

Alan stood up and went to the front, flushing as he became the center of attention. As he turned around and faced the squadron, he noticed that everyone was smiling except Durham, who had a deadpan expression and was looking down at the deck.

"Ericsson, you are the first man from the *Yorktown* to strike a blow against the enemy. You have brought credit both to the ship and to this squadron. As the squadron skipper, it is my privilege to be the first to congratulate you," Armiston declared, holding out his hand. Alan grasped it firmly as a big smile spread across his face. "Now, Ericsson," Armiston continued, "I think that I am not the only person here who would like to hear a first-hand, blow-by-blow account of your attack."

Alan cleared his throat and told the story again, adding a few more details that he thought the pilots would appreciate.

Armiston said, "Well, Ericsson, you did get some lucky breaks, but you grabbed the opportunity those breaks presented and made the fullest possible use of it. It is a fine achievement—congratulations, again!"

They shook hands again, and Alan returned to his seat. Armiston dismissed the squadron, and Durham dived out the door.

Suddenly, Alan realized that all the clouds of doubt about his place in the squadron that had been hovering in the back of his mind since his carrier qualification were gone. Until now, he had felt like he was on probation, not really a member in good standing. He had not been aware of how much his doubts had been bothering him until they had melted away, and he felt a glow of great satisfaction. He had truly made the grade at last. He thought about where he had been one year earlier—he had not even started flight training. He had come a long way.

Sunday, November 2, 1941

USS Yorktown
c/o Fleet Post Office
New York, NY
November 2, 1941

Dear Jennifer,

This letter will not get into the mail for a while, because we are out on patrol. I wanted to write anyway because I had an adventure yesterday. I was able to strike a blow against the enemy. I can't tell you any more, but I think you can imagine the situation. There were several lucky breaks with the lighting and cloud cover that helped a lot. We have reason to think there was some damage at least. This was the first time this had happened aboard the ship, so I was congratulated by the captain and the squadron skipper. Now I feel completely accepted as a carrier aviator for the first time, and you know how much that means to me.

The last letter I have from you was written on October seventeenth. I was very glad to hear you are so happy with where you are working. That implies that the unit is doing important work, which is also good to hear.

Thank you for telling me in detail about your car, you scalawag. It's great that you were able to find a car you are happy with. Let me know how it works out.

Thanks for telling me about the air traffic also. There are many important implications, as you know. Let's hope the time bomb does not go off for a few more months at least.

I will write again when we reach port.

Tons of love,

Alan

CHAPTER TWENTY-SEVEN

The Time Bomb Goes Off

Tuesday, December 2, 1941

Alan was off duty in the afternoon, and the *Yorktown* was turning west to enter Chesapeake Bay on her way back to Norfolk from Casco Bay. He went up to the bow to watch the ship's passage from the Virginia capes across the south end of Chesapeake Bay. By late afternoon, she was back at Pier Seven. Nearby, at Pier Four, was the *Hornet*, which had been commissioned only six weeks before and was working hard at her shakedown.

Although the *Yorktown* had not gone on another long patrol into the Atlantic during November, she had been kept busy in and around Casco Bay. All hands now looked forward to this period of rest in port, while the ship received weeks of overdue maintenance. Many, including Alan, were thinking about plans to visit their homes and families at Christmas. He wished he could visit Jennifer, but now she was much too far away for that. At least he would probably find a letter from her waiting in Norfolk and he looked forward to replying.

The *Yorktown* herself was scheduled to go into a period of overhaul and modification soon. The overhaul had originally been scheduled for August at Pearl Harbor, then for October at Norfolk, but it had been postponed again until now.

Wednesday, December 3, 1941

In the morning, the *Yorktown* air group was transferred ashore to the Norfolk Naval Air Station. The aircraft were hoisted onto the

CHAPTER TWENTY-SIX ~ ANTI-SUBMARINE PATROL

pier and made the long taxi to East Field, and aviation personnel moved into their shore quarters while their wives returned from Portland. Alan noticed that there was a lot more activity in the air around Norfolk than there had been when they left, which he found out was the result of the Advanced Carrier Training Group at Norfolk having been activated. There were already rumors that some of the materials needed for the *Yorktown*'s overhaul would not be available until January.

On the pier, Alan ran into Jack Casey, the former exec of Bombing Five, who was now skipper of Scouting Eight aboard the *Hornet*. As they were catching up, Casey said that the other squadron commanders aboard the *Hornet* were good men, but her air group as a whole was pretty green, including the air group commander, which made it frustrating at times.

Reading the newspapers that evening, Alan was surprised to find that there was a lot of discussion of the possibility of the outbreak of war in the Pacific, which was a big change from a few months earlier. On the other hand, nobody seemed to be concerned about the dangers of trying to defend the Philippines. He hoped that the time bomb would not go off until after the holidays. He was looking forward to visiting his family and Jennifer's at Christmas, but no leave had been announced yet.

Sunday, December 7, 1941

After a pleasant lunch, Alan and Jim Lowery were relaxing with other officers in the Officers' Club. A local radio station was being piped in and was playing Benny Goodman. As he often did, Alan was thinking of Jennifer. He was pleased that he had been able to find a nice silver necklace on Saturday in Norfolk to give to her as a Christmas present. The shop had even gift wrapped it and mailed it to her for him.

Alan had just finished reading an article in *Collier's* magazine about an interview with the Secretary of the Navy. The article was titled, "The Navy is Ready," and it painted a rosy picture that Alan thought was a gross distortion of the situation, probably written to boost public morale. Alan was flipping through the December 8 issue of *Life* magazine, which had appeared before the marked date, as usual. On the cover was a picture of General MacArthur, which reminded Alan of the folly of defending the Philippines. MacArthur was a leading advocate of that strategy. The news section led off with an article about Japan, stating that the US embargo on oil and steel would make war a disaster for Japan. *Eventually, maybe*, thought Alan, *but in the meantime, look out!* A few pages further, there was an article under the heading, "U.S. Cheerfully Faces War with Japan." It seemed to epitomize the public's overly trusting attitude, in Alan's view. He was so engrossed in the article that he did not notice when the music stopped and an announcement was made on the radio. It was about 1430.

Alan heard someone say in a loud voice, "What did he say?"

"Something about an attack on Pearl Harbor," exclaimed another.

"Bullshit! Probably another exercise," said yet another officer.

An officer headed over to the bulkhead where the controls for the public address system were located. A moment later, the volume was turned way up and silence fell on the group.

"Repeating this CBS News Bulletin, just in: Japanese aircraft made a surprise attack on our naval base at Pearl Harbor, in Hawaii, at dawn today. Heavy damage to our ships is reported. We will have further news as it becomes available. Stay tuned to CBS." The music resumed.

Instantly, the room was filled with sound as everyone started talking at once. Alan felt a cold wave of fear and regret wash over him. *Jennifer! Why did I agree with her that going there was a good idea? I warned her several times of this possibility, but I never thought that an attack there was really likely.* He felt tears coming, and he put his face in his hands.

"Hey, Stringy, are you okay?" called Jim. He got up from where he had been and sat next to Alan.

Alan looked up and wiped away the tears. "No," he said softly. He tried to pull himself together.

"It's your wife, isn't it? Well, it's Sunday. None of the civilians will be on the base today, especially early in the morning. There's no reason for the Japs to attack the city. They would stick to military targets: ships, airplanes, airbases, port facilities, and so on. She should be safe and sound." Then Alan remembered Rochefort's unit was on a seven day week, so Jennifer could have been on the base.

"You might be right, but her unit is on a seven-day week. It's just that I agreed that it was a good idea for her to move there, and I knew that an attack there was a possibility. It seems crazy now . . . . How could I have done that? If anything has happened to her, I'll die."

"I think I know how you feel—helpless. I guess that you'll just have to sit tight and wait for some news."

"Yeah, I guess you're right." Alan sat up and collected himself, and Jim moved back to his armchair.

Alan thought for a while about how he could try to find out if Jennifer was all right. He knew that in a time of national crisis like this, most forms of communication would be overloaded. In particular, the few cables connecting Hawaii to the mainland would be backlogged. Military communications would have priority. Everyone who had friends or relatives there would be trying to find out what happened, so he decided that there really was nothing he could do to make the news get to him faster. *If Jennifer is all right, she might be able to use her intelligence connections to get word out to me soon.* He hoped that she would not hesitate to do that.

Then another terrifying thought struck him: Would the Japanese follow up the raid with an invasion of Hawaii? They were probably capable of doing it, but how much would it help their cause? It seemed that they had already dealt the US Navy a severe blow, and if it was a vulnerable outpost for the United States, it seemed it would be at least as vulnerable for the Japanese. With fairly dependable poor weather to the north in winter, the United States could mount a surprise attack on them, although they would surely be better prepared than the US forces had been. It did not seem likely that they would invade, but it could not be ruled out. If they were going to do it, they would do it right away, before the defenses could recover. If nothing happened in the next day, they would probably not come back.

Roger and Marjorie must be as anxious as I am, he thought. He decided that he would try to call them to reassure them as soon as he could get through, which he knew might not be for a day or two.

After getting *that* somewhat settled in his mind, Alan began to think about the other implications of this cataclysmic event. He had been dreading the possibility of the United States being caught unprepared by such rapidly unfolding events, particularly a sudden move by the Japanese in reaction to the oil embargo, and now they had hit the United States with a thunderbolt. Although it was a terrible surprise, Alan had some sense of relief. The long wait for the time bomb to explode was now over.

Suddenly, Alan remembered the British raid on the Italian fleet at Taranto about thirteen months earlier. The Pearl Harbor raid was the Taranto raid writ large. If the US Navy had digested the lessons of Taranto, they should have been better prepared.

It also appeared to Alan that, in a single stroke, the Japanese had pulled the rug out from under the isolationist movement in the United States. Until now, the movement had enjoyed a lot of clout. He doubted that the Japanese government fully understood that this would present them with an angry, determined, and united America. It would probably be more difficult to stay out of the European war now, as well.

Even if the United States declared war on Germany, it seemed likely that the *Yorktown* would be sent back to the Pacific, perhaps quite soon and without the planned overhaul. In that case, combat for the *Yorktown* air group could come up a short time later. It would mean no Christmas leave, but that was greatly outweighed by the possibility of getting to see Jennifer, if she was okay.

The music was interrupted again by another announcement. "CBS News has another report from the Navy Department regarding the attack on our base at Pearl Harbor in Hawaii. There was damage to the Pacific Fleet, which is based at Pearl Harbor, and some battleships are temporarily out of action. A powerful force of our battleships and aircraft carriers is now in pursuit of the attacking force. We will have further news as it becomes available. Stay tuned to CBS."

Alan had heard the old adage "The first casualty in war is the truth" many times. He thought that he detected the firm hand of wartime news control in the second announcement. The earlier announcement of heavy damage was probably closer to the truth. This broadcast mentioned damage to battleships, but not to aircraft carriers, and he wondered if any of them were in the harbor at the time of the raid. He hoped that all his friends who were in the Pacific, both submariners and pilots, were okay.

Monday, December 8, 1941

A hectic period for the men of the *Yorktown* had begun. After the Sunday raid at Pearl Harbor, apparently someone higher up thought that the Germans might make a surprise attack on Norfolk. Alan knew that there were two British aircraft carriers in the Navy Yard for repairs, so perhaps that had something to do with it. Early in the morning, the air group had been ordered to board the *Yorktown* in preparation for a rapid departure. The air group's aircraft had been taxied over to the pier and hoisted aboard the carrier. That evening, the departure was cancelled.

Meanwhile, more bad news started to pour in from the Pacific. About nine hours after the Pearl Harbor attack, the Japanese attacked the northern Philippines with land-based airplanes from Formosa, simultaneously attacking the southern Philippines with carrier aircraft. It was reported that there had been significant losses of aircraft on both sides.

Tuesday, December 9, 1941

In the morning, the air group's aircraft had been hoisted back onto the pier and taxied back to East Field. This sign of confusion in high places within the navy was nothing when compared to the wild reports of air raids and invasion threats on the radio and in the newspapers, though. One report said that California was indefensible and that the army would fall back to the Rocky Mountains, or even the Mississippi River. In another report, an army general verified a report of sixty Japanese airplanes over the Golden Gate Bridge, though the report was soon retracted. Hoarders cleared the shelves of some food markets.

In a follow-up article about the Japanese attack on the Philippines, the *New York Times* reported that US airbases on Luzon in the Philippines had been, "put out of commission for the time being." This was a disaster, in Alan's view, which was perhaps even greater than the one at Pearl Harbor, since the primary means for defense of the Philippines had swiftly collapsed. Since the US forces had plenty of warning after the earlier attack at Pearl Harbor, he wondered how the US air power had been so quickly overwhelmed.

News came that Japanese troops had landed in Thailand and Malaya. Obviously, the Japanese were carrying out a carefully planned offensive to the south, executing simultaneous moves in various locations. The newspapers also reported that the mail to and from Hawaii had been stopped until further notice.

In the evening, Alan ran into a classmate from submarine school at the Officers' Club. They had supper together and got caught up on what each had been doing since submarine school. Alan's classmate had just been rotated back from the Asiatic Fleet about a month earlier. He confided to Alan that—according to reports he had heard from other submariners—only five hours after the Pearl Harbor attack, orders had gone out from main navy to all Pacific commands to execute unrestricted submarine warfare against Japan. Naturally, this was not publicly announced both because it was a major reversal of policy and because most matters connected with the submarine service were kept secret.

Alan's classmate added that, two months before the attack, it had become the understanding among all the submarine officers in the Asiatic Fleet that in the event of war with Japan, unrestricted warfare would be authorized. Evidently, the idea had been per-colating around the navy and the submarine service quietly for some time. The surprise attack at Pearl Harbor made a convenient excuse if anyone asked for an explanation, but the truth was that the decision to make such a major policy change had been made long before the attack.

At 2200, President Roosevelt addressed the country on the radio. He did not deny the harm of the Japanese attack, but he projected calmness and determination and warned people not to believe all the rumors they were hearing. Alan thought that the speech was a good antidote to the hysteria that was evident in some quarters.

Wednesday, December 10, 1941

At 0610 on Wednesday morning, Alan finally reached Roger Warren at home by telephone. He used his knowledge of the layout at Pearl Harbor to try to minimize the possibility of Jennifer being harmed. Roger was still worried, but he thanked Alan for the call.

Later that morning, it was announced that the *Yorktown* would be going into dry dock at the Norfolk Navy Yard on Friday, returning early on the following Tuesday. Later on Tuesday, the *Yorktown* would depart for the Pacific, which left less than two full days before going into dry dock to make preparations aboard for the long voyage. Alan had been hoping since August that the *Yorktown* would be sent back to the Pacific. Now it was going to happen, bringing the possibility of seeing Jennifer—but he could not rejoice until he got some confirmation that she was unharmed in the attack.

Alan knew that he and Scottie would have to work furiously, spending every available moment inventorying the squadron's spare parts aboard the carrier and laying in supplies.

Thursday, December 11, 1941

On Thursday morning, the news spread rapidly through the base that Germany and Italy had declared war on the United States. It seemed that Germany was working closely with Japan, because there was nothing compelling them to declare war other than the attack on Pearl Harbor.

A few hours later, the United States declared war on Germany and Italy in return. Although this was not a complete surprise like the Pearl Harbor attack, it meant that the United States was suddenly thrown into the two-ocean war that many had sought to avoid—a war which Alan still thought that the United States was not ready to fight. There were probably some German submarines that had enough range to do at least short patrols along the east coast of the United States. Thus unrestricted submarine warfare would probably soon be happening nearby. By then, however, the *Yorktown* would probably be in the Pacific.

The morning also brought news that Japanese land-based aircraft had sunk both the British battleship *Prince of Wales* and the battle cruiser *Repulse* off the coast of Malaya. This confirmed for Alan beyond any doubt that aircraft could sink a battleship maneuvering in the open ocean. Therefore, in Alan's mind, the aircraft carrier was the new capital ship in most circumstances.

Alan found a letter from Jennifer waiting for him when he returned to the BOQ in the late afternoon. He had a surge of relief that he was hearing from her, but then he quickly realized it had to have been written before the attack, probably several days at least, to have been carried out on an airplane before the attack.

> *Honolulu, T. H.*
> *December 3, 1941*
> *Dear Alan,*
>
> *I hear you are back in home port, and the ship may go into overhaul. That should give all hands a nice break. Let's hope the time bomb does not go off until after the holidays, at least.*
>
> *My work continues to go well. Joe Rochefort even personally complimented me on what I was doing, which made me feel very good. The difference between the atmosphere in this unit and that in my previous office is stark. Not only are the people happier, they are more productive.*
>
> *It does feel strange that I am still spending time at the beach, with the holidays approaching. The weather is a little cooler, which is a relief to me. I miss my friends in New England, even though I keep up with some of the submariners and I have made some new friends among the wives of people in the office and their friends. The Holmes have invited me to have*

Christmas dinner with them. I look forward to the time when you and I can spend Christmas together.

I imagine you are thinking of going to Boston for Christmas. Have they announced any leave yet? If you do get there, please give my love to my family and yours. I mailed your Christmas present last week, but I did not send it air mail, so it may be late.

I love you very much, you rascal. Merry Christmas!

Oodles of love,

Jennifer

Alan savored this letter, as he had all the others, but it made him more anxious to hear if she was ok. It also underlined how much everything had changed in the past week.

Late that evening, Alan was relaxing and having a beer with Jim Lowery in the bar at the Officers' Club when an orderly appeared in the doorway of the bar. "Telegram for Lieutenant j.g. Ericsson," he announced in a loud voice.

Conversation ceased, and the other officers in the bar looked around. Alan's heart skipped a beat. He knew that a telegram at a time like this would probably contain news of great portent, whether good or bad. Maybe it was news about Jennifer. He broke out in a cold sweat, and Jim put down his beer. Alan stepped away from the bar and headed toward the doorway.

"I'm Lieutenant j.g. Ericsson," he said. He got out his wallet and showed the orderly his navy ID card.

The orderly handed him the telegram. "If you want to make a reply, sir, you'll need to come to the mail room and fill out a lot of paperwork. It's all changed since Sunday," the orderly informed him.

"Okay, thanks," said Alan. The orderly left.

His hands trembled as he opened the familiar yellow envelope and pulled out the message. His glance fell on the message of just seven words:

SAFE SOUND TELL ALL YOU RASCAL STOP JENNIFER

He glanced quickly to the top of the paper. The origin of the telegram had been blacked out, but the "you rascal" part provided all the confirmation he needed that it was really from Jennifer. To him, it also conveyed her love and her undaunted spirit. She had obviously given careful thought to putting as much as possible into six words.

He felt his eyes becoming teary and a glow of intense relief pervaded him as he quickly sat down on a nearby chair. As he stared at the message, among the many things that flashed through his mind was the fact that he would have several phone calls to make—starting with one to Roger and Marjorie—and letters to write—but all that could wait until he had at least collected himself.

Jim came over from the bar. "What is it, Stringy?" he asked.

"The best possible news," Alan said, reaching for a handkerchief and handing the message to Jim.

ILLUSTRATIONS

A note of explanation is in order regarding the cover photograph. It was taken in 1941 and shows a Northrop BT-1 aircraft of Bombing Squadron Six aboard USS *Enterprise*. The *Enterprise* was the sister ship of the *Yorktown*. The airplane paint scheme is the one which was used by the US Navy in the 1930s and which was phased out during 1941 in anticipation of joining World War II. If the photograph had been taken aboard the *Yorktown*, everything would look the same, except that the tails of the airplanes would be painted red, instead of blue, and the label on the aft fuselage would say "5B10", instead of "6B10".

Modern photo of a Tatra 75 convertible (Michal Maňas/CC-BY-2.5)

Modern photo of a 1933 Ford 5 window coupe (Sicnag/CC-BY-2.0)

Wartime photo of a Curtiss P-40 Tomahawk army fighter
(US Army/PD-USGOV-MILITARY-ARMY)

1942 photo of a Grumman F4F-3 Wildcat navy fighter
(US Navy/PD-USGOV-MILITARY-NAVY)

1940 photo of the Vought-Sikorsky XF4U-1 Corsair navy fighter prototype
(NACA/PD-USGOV-NACA)

Modern photo of an Aeronca C3 Razorback light airplane
(Dave Welch, used with permission)

Wartime aerial photo of the Pensacola Naval Air Station, looking north
(from Shettle, M. L. Jr. United States Naval Air Stations of WWII, Volume
1: Eastern States. Bowersville, GA: Schaertel, 1995, with author permission)

1943 photo of a Stearman N2S-2 navy trainer showing the starting procedure (The N2S-2 was identical to the N2S-3 except for the engine and the two were considered interchangeable.)
(US Navy PD-USGOV-MILITARY-NAVY)

1936 photo of a Vought-Sikorsky SBU navy dive-bomber
(US Navy/PD-USGOV-MILITARY-NAVY)

Wartime photo of a Link Trainer with the instructor in the foreground
(William Zuk/released to the public domain)

March 1942 photo of a North American SNJ-2 navy trainer in use at
Pensacola Naval Air Station (US Navy/PD-USGOV-MILITARY-NAVY)

Late 1930s photo of three Grumman F2F-1 navy fighters in formation
(US Navy/PD-USGOV-MILITARY-NAVY)

Wartime aerial photo of the Norfolk Naval Air Station, with northeast toward the top (from Shettle, M. L. Jr. United States Naval Air Stations of WWII, Volume 1: Eastern States. Bowersville, GA: Schaertel, 1995, with author permission)

1938 photo of a BT-1 navy dive-bomber, recently delivered to Squadron
VB-5 and undergoing maintenance with dive flaps open
(US Navy/PD-USGOV-MILITARY-NAVY)

1930s photo of the aircraft carrier USS *Ranger*, CV-4
(US Navy/PD-USGOV-MILITARY-NAVY)

1941 photo of SBD-2 and SBD-3 Dauntless navy dive-bombers, warming up with the rest of the air group aboard the aircraft carrier USS *Saratoga*, CV-3 (US Navy/PD-USGOV-MILITARY-NAVY)

Photo looking down at the SBD-3 navy dive-bomber pilot's cockpit
from the "Pilot's Flight Operating Instructions" manual
(US Navy/PD-USGOV-MILITARY-NAVY)

1940 photo of the aircraft carrier USS *Yorktown*, CV-5, docked at the North Island Naval Air Station with a full deck load of airplanes and a BT-1 on the ship's crane (US Navy/PD-USGOV-MILITARY-NAVY)

Recent photo of the World War Two aircraft carrier ready room exhibit at the National Museum of Naval Aviation (Photo taken by author)

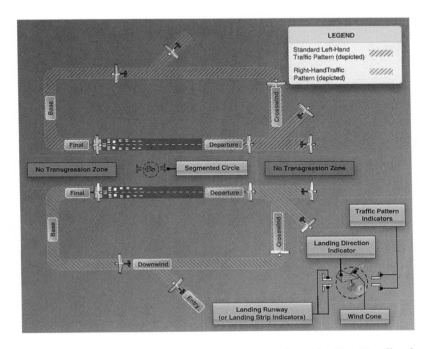

US standard right and left airport traffic patterns from the FAA Handbook
(FAA/PD-USGOV-FAA)

Glossary

Note to the reader: The Appendix which follows this Glossary also defines a number of abbreviations, codes and names.

abeam   in a position off to one side, ninety degrees from straight ahead

aft   adverb meaning farther toward the back or stern of a vessel or vehicle

after   adjective meaning farther toward the back or stern of a vessel or vehicle

ailerons   panels on the outer wing trailing edge which can be angled up and down; those on opposite wings move in opposite directions when the control stick is moved sideways, causing the airplane to roll

amidships   in or toward the middle of a ship

approach plate   a standardized single sheet of paper, showing diagrams and data which specify an instrument approach procedure to a particular runway

athwart his hawse literally "across his bow"; used to mean "at cross purposes"

attitude   the orientation of an airplane relative to the horizon

beam   the maximum width of a ship or boat

bear off   to turn a sailboat farther away from heading into the wind

bilge   noun meaning the inside of the bottom of a ship, which usually has some water and refuse in it, and, hence, anything disgusting;

	or, in US Navy slang, verb for failing a test, or for a superior to rate an inferior as a failure, and also to expel that person from the unit under the superior's command
buffet	strong vibration of part of an airplane due to turbulent airflow passing over it
bulkhead	the wall of a ship's compartment, separating it from the adjacent compartment
ceiling	height of the bottom of a cloud layer from the ground
conning tower	the compartment in a submarine where the motion of the ship through the water is normally controlled when submerged
course	the direction of travel in degrees, due north being 0 or 360, and due south being 180
dead reckoning	navigation by keeping track of courses, speeds, and times to estimate position, with the course estimated by correcting heading for drift due to outside influences, such as the influence of wind on airplanes
draft	depth below the waterline of the lowest part of a ship
elevators	panels on the trailing edge of a plane's horizontal stabilizer, which can be angled up or down by moving the control stick forward or back, to change the pitch of the airplane
empty weight	the weight of an airplane with no crew, cargo, munitions, or fuel
escort	maneuverable armed ship that accompanies other ships to protect them from submarines

fairing	a smooth aerodynamic cover over a protrusion on an airplane, or a filler panel used to make a smooth curve between two surfaces having a sharp angle between them, such as the junction of the wing and the fuselage
fetch	nautical term for the distance a wind blows over the sea surface without interference, allowing the wind to raise waves
flare	part of the sequence of maneuvers to land an airplane, in which the angle of descent of the final approach is shallowed out until the airplane is flying level, with the wheels just above the runway
fleet up	move up to fill a vacancy in the next higher position in a naval unit
funnel	smokestack of a ship
gross weight	total weight of an airplane, the sum of the empty weight and the useful load, including crew, cargo, munitions, and fuel
head	ship's toilet or restroom
heading	the direction in which a ship or airplane is pointed, in degrees from north, which may differ from the actual course due to influences such as the wind, or tides and currents for ships
heel	temporary inclination of a ship toward the outside of a turn, caused by inertia
horizontal stabilizer	a small horizontal wing-like structure on the tail of an airplane
hulk	a retired ship, stripped of useful equipment

in trail	a formation of airplanes in which they follow one right behind the other
ketch	a fore and aft rigged sailboat with two masts, in which the forward, or main, mast is larger and the aft, or mizzen, mast is forward of the rudder post
leeward	in the direction the wind is blowing
list	a steady inclination of a ship to one side or the other caused by an imbalance or uneven support from below
magnetic	when applied to directions, relative to magnetic north, the direction from the current position to the magnetic north pole, differing from true directions by the variation
magnetic north pole	a position in northern Canada that is the north pole of the earth's magnetic field, causing compasses to point to it
mountain telegraph	slang expression similar to grapevine, gossip, or rumor mill
NACA	National Advisory Committee for Aeronautics, the federal agency assisting with aeronautical research; a predecessor of NASA
oiler	naval term for a tanker, a cargo ship designed to carry petroleum or petroleum products
overhead	the deck on top of a ship compartment, separating it from the compartment above; the equivalent of the "ceiling" in a land-based structure
plane captain	person assigned to and responsible for the maintenance and material condition of a particular airplane

plebe	a member of the freshman class at the US Naval Academy, customarily harassed by the upper classmen
pitch	the orientation of an airplane around the transverse axis, causing the nose to point up or down relative to the horizon
power loading	gross weight of an airplane divided by its engine's horsepower; a measure of the responsiveness of the airplane to its engine
reach	a sailing maneuver in which the boat moves at an angle roughly ninety degrees from straight into the wind
roll (airplane)	the orientation or rotation of an airplane around the longitudinal axis, in which the wings rotate downward on one side and upward on the other
roll (ship)	the unsteady inclination of a ship to one side or the other caused by wave action
rudder (airplane)	a panel on the trailing edge of the vertical stabilizer, which can be angled to the right or left, causing the airplane nose to turn toward the right or left
sheet in	pull in the rope that controls the angle of a sail to bring it in closer to the center of the boat
squawk	a discrepancy or defect in an airplane
tack	a sailing maneuver in which the boat moves at an angle substantially less than ninety degrees from straight into the wind, often preceded by port or starboard to indicate the side of the boat that is more toward the wind

talker	man posted at a navy ship duty station to relay messages by telephone to and from other duty stations
tender (naval)	a ship equipped with personnel and supplies to maintain and repair small vessels or flying boats at locations away from naval port facilities
tender (railroad)	a special railroad car, pulled right behind a steam locomotive, that carries fuel and water for the locomotive
threshold	the approach end of a runway
true	when applied to directions, relative to true north, the direction to the north pole
useful load	the weight of the crew, cargo, munitions, and fuel in an airplane
variation	the difference, in degrees, between the direction to the north pole and the direction to the magnetic north pole
wardroom	the compartment in which officers gather to eat and relax aboard ship
wing loading	gross weight of an airplane divided by its wing area; an inverse measure of responsiveness of an airplane to its wings
yaw	the orientation of an airplane around the vertical axis, in which the nose of the airplane turns toward the right or left
yeoman	naval term for an enlisted man who performs secretarial and clerical duties

APPENDIX

Miscellaneous Abbreviations, Codes and Names

(All information is for the US military forces as of late 1941.)

Fleet Aircraft Carriers and Their Designations

The US Navy had built eight fleet (large) carriers by the end of 1941, as follows:

CV-1 *Langley*   First experimental carrier; converted from a collier (bulk coal carrier ship); commissioned: 1922; 14,000 tons; converted to a seaplane tender in 1936.

CV-2 *Lexington*   First of class; built on a battle cruiser hull that was surplus due to the Washington Naval Treaty of 1922; commissioned: 1927; 41,200 tons.

CV-3 *Saratoga*   Second of class; built on a battle cruiser hull that was surplus due to the Washington Naval Treaty of 1922; commissioned: 1927; 41,200 tons.

CV-4 *Ranger*   Smaller carrier; first carrier designed completely as such; commissioned: 1934; 16,600 tons.

CV-5 *Yorktown*   First of class; commissioned: 1937; 23,500 tons.

CV-6 *Enterprise*   Second of class; commissioned: 1938; 23,500 tons.

CV-7 *Wasp*   Smaller carrier to fit within treaty limitations; commissioned: 1940; 18,300 tons.

CV-8 *Hornet*   Nearly identical to *Yorktown* class; commissioned: 1941; 23,500 tons.

Aircraft Carrier Deck Crew Color Coding

Carrier deck crewmen wore shirts and caps whose color indicated the crewman's function as follows:

Brown	plane captain
Yellow	deck control
Red	ordnance
Purple	oil and gasoline
Green	arresting gear and catapults
Blue	plane movers
White	medical corpsmen

Aircraft Carrier Squadron Nomenclature

Carrier squadrons had an alphanumeric designator. The first letter was always V, which stood for heavier-than-air, as opposed to lighter-than-air aircraft such as dirigibles and blimps. The next letter designated the purpose of the squadron as follows:

F	Fighting
S	Scouting
B	Dive-bombing
T	Torpedo bombing

By late 1941, separate scouting and bombing squadrons continued to exist, but their aircraft, capability, and operations had become essentially identical.

Following the letter representing the purpose of the squadron, there was a dash, followed by a number that was originally the number of the carrier on which the squadron was normally embarked, but there was the occasional swapping of squadrons between carriers. If there were two squadrons of the same type on a single carrier, there was another digit, either a one or two, to designate those.

Examples:

VB-5   Bombing squadron from carrier CV-5, *Yorktown*.

VF-42   Second fighting squadron from carrier CV-4, *Ranger*.

Airport Runways (Still applies today in 2014)

Runways were denoted by numbers which are the magnetic heading of the runway rounded to the nearest ten degrees with the zero dropped. Example: Runway twenty-nine (or "two nine") has a nominal magnetic heading of 290, though the actual heading is between 285 and 295; runway thirty-six (or "three six") has a nominal magnetic heading of 360.

Airport Traffic Patterns (Still applies today in 2014)

Airport traffic patterns are rectangular, with the runway on one of the long sides of the rectangle (see Illustration, which shows a plan view with the various legs of the traffic pattern labeled). Turns are to the left unless otherwise noted. The pilot may enter the pattern at the cross-wind leg, or he may enter the downwind leg directly. The traffic pattern altitude is normally around 1,000 feet above the runway.

Army Aircraft Nomenclature

The army used an entirely different aircraft indicator system from the navy. The first letter designated the type (purpose) of the aircraft, as follows:

A   Attack (light bomber)

B   Bomber

O   Observation (reconnaissance)

P   Pursuit (fighter)

T   Trainer, with a preceding letter P (primary), B (basic), or A (advanced)

In the case of experimental aircraft, the letter X preceded all other characters.

The first letter was followed by a dash and then a number that indicated the sequence of all designs of that type considered by the Army. This was followed by a letter indicating the version, and there was no indication of the designer or manufacturer.

Example:

P-40B   The fortieth pursuit type considered by the army, third version (after two revisions).

Military Aircraft Piston Engine Nomenclature

Army and navy aircraft often had engine types in common, and they used the same nomenclature. Military aircraft piston engines had an alphanumeric designator. The first character was a letter designating the cylinder arrangement, as follows:

I   Inline; a single bank or line of cylinders with crankcase; air cooled.

O   Opposed; two banks of cylinders are arranged on a single crankcase directly across from each other; usually two or three cylinders in each bank; air cooled.

R   Radial; each row, or disk, had cylinders arranged radially, like spokes of a wheel around a crankcase; most radials had only one row of three, five, seven, or nine cylinders, though a few had two rows of seven or nine, and one had four rows of seven; air cooled.

V   Vee type; two banks of cylinders that were angled in a vee and joined on a single crankcase; usually six cylinders in each bank; liquid cooled.

This letter was followed by a dash and then a three- or four-digit number, designating the engine's total displacement in cubic inches. The displacement is the total volume swept by the pistons and was the accepted measure of engine size. The "volume swept" is the volume of the space that the top of the piston moves through as it goes up and down in the cylinder.

Military Aircraft Engine Cooling:

Air cooled	Ambient air was brought in and ducted to flow around the engine cylinders and particularly the cylinder heads; the cylinders and cylinder heads were extensively finned on the outside to increase the surface area for heat transfer. The heated air then exited through ducts. Air cooling was always supplemented by cooling the engine-lubricating oil in an oil radiator. This arrangement was reliable because it had few moving parts, and, except for the small oil-cooling system, it was free from leaks. However, this arrangement tended to have greater aerodynamic drag.
Liquid Cooled	Ambient air was brought in and ducted to flow through a radiator (heat exchanger) to cool a liquid coolant. The liquid coolant was circulated by a pump around the engine cylinders and cylinder heads and then back to the radiator. In military engines, liquid cooling was always supplemented by cooling the engine-lubricating oil in an oil radiator. This arrangement tended to have less drag than an air-cooled system because the cooling radiator was relatively small and could be positioned and ducted

to minimize drag, but this arrangement was less reliable and more vulnerable to combat damage. For this reason, the US Navy avoided it after radial air-cooled engines became available in the 1920s.

Examples (these three engines competed directly with each other):

V-1710	Vee type; 1,710 cubic-inch displacement; two banks of six cylinders; liquid cooled; made by the Allison division of General Motors.
R-1820	Radial; 1,820 cubic-inch displacement; one row of nine cylinders; air cooled; made by the Wright division of Curtiss-Wright.
R-1830	Radial; 1,830 cubic-inch displacement; two rows of seven cylinders each; air cooled; made by the Pratt & Whitney division of United Aircraft.

Military Ranks

Navy	Marines and Army Equivalent
Officers	
Admiral (Adm.)	General
Vice Admiral (VAdm.)	Lieutenant General
Rear Admiral (RAdm.)	Major General
Commodore (rarely used)	Brigadier General
Captain (Capt.)	Colonel
Commander (Cdr.)	Lieutenant Colonel
Lieutenant Commander (Lt. Cdr.)	Major
Lieutenant (Lt.)	Captain
Lieutenant Junior Grade (Lt. j.g.)	First Lieutenant

Ensign (Ens.)	Second Lieutenant

Enlisted Men

Chief Petty Officer	Master Sergeant
Petty Officer First Class	First Sergeant, Technical Sergeant
Petty Officer Second Class	Staff Sergeant
Petty Officer Third Class	Sergeant
Seaman First Class	Corporal
Seaman Second Class	Private First Class
Seaman Third Class	Private

Naval Aviation Petty Officer Abbreviations for Chief, First Class, Second Class, Third Class:

Aviation Ordnance Man	ACOM, AOM1c, AOM2c, AOM3c
Aviation Machinist's Mate	ACMM, AMM1c, AMM2c, AMM3c
Aviation Pilot	CAP, AP1c, AP2c
Aviation Radioman	ACRM, ARM1c, ARM2c, ARM3c

Naval Abbreviations

BOQ	Bachelor Officers' Quarters
BuAer:	Bureau of Aeronautics: Oversees the development and production of aircraft, both heavier- and lighter-than-air.
BuOrd:	Bureau of Ordnance: Oversees the development and production of naval guns, bombs, and torpedoes.
CINCPAC	Commander in Chief of the Pacific Fleet

CINCLANT	Commander in Chief of the Atlantic Fleet
CNO	Chief of Naval Operations
CO	Commanding Officer
COMCRULANT	Commander of the Cruisers in the Atlantic
XO	Executive Officer, assistant to the CO and second in command
USN	Designates regular navy, meaning Naval Academy graduates or those promoted from enlisted men
USNR	Designates Naval Reserve

Naval Aircraft Nomenclature

The navy used an entirely different system from the army. The first one or two characters are letters that designate the purpose of the aircraft, as follows:

F	Fighter: Single engine (except for one experimental example); designed primarily for combat against other aircraft, but can be used for light attack on surface targets.
B,SB	Dive-bomber: Single engine; designed to attack surface targets with a single bomb that is dropped in a very steep dive; armed for defense against other aircraft. The S indicates that the aircraft is also designed for scouting (reconnaissance).
J	Utility aircraft: Usually a single-engine amphibian for communication among multiple ships or between ships and the shore.
N, SN	Trainer: Designed for pilot or aircrew training. The S indicates that the aircraft is also designed for scouting (reconnaissance).
PB	Patrol bomber: Multiengine flying boat designed for long-range patrol and horizontal bombing; armed for defense against other aircraft.

SO, OS   Scout observation: Single-engine float plane carried on a battleship or cruiser, mainly for scouting (reconnaissance), or spotting the fall of naval gun fire.

TB   Torpedo bomber: Single engine; designed to attack surface ships with a torpedo that is dropped from horizontal flight at very low altitude; larger than a dive-bomber because the torpedo weighs twice as much as the largest bomb; may also be used to drop bombs from horizontal flight; armed for defense against other aircraft.

X   Experimental: In the case of experimental aircraft, the letter X preceded all other characters.

The next character is a single digit that designates the sequence of the designs for that purpose or type that were built by that manufacturer. For example, if the designation started off with "F4" it would mean that this was the fourth fighter design by that manufacturer. In the case of the first design (number 1), the digit is omitted.

The next character is a letter designating the manufacturer; before 1942, this also would have indicated the firm that designed the aircraft, as follows:

A Brewster
B Boeing
C Curtis
D Douglas
F Grumman
J North American
M Martin
N Naval Aircraft Factory
S Stearman (a division of Boeing)
T Northrop

U Vought-Sikorsky (a division of United Aircraft)

Y Consolidated

Next, there is a dash followed by a single digit, which designates the sequence of revisions of that design.

Examples:

XF4U-1 Experimental example of the fourth fighter design built by Vought-Sikorsky, first version (no revision).

N2S-3 Second trainer design built by Stearman, third version (second revision).

XBT-2 Experimental example of the first dive-bomber design built by Northrop, second version (first revision).

SBD-3 First scout bomber design built by Douglas, third version (second revision).

F4F-3 Fourth fighter design built by Grumman, third version (second revision).

On October 1, 1941, the secretary of the navy approved the official use of manufacturer's names for naval aircraft, such as "Dauntless" for the SBD and "Wildcat" for the F4F.

Naval Combatant Ship Types

CV-x Fleet Aircraft Carrier: Large aircraft carrier designed to operate with the fleet or in a separate task force; maximum speed: thirty-plus knots; after the first carrier, they were named after early US naval ships.

BB-x Battleship: Large surface-combat ship; heavily armed and armored; able to easily defeat other surface-combat ships except battleships; before 1942, maximum speed: twenty-one knots, except for two ships newly commissioned; named after US states.

CA-x Heavy Cruiser: Smaller than battleship; able to easily defeat other surface-combat ships except battleships and heavy cruisers; maximum speed: thirty-plus knots; named after US cities.

CL-x   Light Cruiser: Smaller than heavy cruiser; able to easily defeat destroyers and small surface-combat ships; maximum speed: thirty-plus knots; named after US cities.

DD-x   Destroyer: Smaller than light cruiser; able to easily defeat small surface-combat ships; able to detect and attack submarines with depth charges; very maneuverable; maximum speed: thirty-plus knots; named after prominent navy and marine persons.

SS-x   Submarine: Designed for torpedo attack against other ships while surfaced or submerged; for fleet boats of mid-1930s and later, maximum speed: twenty knots on the surface, ten knots submerged; many older types of lesser capability in service in 1941; fleet boats named after fish species, with first letter indicating class or type.